THE WAREHOUSE

THE WAREHOUSE

A NOVEL

Rob Hart

BALLANTINE BOOKS
NEW YORK

2020 Ballantine Books Trade Paperback Edition

Published in the United States by Ballantine Books, an imprint of Random House, a division of Penguin Random House LLC, New York.

BALLANTINE and the HOUSE colophon are registered trademarks of Penguin Random House LLC.

Originally published in hardcover in the United States by Crown, an imprint of Random House, a division of Penguin Random House LLC, in 2019

ISBN 978-1-9848-2380-9
Ebook ISBN 978-1-9848-2381-6

Printed in the United States of America on acid-free paper

Art by Slavica/Istock

randomhousebooks.com

9 8 7 6 5 4 3 2 1

FOR MARIA FERNANDES

I pity the man who wants a coat so cheap that the man or woman who produces the cloth or shapes it into a garment will starve in the process.

—*U.S. President Benjamin Harrison, 1891*

PROCESSING¹

GIBSON

Well, I'm dying!

A lot of men make it to the end of their life and they don't know they've reached it. Just the lights go off one day. Here I am with a deadline.

I don't have time to write a book about my life, like everyone has been telling me I should, so this'll have to do. A blog seems pretty fitting, doesn't it? I haven't been sleeping much lately, so this gives me something to keep myself occupied at night.

Anyway, sleep is for people who lack ambition.

At least there'll be some kind of written record. I want you to hear it from me, rather than from someone looking for a buck, making educated guesses. From my line of work, I can tell you: guesses are rarely educated.

I hope it's a good story because I feel like I've lived a pretty good life.

You might be thinking: Mr. Wells, you are worth $304.9 billion, which makes you the richest man in America, and the fourth-richest person on God's green earth, so of course you've lived a good life.

But, friend, that ain't the point.

Or, more important, one thing has nothing to do with the other.

Here's the real truth: I met the most beautiful woman in the world and convinced her to marry me before I had a penny to my name. Together we raised a little girl who grew up blessed, yes, but has been taught to appreciate the value of a dollar. She says *please* and *thank you* and she means it.

I've seen the sun rise and set. I've seen parts of the world my daddy never even heard of. I've met three presidents and respectfully told them all how they could do their job better—and they listened. I bowled a perfect game at my local bowling alley and my name is still up on that wall to this day.

There's been some tough stuff mixed in, but sitting here right now, my dogs resting at my feet, my wife, Molly, asleep in the next room, my little girl, Claire, safe and secure in her future, it's easy to feel like I can be satisfied with the things I've accomplished.

It's with great humility I say Cloud has been the kind of accomplishment I can be proud of. It's the kind of accomplishment most men don't get to make. The freedoms of my childhood disappeared so long ago, it's like you can barely remember them. Used to be earning a living and settling down somewhere wasn't so hard. After a while it became a luxury, and finally, a fantasy. As Cloud grew, I realized it could be more than a store. It could be a solution. It could provide relief to this great nation.

Remind people of the meaning of the word *prosperity*.

And it did.

We gave people jobs. We gave people access to affordable goods and health care. We've generated billions of dollars in tax revenue. We've led the charge in cutting carbon emissions, developing standards and technology that will save this planet.

We did that by concentrating on the only thing that matters in this life: family.

I've got my family at home and my family at work. Two different families I love with all my heart, and I will be sad to leave them behind.

The doc tells me I've got a year, and he's a pretty good doctor so I trust what he says. And I know the news is going to come out pretty soon, so I figure I might as well be the one to tell you.

Stage-four pancreatic cancer. Stage four means the cancer has spread to other parts of my body. Specifically, my spine, lungs, and liver. There's no stage five.

Here's the thing about the pancreas: it's hidden way back in your abdomen. For a lot of people, by the time you find out something's wrong, it's like fire across a dry field. Too late to do much about it.

When the doc told me, he put on that stern voice and placed his hand on my arm. And I'm thinking, Here we go. Time for some bad news. So he tells me what's wrong and my first question, swear to truth, was: "What the hell does a pancreas even *do*?"

He laughed, and I laughed, which helped lighten the mood a bit. Which was good because it took a hard turn after that. In case you were wondering, the pancreas helps digest food and regulate blood sugar. Now I know.

I got one year left. So starting tomorrow morning my wife and I are hitting the road. I'm going to visit as many MotherClouds in the contiguous United States as I possibly can.

I want to say thank you. There's no way I can shake the hand of every person who works in every MotherCloud, but I'm going to damn well try. That sounds a lot nicer than sitting at home and waiting to die.

Just like always, I'll be traveling by bus. Flying is for the birds. And anyway, have you seen how much it costs to fly nowadays?

It's going to take some time, and as the tour winds on, I suspect I'll be a bit more tired. Maybe even a little depressed, because despite my sunny disposition, it's hard for a man to be told he's going to die and then just carry on. But I've been the recipient of a lot of love and goodwill in my life, and I have to do what I can. Otherwise, I'm just going to sit and mope every day for the next year or so, and we can't have that. Molly would sooner smother me just to get it over with!

It's been about a week now that I've known, but something about writing it down makes it so much more real. No taking it back now.

Anyway. Enough of that. I'm going to walk the dogs. Could do with some fresh air. If you see my bus driving by, give it a wave. That always makes me feel pretty good, when people do that.

Thanks for reading, and I'll speak to you soon.

PAXTON

Paxton pressed his hand against the front window of the ice-cream parlor. The menu board on the wall inside promised homemade flavors. Graham cracker and chocolate marshmallow and peanut butter fudge.

Flanking it, on one side, was a hardware store called Pop's, and on the other was a diner with a chrome and neon sign he couldn't quite make out. Delia's? Dahlia's?

Paxton looked up and down the stretch of the main road. It was so easy to imagine the street bustling with people. All the life this place used to hold. It was the kind of town that could inspire feelings of nostalgia on the first visit.

Now it was an echo fading in the white sunlight.

He turned back to the ice-cream parlor, the only business on the strip not boarded up with weathered plywood. The window was hot to the touch where the sun hit it and coated in a layer of grit.

Looking inside, at the dusty stacks of flared tin cups and the empty stools and the fallow refrigerators, Paxton wanted to feel some kind of regret, about what this place must have meant to the town that surrounded it.

But he had reached the limit of his sadness when he stepped off the bus. Just the act of being there was stretching his skin to bursting, like an overfilled balloon.

Paxton hitched his bag over his shoulder and turned back into the horde shuffling down the sidewalk, trampling the grass jutting through the cracks in the concrete. There were still people coming up in the rear—older folks, people nursing injuries so they couldn't walk as well.

Forty-seven people had gotten off the bus. Forty-seven people, not including him. About halfway through the two-hour ride, when there was nothing left on his phone to capture his attention, he'd counted. Heavy-shouldered men with the callused hands of day laborers. Stooped office workers grown soft from years of hunching at keyboards. One girl couldn't have been more than seventeen. She was short and curvy, with long brown braids that reached down to her lower back and skin the color of milk. She wore an old lavender pantsuit, two sizes too big, the fabric faded and stretched from years of washing and wear. The sliver of an orange tag, like the kind used in secondhand stores, stuck out from its collar.

Everyone carried luggage. Battered roller suitcases wobbling on uneven pavement. Bags strapped to backs or slung over shoulders.

Everyone sweating from exertion. The sun baked the top of Paxton's head.

It must have been well past a hundred degrees. Sweat ran down Paxton's legs, pooling in his underarms, making his clothes stick. Which was exactly why he wore black pants and a white shirt, so the sweat wouldn't show as much. The white-haired man next to him, the one who looked like a college professor put out to pasture, his beige suit was the color of wet cardboard.

Hopefully the processing center was close. Hopefully it was cool. He just wanted to be inside. He could taste it on his tongue: dust blowing from ruined fields, no longer strong enough to keep a grip on anything. It had been cruel of the bus driver to drop them at the edge of town. He was probably staying close to the interstate to conserve gas, but still.

The line ahead shifted, drifting to the right at the intersection. Paxton dug in harder. He wanted to stop to pull a bottle of water out of his bag, but pausing at the ice-cream parlor had been an indulgence. There were now more people ahead of him than behind.

As he neared the corner, a woman launched past him, clipping his side, making enough contact he almost stumbled. She was older, Asian, with a mop of white hair on her head and a leather satchel looped around her shoulder, making a hard push for the front of the pack. But the effort proved to be too much and within a couple of feet she tripped, went down hard on her knee.

The people around her stepped to the side, gave her room, but didn't stop. Paxton knew why. A little voice in his head screamed, *Keep walking*, but of course he couldn't, so he helped her get to her feet. Her bare knee was scratched red, a long trail of blood running down her leg to her tennis shoe, so thick the line was black.

She looked at him, barely nodded, and took off. Paxton sighed.

"You're welcome," he said, not loud enough for her to hear.

He checked behind him. The people at the back were picking up the pace. Walking with a renewed sense of effort, probably at the sight of someone going down to the ground. There was blood in the air. Paxton hitched the bag again and took off at a brisk pace, aiming hard for that corner. He turned and found a large theater with a white marquee. The stucco on the front of the building was crumbling to reveal patches of weather-worn brick.

Broken neon glass letters formed an uneven pattern along the top of the marquee.

R-I-V-R-V-I-E.

Paxton figured it was supposed to spell out *Riverview*, even though there didn't seem to be any rivers nearby, but then again, maybe there used to be. Parked outside the theater was a mobile air-conditioning unit, the sleek vehicle humming, pumping cold air through a sealed tube into the building. Paxton followed the crowd toward the long row of open doors. As he got closer, the doors on the end closed, leaving a few in the middle still open.

He pushed forward, nearly running the final few steps, aiming for the middle. As he stepped through, more doors slammed behind him. The sun disappeared and the cool air enveloped him and it felt like a kiss.

He shivered, looked back. Saw the last door close, and a middle-aged man with a pronounced limp was left out in the blazing sun. The first thing the man did was deflate. Shoulders slumped, bag dropped to the ground. Then the tension returned to his spine and he stepped forward, smacking his palm against the door. He must have been wearing a ring because it made a sharp crack, like the glass might break.

"Hey," he yelled, his voice muffled. "Hey. You can't do this. I came all the way out here."

Crack, crack, crack.

"Hey."

A man in a gray shirt that said *RapidHire* on the back in white letters approached the rejected applicant. He placed a hand on the man's shoulder. Paxton couldn't read lips, but he assumed it was the same thing spoken to the woman who'd gotten turned away from the bus. She was the last person on line and the doors closed in her face, and a man in a RapidHire shirt appeared and said: "There is no last place. You have to want to work at Cloud. You are free to apply again in one month's time."

Paxton turned away from the scene. He couldn't find more room for his own sadness—certainly he couldn't muster space for anyone else's.

The lobby was filled with men and women in the RapidHire shirts. Some stood with tweezers and small plastic bags, smiling happy, friendly smiles. Each applicant was instructed to allow a person in gray to pluck a few hairs and place them into a plastic bag. Then the applicant was invited to write his or her name and Social Security number on the bag in black felt marker.

The woman collecting Paxton's sample was almost perfectly round and shorter than him by a head. He had to bend down so she could reach. He winced as she ripped a few hairs from their roots, and he wrote his name on the bag, which he passed to another man who was waiting to run it off. As Paxton stepped over the threshold from the lobby to the theater, a stick-thin man with a bushy mustache handed him a small tablet computer.

"Take a seat and turn it on," he said, his voice a practiced, disinterested monotone. "The interview process will begin shortly."

Paxton hitched his bag on his shoulder and made his way down the aisle, the path worn almost to the subfloor. The space smelled like old, leaky pipes. He picked a row toward the front and moved to the middle. By the time he was settled into the hard wooden seat, his duffel next to him, there was a series of hard clicks at the rear of the theater as the doors latched shut.

His row was empty, save a woman with skin the color of baked earth and springy coils of dark brown hair piled high and unevenly atop her head. She wore a butterscotch sundress and matching flats, and sat toward the far end of the row, by the wall of the theater, where the ornate maroon wallpaper was marred by water stains. Paxton tried to catch her eye, smile at her, wanting to be polite, but also wanting to see more of her face, too. She didn't notice him, so he looked down at the tablet. Pulled a bottle of water from his bag, downed half of it, and pressed the button on the side.

The screen flared to life, large numbers at the center of the display.
Ten.
Then nine.
Then eight.

When it hit zero, the tablet buzzed and flashed, and the numbers were replaced by a series of empty fields. Paxton balanced it on his lap and focused.

Name, contact information, brief work history. Shirt size?

Paxton's hand hovered over *Work History*. He didn't want to explain what he had done before this, and the confluence of events that had brought him to a broken theater in a broken town. Because to do that meant having to explain that Cloud had destroyed his life.

Anyway, what would he write?

Would they even know who he was?

If they didn't, was that better or worse?

Paxton found he did, in fact, have more room for sadness, at the thought of applying for this job with *CEO* in the work history field.

His stomach knotted and he settled on the prison. Fifteen years. A long enough time to demonstrate loyalty. That's what he would call it, if he were asked: loyalty. If someone wanted to know about the gap, those two years between the prison and now, he'd deal with it.

After he filled in all the fields, the next screen appeared.

Have you ever stolen anything?

Underneath were two buttons. Green Yes and red No.

He rubbed his eyes, the brightness of the screen making them ache. Thought back to when he was nine, standing by the spinning wire comic rack in Mr. Chowdury's deli.

The comic book Paxton wanted was four dollars and he only had two. He could have gone home and asked his mother for the money, but instead he waited, his leg shaking, until a man came in and asked for a pack of cigarettes. As Mr. Chowdury bent down to where he kept the cigarettes underneath the counter, Paxton rolled up the comic, held it flush to his leg so it'd be out of view, and headed for the exit.

He walked to the park and sat on a rock and tried to read the comic but couldn't concentrate enough to understand it. The artwork blurred and got muddy as he obsessed over what he had just done.

Broken the law. Stolen from someone who had always been kind to him.

It took him half the day to work up the nerve, but he went back to the deli; stood outside, waiting until he was sure there was no one else in there; then brought the comic book to the counter, carrying it like a dead pet. He explained through a hot gush of tears and phlegm that he was sorry.

Mr. Chowdury agreed to not call the police, or worse, his mother. But every time Paxton went into the deli after that—and it was the only deli within walking distance, so he had no choice—he could feel the old man's eyes burning on his back.

Paxton read the question again and touched the screen over the red box marked No, even though it was a lie. It was a lie he could live with.

The screen flashed and a new question appeared.

Do you believe it's morally acceptable to steal in some circumstances?
Green Yes, red No.
That was easy. No.

Do you believe it's morally acceptable to steal under any circumstances?
No.

If your family were starving, would you steal a loaf of bread to feed them?
Real answer: probably.
No.

Would you steal from your job?
No.

What if you knew you wouldn't be caught?
Paxton wished there was an I'm-not-going-to-steal-anything-please-let's-move-on button.
No.

If you knew someone stole something, would you report him or her?
He almost pressed No, having gotten used to the repetitive tap, then jerked his hand away and pressed Yes.

If the person threatened to harm you, would you still report him or her?
Sure. Yes.

Have you ever used drugs?

This one was a relief. Not just for the change of subject, but because Paxton could answer this one honestly.

No.

Have you ever had alcohol?

Yes.

How many alcoholic drinks do you consume per week?

1–3
4–6
7–10
11+

Seven to ten was probably more accurate, but Paxton picked the second option.

After that, the questions shifted.

How many windows are there in Seattle?

10,000
100,000
1,000,000
1,000,000,000

Should Uranus be considered a planet?

Yes
No

There are too many lawsuits.

Agree a lot
Agree a little
No opinion
Disagree a little
Disagree a lot

Paxton tried to give each question serious consideration, even if he wasn't sure what it all meant, though he figured there was some kind of algorithm—something that would reveal to them the core of his personality through his opinion on astronomy.

He answered questions until he lost count. Then the screen went blank, and it stayed blank long enough that he wondered if he had done something wrong. He looked around for help but, finding none, looked back to the screen, where there was more text.

Thank you for your answers. Now we ask for a brief statement. When you see the timer appear in the lower left-hand corner, the recording will start, and you'll have one minute to explain why you want to work at Cloud. Please note, you don't need to speak for the entire minute. A clear, simple, and direct explanation will suffice. When you feel that you are finished, you may hit the red dot at the bottom of the screen to end the recording. You will not have the opportunity to rerecord.

Paxton's face appeared reflected back to him, distorted by the tilt of the screen, his skin washed to a sickly gray by the glow. A timer appeared in the bottom left-hand corner.

1:00

Then:

:59

"I didn't realize I would have to give a speech," Paxton said, giving his best this-is-a-joke smile, which looked sharper than he intended. "I guess I would say that, uh, you know, it's tough to get a job in this day and age, and between that and looking for a new place to live I figure it's kinda perfect, right?"

:43

"I mean, I really do want to work here. I think, uh, it's an incredible opportunity to learn and grow. Like the commercial says, 'Cloud is the solution to every need.'" He shook his head. "I'm sorry, I'm not great at talking off the cuff."

:22

Deep breath.

"But I'm a hard worker. I take pride in my work and I promise to give this my all."

:09

Paxton pressed the red button and his face disappeared. The screen flashed to white. He cursed himself for stumbling through that. Had he known this would be part of the application he would have practiced.

Thank you. Please wait while the interview results are tabulated. At the end of the process your screen will turn either green or red. If red, we are sorry, either you failed the drug test, or you did not meet the standards expected at Cloud. You may exit the building and you must wait one month before reapplying. If green, then please stay and await further instructions.

The tablet turned black. Paxton raised his head and looked around, to see everyone else raising their heads and looking around. He caught eyes with the woman in his row, gave a little shrug. Rather than return it, she put the tablet on her lap and dug a small paperback out of her purse.

Paxton balanced the tablet on his knees, not sure whether he wanted to see red or green.

Red meant leaving here and standing in the sun until another bus arrived, if there was even one coming. It meant scratching through want ads for jobs that didn't pay enough to survive, and apartment listings for places that were either out of his price range or so decrepit as to be unlivable. It meant finding himself back in that rotten pool of frustration and emotion where he'd been treading for months, his nose barely above the waterline.

It almost seemed preferable to working for Cloud.

A sniffle erupted behind him. Paxton glanced back and saw the Asian woman who'd pushed past him earlier, face down, features washed in red light.

Paxton held his breath as his screen flashed.

ZINNIA

Green.

She pulled out her cell phone and ran a quick scan of the room. Nothing on intercept. Once they got to MotherCloud she'd have to go full radio silent, because who knew what they'd be able to pluck out of the air? Being careless with transmissions was a good way to get got. She tapped out a text to give an update on her status: *Hey, Mom, great news! I got the job.*

She put the phone in her purse, glanced around the room. Seemed to be more people staying than leaving. Two rows back a young woman in a lavender pantsuit and long brown braids gave a little whoop and a smile.

The test wasn't hard. You'd have to be a dummy to fail. A lot of the answers didn't even matter, especially when you got into the abstract stuff. Windows in Seattle? What mattered was timing. Answer too quickly, you were powering through and trying to get it done with. Wait too long, and your relationship to reason was wanting. Then, the video. No one actually watched them. As if there were a crew of people sitting in the back. It was all facial and audio scanning. Smile. Eye contact. Use key words like *passion* and *hard worker* and *learn* and *grow*.

The way to win the test was to land in the middle. Just enough to show you were thinking about the questions.

That, and don't fail the drug test.

Not that she used anything on the regular, outside a little pot to unwind, and the last time she'd indulged was more than six months ago, the THC long since flushed from her system.

She glanced to her right. The goofy guy sitting eight seats down, he'd made the cut. Tilted his green screen toward her and smiled. She gave in and threw a little smile back. It helped to be polite. Being rude made you stand out.

The way he looked at her, as if they were friends now, he was going to sit next to her on the bus. She was sure of it.

While waiting for the next set of directions, she watched the people who hadn't made the cut heading toward the door. Trudging up the aisles, dreading a return to the daytime heat. She tried to muster a little sympathy for them but found it hard to feel bad they didn't get picked for a monkey job.

Not that she was heartless. She had a heart. She was sure of it. If she pressed her hand to her chest she could feel it pumping.

After the room had cleared of rejects and the doors were shut again, a woman in a white polo shirt with a Cloud logo on the right breast moved to the front of the auditorium. She had a bonnet of gold hair like it had been spun off a loom, and she raised her singsong voice to be heard in the cavernous space.

"Everyone, could you please collect your things and follow us toward the rear exit? We have a bus waiting. If you prefer to defer your processing by a few days, please see a manager immediately. Thank you."

The room stood as one, hinge seats snapping back on their springs like a volley of gunshots. She slung her purse over her shoulder, grabbed her gym bag, followed the line toward the rear of the theater, keeping pace with the crowd as it made its way through a harsh, glowing rectangle of white light.

As she approached the door, a group of people in RapidHire shirts appeared. They moved with purpose, wearing serious faces, scanning the people who passed by. Her stomach fluttered but she kept walking, careful not to draw attention.

As she reached the scrum of employees, one of them reached out, and she paused, ready to evac. She had an escape route mapped. It would involve some running and then a lot of walking. And not getting paid.

But the man was aiming for the person in front of her: the girl in the lavender pantsuit with the long braids. He gripped her arm, yanking her out of the lineup so hard she yelped. People continued to walk past, eyes turned toward the floor, moving faster, desperate to disentangle from the disturbance. The RapidHire team led the girl away, using words like *misrepresented* and *work history* and *inappropriate* and *barred*.

She allowed herself the indulgence of a smile.

Stepping outside was like opening an oven door midbake. A bus idled at the curb, big and blue, shaped like a bullet, the top stacked with solar panels. Emblazoned on the side was the same logo as on the woman's polo: a white cloud, with another blue cloud staggered slightly behind it. This bus was cleaner than the battered old diesel that'd brought them to town, which had made a sound like it was crying when the driver started the engine.

It was nicer on the inside, too. It made her think of a plane. Two rows of three seats, everything sleek and plastic and stiff. Screens set into the rear of the headrests. Tossed haphazardly on each seat were some pamphlets and a pair of cheap, disposable earbuds, still wrapped in plastic. She moved toward the back, slid in next to the window. The air inside was frigid, but the glass was frying-pan hot.

She checked her phone and found a return text.

Congratulations! Best of luck. Dad and I will see you at Christmas.

Translation: proceed as planned.

There was a shuffling sound next to her. The feel of a presence displacing the air. She looked up, into the face of the goof from the theater. He was smiling in a way that made it seem like he wanted her to think he was suave. It was minimally effective. He looked as if he enjoyed khaki pants and light beer. He looked like the kind of person who thought it was important to talk about one's feelings. His hair was parted.

"Seat taken?" he asked.

She played the odds in her head. Her preferred method was to get in, get out, make as little noise and personal connection as possible. But she also knew things as basic as social interaction could affect her ranking. The more she resisted socializing, the more she risked standing out, or worse, getting fired. Navigating this was going to mean making a few friends.

Probably a good time to start.

"Not yet," she said to the goof.

He slung his bag onto the rack over their heads and sat down on the aisle seat, leaving a free seat between them. He reeked of dried sweat, but so did everyone. So did she.

"Well . . . ," he said, looking around the bus, which was filled with the sound of shuffling and crinkling plastic and hushed conversations, trying desperately to make the empty space between them less awkward. "How did a girl like you end up in a place like this?"

After he said it, he gave a pained little smile, realizing how silly the line sounded.

But there was something deeper. An undercurrent of disdain beneath the words. *How did you screw up so bad, too?*

"I was a teacher," she said. "When the Detroit school system went full charter last year they decided instead of a math teacher in every school, they could have one math teacher for each district, video-conferenced into the classrooms. There used to be fifteen thousand teachers. Now there are less than a hundred." She shrugged. "And I did not get to be one of them."

"I heard that's happening in some other cities, too," he said. "Municipal budgets are strapped everywhere. It does make a little sense as a cost-saving measure, right?"

Why does he know about municipal budgets?

"Let's revisit that in a few years when kids can't solve a simple math problem," she said, giving him a little eyebrow.

"Sorry. Didn't mean any offense. What kind of math did you teach?"

"Basic stuff," she said. "Mostly worked with the younger kids. Multiplication tables. Geometry."

He nodded. "I was a bit of a math geek myself."

"What did you do, before this?" she asked.

He grimaced, like someone had shoved a fingertip into his ribs. It was almost enough to make her regret asking, because he was probably going to unload some bullshit sob story on her.

"I used to be a prison guard," he said. "One of the for-profits. Upper New York Correctional Center."

Okay, she thought. *Municipal budgets.*

"But after that . . . ," he said. "Ever hear of the Perfect Egg?"

"Nope," she said, truthfully.

He opened his hands in his lap, as if he were about to give a presentation, but then folded them again when he found they were empty. "It was this thing you put an egg in, and you put it in the microwave, and it would cook a perfect hard-boiled egg, to the exact doneness you'd want, depending on how long you put it in for. It came with a little chart, for the timing. And then, when it was done, the shell would peel right off when you opened it up." He looked up at her. "Do you like hard-boiled eggs?"

"Not really."

"You wouldn't think so, but a gadget to make them easier . . ." He looked past her, out the window. "People like kitchen gadgets. It turned out to be pretty popular."

"What happened?" she asked.

He looked at his shoes. "I had orders from all around, but Cloud was the biggest account. Thing was, they kept on asking for discounts so they could charge less. Which, in the beginning, was not so bad. I streamlined the packaging, cut waste. We did it out of my garage. It was me and four other people. But it got to a point where the discounts got so deep I couldn't turn a profit. When I refused to go any lower, Cloud pulled their account, and the other accounts weren't enough to make up for it."

He paused, like he wanted to say more, but didn't.

"I'm sorry to hear that," she said, not really truthfully.

"It's fine," he said, looking up at her, smiling, the storm clouds receding. "I just got hired by the company that destroyed my livelihood, so I've got that going for me. The patent is pending. I figure once that gets approved I can sell it to them. I think that's what they were hoping for anyway, that they'd put me out of business and they could introduce their own version."

She had been approaching the boundaries of pity, but his attitude forced her to take a hard left into annoyance. She resented the way he carried himself. Slumped, weepy, like all those sad sacks who hadn't gotten their monkey job. Tough luck, dude. Learn a skill that doesn't involve babysitting criminals or cooking eggs in microwaves.

"Well, at least there's that," she said.

"Thanks," he said. "Hey, the way it goes, you know? Something doesn't work, you press on. You want to get back to teaching? I hear the schools on site are pretty good."

"Yeah, I don't know," she said. "Honestly just wanted to earn a little money, get out of the country for a bit. Build up a bit of a cash reserve, go teach English somewhere. Thailand. Bangladesh. Someplace not here."

The doors of the bus closed. She whispered a silent prayer of thanks that the seat between her and the goof remained empty. The woman with the singsong voice stood at the front and waved her hand. Most of the hushed getting-to-know-you conversations on the bus stopped, heads snapping to attention.

"Okay, everyone, we're about to take off," she said. "If you'll please put on your headphones, there's an introductory video we'd like you to watch. The trip will take approximately two hours. There's a bathroom at the back and water available up front here if anyone needs it. After the video please take some time to flip through the pamphlets, and when we arrive you'll receive your housing assignment. The video will begin in three minutes. Thank you!"

A countdown clock appeared on the screens in the headrests.

3:00
2:59
2:58

They both reached for the middle seat, where they'd pushed the pamphlets and earbuds. Their hands brushed and the plastic wrap crinkled. The goof seemed to be looking at her, so she was careful not to return the eye contact, just in case, though she could feel the warmth of where he had touched her skin.

Close, but not too close.

Get in, do the job, get the hell out.

"Can't wait for this video to be over," she said. "I'd love to take a nap."

"That's not a bad idea."

As she plugged the buds into the port under the screen, she wondered again about who had hired her.

The initial call and all communication had come in anonymously and encrypted. The offer had blown her hair back. She could retire on it. She would have to, probably, after handing over her genetic material. As much as it pained her to let someone pluck her hair and log her in a database, after this it wouldn't even really matter. She could spend the rest of her life on some beach in Mexico. A big, beautiful beach with no extradition laws.

This wasn't her first anonymous job, but it was definitely her biggest. And it wasn't her job to know, but she couldn't help but wonder.

The way to answer the question of "who" meant expanding on it slightly: who benefits? That didn't narrow it down. When the king is dying the entire kingdom is suspect.

"I'm so sorry," the goof said, breaking her train of thought. "I should have introduced myself." He offered his hand across the empty seat. "Paxton."

She considered the hand for a moment, before reaching over with her own. His grip was stronger than she would have guessed, his hand mercifully free of sweat.

She reminded herself of her name for this gig.

"Zinnia," she said.

"Zinnia," he repeated, nodding. "Like the flower."

"Like the flower," she agreed.

"Nice to meet you."

It was the first she'd said it out loud to anyone other than herself. She liked the way it sounded. Zinnia. It sounded like a smooth rock pinging off the surface of a still pond. It was her favorite part of each new job. Picking a name.

Zinnia smiled and turned from Paxton, slid the buds in her ears as the timer hit zero, and the video began.

WELCOME

A well-appointed suburban kitchen. Stainless-steel surfaces sparkling in sunlight through big bay windows. Three children, two girls and a boy, run across the screen laughing, playfully chased by a mother, a young brunette, barefoot, wearing a white sweater and jeans.

The mother stops and turns to the screen, putting her hands on her hips, speaking directly to the audience.

Mother: "I love my children, but they can be a lot to handle. Just getting them dressed and out the door can take forever. And after the Black Friday Massacres . . ."

She pauses, presses her hand to her chest, closes her eyes, and looks on the verge of tears, before opening them again, and smiling.

". . . after that, the thought of going outside to shop just scares me to death. Honestly, if it wasn't for Cloud, I don't know what I'd do."

She smiles, soft and sure, the way a mother is supposed to smile.

Cut to the little boy on the floor, face twisted in pain, holding on to his knee, scraped red and raw. The child wails.

Child: "Mommeeeeeeeee."

Cut to a man in a red polo shirt, leaping to the ground from someplace above. He's lean, handsome, blond. He looks grown in a lab. The camera zooms in on the item in his hand: a box of adhesive bandages.

He takes off, sprinting between two massive aisles in a cavernous warehouse, the shelves stacked neatly with a diverse array of items.

Mugs and toilet paper and books and soup. Soap and bathrobes and laptops and motor oil. Envelopes and playsets and towels and sneakers.

The man stops in front of a long line of conveyor belts, puts the box of bandages in a blue bin, and pushes it down the belt.

Cut to a drone buzzing across a brilliant blue sky.

Cut to the mother, tearing open the cardboard container emblazoned with the Cloud logo. She takes out the box of bandages and removes one, which she applies to the child's knee. The boy smiles and kisses his mother on the cheek.

The mother turns back to the screen.

Mother: "Thanks to Cloud, I'm always ready for whatever life throws at us. And when it comes time for a treat, Cloud has me covered there, too."

The man in the red polo is back, this time a box of chocolates tucked under his arm. He takes off running again. The camera doesn't follow him. He grows smaller and smaller between the cavernous aisles, until he hangs a hard right and disappears, and it's just the monolithic shelves overlooking an empty floor, stretching into the distance.

Cut to a white screen. A lean, older man walks out. He's wearing jeans, a white button-down shirt with the sleeves rolled up, and brown cowboy boots. Silver hair cut high and tight. He stops in the center of the screen and smiles.

Gibson: "Hi. I'm Gibson Wells, your new boss. It's a real pleasure to welcome you to the family."

Cut to Wells roaming the massive aisles, this time with men and women in red whipping around him. No one stops to acknowledge him, as if he's a ghost on their periphery.

Gibson: "Cloud is the solution to every need. It's a point of relief in a fast-paced world. We aim to assist people and families who can't make it out to a store, or don't have one nearby, or don't want to take the risk."

Cut to a room gridded by massive tables, covered with blue tubing, like industrial air pumps, except when the workers in the red polos spray the items on the table, they're encased in swelling foam that quickly dries into cardboard.

They affix labels and a sticker of the Cloud logo to the packages, and put them onto a series of pulleys moving endlessly toward the ceiling.

Wells is still roaming, the workers running with speed and precision, oblivious to him.

Gibson: "Here at Cloud, we believe in offering a safe, secure work environment where you can be the master of your own destiny. We have a wide array of positions available, from the pickers—those handsome folks in red—to our boxers, to our support staff . . ."

Cut to a giant room full of cubicles, everyone wearing canary-yellow polo shirts and phone headsets, looking at small tablets bolted onto desks. Everyone is smiling and laughing, catching up with old friends.

Gibson: ". . . to the assistants . . ."

Cut to a gleaming industrial kitchen where employees in green polo shirts prepare meals and empty trash cans. Still smiling and laughing. Wells is wearing a hairnet, chopping an onion next to a small Indian woman.

Gibson: ". . . to the tech team . . ."

Cut to a group of young men and women in brown polos examining the exposed guts of a computer terminal.

Gibson: ". . . to the managers . . ."

Cut to a table at which a group of men and women in bright white polo shirts hold tablets and discuss something very important. Wells stands off to the side.

Gibson: "At Cloud, we evaluate your skill set, and we place you in the position that's best suited for both of us."

Cut to a tidy, catalog-pretty apartment, where a young man lifts his daughter onto his shoulders while he stirs a pot of sauce on the stove.

The walls feature cursive decals that say LOVE and INSPIRE. The couch is sleek and modern. The galley kitchen is big enough to fit four people cooking together and looks onto a sunken living room suited for a cocktail party.

Wells is gone now, but his voice remains.

Gibson: "Because Cloud isn't just a place to work. It's a place to live. Trust me, when your friends and family come to visit, they just might want to work here, too."

Cut to a clogged superhighway, the cars not moving, fumes turning the sky to ash.

Gibson: "The average American's commute used to be two hours, roundtrip. That's two hours of time wasted. Two hours' worth of carbon pumped into the atmosphere. Every employee who chooses to live in our residential facilities can make it from their spot on the floor to home in less than fifteen minutes. When more of your time belongs to you, that's more time for you to be with your family, or pursue a hobby, or just get some much-needed relaxation."

Cut to a montage of quick scenes: Shoppers roaming a white marble corridor surrounded by brand-name stores. A doctor pressing a stethoscope to a young man's chest under his shirt. A young couple munching popcorn, movie screen light flickering across their faces. An older woman running on a treadmill.

Gibson: "We offer everything from entertainment, to health and wellness services, to education that meets the highest standards. When you're here, you'll never want to leave. And I want this to feel like home. A real home. That's why, while we always make your safety a top priority, you won't see cameras everywhere you look. That's no way to live."

Cut to white. Wells is back. The background has dropped away, so he's standing in a void.

Gibson: "Everything you see here, and more, will be available to you when you've started at Cloud. And you can trust that your job will be secure. While some of our processes are automated, I don't believe in employing robots. A robot will never replicate the dexterity and critical reasoning skills of a human being. And on the day that they can—we won't care. We believe in family. That's the key to running a successful business."

Cut to a shuttered storefront, the windows boarded with plywood. Wells walks onto the sidewalk, looks up at the store, shakes his head, and turns to the camera.

Gibson: "Things are tough. No doubt about that. But we've faced adversity before, and we've come out on top, because that's what we do. We achieve and we persevere. It's my dream to help get America back on its feet, and that's why I've been working with your local elected officials to ensure we have the room and ability to grow, so we can get more Americans earning a living wage. Our success starts with you. You are the gears that keep our economy moving. I want you to know that sometimes your job might be hard, or feel repetitive, but you should never forget how important you are. Without you, Cloud is nothing. If you really think about it . . ."

The camera closes in. He smiles and extends his arms, as if welcoming the viewer in for a hug.

Gibson: ". . . I work for you."

Cut to a table in a restaurant. Seated around it are a dozen men and women, many of them overweight. The men clutch cigars, the air hazy with curls of gray smoke. The table is littered with empty wineglasses and plates of half-eaten steak.

Gibson: "Some people will tell you it's their job to fight for you. It's not. Their job is to fight for themselves. Their job is to enrich themselves off of your hard work. At Cloud, we're here for you, and we mean that."

The camera backs out, showing Gibson standing in a small apartment.

Gibson: "Now, you might be wondering, what happens next? When you arrive at Cloud you'll be issued a room and a CloudBand."

Gibson holds up his wrist to show a small glass square with a rugged leather strap.

Gibson: "Your CloudBand will be your new best friend. It'll help you get around the facility, open doors, pay for items, provide directions, monitor your health and heart rate, and most important, assist you in your job. And when you arrive at your room, you're going to find some more goodies. . . ."

He holds up a small box.

Gibson: "The color of your shirt will tell you where you're working. We're still processing your test information, but by the time you get to your room, we'll have it figured out. Once you arrive, drop your stuff, take a walk around. Get yourself acquainted. Tomorrow is orientation, where you'll be teamed up with someone in your section to show you the ropes."

He puts down the box and winks at the camera.

Gibson: "Good luck, and welcome to the family. We have more than a hundred MotherCloud facilities throughout the United States, and I'm known to visit from time to time. So if you see me wandering the floor, feel free to stop me and say hello. I'm looking forward to meeting you. And remember: call me Gib."

GIBSON

So now that we got all the depressing stuff out of the way, probably the best way to start is to tell you how I got into this business in the first place, right?

There's a problem with that: I don't right know. There is not a kid on this planet who grows up thinking he wants to run the biggest electronic retail and cloud computing company in the world. When I was a kid I wanted to be an astronaut.

Remember the Curiosity rover? The one sent out to poke around Mars, way back in 2011? I loved that thing. I had a model of it, big enough I could put the family cat on top and drive him around the living room. All this time later I can remember stuff about Mars, like how it's got the tallest mountain in the solar system—Olympus Mons—and an object that weighs one hundred pounds on Earth would weigh only thirty-eight pounds up there.

Hell of a weight-loss plan, if you ask me. Easier than giving up red meat.

So I was convinced I'd be the first person to step foot on that planet. Spent years studying. It wasn't really that I wanted to go. I wanted to be first. But by the time I got to high school, someone else did it, so that dream went out the window.

Not that I still wouldn't like to go if someone offered, but the mystique of it was sort of gone. There's a big difference between being the first person to do a thing and being the second.

Anyway, the whole time I was pretending to bounce around an alien planet, I was already on track to be where I am today. Because the thing I always really liked to do was take care of people.

In the town where I grew up, there was this general store, about a mile away from our house. Coop's. Saying used to be that if Mr. Cooper didn't have it, you probably didn't need it.

The place was a marvel. Not big the way you expect a store to be. Just big enough, everything stacked to the ceiling, like everything was balancing on itself. You could ask Mr. Cooper for any old thing and he'd find it right away. Sometimes it meant digging through to the back of the shelves, but he always had what you were looking for.

By the time I was nine, my mother would let me go to the store by myself, so of course I was always offering to go. Even for the littlest thing. I would run there. She'd say she needed a loaf of bread and I'd be out the door before she could tell me it could wait until her next trip.

It got to be I was going back and forth so much, I started running errands for people in the neighborhood. Mr. Perry next door would see me take off and he'd stop me, ask me to pick up a can of shaving cream or something. He'd give me a couple of bucks, kick me the change when I got back. This turned into a lucrative little side business. After a bit, I was swimming in comic books and candy.

But you know what the big moment was? The moment that changed everything? There was this kid on my block. Ray Carson. He was a big kid, built like an ox, and kind of quiet, but real nice. So one day I come out of the store with an armload of groceries—I had probably six or seven stops to make before going home—and it damn near felt like my arms were going to fall off.

Ray is standing there up against the wall of the store, eating a candy bar, and I say to him, "Ray, want to give me a hand? I'll give you a little money for your trouble." Ray says sure, he'll help, because what kid doesn't want a little spending money?

I give him a couple of the bags and we get everything dropped off, faster than I would have been able to do it by myself. At the end I took all my tip money and gave some of it to Ray, and he was pretty happy, so we kept on doing that. I'd take the orders and do the shopping; he'd help me carry everything and deliver. Got to be I upgraded from candy and comic books to video games and model rockets. The nice ones with a million parts that never all seemed to be in the box.

After a little while I had kids who saw how well Ray Carson was making out, and they'd ask if they could work for me, too. So I said sure, and it got to be where the people living on my block never really had to leave the house.

And it made me feel good. It was nice to see my mom be able to sit down and paint her nails rather than run around like a lunatic, which is what she was doing most days, on account of me and my dad.

Things were going so well that one night, I decide, I'm going to take my parents out to dinner.

We went to the Italian place next to Coop's. I wore a white shirt and a black tie I bought special for that night, except I didn't know how to tie it. I wanted to surprise my mom, come downstairs wearing it, but I ended up calling her upstairs to tie it for me. When she saw me standing there, trying to get the thing right, I thought her face would just about burst.

So we head out, and we walked because it was a nice night, and the whole time my daddy was kidding around, thinking that when the bill came I'd get scared and he'd swoop in to save the day. But I'd checked the menu online and knew I had enough money to cover it.

I got the chicken parmigiana. My mom got the chicken marsala and my daddy made a big show of it, got the surf and turf. When the bill came I picked it up and I took the bill folder and figured out the tip—10 percent, because my parents' drinks came out late, and the waiter forgot to refill the bread bowl when we asked, and like my dad said, a tip is a reward for good service.

I put the money in the bill folder and let the waiter take it, told him to keep the change, and my dad is just sitting there with his wallet in his hand, this look on his face like, I don't know, the cat just rode in on the Curiosity rover or something. Here I was, twelve years old and buying my daddy dinner at a restaurant with a candle on the table.

After the waiter was gone, before we left, he patted me on the shoulder and looked at my mom and he said, "Our boy."

I can remember that moment exactly. Everything about it, down to the last detail. The way the candle made this orange light dance on the wall behind him. The purple stain on the white tablecloth from the little bit of wine that spilled out of his glass. This soft look he had in his eyes, which he only ever got when he was being really honest about something. The way his hand felt on my shoulder.

"Our boy," he said.

Now, that's a hell of a thing. It made me feel like I'd done something special. Like even though I was a kid I could take care of them.

That's it, I guess. It started with a need to please my parents. Though I guess that's why most people do anything. It would be brutally dishonest to say this has nothing to do with wanting to live a comfortable life, to make some money, to be successful. Everyone in this world wants that. But simply put, it seems I have a need to please.

I remember, years and years later, we were opening our first MotherCloud. We started pretty modestly, with only something like a thousand people, but it was a pretty big deal at the time, being the first modern live-work facility in the United States.

My daddy came out. It was a tough trip for him, because he was pretty sick at that point, and Mom had passed a few years back, but he came out anyway, and I remember, after we cut that ribbon, me and him took a little stroll through the dormitory so I could show him around.

After we were done, he patted me on the shoulder and he said, "Our boy."

Even though Mom was gone.

He died a few months later and I miss them both like crazy, but if there's any silver lining to this cancer gnawing at my gut, it's that at least I'll be seeing them soon. Fingers crossed I head in the same direction as them!

So that's what's been on my mind. Lots more to talk about, but I've never really articulated that beginning part of it. And now I have, and it feels good to see it in writing. Tomorrow Molly and I will make it to the MotherCloud outside Orlando. It was the twelfth one we built, and the first one that was on the kind of scale we build them to now, so it's pretty special to me, but then again, they all are.

And, listen, I know a lot of people are expecting me to announce who's going to take over in my stead. I had to turn off my phone because it won't stop ringing. I'll get to it soon enough. I'm not dying tomorrow, okay? So all you reporters out there, pour yourselves a drink, take a deep breath. I still have full control of the board and I'll be announcing it here, on the blog, so it's not like any of you are getting an exclusive.

That's all for now. Thanks for reading. After unloading all this stuff, I am just real excited to get off this bus and stretch my legs and walk around a bit.

PAXTON

Mass migrations continue out of Kolkata, India, where more than six million people live in low-lying areas that, in the past few years, have fallen below sea level. . . .

The accompanying picture showed a group of people floating on a makeshift boat assembled from driftwood. Two men, a woman. Three children. All of them, their skin stretched taut like drums. Paxton closed the browser on his phone.

The sky darkened. He thought maybe a storm was coming in, but when he leaned over to peek past Zinnia's sleeping form, the air looked full of insects. Great black swarms moving back and forth across the sky.

The roadway was getting busier, too—they had been alone for so long, barreling through nowhere, but then a driverless tractor-trailer had whipped past them, the roar of it ripping Paxton from the edge of a nap. The trucks increased in frequency after that, one every ten minutes, then five, and now maybe every thirty seconds.

The horizon ahead was a flat line with a single large box sticking out of it. Too far away to make out the details just yet. He leaned back in his seat, picked up the brochures explaining the credit system and ranking system and housing system and health care system. He'd read them all twice but it was a lot of information. His eyes were bouncing off the words.

The intro video was playing on a loop. Must have been shot years ago. Paxton knew what Gibson Wells looked like. The man was in the news nearly every day, and the Gibson in the video was taller, had less gray hair.

Now he was dying. *The* Gibson Wells. It was like being told New York City was going to remove Grand Central Terminal. Just pick it up and toss it out. How would things function without it? The enormity of the question overshadowed his anger.

He couldn't stop thinking about what Wells had said at the end. About visiting MotherClouds across the country. Wells still had a year to live. How many would he visit? Could Paxton meet him? Confront him? What would he say to a man who was worth three hundred billion dollars and thought that wasn't enough?

He stuck the pamphlets into his bag and took out a bottle of water, cracked the plastic cap. Took out the only pamphlet that was making his chest ache with anticipation.

The color-coded job assignments.

Red was the pickers and placers, the swarm of people responsible for moving goods around. Brown for tech support, yellow for customer service, green for food service and cleaners and other odd jobs. White was for managers, though no one started at that level. There were other colors, too, not in the video, like purple for teachers and orange for the drone field.

Any of those would do just fine, but he hoped for red.

And he feared blue. Blue was security.

Red would mean a lot of time on his feet, but he was in good enough shape to handle it. Hell, he could stand to lose some of the soft skin from around his midsection.

But his background was in security. Not his real background. His degree was in engineering and robotics. But when he couldn't get a job out of college, when he got desperate, he'd answered a want ad from a prison and ended up there for fifteen years, carrying a retractable baton and pepper spray while he scrimped and saved and tried to launch his own business.

That first day at UNYCC he was so scared. He thought he'd be walking into a place where everybody was covered in tattoos and they ground down toothbrushes into shivs. What he found were a few thousand low-level, nonviolent offenders. Drug violations and outstanding parking tickets and failure to pay mortgages or student loans.

His job was mostly to tell people where to stand and when to go back to their cells and to pick up something they'd dropped on the floor. He hated it. He hated it so much that some nights he would come home and go immediately to bed, dig his head into his pillow, his stomach a pit, the rest of his body falling into it.

The last day, the day he handed in his two-week notice and his supervisor shrugged and told him to just go home, it was the best day of his life. He'd promised himself he'd never return to a place where he'd have to answer to someone.

And yet.

As the bus barreled closer, Paxton flipped through the pamphlet, reread the security section. Apparently Cloud had its own team, deputized to handle screening and quality-of-life issues, and in the event of actual crimes, would liaise with local law enforcement. He looked out the window, at the rolling, empty fields. He wondered about local law enforcement.

The Cloud campus came into view as the bus crested a slight incline, affording a spectacular view of the surroundings.

A scatter of buildings sat before them, but at the center, the source of the drones buzzing back and forth across the sky, was a single structure so big you couldn't look at the entire thing at once, you had to do it in stages. The side of it facing Paxton was almost perfectly smooth and flat. Tubes ran between the behemoth and the smaller buildings that surrounded it, snaking across the ground, and the architecture had a feel of being both childish and brutal—hastily arranged after being dropped from the sky by an uncaring hand.

The woman in the white polo who'd been handling the announcements thus far stood up and said, "Attention, everyone."

Zinnia was still zonked out, so Paxton leaned over and said, "Hey." When she didn't stir, he put a finger on her shoulder and applied slight pressure until she woke up. She sat up with a start, eyes wild. Paxton put up his hands, palms out. "Sorry. Showtime."

She breathed in through her nose, nodded, shook her head as if she were trying to rattle a thought loose.

"There are three dormitories at MotherCloud: Oak, Sequoia, and Maple," the woman said. "Please listen carefully as I'll be reading a list of housing assignments."

She launched into a series of last names.

Athelia, Oak
Bronson, Sequoia
Cosentino, Maple

Paxton waited his turn, down at the end of the alphabet. Finally: Oak. He repeated it to himself: Oak, Oak, Oak.

He turned to Zinnia, who was riffling through her bag for something, not listening.

"You get yours?" Paxton asked.

She nodded without looking up. "Maple."

That's too bad, Paxton thought. There was something about Zinnia he liked. She seemed attentive. Compassionate. He hadn't expected to tell her what happened with the Perfect Egg, but he'd found that when he did, the saying of it, he was able to relieve some of the pressure, like letting air out of the balloon. It didn't hurt that she was pretty, though in an odd way. Her smooth neck and long, skinny limbs made him think of a gazelle. And when she smiled, her top lip arched in an exaggerated curve. It was a good smile and he wanted to see more of it.

Maybe Maple and Oak were close to each other?

A thought seized him. He wanted to say it was sudden, but it wasn't. The thought had climbed onto the bus with him and sat behind them until just now. Everything was about to change. A new job and a new place to live all at once. A seismic shift in the landscape of his life. He found himself stuck between a feeling like he couldn't wait to be there and hoping the bus would turn around.

He told himself he wouldn't be here for long. That this was just a temporary stop, like what the prison was supposed to be. Except this time he would stick to that.

The bus cruised toward the closest building, a large box with a gaping maw that the roadway ran into. Inside, the road split into dozens of lanes. Almost all of them were filled with tractor-trailers, making a careful, choreographed dance underneath metal scanners extending over the roadway. Paxton couldn't see any trucks coming the other way. There must have been a different route for exiting.

The bus drifted to the right, into its own lane away from the trucks, and sped past the gridlock, then came to a stop amidst a cluster of similar buses sitting in a lot. The woman who'd been leading the pack stood again and said, "As you exit the bus you'll receive your watch. It'll take a few minutes, so you folks in the back get comfy. We'll have you all off soon. Thank you and welcome to MotherCloud!"

The people on the bus stood and grabbed their bags. Zinnia remained seated, gazing through the window at the scene outside, which was mostly just other buses, the tops of their roofs visible, the black surfaces of the solar arrays rippling in the light.

Paxton considered asking her to go for a drink. It might be nice to know some people. But Zinnia was pretty, maybe a bit too pretty for him, and he didn't want to mar his first day with a rejection. He stood and got his bag, stepped aside, and let her walk ahead of him.

Outside the bus was a tall man with his gray hair pulled back into a neat ponytail, wearing a white polo shirt. He was flanked by a tall black woman, her head wrapped in a purple bandana, holding a box. The man would ask a question, tap the screen of his tablet, then reach in the box and hand each person something. One after another. When it was Paxton's turn, the man asked his name, checked the tablet, and handed him a watch.

Paxton stepped away from the throng to examine it. The strap was dark, dark gray, almost black, with a magnetic clasp. On the inside of the band was a series of metal discs. When he laid it over his wrist and secured the clasp, the screen flashed.

Hello, Paxton! Please place your thumb on the screen.

The message was replaced by the outline of a fingerprint. Paxton pressed his thumb against the screen and after a moment the watch buzzed.

Thanks!

Then:

Use your watch to get to your room.

Then:

You've been assigned to Oak.

He followed a queue of people to a series of body scanners, staffed by men and women in blue polo shirts wearing blue latex gloves. One of the men in blue called out, "No weapons," as one person after another deposited their luggage on a scanner, stepped into one of the machines, put their arms in the air, and allowed the machine to spin around them, before stepping out and getting their bags.

Beyond the scanners was an elevated platform overlooking a set of tracks, fronted by turnstiles. On each turnstile was a small black-mirrored disc with a white light around the circumference. People waved their CloudBands in front of the disc and the light turned green and made a comforting, satisfying sound. A warm little *ding* that seemed to say, *Everything is going to be okay.*

Paxton made it onto the platform and found Zinnia and stood next to her, watched as she fiddled with the watch, running her thin fingers along it.

"Not a watch person?" he asked.

"Hmm?" She looked up and squinted, as if she'd forgotten who he was.

"Sorry. Just an observation. Seems like you don't like wearing it."

Zinnia stretched out her arm. "It's light. It's like you can barely feel it."

"That's good though, right? If we're going to have to wear it all day long."

She nodded as a tram car shaped like a bullet pulled into the station. It moved silently on magnetic tracks and came to a stop with all the force of a leaf hitting the ground. The assembly of people climbed on, squeezing into the packed space. There was a series of yellow poles for people to hold on to, and a few disability seats along the wall that could be pulled down, but no one took them.

Paxton was pushed away from Zinnia by the force of the crowd, and when they'd settled and the doors closed, she was on the other side of the car, everyone crammed in shoulder to shoulder. Bodies pressed against him, smelling of sweat and aftershave and perfume, a toxic mix in the confined space. He wanted to kick himself for not saying something to Zinnia. At this point it felt like it was too late.

The tram rocketed through darkened tunnels before blasting into the sunlight. A few sharp turns nearly threw people from their feet.

The tram slowed and the large tinted windows flickered. The word *OAK* appeared in ghost-white letters, superimposed over the landscape. A cool male voice chimed in, announcing the station.

Paxton followed the crowd off and threw a quick salute to Zinnia, saying, "See you around?" It sounded more like a question than he would have wanted—he wanted to sound more bold—but she smiled and nodded.

Just off the tram was a tiled, subterranean station with a bank of three escalators, flanked by staircases on either side. One of the escalators wasn't working, orange cones placed around the mouth of it like teeth. Most people were opting for the escalator, but Paxton slung his bag onto his shoulder and braved the stairs. At the top was a blank cement space with a bank of elevators. One entire wall was a large screen, playing the introductory video from the bus.

As the mother placed an adhesive bandage on her son's knee, his wrist buzzed.

Floor 10, Room D

Efficient, at least. He proceeded to the elevators, found there weren't any buttons on the inside, just another disc surrounded by a circle of light. As people waved their wrists in front of it, the floor numbers appeared on the surface of the glass. Paxton waved his and the number 10 appeared.

Paxton was the only one to get off on the tenth floor. When the doors closed behind him he was surprised at the silence of the hallway. Pleasant, after hours of talking and videos and the bus and the road and the forced proximity to strangers. The walls were cinder block, painted white, the doors forest green, a little placard indicating the direction of restrooms and apartment numbers. The alphabet started at the far end of the hallway, which meant a long walk down the linoleum, his shoes squeaking against the reflective surface.

At the door marked D he held his wrist near the knob and there was a deep click. Paxton pushed the door open.

The room was more like a crowded hallway than an apartment. The floor was the same hard material of the hallway, the walls the same white-painted cinder block. Immediately to the right was a kitchen area: a countertop with a microwave built into the wall, as well as a small sink and a hot plate. He popped open a cabinet to find cheap plastic dishware. To his left were sliding doors, which he opened to find a long shallow closet.

Just past the counter and the closet was a futon built onto the left wall, with storage cabinets underneath. The mattress was a smooth, plastic-like material, like you would give a kid who still wets the bed. There was a small notecard on the edge of the futon, indicating he could pull it out into a bed.

On the wall opposite the bed was a mounted television, underneath which was a narrow coffee table, barely deep enough for a cup of coffee. At the far end of the room was a window of frosted glass, letting sunlight filter through the room, with a shade above it that could be drawn down.

Paxton put his bag next to a series of boxes and folded sheets and an anemic pillow. He stood next to the futon and could barely touch either wall with his fingertips.

No bathroom. He recalled the signs in the hallway for the restrooms and sighed. Shared bathrooms. Like being back in college. At least he didn't have a roommate.

Paxton's wrist buzzed.

Turn on the TV!

He found a remote on the futon, sat down, and turned on the television, which was at a high enough angle he had to crane his neck. A small woman wearing a white polo shirt and a megawatt smile stood in a room not dissimilar to Paxton's.

"Hello," she said. "Welcome to your introductory housing. As I'm sure you know from reading your housing material, room upgrades are available, but for now, you'll be here. We've provided you with some basics, and you can head over to the shops to fill in anything else you might need. During your first week at MotherCloud you're entitled to a ten percent discount on all apartment and wellness items. After that, you receive a five percent discount on all items purchased through the Cloud website. You'll find bathrooms at the end of the hall—male, female, and gender-neutral. If you need anything, please contact your resident adviser, who lives in apartment R. Now drop your stuff, take a walk around, and get acquainted with your Cloud family. But first, you might want to check your bed." She clapped her hands. "There's a job assignment—and a shirt—waiting for you."

The screen went black.

Paxton regarded the box sitting on the mattress. He hadn't noticed it when he first came in, even though it was sitting there, right in the open. He hadn't noticed it because he didn't want to notice.

Red. Please be red.

Really anything but blue.

He picked up the box and cradled it on his lap. Thought back to the prison. A short time after he got the job, he read about the Stanford prison experiment. A bunch of scientists stuck some folks into a role-playing environment where some were prisoners and some were guards. Though regular people, they took to their roles in earnest, the "guards" growing authoritative and cruel, the "prisoners" submitting to rules they really had no reason to submit to. It fascinated Paxton on a couple of levels, the deepest being that, even in a guard's uniform, he always felt like one of the prisoners. Authority was a too-big shoe that rubbed his foot raw and threatened to tumble off if he took too wide a step.

So of course, upon tearing open the box, he found three blue polo shirts.

They were neatly folded, the material smooth like athletic wear.

He sat there for a long time staring at them before tossing them against the wall and falling backward on the futon, letting his attention drift into the rough texture of the ceiling.

He considered leaving the room, going outside, somewhere, anywhere, but he couldn't bring himself to do it. He grabbed the pamphlets he'd gotten on the bus and reread the payment structure. The sooner he could get out, the better.

PAYMENTS AT MOTHERCLOUD

Welcome to MotherCloud! You probably have some questions about our payment structure. That's okay—it can be a little confusing! The following is an overview of how our system works, but if you need further assistance, you're welcome to make an appointment with a banker in our Admin building.

Cloud is 100 percent paperless—this includes money. Your CloudBand, which features the latest in near-field communication technology, is coded to you and you alone. It will only work when the clasp is done and it is in contact with your skin, so we recommend you only take it off for charging at night.

Your watch can be used for all transactions at MotherCloud. As an employee you are granted a special account in our banking system you can use while you work here. If you leave Cloud, you are welcome to maintain your account here—we're FDIC insured and funds are accessible through any standard ATM.

Your salary is paid in credits. One credit is roughly equivalent to $1 US, subject to a small conversion fee of a few fractions of a cent (see online banking portal for latest conversion figures)—and will be deposited in your account every Friday.

Taxes, along with modest housing, health, and transit fees, will be removed for you. As you know, because of the American Worker Housing Act, and the Paperless Currency Act, you do not earn minimum wage. But you get that money back in a variety of ways—through generous housing and health care plans, and through unlimited use of our company transit system, as well as our matching retirement fund.

Your account balance starts at zero, but you can use any current bank account to transfer money over, subject to a modest processing fee (see online banking portal for latest fee rates). We also offer temporary relief for those who don't have any cash to help them get started, on a credit basis. Please contact our banking department for more information.

You should also be aware that, due to the Worker Responsibility Act, you can be docked pay for the following offenses:

- Damage to Cloud property
- Arriving to work late more than twice
- Not meeting monthly quotas as set by a manager
- Personal health care negligence
- Going over your allotment of sick days
- Losing or breaking your watch
- Disorderly conduct

In addition, you can receive additional credits for the following:

- Meeting your monthly quotas for three months or more
- Using no sick days for six months or more
- Receiving a health checkup every six months
- Receiving a teeth cleaning once a year

Also, your pay is automatically increased by .05 credits for every week you maintain a five-star rating. The rating must be maintained for the entire week for the raise to take effect.

Your account also works as a credit card. If you go below the amount of credits in your account, you can still make charges. Any credits earned once you're in a deficit will go toward paying interest (see online banking portal for current rates) and then the principal.

You're also welcome to join our pension retirement program, in which, after a certain amount of years, you will be eligible for a reduced twenty-hour workweek, as well as subsidized housing and a 20 percent discount on anything purchased from the Cloud store.

Bankers are available between the hours of nine a.m. and five p.m. in Admin to help you with any needs you might have. You can also access your account at any time from the online banking portal, on CloudPoints located throughout MotherCloud, or through the browser on your apartment's television.

ZINNIA

Zinnia ran her finger over the screen of the watch. So smooth it was slippery. She clasped it, the magnets snapping against the thin membrane of skin on the inside of her wrist.

Charge it at night. Other than that, don't take it off, because it provides health tracking data, opens doors, registers ratings, delivers job assignments, processes transactions, and probably a hundred other things someone would need to do in MotherCloud.

Might as well have been a manacle.

In her head she recited the paragraph from the CloudBand manual that had sent her blood pressure up a few clicks.

CloudBands must be worn outside your room at all times, and your band is coded to you. Due to the sensitive personal information stored on each CloudBand, an alarm will sound—both audibly and in the Cloud security system—if it is off for too long, or if someone else is wearing your band.

She looked up at the door. On the inside wall was a disc—even to get out, you had to swipe. Probably to ensure people weren't leaving without wearing them, since they served as your key to everything, from the elevator to your apartment to the bathrooms.

It wasn't just about wearing it or not wearing it—it was tracking her location. Step into the wrong section, probably a blip would appear on a screen in a dark room. Someone would be alerted.

She glanced at the red polo shirts she'd pulled from the box on her bed, still annoyed they hadn't been brown.

She'd known about the watches of course. And she thought she'd figured out Cloud's job placement algorithm, giving them answers and a background that would place her on the tech crew. Which, in turn, would have provided ample access to what she needed.

Now, not so much.

It left her with three options:

First, tamper with the watch to alter the location data. Not impossible but also not something she was excited about. She was good, but maybe not that good.

Second, she could find a way to move without the watch on. Except, she wouldn't be able to open any doors. She couldn't even get out of her room.

Third, get reassigned to maintenance or security, since those jobs had the most access. Though she didn't even know if that was possible.

Which meant this whole gig was going to be a hell of a lot harder.

So why not start now, with some penetration testing?

She knelt down at the disc on the wall. Ran her fingers over it. Considered prying it off, but she figured it would trip some kind of alarm. She swiped so the door would open, then kept her foot in the door as she leaned over to the CloudBand charger. Placed the watch on the mat and then stepped into the hallway.

She stood there for a moment, until she realized it looked weird to just stand there, so she made her way to the bathrooms. By the time she reached them, a hunk of meat in a blue polo with tribal forearm tattoos had appeared from the elevators. He stopped a safe distance away from her and put his hands up in a *Calm down* gesture. He seemed to understand how the way he looked could set people on edge.

"Miss?" he asked, his voice slightly dopey. "You're not supposed to be out of your room without your CloudBand."

"Sorry. First day."

He smiled a gee-whiz smile. "It happens. Let me swipe you back into your room though, because otherwise you'll be locked out."

She let him escort her down the hallway. He kept a respectful distance. At the door he waved his watch in front of the disc and it lit up green. Then he stepped away from the door as if there were a wild tiger behind it. It was sweet.

"Thank you," she said.

"No worries, miss," he said.

She watched him trudge down the hallway and stepped back in the room. Went to her makeup kit, pulled out the tube of red lipstick she'd never worn. Unscrewed the bottom and pulled out a radiofrequency detector the size and shape of her thumb. She pressed the button on the side and a green light flashed to indicate it was charged.

She ran it over every surface in the room. The light turned red at the television and light fixture, which was where she expected it would, but no place else. Nothing in the air vents or the cabinets.

Next she popped open the door and ran the scanner around the jamb. The light turned red at the latch. There was something there, embedded behind the thin metal of the frame. Thermal scanner? Motion detector? She took her CloudBand off the charger and strapped it around her wrist. Checked the door again. No red light. Put the CloudBand on the charger. Red light.

There it was. It seemed fair to assume, then, that the problem point was the door. Some kind of sensor that could read her leaving the room if she wasn't wearing the watch. If she could dock her watch and find another exit, she'd be okay.

She looked around the room and it looked even smaller, like a child's clubhouse. She'd get there. First, a little recon. She strapped the watch to her wrist and ambled down the empty hallway to the bathroom. Picked the gender-neutral door—half man, half woman-with-skirt—where she found a long row of sinks and toilets and urinals. One of the toilet stalls was taken, small sneakers visible underneath the gap. Probably a woman, given the size and style.

Zinnia walked to the sink and ran the tap. The faucet felt loose in the housing. She gave it a tug and it nearly came out. She went to the next sink and splashed some water on her face. Looked up and found the bathroom had a drop ceiling.

Good.

On her way to the elevator she crossed paths with a young woman, pretty in a cheerleader way, and delicate, too, which made the brown polo shirt appear out of place on her slender frame. Her hair, the same color as her polo, was tied in a ponytail pulled back so tight it looked painful. She locked her big cartoon eyes on Zinnia and said, "You're new on the floor?"

Zinnia paused. The law of social niceties demanded she offer platitudes in exchange.

"I am," Zinnia said, forcing herself to smile. "Just this morning."

"Welcome," the girl said, offering her hand. "I'm Hadley."

Zinnia shook. The girl's hand was fragile, like a small bird.

"How are you getting on?" the girl asked.

"Fine," Zinnia said. "You know, it's a lot, but I'm getting settled."

"Well, if you need anything, I'm in Q. And there's Cynthia in V. She's, like, the mayor of the hall." The girl gave a conspiratorial smile. "You know how it is. We girls have to stick together."

"Is that how it is?"

Hadley blinked. Once, twice. Then she nodded and widened her smile, hoping the glow would distract from the unsaid thing hanging in the air, and Zinnia filed that away in her brain as potentially interesting.

"Well, nice to meet you," she said, and she spun around in her cute little red flats. Zinnia called after her, "Nice to meet you, too," and turned toward the elevator, her guard still up, trying to figure out exactly what that was, and by the time she was halfway down to the lobby she decided the girl was just being nice and she should probably calm down.

Once downstairs, Zinnia stopped in front of a large freestanding computer screen that showed a map of the entire campus.

The dorms ran in a straight line, north to south: Sequoia, Maple, Oak. North of Sequoia was a teardrop-shaped facility called Live-Play, which the map indicated had restaurants and movie theaters and a whole bunch of other crap for the people here to anesthetize themselves with.

The tram ran in a loop. It stopped in each of the three dorms. The dorms were also connected by halls of shops, so you could walk from Oak on one end to Live-Play on the other on what the map called the promenade. It looked to be about a mile.

The tram then looped around to two more buildings—one of which was for administration and banking and schools, Admin, and the other for health and hospital, Care. Then it went through the main warehouse facility, before returning to Incoming, the building where they'd gotten off the bus. Finally, back to the dorms.

The map showed there were also emergency tracks. Each facility had multiple medical bays, all of which led directly to Care. There was also an entirely separate system that took maintenance workers across the solar and wind fields to the far edge of the property, to the cluster of water, waste, and energy processing facilities.

It was exactly where she needed to be.

Zinnia turned and walked, figured she would go down to Oak, then loop back up to Live-Play. Get a feel for the promenade, at least. The lobby of Maple was stark, plain polished concrete. Zinnia found doors to a laundry room as well as a gym, which was nicely stocked—free weights and machines and treadmills. No one was using it.

The promenade was airport chic, a massive, bi-level hall with the occasional elevator or escalator or winding staircase. There were quick-stop food joints, drugstores, a delicatessen, a nail salon, a foot massage parlor. Lots of foot massage parlors, full of people in red or brown or white polo shirts, sprawled on long chaise lounges while women in green shirts worked their hideously exposed feet. Built into the walls were massive video screens, the color saturation torqued up so high it hurt her eyes to look at them, advertising jewelry and phones and snacks.

Everything was polished concrete and glass, the feel of the color blue, and Zinnia had a sense of every surface being violent. She climbed a staircase and walked along the railing, the barrier a perfectly clear plate of glass, and her stomach lurched as if she might fall; if she did, she would surely be grievously injured on the unforgiving floor. She passed an escalator that was out of service, the teeth of it pulled up, men in brown polos standing inside its guts, not really trying to fix it, more looking around like they were just discovering how it worked, while long lines of people queued up at the elevator.

She passed through the final dormitory and entered a corridor that turned at a ninety-degree angle, leading to Live-Play. It was lined with video screens and restaurants a little more eclectic than the sandwich and soup fare in the earlier halls. Tacos and barbecue and ramen, all of the storefronts with stool seating and limited menus, all of them half-full of people eating with their faces down.

She stopped into the taco shop and sat at the bar. A stout Mexican man raised his eyebrows at her and she asked in Spanish if he had *cabeza*. He frowned and shook his head, pointed to the small menu over his head. Chicken, pork, and of course beef that was four times the cost of the other two. She settled on three pork tacos and the man got to work, throwing precooked meat onto the stainless-steel griddle to warm it up, tossing down some corn tortillas alongside.

Zinnia worked some money out of her pocket and put enough on the bar to cover her tab, plus a little extra, as the cook scooped the meat onto the tortillas, along with a heap of chopped onion and cilantro. He placed the plate in front of her, along with a small black disc. He shook his head at the money and said he couldn't make change. Zinnia waved him off, said to keep it. He smiled and nodded, pulling the cash off the counter, looking around briefly, and placing it in his pocket.

"*Es tu primer día?*" he asked.

"*Sí,*" Zinnia said.

He smiled, his eyes going soft, like a parent who'd gotten disappointing news about a child. He nodded his head slowly and said, "*Buena suerte.*"

She didn't like the way he said it. He turned his back and Zinnia dug into the tacos. Not the best she'd had, but good enough for Middle of Fucking Nowheresville. When she was done with her food she slid the plate across the bar and waved to the cook, who waved back and gave another pained smile. Then she wandered down the corridor until it opened into a large hall.

Live-Play smelled like fresh running water. Air filters working overtime. It reminded her a little bit of a shopping mall, or at least, how shopping malls were back before they fell out of vogue. When she was a child, and it felt as if everything she could ever want was there in one place. There were three levels, one above her and one below, accessible by a jumble of elevators and escalators. Shops and stores hugging the walls, walkways looking out over a chasm. A large portion of it was taken up by a casino. At the roof, a series of glass panels let in a filtered view of the sky, muted dark blue.

There was a British pub and a sushi joint—sushi, sure, fresh fish all the way out here. And a CloudBurger, which was supposed to be quite good, and included an actual piece of beef that didn't cost as much as an entire dinner.

Besides food, there was a retro arcade and a more advanced VR room. Plus a movie theater, nail salon, massage parlor, candy store. The seating areas along the floor were dotted with people. More people milled in and out of the stores.

She passed a deli and felt a little pang in her stomach. She could eat more. A piece of fruit would be nice. Something fresh. She stepped inside and wandered the short aisles, found packages of processed food, drinks in the fridge case. But no apples, no bananas. She left. Kept walking until she crossed the retro arcade. She abandoned her quest for fruit, stepped into the maze of glittering and buzzing machines.

All the games had little metal discs on the front. She searched the place for a coin machine but couldn't find one, so she ducked back into the hallway, found a CloudPoint kiosk. They were everywhere. She could see half a dozen more from where she was standing.

She logged into the banking portal, which prompted her to swipe her watch. The screen lit up—*Welcome, Zinnia!*—and she got to work linking the dummy bank account on the outside, putting credits into her account. She transferred $1,000 and ended up with $994.45. As she worked she examined the kiosk—like an ATM, big and heavy and plastic, with a touchscreen. No visible access ports.

There was a panel toward the bottom of the machine, probably with at least a USB connection, probably some other tech she could play with, but a few problems presented themselves: how to open the panel, how to keep the near-field communication tech from registering her watch, how to do it so no one would see. Still, probably a good option to get the entrée she needed.

She scrolled around the screen and found that the current rate for pickers was nine credits per hour, which probably translated to somewhere between eight and nine bucks. Once that was finished, her watch now loaded with some money, she went back to the arcade, spent a little more time wandering the empty aisles until she found what she was looking for.

Pac-Man. The classic version. First released in Japan in 1980. The Japanese name was *Pakkuman*. *Paku-paku* described the sound of a mouth opening and closing in rapid succession. Zinnia liked video games, and this was her favorite.

She swiped her CloudBand and started, pushing the little yellow form through the maze, gobbling white dots while avoiding candy-colored ghosts, jerking the joystick to the left and the right, the sound of it slamming against the cabinet loud, as if she might break it.

The machine, and everything else around her, supposedly powered by the sun and the wind.

Supposedly.

The technical term for what she did was "competitive intelligence." The romantic term was "corporate espionage." She infiltrated the tightest security systems, the most secretive companies, to abscond with their best-kept secrets.

And she was good at it.

But she'd never worked Cloud before. Never even thought of it. That was like climbing Everest. Though with the way things were going, it was only a matter of time. Cloud hoovered up businesses so fast, soon there wouldn't be anyone left who needed to spy on someone else. It used to be she could work a job every few months and that was more than enough. Lately she was lucky to pull a gig a year.

Still, when she'd accepted this, she'd figured there wasn't much to it. Probably a miscalculation on someone's part. But then she examined the satellite photos. The square acreage of the solar farms. The specs of the photovoltaic panels. The number and output of the wind turbines. And she realized her employers were right: there didn't seem to be any way Cloud could produce the amount of energy required to run this place.

One of the reasons Cloud enjoyed tax-free status was the company's green initiatives. The company had to meet government-mandated energy benchmarks in order to qualify for huge tax breaks. So if it was true—if the infrastructure on site wasn't enough to produce the energy needed to sustain it—Cloud was using something else. Probably something that wasn't green. Which meant they could stand to lose millions—maybe billions.

The orange ghost got on her tail. Zinnia moved Pac-Man up and down the alleys on the screen, mostly ones she had already cleared, trying to shake him, trying to avoid the others, until she reached the larger glowing orb that flipped the table. The ghosts went blue and she gave chase.

So, who benefits?

Not that she needed to know in order to do her job. But the question was like an itch. It could have been one of the journalism or good-government groups that were always up Cloud's ass about labor practices or the monopoly it held on online retail. Newspapers had been trying to sneak people into these facilities for years, but the algorithms and work histories had always weeded them out. It had taken Zinnia a month to build a fake history with a solid-enough foundation to pass muster.

But she figured it was more likely one of the brick-and-mortar superstore companies, wanting to take Cloud down a few pegs. Regain some of the foothold they'd lost after the Black Friday Massacres.

Zinnia found herself with most of the screen cleared, just a few dots up in the left-hand corner still to munch. She made for them.

All that mattered was this: A facility of this size with this many people ought to have required fifty megawatts per hour to operate. And the capacity of the solar and wind fields was fifteen, maybe twenty. Something was off. She just had to figure out what. Which meant making it inside their infrastructure. She had a few months to do it and until then she was on her own. No communication with her employers. Not even through the encrypted app on her phone. She had no idea how capable Cloud was.

Zinnia jerked Pac-Man down another alley, going for those last dots, the ghosts flanking her. She aimed for the next hard left but knew she wouldn't make it in time. Within seconds she was trapped, and the orange ghost ran into Pac-Man and the little yellow orb made a whistle-and-splat sound as it deflated and disappeared.

ORIENTATION^2

GIBSON

There are a lot of days at Cloud I remember, but the one I remember most fondly is the first day. I remember it because it was the hardest. Every day after that was a little easier.

People thought I was nuts to start this company. A lot of people probably don't even remember, back in the day, there was another company that did some of the same stuff we do now, except on a much smaller scale. Problem was, their interests were too earthbound.

Ever since I was a kid, I was obsessed with the sky. The broadness of it. Like we had this giant resource over us every day and we weren't really using it. Sure, we had planes flying this way and that, but there seemed to be so much more potential.

At a pretty young age I knew the future was in drone technology. The air and the roads had been all gummed up by these giant trucks, taking up space, spitting out poison. If we could solve the truck problem, we could solve a lot of other problems. Traffic, pollution, crash fatalities.

Do you know what traffic costs? About ten years ago, when it reached epidemic proportions, you're talking about something like $305 billion in direct and indirect losses in a single year. This was according to the Institute for Economics and Business Research.

Now, what does that mean? Losses include time wasted while sitting in traffic, the cost of fuel, impact on the environment, road maintenance, traffic fatalities. Mass transit helps, but only so much. Even way back when I was young, a lot of our mass transit infrastructure was already falling apart, and the cost to fix it was astronomical. We all remember when the New York City subway system finally fell apart. That city has never been the same since.

The key was getting drones into the sky for more than just fun and games.

I remember my first drone. This dinky little thing that couldn't go more than a hundred feet without dipping down and crashing. It certainly wasn't strong enough to carry much. But as time went on, as the mechanics got better and they could carry more weight, I began to tinker with them, and then invested in a company that made them—lucky for me, right before the company took off, so I ended up with a nice little chunk of cash.

That company was called WhirlyBird. I hated that name, but they did something real smart. Rather than take drones as they were, they thought, If we were to design these today, knowing what we know now, how could we make them better?

They started from scratch. Redistributed the way the motors were laid out. Experimented with new kinds of materials. Lighter composites. World-changing technology, the *New York Times* called it. And I was damn proud to be a part of it.

From there, it took a lot of lobbying with the Federal Aviation Administration to figure out how to keep planes and drones in the air at the same time, without anyone crashing into each other. Drones don't go that high, but you don't want to screw with takeoff and landing.

And to be honest, that was damn hard. Not so much the crashing—the guys and gals at WhirlyBird developed some pretty good detection technology. The problem was, well, you know we started with ground delivery, but when we wanted to move Cloud over to majority-drone delivery, we had to work with the federal government. And it was pretty much a nightmare. Years and years of problems. Until finally, we made an agreement to take control of the FAA. We privatized it, we staffed it with competent people—and it got better.

You can build one government-funded building in the time it takes to develop a hundred privately owned properties, because of one key difference—private developers want to make money, while governments want to keep people employed. Which means dragging things out as long as possible.

Anyway, a lot of people think I named my company Cloud because of the way the drones look coming off the processing centers, these great big clouds of machines flying packages this way and that. But I went with Cloud because that was my mission statement.

The sky wasn't the limit anymore.

So, back to that first day, it was me and Ray Carson—yes, Ray, there from day one. Besides having a strong back, Ray was real tech-savvy, more so than me, so he was a big help, able to translate whenever someone started throwing out words with more than three syllables. So I named him my VP. It was him and me and a couple of other folks. First thing we had to do was sign up a bunch of companies, get them to agree to let us deliver their goods. If we got some good companies and did a good job for them, I knew more would follow.

We rented this office building in the downtown area, not too far from where I grew up, which was important to me, because I wanted that connection to my hometown. I didn't want to forget where I came from.

So we show up to the office, and the place is empty. I swear to truth, all these years later, I know for a fact the Realtor told us the office would be furnished. It wasn't a big space—or even a very nice space—but it was a space, and we wouldn't have to scramble to fill it. But we walk in and the place is stripped bare. Nothing but walls and floors and wires hanging from where the lighting fixtures used to be. The previous company, this old accounting firm, they were supposed to leave their stuff behind.

They even took the damn toilets!

So I get on the phone with the Realtor, a real crook whose name I wish I could remember, because I would just love to plaster it all over the internet right now. He swore to me up and down that no, he never said the place would be furnished. And this was back in my youth, when I was a little more energetic but, I guess you could say, easily distracted. I didn't get any kind of promise in writing, just a handshake deal.

Which apparently, to this guy, wasn't worth anything.

So it's me and Ray and about a dozen people standing around with not much to do but stare at all this empty space. This is where Renee stepped up big-time. Renee was a former military gal, as smart and tough as they come. If you were to tell her something wasn't possible, she would give this cute little laugh and then tell you: "Make it possible." I learned a lot from her.

She gets on the horn, calling up everyone in creation, trying to find us what we need. After all the money I'd laid out on the building and licensing and a bunch of other start-up costs, it just about wiped out my windfall from the WhirlyBird investment. I was really relying on her. And Renee finds out there's this school nearby that's being closed down, on account of it's consolidating with another school in the district, and a lot of the furniture is getting piled up outside to get hauled off.

Jackpot! I'm not the kind of guy who needs fancy things. I don't need some desk that changes heights and makes my coffee and tells me I look nice. All I need is a phone, a computer, a pad, a pen, and a place to sit. End of list.

Me and Ray and a few of the other men trek out to the school, and sure enough, there's a big pile of stuff. We took everything. At that point I didn't want to be picky. I didn't know exactly how much of it we even needed. I figured, anything that we can take, let's take it and see if we can use it.

There were a couple of teacher's desks, metal behemoths that weighed a million pounds, but there weren't enough of them to go around. We did find a lot of school desks. The kind with the top that would flip up and you could store stuff inside. We got dozens of those. And what we did was line them up in rows of three and bolt them together.

We got to calling them triplets. I took one for myself. It felt important that I didn't take one of those big old desks. I didn't want to give people the wrong idea about how things were, like I needed special treatment. If I'd had my way, everyone would have taken a triplet, but Ray just fell in love with a big desk we dragged over. He liked to put his feet up when he was thinking, so I figured, I'll let him have it.

I still have my triplet, down in the basement of my house. And that's why, when you go to our corporate offices, you'll see that everyone works on one. No $10,000 mahogany slabs carved from a single tree for us. Over time I came to appreciate the look of them. I think it's a good reminder. Stay humble. No one needs a big fancy desk except for someone who wants you to think he's more important than he really is.

We found a lot of discarded computer equipment, too. We had this kid working for us, Kirk, a real whiz. He basically took all this stuff and built a big Frankenstein of a computer network, just so we could get on our feet.

I think that's what needed to happen. It was our first real test.

Technically, the first test was my having this idea, and convincing enough people I had enough wits that maybe I could pull it off. But this was our first physical test. One of those moments when a lot of folks would throw their hands up and say they were done. My team dug in and found a solution to a problem.

I remember, after we finished up, it was well past sundown, and me and Ray wandered over to this local bar we went to sometimes, the Foundry. Both of us were aching, dragging ourselves onto bar stools like old men, and we figured, we ought to toast. Get a nice glass of scotch or something. So I went into my wallet and found it was empty—I had bought everyone lunch that day. And my cards were maxed out.

Ray, God bless him, put his card down on the bar and ordered us two scotches on the rocks. But his cards were close to maxed out, too, so he got well scotch, which tasted like battery acid that had been lit on fire.

To this day, the best drink I ever had.

Before we called it an early night—believe me, we weren't the type to tie one on, especially when we had to be in to work early the next day—Ray patted me on the back and said, "I think this is the start of something."

This is a hard thing to say, especially with how much faith everyone put in me at that point, but I didn't believe him. Sitting in that bar, thinking of my school desk and our computer network that seemed to switch off if the wind blew too hard—I was so scared. Like I'd convinced these people I wasn't nuts, and now they were depending on me.

Ray gave me a second wind. There from the beginning. I don't have any brothers or sisters, but I have Ray, and that's the next best thing.

ZINNIA

Zinnia pulled on a pair of jeans and her red polo, then sat down to put on some shoes, and found herself with two not-so-great choices.

She'd brought a sturdy pair of boots, because she thought she'd be on the tech team, and a pair of flats so thin they were practically socks. She liked them because she could ball them up and stick them into her purse, but for a job like this, lots of standing and walking, they weren't going to cut it. Plus, her ankle still felt a little wonky from that spill in Bahrain last month. She needed the support, so she opted for the boots.

She grabbed the CloudBand off the charging mat and strapped it around her wrist. It buzzed and said: *Good morning, Zinnia!*

Then: *Your shift is due to start in 40 minutes. You should leave soon.*

The words were replaced by a pulsing arrow that pointed toward the door. She stood, turned in a circle. The arrow spun, never leaving the door. As she stepped outside the watch buzzed against her wrist and the arrow swung to the left, pointing toward the elevators.

She followed the arrow down to the tram, where a massive group of people waited. There was a spectrum of polo colors, but mostly red. A tram car slid into the station, filled up, and left. Zinnia watched two more. When she managed to make it aboard the fourth, the space filled until she was shoulder to shoulder with the people around her, all of them doing the commuter shuffle, elbows tight to their bodies, shifting their weight with the movement of the car to keep upright.

The crowd getting off at the main warehouse facility were mostly young, fit. No older folks, no heavy folks, no one with any clear disabilities. They all drifted toward the end of a long queue that snaked around a large room, marching through lanes cordoned off by stanchions.

At the end of the line were three turnstiles, a revolving set of metal arms that only one person could step through at a time, after scanning their watch at the disc on the front.

A series of video monitors was built into the walls, all of them showing a clip in which a man bent over to pick up a box, arching his back. A buzzer sounded and a red X appeared on the image. The same man bent at the knees, keeping his spine straight, and there was a ding and a green check mark appeared.

Then, a woman calmly walking with a box to a conveyor belt. The screen froze, and the words *Walk, don't run* appeared.

Then, a man carrying a box that seemed to be too heavy for him. *Inform a manager if you can't lift an object heavier than 25 pounds.*

Then, a woman climbing the side of a shelving unit, like a monkey. Buzz. Red X. *Always use your safety harness.*

When it was Zinnia's turn at the turnstile, she stepped through and walked down a hallway into a space so massive it made her a little dizzy, trying to process it all.

Shelving units stretched as far as she could see. The inside of the place had a horizon line. She couldn't see the outer walls from where she was standing, just mammoth support columns, reaching up to the vastness of the ceiling, which was lower than she would have expected. Three stories. Maybe four. The shelving units themselves were twice her height, and they slid across the polished concrete floor, spinning around and switching spots with each other. Men and women in red polo shirts dashed back and forth between them, digging out packages. The space was snaked with conveyor belts marked in yellow, items flying across the rollers.

Spinning metal and slapping feet and the soft whir of machinery melded into a symphony of chaos. It smelled of motor oil and cleaning supplies and something else. That gym smell. Aerosolized sweat and rubber. The air was both cool and slightly humid. Zinnia stood and watched this great machine, dancing, oblivious to her, almost to itself.

Her wrist buzzed. Another arrow. It prompted her to walk forward, until it buzzed again, the arrow switching, moving her to the right. She glanced up and down, from the watch to the space in front of her, careful to avoid the red runners and the spinning machines, having to stop every dozen steps to let someone pass so she wouldn't get knocked on her ass.

So much for *Walk, don't run.*

After a few more turns she realized the buzzing was different for each new direction. The side of the watch closest to her wrist joint buzzed when it wanted her to go right. Back or forth, it would buzz the bottom or the top. It took a minute, but once she noticed it, she couldn't not notice. A few more turns and she found she could navigate by feel without looking down.

"Pretty cool, huh?"

She found herself at a far wall, or maybe just a freestanding structure in the middle of the warehouse floor. She couldn't tell. Leaning against the wall was a young Latino man. Strong, hammered forearms with curly black hair.

"Miguel," he said, extending his hand. The band of his watch was fabric, and dark green, like fresh leaves. "I'm here to help you get acclimated."

"Zinnia," she said, returning the shake. The skin of his hand was cracked and callused.

"Okay, *mi amiga,* you seem to have gotten the knack of the directionals. So, let's walk around a bit and I'll explain the mechanics of all this. Then we can get started."

Zinnia held up her wrist. "So this really is your lifeline, isn't it?"

"Only thing you'll ever need to get around. Follow me."

Miguel pushed off the wall and strode along it, the expanse of the warehouse floor to their left, and to their right: offices, break rooms, bathrooms, broken up by long stretches of walls that featured video screens playing a clip of the commercial they'd watched on the bus ride over.

The young mother. The bandages.

"Honestly, if it wasn't for Cloud, I don't know what I'd do."

There was added footage. Happy, shiny people working at Cloud. People picking items out of bins, placing them on conveyor belts. The occasional testimonial from a satisfied customer.

An Asian kid in a dorm room.

"I'd never have passed my midterm if I didn't get that textbook in time."

A young black girl in front of a dilapidated house.

"There are no bookstores or libraries in my neighborhood. If it weren't for Cloud I wouldn't have any books at all."

An elderly white man sitting in an old-fashioned living room.

"It's hard for me to make it to the store these days. Thank you, Cloud."

"Welcome to the floor," Miguel said, spreading his arms. "That's what we call it. All these pretty folks are reds." He pinched the fabric of his polo shirt. "The whites are the managers. They roam around and keep an eye on things. Speaking of, if you have an issue, just press the crown of the watch and say *manager*. It'll send you to the closest one who's free."

Zinnia looked down at her watch. Wondered if it listened only when the crown was pressed. Probably not.

"So the gig is pretty simple," Miguel said. "Seriously, the watch does most of the work for you. It'll give you directions to an item. You find the item. You pick it up. It'll give you directions to a particular belt. You drop the item. Boom. Next one. You do that for nine hours. Two fifteen-minute breaks for the bathroom, plus a half hour for lunch."

"You can't just go to the bathroom?" Zinnia asked.

"Let me introduce you to the yellow line, *mi amiga*." Miguel held up the watch, tapped the face. Running along the bottom, hair-thin, was a green line. "It doesn't look so bad now, but once you get started, this tracks your progress. Green means you're making rate. If you're lagging behind, you drop into yellow. You hit red, your employee ranking plummets. So don't hit red."

"These folks are really obsessed with their colors, aren't they?"

Miguel nodded. "Lot of people here who don't speak a word of *inglés*. Anyway, to your question, too much time in the bathroom, you fall behind. Best to hold it. And a thing about breaks . . ." He stopped. Raised an eyebrow, as if he needed to emphasize the point. "You get a half hour for lunch. If you're all the way out in the hinterlands, it could take up to twenty minutes to make it to a break room. The algorithm is supposed to keep that from happening, but it happens. My advice—the protein bars in the vending machines keep pretty well. Carry one in your back pocket. Better to get the calories."

"What about water?"

Miguel shrugged. "There are water fountains everywhere. Stay hydrated. You'd be amazed with so much space, but it can get hot as hell in here sometimes." He looked down at her feet and grimaced. "And get some sneakers. Order them tonight. Trust me—those boots are not going to feel nice in a few hours."

"Yeah, I figured that," Zinnia said. "So you pick stuff up, drop it on the conveyor. What about larger items?"

"Different part of the floor," Miguel said. "And you only ever get there once you've been here a bit. Entry level is strictly stuff under twenty pounds. Hold on . . ."

He put his arm up, not touching Zinnia, but making sure it was close enough to get her to stop walking. A girl in a red polo flew past. Zinnia had barely seen her in her peripheral vision. The girl's hair was whipping around her face and she was sprinting, hard, something tucked under her arm. Face nearly purple from exertion, and maybe tears. She hit a corner, turned, and disappeared.

"Building on fire?" Zinnia asked.

"Getting to the end of her shift," Miguel said. "Way the algorithm works, you're supposed to have enough time to walk to your item, pick it up, and bring it to a belt, all at a brisk and deliberate pace, right? Doesn't really work like that. Sometimes the bugs have things moved around. Sometimes stuff isn't shelved right, so you lose time looking for it. Sometimes by the end of your shift, you're motoring to replenish that line." He pointed to another young man hauling ass down a row and disappearing. "You come in too far behind too many times, your rating goes down."

"Bugs?" Zinnia asked.

Miguel stepped down an aisle, waved for her to follow. He brought her to a shelving unit, crouched, and pointed underneath, to a little yellow dome on wheels, hooked into the bottom of the unit. Then he kept pointing, along the floor, to stickers with scanner codes placed on the concrete.

"The little yellow things that move them around, we call them bugs," he said. "So, how about we do our first pick, so you can get a feel for it?"

"Sure."

Miguel raised his wrist to his face, pressed the crown. "Preliminary training complete, on to step two."

Zinnia's wrist buzzed. Another arrow. Miguel placed his hand in the air, palm up, and bowed.

"After you, *mi amiga*."

Zinnia let the buzz of the watch tell her which way to go. She understood the importance of a directional technology that didn't involve looking down. Between the moving shelves, the dashing reds, and the conveyor belts, it was an easy place to get creamed if you weren't paying attention.

"You're a natural," Miguel said.

"So why is it you're training me, and not one of the managers?"

"Managers have more important stuff to do," he said in a tone that indicated he didn't believe it. "This is a voluntary program. You don't really get anything, except an hour or two where you don't have to run around. I like it. You're a relief. Most people don't pick up on the directional thing until the end of their first shift."

Zinnia stepped around a shelving unit as it slid into their path.

"Doesn't seem too hard," Zinnia said.

"You'd be surprised."

Probably not, Zinnia thought.

"How long have you been here?" Zinnia asked.

"Going on five years."

"You like it?"

Long pause. Zinnia glanced over. Miguel had a look on his face as if he were chewing something soft and unpleasant. Zinnia kept looking, not giving up, so he shrugged. "It's a job."

Answer enough. She figured that was the end, but then he kept going. "My husband wants me to take the manager's test. Try and move up. But I like this just fine."

Zinnia wondered about the managers. The ratio was extreme. She saw hundreds of people in red, but only the occasional man or woman in white, carrying a tablet, walking like they had someplace to be.

"I would figure being a manager is a little less intense," Zinnia said.

"And more money. But I don't know . . ." Miguel looked at Zinnia, speaking slowly. Choosing his words. "They have this program, the Rainbow Coalition, supposed to be all about minority empowerment. Getting us up in the ranks. Diversification. I don't know how effective it is. Most of the people who wear white . . . they tend to match their shirts, if you know what I'm saying?"

Zinnia gave a conspiratorial nod.

"You Latina, or . . . ?" Miguel asked, then shook his head and dropped his chin. "Sorry, I shouldn't ask."

Zinnia gave him a *Don't worry* smile. "My mother."

"You should think about applying then."

The watch buzzed again, several times in rapid succession. She looked down, saw it said 8495-A. Looked up and saw the same number on the shelving unit in front of her.

"Okay," Miguel said. "Now tap the watch."

Zinnia did, and the numbers changed.

Bin 17.

Electric razor.

Then, a picture of an electric razor in plastic clamshell packaging.

"Seventeen?" Zinnia asked.

"Toward the top of the spinner," Miguel said. "Hold on . . ." He pulled a bundle from his pocket. "Sorry, was supposed to give this to you at the start. Safety harness."

Zinnia looped it over her belt, and found a carabiner clip on one end. She pulled the clip and a gauge of heavy nylon wire came out from inside the belt. It was thin and sleek and she immediately thought of a million different uses for it. Like not going ass-over-elbow in Bahrain.

"Attach it to the hooks as you climb," Miguel said, taking the carabiner and latching it to a curved piece of metal protruding a few inches above Zinnia's head. There were more hooks, running up the side of the unit. "Though honestly, in a few days you'll stop using the thing. Takes too much time. But if you see a manager around, use it. You can get a strike for that. Three strikes, you lose a credit."

Jesus, this system. Zinnia climbed the side of the unit, treating the individual shelves like a ladder, and found the bin. She grabbed the hard plastic clamshell holding the razor that had appeared on the watch and leapt to the ground. The watch buzzed with a smiley face.

"I guess this means I did it right," Zinnia said, holding up her wrist.

Miguel nodded. "Everything is chipped. It'll let you know if you didn't pick the right item. The way they stock them is pretty clever—they don't usually put things next to each other that could easily be confused. Still, mistakes happen. Now . . ."

The watch buzzed again, pointing her away from the shelving unit, down another long row. They walked until they reached a conveyor belt. The watch gave several buzzes again. Underneath the belt were piles of plastic bins nested inside each other. She took one, placed the package inside, and it whisked off, disappearing from sight.

"On to the next," he said.

"That's it?"

"That's it. Like I said, you're new, first couple of weeks all you're going to do is carry smaller stuff. Longer you're here, the more complicated the work gets. Heavier items, or you get assigned to placing, which means you carry items from where they come in to the appropriate shelving unit. Word of warning: the bugs aren't supposed to move when someone is hooked onto a shelving unit, but since we don't always hook ourselves in . . . sometimes they do, and it's like riding a bronco."

"So what now?"

Miguel looked down at his own watch. "Technically, we have another hour free, where you can ask me questions. How would you feel about walking over to a break room, grabbing some water? Breaks are rare enough around here. Got to take them where you can."

"Sure," Zinnia said. She preferred to get to work—the mindless tedium of it would give her space to think—but she figured he might say something useful.

Miguel wasn't exaggerating about what a haul it was to get to the break room. It took them fifteen minutes to find one. She had no sense of space, but he seemed to know the way. Halfway through the walk, Miguel pointed out she could say *break room* into her watch and it would direct her to the closest one.

They got to a room, found it mostly empty. A row of vending machines along one wall, two of them out of order, and a series of flat tables with stools bolted to them. On the wall, in great big cursive, it said: YOU MAKE ALL THINGS POSSIBLE!

Miguel got two bottles of water from a machine and placed them on a table. As Zinnia sat, he pushed a bottle toward her.

"Thanks," she said, cracking the plastic top.

"I can't stress it enough," he said. "Make sure to stay hydrated. That's what gets most people. Dehydration."

Zinnia took a sip, the water so cold it stung her teeth.

"Anything else I should know?" she asked.

Miguel looked at her. Blinked a few times. As if maybe there was something he wanted to tell her but he wasn't sure if he could trust her.

She tried to think of something that would translate to *Hey, I'm cool*, but finally, Miguel said, "Stay hydrated. Hit your numbers. Don't complain. If you get hurt, walk it off. The less you have to talk to the managers, the better." He took out his phone, typed something, and held it up for her to see.

Don't even SAY the word union.

Zinnia nodded. "Got it."

Miguel cleared the text from his phone. "How's the apartment working out for you?"

"The shoebox?"

"You have to think vertically. I get these wire baskets and hang them from the ceiling. Makes for easy storage."

"You still live in one of those?" Zinnia asked. "Didn't you say you were married?"

"We make it work."

"I thought you could upgrade housing."

"You can," Miguel said. "But it's expensive. My husband and I—he blew out his ankle so now he works in customer service—we're saving our credits. He's from Germany. We're thinking of leaving, going there."

Zinnia nodded. "Germany is nice."

Miguel breathed in, let it out in a long, sad stream of air. "One day . . ."

Zinnia gave him a small smile. Something he might find comforting but that would also cover up the awkwardness, the pity she felt for this man, stuck in his monkey job, dreaming of leaving the country when there was a very good chance it was never going to happen.

Miguel looked at his CloudBand. "I guess that's it. If you get jammed up on something you can say *Miguel Velandres* into the watch and it'll find me. And like I said, you can say *manager* to find a white, but it's better the less you have to bother with them."

They dropped their water bottles into an overflowing recycling bin—a sign above it that said, THANK YOU FOR RECYCLING!—and stepped onto the floor.

"You ready?" Miguel asked.

Zinnia nodded.

He raised his wrist. "Orientation complete."

Zinnia's wrist buzzed. Another arrow, beckoning her to move forward.

Miguel raised his hand. "Don't linger. Never linger."

They shook hands, and Zinnia took off, letting the gentle vibration of the watch carry her. From over her shoulder Miguel called out, "Don't forget, *mi amiga*. Get some sneakers."

PAXTON

Paxton sat alone against the back wall of the briefing room. Two women and four men, all in blue polo shirts, sat at its front, separated from him by three empty rows of classroom-style desks.

The other people talked like they knew each other. Paxton wasn't sure how that was possible, considering this was orientation. Maybe they were housed near each other.

Paxton hadn't planned to sit by himself. But he'd been the first to arrive and sat in the back. The others filtered in and sat near the front, already engaged in conversation, not really noticing him. To get up and go over to them might come off as desperate. So Paxton stayed where he was, watching the partially closed blinds covering the large window overlooking the main room.

It was a command center. Lots of cubicles. Lots of folks in blue polo shirts talking on phones, tapping at tablets bolted into the desks. Everyone looking over their shoulders like someone might be watching. Video screens covering the walls, all of them showing maps and wireframe schematics.

A figure moved along the window and the door opened. A man with a face like the side of a tree walked in. His slate hair was cut short and sharp. The top of his lip was obscured by a thick, bushy mustache. He wore a tan shirt with the sleeves rolled up and forest-green khakis. No gun, but a heavy-duty flashlight hung from the holster of his belt. The gold star pinned to his chest was so polished it cradled the light. He had the straight spine and hundred-yard stare of a real-deal law enforcement officer. The kind of person who made you immediately want to apologize, even if you hadn't done anything wrong.

He strode to the lectern and looked around the room, making eye contact with each person in turn. He got to Paxton last, lingered for a moment, and nodded his head, as if the seven people before him were acceptable.

"My name is Sheriff Dobbs, and I'm the man responsible for this county," he said, speaking like he had somewhere else to be. "As sheriff, it is my job to come here and do two things when we got a group of new recruits such as yourselves. First, I am to deputize you under the authority of the MotherCloud Security and Safety Act." He waved his hand like a bored magician. "Consider yourself deputized.

"Second," he said, "I'm supposed to explain to you all what the hell that means."

He gave a little smirk. Permission for sphincters to unclench. A few people laughed. Paxton didn't, but he did flip open a small notebook. He wrote at the top of the page: *Sheriff Dobbs.*

"Now, you may be asking, can I make arrests?" he asked. "And the answer is: not really. What you can do is detain. You got yourself a perp—maybe someone stole something, started a fight, whatever— you bring him over to holding in Admin. The Safety and Security Act mandates ten officers from the local jurisdiction must be in the office at all times in order to address criminal matters. But ten people ain't enough to cover as much ground as we got here, so you are the eyes and ears."

Detain. Eyes and ears. Real cops handle serious shit.

"Most of the time, things are pretty quiet," he said. " 'Cause here's the truth. You fuck up at Cloud, you're out. You get caught stealing, you earn enough strikes to get turfed, you are not welcome at a single Cloud-affiliated company in these United States, or even on the rest of God's green planet. I don't have to tell you that means your employment options will become severely limited. And that means most people are smart enough to not shit where they eat."

Screw up, you're out. Keeps people in line.

"Most of your responsibility is to be seen," Dobbs said. "Be out there, a part of the community." He tugged at the collar of his tan uniform. "This is a line of demarcation. This is why you wear the polo shirts. We want to encourage a friendly atmosphere. That's why you don't get some kind of fancy uniform."

Shirts are a system of equality.

"Most of y'all are here because you have some kind of law enforcement or security on your CV," he said. "Still, every place does things differently, and that means we have training and education sessions. Twice a month. Today is going to be the longest. We're going to make you sit and watch some videos about what to do in the event of conflict, if you suspect someone of stealing, etcetera, etcetera. But I made some popcorn, if that helps."

Some more laughs.

Dobbs seems okay.

"Now everyone head on down the hall and get yourself a seat," he said. "I'll be there and we'll get started in a few minutes. But first . . . is there a Paxton here?"

Paxton looked up. Dobbs made eye contact and smiled.

"Hang around for a second, son," he said. "I got a question for you."

The other six people in the room stood, throwing glances at Paxton on their way to the door, wondering what made him special. Paxton wondered that, too.

When the room was empty Dobbs said, "Follow me."

He turned and left. Paxton jumped to his feet, scrambling into the bullpen, and followed Dobbs through a door at the rear of the room, next to which was a large pane of reflective glass.

Paxton stepped inside the darkened room, which consisted of a desk, two chairs in front of it, some pictures, and a few maps of the facility. Each one seemed to have a different focus. At a quick glance Paxton could tell one was the transit system, another was the electrical grid, a third, topographical maybe? Not much else. It was the kind of office for someone who didn't feel much need to keep an office.

"Take a seat," Dobbs said, falling into the worn roller chair behind the desk. "I don't want to leave the rest of them waiting too long, but I couldn't help but notice your work history. You were a prison guard."

"I was," Paxton said.

"Bit of a gap between then and now."

"I owned my own company," he said. "But it didn't work out. You know, this economy is a full-contact sport."

Dobbs didn't acknowledge the sarcasm. "Listen, tell me something. Why'd you become a guard?"

Paxton sat back in the chair. He wished he had a better answer, something about a higher calling, but that would be a lie, so he told the truth. "I needed a job. I saw an ad. Ended up staying longer than intended."

"And how do you feel about being here?" Dobbs asked.

"Honestly?"

"No wrong answers, son."

"I was hoping for a red shirt."

Dobbs smiled, his lips drawn tight. "Look, I don't have time to sit here and bullshit around the bush with you. I like that you're not gung-ho for this job. Job like this, the more enthusiasm you have, the more my flags go up. Some people like authority a bit too much. It's a sport for them, or a coping mechanism, or just a way to get back at the world. You understand?"

Paxton thought about every guard he'd worked with who smiled too much as they swung their stick, who poked and prodded the volatile prisoners, who hooted and hollered when it was time to throw someone in the box.

"I do," he said. "I know exactly what you mean."

"In that prison where you worked, how much did you deal with contraband?"

"We had some drug issues," he said. "I worked under a few wardens. Some had zero-tolerance policies; some looked the other way, figured doped-up prisoners were easier to control."

"Were they?" Dobbs asked.

Paxton chose his words carefully. Now he felt like he was taking a test. "Yes and no. Get someone high enough, they can be pretty easy to deal with. Get them too high, and they OD or tear stuff up, and that's no good either."

Dobbs leaned back in his chair, tenting his hands and pressing his fingertips together. The band of his watch was the standard-issue, same as Paxton's. "We got a little problem here, and I'm setting up something . . . I don't want to call it a task force. Not that official. Just some folks to keep their eyes and ears open. Maybe ask around if they find themselves in a position where they might be able to do some good."

"What's the problem?"

"Oblivion. You know what that is?"

"I know it's a drug, but it didn't really come into vogue until recently. After I left the prison."

Dobbs glanced toward the waiting blues and gave a little shrug, as if he could risk another few minutes. "It's a modified form of heroin that's not physically addictive. See, the reason heroin is so heinous is, it rewires your brain. Makes it so your body can't function without it. That's why withdrawal is so hard. Oblivion is the same high, but without the hook. It's psychologically addictive, same way anything feels good so you want to do it again. So people OD, just not as many. Right now we are seeing a lot of it. And sometimes it ain't mixed right so people get sick just from taking it. Sometimes it kills them.

Word from on top is, we have to shut this shit down." Dobbs dropped his voice. "And I'm going to level with you. The county can't spare any more officers. The men upstairs want me to handle it with the on-site men and women in blue. So that's where I'm at. I need a few good folks who can poke around in a . . . relaxed manner. And someone who's got an eye for contraband could be helpful."

"Why relaxed?" Paxton asked.

Dobbs stared at him for a moment before responding. "I like it when things are relaxed."

Paxton sat back, at a loss for what to say. He'd been half-hoping that Dobbs was going to tell him a mistake had been made, that he'd be getting his red shirt and would be shipped off to the warehouse floor, where he could outrun his stress and maybe get the hell out of here in a timely fashion. Now he was being asked to do extra-credit work for a job he didn't want in the first place.

And yet, there was something he liked about Dobbs. He spoke carefully, and clearly, and with respect, three things in short supply among the supervisors at the prison. Plus, it was nice to be asked, like Paxton had some special skill. Like he was needed.

Dobbs gave another pained smile, put his hand up. "Don't decide anything now. I know it's a lot to ask. It's your first day. All I know is, you got a clean record and you got an eye for details. You were the only person in there taking notes. I appreciate things like that. So, you think on it and maybe in a day or two, as we're sorting stuff out, we'll touch base."

Paxton stood. "That's fair."

"Just so you know, job like this, there's room for advancement," Dobbs said. "Plus, you'd be doing some real good work, helping people who need help. Now." He waved his hand down the hall. "Get on and grab a seat. Let them all wonder why the hell I pulled you out. I'll be down with that popcorn in a minute."

SECURITY TRAINING VIDEO

A man and a woman walk hand in hand along a field of bright green artificial turf. Above them is a glass dome, yellowed sunlight filtering through the frosted panels.

Two children, a boy and a girl, run ahead of the adults. They pick a spot on the turf and unfurl a picnic blanket. The boy stops to wave to someone. The camera turns to find a woman in a blue polo shirt, walking along a nearby pathway.

Cut to workers in red polo shirts dashing back and forth with items tucked under their arms in search of conveyor belts. Men and women in blue polo shirts appear and disappear among the stacks, unseen, like ghosts, or guardian angels, not interfering. Protecting.

An old woman wearing a green polo pushes a cart through a gray-carpeted office, emptying trash cans. She stops to salute a man in a blue polo shirt, who laughs it off and gives her a hug.

Voice-over (VO): Hello, and welcome to the first in a series of videos designed to help you understand your role as a security officer at Mother-Cloud. No doubt you've already been deputized. Congratulations! Now it's time to talk about what that means.

A young couple walks down a brightly lit white staircase, hand in hand.

A woman in a blue polo shirt patrols a residential hallway.

A line of people wait to pass through metal detectors on their way off the warehouse floor. Workers in blue polos wearing baby-blue latex gloves wave them through, one after another.

Everyone is smiling.

VO: Your job is to support the safety and security of this facility, while keeping it open, friendly, and welcoming to the people who live and work here. You do this through patrolling, monitoring, observing, and reporting.

A group of teenagers play video games in a retro-style arcade. They look like they could be loud, raucous. But they stop to wave to a man in a blue polo shirt, who waves back.

They are all friends.

VO: This video series will explore demeanor and ethical behavior, crisis intervention, criminal and civil laws that pertain to your position, and how best to aid your facility's sheriff and his officers. First, and most important . . .

The screen goes black. The words RESPECT IS EARNED appear in large white type.

VO: Treat everyone with dignity and respect, and they'll treat you with dignity and respect in return. The simple use of *sir* or *ma'am* goes a long way. Your primary goal should always be prevention and deterrence.

The words VIGILANCE IS KEY appear.

VO: Again, your primary goal should always be prevention and deterrence. And to do that you must be aware of your surroundings. Even when you're not working—if you see something that requires attention, please notify on-shift security officers immediately.

Cut to an image of a man peering down an empty hallway, as if he's doing something wrong. He pulls his collar up and ducks through a door, where he finds a group of people sitting around a small table in what appears to be a repurposed storage room.

VO: Cloud works tirelessly with local and government officials to promote a safe and secure work environment. Fair treatment of our workers is priority number one—we take every comment and complaint seriously. If you suspect employees of organizing over grievances outside the traditional channels of human resources, please notify your local sheriff immediately.

Cut back to the family having the picnic.
They wave over the woman in the blue polo shirt. She strides across the artificial turf and the little boy reaches up, handing her a fat chocolate chip cookie.

The security officer takes it, bends down, and gives the little boy a hug.

VO: **MotherCloud is a new paradigm for the American economy, and more important, the American family. You are their first line of defense. We thank you for the responsibility you are about to undertake.**

The screen goes black. The words ROLES AND RESPONSIBILITIES appear in large white type.

VO: **Now, on to the first installment in the induction series. . . .**

ZINNIA

Zinnia's foot slipped and her stomach lurched. She managed to grab the side of the shelving unit before she fell backward and cracked her head on the floor.

It hadn't taken long to stop using the carabiner. The clip took precious seconds to engage and disengage, which weren't worth spending. She was less concerned with falling and more concerned with the yellow line.

After she'd finished with Miguel, she was tasked with picking her first item. A three-pack of deodorant. She walked briskly to the shelving unit. It took more than ten minutes to get there, crossing the massive floor, dancing around the other reds and the sliding shelves. By the time she delivered the package to the conveyor belt, the green bar on her CloudBand had turned yellow.

The next item was a book. She took off, walking a little faster, the shelving units eventually giving way to a rotating library, titles spinning around her. It was a little harder to find, the way the books were packed spine-out on the shelf, but she tracked it down and got it to where it needed to go. The bar was still yellow, but it had replenished a bit.

The next item: a six-pack of soup cans, wrapped in plastic.

Then: Alarm clock. Shower radio. Book. Digital camera. Book. Phone charger. Snow boots. Sunglasses. Medicine ball. Designer messenger bag. Tablet. Book. Salt scrub. Infinity scarf. Pliers. Curling iron. Vacuum sealer. Christmas lights. Package of pens. Set of three silicone whisks. Noise-canceling headphones. Digital scale. Sunglasses. Vitamins. Flashlight. Umbrella. Vise grip. Wallet. Digital meat thermometer. Dog biscuits. Doll. Compression socks. Shampoo. Book. Rubber ducky. Sports watch. Sippy cup. Knife sharpener. Drill battery. Shower caddy. Travel coffee mug. French press. Measuring tape. Kids' socks. Magic markers. Swaddling blanket. Knee brace. Cat bed. Scissors. Sunglasses. Christmas lights. Dremel kit. Teddy bear. Books. Protein powder. Nose-hair trimmer. Playing cards. Tongs. Phone charger. Baking sheets. Bracelet. Multi-tool. Wool cap. Nightlight. Package of men's undershirts. Chef's knife. Yoga mat. Hand towels. Christmas lights. Leather belt. Salad spinner. Ream of printer paper. Fiber pills. Set of spatulas. Book. Hoodie. Tablet case. Immersion blender. Cookie cutters. Tablet. Keyboard. Phone charger. Action figure.

With each item, Zinnia's feet ached a little more. Soon her shoulders joined in, creaking in the joints, muscles throbbing. She stopped a few times along the wall or in a quiet corner, so she could loosen or tighten her boots, looking for a sweet spot that would keep them from ripping apart her feet. But the yellow bar was relentless. If she stopped long enough she could watch the slow creep of it. Once or twice, when she really hoofed it, it turned green, but only ever for a moment.

The work was mindless. Once she fell into the rhythm of the watch, she was able to make it from shelving unit to conveyor belt to shelving unit on autopilot. Occasionally she was a little thrown by the placement of an item, pushing bins around, wasting a few seconds searching for the right thing. But mostly the system worked.

She distracted herself from the pain in her feet and the monotony of the job by working on her plan.

The goal was simple: get inside the energy processing facility.

It was simple to say. She had to get inside a building.

In practice, it was a nightmare.

The facility was on the other side of campus. It was only accessible by a tram system she couldn't board—unlikely her CloudBand permissions would allow it. She couldn't go on foot. She'd memorized those satellite photos down to blades of grass. The terrain was flat. There was a lot of open ground between the dorms and the warehouse facility, and then even more through the wind and solar farms before she could reach the processing facilities. The entirety of Cloud's surveillance technology could have boiled down to an old man sitting on a porch with a bottle of moonshine, and she still wouldn't have risked it; she'd be too easy to spot.

The tram was her way in. Or at least, the tram tunnels. She wasn't so worried about being seen. Like Gibson said in the video, there weren't a lot of cameras around. The problem was the damn GPS tethered to her wrist.

One problem at a time.

The watch told her to pick up a phone charger. She jogged to the shelving unit, power walked to the conveyor belt, and looked for the next item, only to find the watch had a new message.

You are now entitled to a 15-minute bathroom break.

Zinnia was in the middle of a vast stretch of health and beauty items. Once she stopped moving, the delicate choreography crumbled. She hopped from foot to foot, getting out of the way of reds sprinting past her, trying to get her bearings, and found she couldn't.

She raised her hand, pressed the crown, and said, "Bathroom."

The watch prodded her to make a left, and she laughed to distract from the general sense of disgust she felt that there was now a record somewhere that at eleven fifteen a.m. on a Tuesday she went to take a piss.

It took nearly seven minutes to make it to a bathroom, and she was thankful she only had to pee. She stepped inside a long room—gray tile, one long mirror above a bank of sinks crowded with women in red, and white lights so bright they buzzed blue. The room was perfumed with the smell of urine. She stepped into one of the few free stalls and found the floor covered with discarded scraps of paper, the toilet full of dark yellow liquid and crammed with more toilet paper.

She sighed, hovered over the seat, relieved herself, didn't bother flushing, because what was the point, and stepped out to the bank of sinks, where she jockeyed among the other reds for position and washed her hands and leaned forward into the mirror.

Her eyelids were heavy. Free from the distraction of inertia, her feet bellowed. She considered taking off her boots but that might make it worse. She didn't want to see the damage. Instead she stepped outside the bathroom, found a CloudPoint. She figured she had two or three minutes left on her break. She pressed the screen and it said: *Welcome, Zinnia!*

She searched for *sneakers* and picked the first pair she saw. Neon green, like alien puke, but they were in stock. She did not give a damn, she just didn't want to spend another day in these boots.

She added thumbtacks and a few large mandala tapestries—the kaleidoscopic drapings you'd find hanging from the wall of a college student who smoked too much weed. Something to help her get out of her room.

The last tool she needed, she didn't want traced back to her.

She set everything to be delivered to her room and turned away from the CloudPoint.

The CloudPoints. Step one of a two-step process.

Cloud's entire infrastructure—from the navigation of the drones to the directions relayed by the watch—fed down through a proprietary network of satellites. Impossible to hack from the outside. Zinnia had tried a few weeks ago, poking around the perimeter, just to see what would happen. It was like trying to scratch through a concrete wall with a fingernail. The only way to access the network was inside a Cloud facility.

What she needed were schematics. Maps. Anything that showed the guts of this place. Which had been impossible to find. She'd tried that, too. Environmental impact studies. Business records. The local department of buildings. The way it used to be, in order to build a place like this, you needed to file endless reams of paperwork. But thanks to something called the Red Tape Elimination Act, sponsored by Gibson Wells, large corporations were excused from having to file all that, because it was an "impediment to creating jobs."

She needed to understand if there was any way to move around while avoiding detection. If she could find a back door into the energy processing facility. Access tunnels, large ducts, anything. But it wasn't as simple as plugging into a CloudPoint to get what she needed. First, she needed to carve off a little piece of Cloud's code.

Her wrist buzzed, the yellow bar back.

You currently have a 73 percent pick rate.

Then:

Falling below 60 percent will result in a negative impact on your Employee Rating.

Then:

Remember to hydrate!

Then:

A unit and bin number, along with a picture of a book.
Zinnia sighed, turned, and took off at a jog.

GIBSON

I'd like to take a minute to talk about our employee rating system.

I've done a lot of controversial things in my career. I wasn't always right, but I was right more than I was wrong. You don't make it this far otherwise. Out of everything I ever did, this is the one that caught me the most flak.

I remember when I first introduced it, we were maybe two or three years into Cloud, and things were finally taking off, and I realized I needed something to set us apart from the pack. Something that would really challenge our employees to work their hardest. A herd is only as fast and strong as the slowest members.

Now, to make sure you understand my thinking, I want to tell you a little story about where I went to school: the Newberry Academy for Excellence. Back then, there were different kinds of schools. Public schools, which were paid for by the government; private schools, usually associated with religious institutions; and charter schools. Newberry was a charter. A charter school gets public funding but is owned by a private company, so they don't have to adhere to all the nonsense that gets handed down by government education boards.

What used to happen was, a bunch of politicians with no experience in education would get together and come up with formulas that were supposed to work for every kid, everywhere. But kids don't all learn the same. You might be surprised to hear that I was a terrible test-taker. I used to get so nervous that on the morning of big exams I'd almost always heave my guts up on the way to school.

Charter schools put power in the hands of educators, to design programs that worked for the kids they were teaching. No more having to live up to some ridiculous standard—the only standards that mattered were decided by the people who were in the trenches, doing the work. My kind of system. It should be no surprise that this is the system of education we have now.

So anyway, in my school, when we got our report cards every semester, they'd come with a star rating at the top. Now, obviously, five stars meant you were doing great, and one star meant you were in some serious trouble. I was generally a four-star student, but sometimes I slipped down to three.

The teachers and the principal liked it because it was a real quick way to look and see how a student was doing. Education is a big, complicated thing, and obviously the report card was a lot longer, with data points and grade-point averages and notes. But there was a simplicity to five stars. Better than the way they *used* to do it, giving letter grades, along with pluses or minuses. All that was too complicated. What is a C+, exactly? Why was it A, B, C, D, and F? Where'd the E go?

People understand five-star rating systems. We see it every day when we go to purchase something or watch a video or rate a restaurant. Why not bring it into the school system? And it was a big help, at least for me. You better believe those days I brought home three stars my daddy sat me down and had a long talk with me about how important it was to work harder. Even when I brought home four-star ratings, even knowing five stars was pretty much near impossible, he wanted me to reach for that.

Four stars meant ice cream. My daddy would take me to Eggsy's, this local place near us, and get me a two-scoop vanilla sundae with hot fudge and melted marshmallow and peanut butter chips, and he'd ask me, "How can you do better?"

He'd ask me that, too, if I got three stars, there just wouldn't be any ice cream.

So it got to where my goal, always, was to bring home five stars, knowing that even if I didn't make it, even if I came in at four, I could still be pretty proud of myself. To my mind, three stars was failing. Which ain't even true! Three stars wasn't bad at all. You're not considered failing until you get down to two. But do you see what it did? It gave me a goal and it encouraged me to set a high standard for myself.

So when I was in Newberry, this was back when a lot of the public schools were transitioning over to charter schools, and there were still a lot of old contracts the districts had to deal with. So for example, a union would have negotiated a pretty sweet deal, that their teachers could go on a killing rampage and burn down the building and they'd still collect their paychecks, with time and a half on holidays.

Which is the problem with unions, right? Biggest scam the world has ever known. Back in the day, when workers were being exploited, when they were being driven into the ground in unsafe conditions, they made a lot of sense. But we're a long way away from the Triangle Shirtwaist Factory fire. That kind of thing doesn't happen anymore. It can't. Not with the way the system works. The American consumer votes with his or her dollar—if a company is truly that bad then no one will work or shop there. Simple as that.

So the school had this janitor, Mr. Skelton. We used to joke around and call him Mr. Skeleton, on account of his age. He looked like he was nearly a hundred, and it was a bit of a sad sight, him pushing his broom down the hallway like he could barely manage it. It got to the point where if there was a mess in the classrooms, most times the teachers would clean it up themselves. Because what would happen was, if you called Mr. Skelton, he usually wouldn't even show up until classes had changed.

He was a holdover. That's what we used to call them. Union folks who had negotiated cozy contracts so they had no incentive to retire.

They just kept on working because they knew they could never be fired. Even if they were too old to do the job, they could just show up and collect their paycheck and their medical insurance and all that. Good work, if you can get it.

You'd think this guy, old as he was, would have taken a little time for himself. Try to enjoy the last of his life. But, no way, he just wanted to ride out that golden ticket. I thought about that a lot as I was building Cloud. Because a company like this, you have so many people working for you, it's incredible.

Do you know how many people work at Cloud? Swear to truth, I can't even tell you. Not an exact number, what with subsidiaries and the way staff rotates on our processing centers and the way we're adding new companies every day. It's north of thirty million. That's the best I can say.

Think about that. Thirty million. You can take half the major cities in America and add them up and you won't even get that many people. And when you have thirty million people to manage, you need to come up with a system to make it a little easier. Hence the rating system. It's a way to gauge performance in a transparent, streamlined way. Because an employee at two or three stars knows they have to work a little harder.

And don't we all want to be five-star people?

If you're a four-star worker, you're in good shape. At three stars, maybe you could pick up the pace. Two, and it's time to buckle down and show what you're worth.

That's why one star is an automatic dismissal.

Every day I get up and go to work, I give it my best. I have to expect the same of my employees. And I don't give a damn about what the *New York Times* says. All those ranting and raving op-eds about how I'm doing this or that to the American worker. That I'm "undervaluing" them. That I'm "oversimplifying a complex system."

That's what I do! Oversimplify complex systems. It's worked pretty well so far.

I'm giving my employees the tools they need to be the masters of their own destiny. And that train runs two ways. A one-star employee doesn't just bring down the average, they're in a position they're not suited for. You wouldn't take a physicist and ask them to blow glass.

Or a butcher and ask them to program a website. People have different skill sets and talents. Yes, Cloud is a big employer, but maybe you're not the right fit for us.

So anyway, that's that. I'm not going to relitigate my entire run at Cloud. But I get asked about that a lot, or I used to when I did more interviews, and it's just something I wanted to get off my chest.

Otherwise, people have been asking how I'm feeling, and I'm feeling pretty good. Trying a new cancer treatment, which my doctor says has shown promising results in mice, except I'm not a mouse, so I don't know why he's so optimistic. The side effects aren't so bad, except it makes me a little more hungry, but when you're shedding weight like I am, that ain't terrible.

I also want to address a report that came out in one of those business blogs yesterday. I'm not even going to name it because I don't want to send traffic their way. They said that I was close to naming Ray Carson to take over the company.

I cannot be more clear about this: I have not told anyone my final decision, because I have not made my final decision. Cloud is running fine and it's got a board and managers and that ain't gonna change. So, everyone, please show a little respect for me and my wishes and my family.

There'll be an announcement about all of this soon enough.

PAXTON

There was a yell and a crash from the other side of the bullpen. Paxton looked up from the tablet screen, where he'd been familiarizing himself with the paperwork for various incidents in and around Cloud—what you have to fill out when someone gets injured, when something gets stolen, when someone dies—and peeked over the wall of his cubicle.

He found a half dozen blues wrestling with a green. The green was all bone and sinew, with a ratty beard that went down to his belly button. He was trying to get away from the others, until a slender blue with a buzz cut dove out of the crowd and clocked him across the jaw.

The guy with the beard went down hard, and the figure spat, "That's right!"

Paxton couldn't tell if it was a man or a woman. The register of the voice seemed to read woman, but the slight body, the efficiently short haircut, the lack of curvature, read more as a young man.

After a moment he realized the person had turned away from the man lying on the floor and was coming toward him, and then they were at the cubicle and asked, "You Paxton? I'm Dakota."

The name didn't help, but then Paxton noticed the smooth curve of throat where there could have been an Adam's apple and wasn't.

He stood, shook her hand. The band of her watch was black leather with metal studs set around the circumference.

"Nice to meet you," Paxton said.

"I would hope so," she said, throwing up an eyebrow. "I'm your new partner. Let's go take a walk."

Dakota made a tight turn on her heel and stalked off. Paxton jogged to catch up and fell in step behind her as they left the bullpen, walking into the blank polished concrete hallways of Admin.

"What's with the pile-on?"

It took her a minute to remember, like the burst of violence had been a passing gesture, something easily forgotten. "Guy was running a rub-and-tug out of one of the massage joints."

"You hit him pretty hard."

"That bother you?"

"Only if he didn't deserve it."

She laughed. "Some of the girls weren't exactly doing it voluntarily, so what do you think?"

"I think you should have hit him harder, then," Paxton said, which earned a smile. "I didn't know people got partnered up here. All those videos we watched, the security officers were generally on their own."

"Blue work is mostly solo, unless it's special projects, or task force stuff." Dakota turned her face a little toward Paxton, looking him up and down. That eyebrow again. "Dobbs tells me you're the man's going to crack our smuggling problem."

"I haven't exactly agreed to that yet. . . ."

Dakota smiled. "Sure you have."

They reached an elevator bank. Dakota swiped her wrist across the panel and placed her arms behind her back, taking another look at Paxton. He truly could not tell whether she was interested in getting to know him or saw him as an inconvenience. She had the demeanor of a blank piece of paper.

"So where are we headed?" Paxton asked.

"Walk around a bit," she said. "Stretch your legs. I hear it's up to three hours now. The introductory videos."

"I wasn't timing it, but that sounds about right."

"It's mostly cover-your-ass stuff," Dakota said. "Not for you, for management. Something goes wrong, they can say they reviewed this stuff, it's not on them, it's on you."

An empty elevator arrived. They stepped on and Dakota selected the bottom floor, which would bring them to the tram station. As the doors slid closed, she said, "I don't need to tell you this. You worked in a prison. But as time goes on, you'll see there's the Cloud way of doing things and the right way of doing things. Sometimes those are the same, sometimes they aren't."

"I am familiar with that concept, yes," Paxton said.

They stepped off the elevator and strode down the corridor, turning the corner into a thick crowd of people lined up at a long row of kiosks against the wall, where they could input their problem—housing issue, banking questions, etcetera—and be directed to the appropriate floor and room.

Dakota didn't speak. Didn't look interested in speaking. She walked, and Paxton followed. A few people threw glances their way. He understood this dance. Dobbs called the polo shirt an equalizer. It wasn't. Didn't matter if the badge was tin, it still shone if it caught the light at the right angle.

A tram car pulled in and they climbed aboard. The crowd seemed to part for them. Still Dakota didn't talk. This, Paxton understood, too. For them to talk, to engage in conversation like normal people, would humanize them too much.

Paxton hated how easy it was to slip back into that mind-set. Like walking the stacks all over again.

They rode the tram through Care, then the warehouse and Incoming, finally arriving in the lobby of Oak. They took the escalator up into the terminus of the promenade, where a tram line came in from Incoming and went out to the processing facilities. There were also loading bays and docks for shipments. Food and goods for the stores running through the promenade. A lot of those goods were moved around by electric golf carts with rolling platforms attached to the back. It was a big, busy space, workers in green and brown dashing around each other, moving goods.

Dakota cleared her throat. "This right here. This is the problem area."

"What do you mean?"

"This is where everything comes in," she said. "I mean, technically, it all comes in at Incoming, but mostly in large packages that get doled out where they need to go. Our theory has been that this is where the oblivion comes in. Maybe different shipments each time. Could be a ring of employees. Could be a single person. There's a lot we don't know about how this works. But my gut tells me that it all comes down to here."

Paxton walked a bit, looking, not at anything in particular, but around. He could see how this might be a good entry point. There were a lot of nooks and crannies. Alcoves where the golf carts were stowed, doors branching off into what he assumed were webs of hallways running behind the storefronts. There were more than a hundred people unloading boxes, putting them on carts. You'd need an army to watch the entire thing.

"Why not just put in more cameras?" Paxton asked.

Dakota shook her head. "The overlords don't like them. That's still in the video, right? Dobbs has had this fight, but this comes right down from the man at the top. Says they're not homey. That it'll make people uncomfortable." She threw up air quotes around the last word and piled on an exaggerated eye roll.

"Right. All the people who are wearing tracking watches everywhere they go."

Dakota shrugged. "When one of us owns the company, we can change it."

Paxton took a few more steps, surveying the surroundings. "Food shipments were always popular. We had this big rush of heroin for a little while. Turned out, everything was coming in shoved down in jars of peanut butter. Dogs couldn't smell it."

"We've been up and down the food deliveries," she said.

"Tell me about oblivion," Paxton said. "Like I said to Dobbs, I don't even know what it is."

"He mentioned that, yeah." She looked around. Made sure they were alone. "Come here."

She led him to a quiet corner, next to a long row of plugged-in, recharging golf carts. She reached into her pocket and came out with a small plastic case, wide as a postage stamp and a little bit longer. She opened it and slipped out a thin piece of film. Tinted green, rectangular, barely smaller than the case. A breath strip.

"That's it?" Paxton asked.

She nodded. He took it and turned it over. Light and thin and a tiny bit sticky.

Dakota took it back, slipped it in the case. "Absorbed in the mouth, goes right into the circulatory system, bypassing the gastrointestinal tract so it doesn't degrade."

"How do you know people aren't just walking in with it? I could have brought ten pounds of it with me when I came in yesterday."

Dakota laughed. Not with him, at him, and he felt blood rush to his face. "Sniffers. Installed on the scanners you came through. More effective than dogs because you don't know they're there. You think we didn't think of that?"

"What about visitors? People coming in and out?"

"First, everyone here comes through the scanners, visitor or resident," she said. "Second, people don't get a ton of visitors here. You know how much it costs to rent a car or fly. I mean, my mom used to visit once a month, when I started working here. Now I see her on Thanksgiving."

"And what about naloxone? Does it stop an oblivion OD?"

"Different chemical process. No way to stop it. Try to keep up, okay?"

The blood that had rushed to his face flashed hot. "I figure the reason you're coming to me is you want a fresh perspective on this, right? So, sure, I'm going to throw out a few obvious questions. If you could do it on your own, you wouldn't be asking me."

The words were caustic in his mouth. Dakota paused. Her eyes got a little wider.

"I'm sorry," he said. "That was a bit much."

"No," Dakota said, lip curling into a grin. "It was exactly enough. C'mon, let's walk some more."

They strolled in silence for a bit, until it became too much, so Paxton asked, "What did you do before this?"

"Odd jobs, mostly. Some night security work, because it was quiet and gave me time to read, which is why I think I got shuffled into this," she said.

They moved onto the promenade, where there was a steady flow of people moving back and forth. Paxton caught stray glimpses of blue polos, in shops, along the upper walkway. A few of them saw him and gave a brief nod.

"To be honest, I didn't want to work security," Paxton said. "I wanted to work the warehouse floor. Any color but blue, really."

"How come?" Dakota asked.

"Wasn't a big fan of the work."

"This is a lot different from a prison," Dakota said. "Probably. And look, I get it. I got here and I wasn't excited either. But I'll tell you, it comes with perks."

The way she said *perks* made it sound like it rhymed with *secret*. Generally, Paxton knew what she meant. The prison had perks. Contraband didn't go into the trash—it usually went home with the guard who found it. Most of the time that was money or drugs.

Not that Paxton ever saw it. But he'd heard stories.

"Like?" he asked.

"You ever want a day off, you're a hell of a lot more likely to get it from Dobbs than from some random white," Dakota said. "He takes care of us. When he sees you're doing the right thing."

There was more to that "right thing." Of course there was more. Paxton knew he hadn't earned more yet. But he wanted to. He was surprised by that feeling. Wanting Dakota to like him. Wanting her respect. Approval was a funny thing. It was like a little pill you could pop in your mouth to make you feel good.

"Security! Security!"

The two of them turned toward the source of the yelling: an overweight, elderly man in a green polo shirt, waving at them from the mouth of a convenience store. Dakota took off at a trot and Paxton followed.

The store was small. Snacks and toiletries. Refrigerator case along the back wall for drinks. Magazine racks. The man was holding a lanky black man in a red polo shirt by the arm. The man—no more than a kid, really—was struggling to get away from him, but the elderly man was big and meaty and had a good grip.

"What happened, Ralph?" Dakota asked.

"Caught this kid stealing," the man in the green shirt—Ralph—said, mostly directing his attention to Dakota, but throwing a few suspicious glances at Paxton.

"I didn't steal nothing," the kid said, giving one final yank to free himself, but once he did that, not running either. Just taking a few steps back, looking for space.

"He pocketed a candy bar," Ralph said.

"No," the kid said, growing agitated. "No, I did not."

"Search him," Ralph said. A demand.

The kid turned out his pockets voluntarily. They were empty. He looked back and forth between Paxton and Dakota. Shrugged his shoulders. "See?"

"Musta eaten it," Ralph said.

"Then where's the wrapper?" the kid asked.

Dakota looked over at Ralph, as if reiterating the question.

"How the hell should I know?" Ralph said. "Kids these days, they're clever. But he took it. I saw it, with my own two eyes. Comes in here, acting all suspicious."

The kid sneered. "Suspicious, right. What's suspicious about me besides the color of my skin?"

Ralph threw his hands up, suddenly offended. "Hey, hey, I'm not racist. Don't go accusing me—"

"It's not an accusation," the kid said, nearly yelling. "It's the truth."

This was the moment. The flash point where it got better or worse. Only way to handle the flash point was separation. "Hey," Paxton said. He pointed to Ralph. "You, go over there. Now, while we sort this out."

Ralph put his hands up, walked back toward the counter.

"Good call," Dakota whispered to Paxton, then nodded at the kid. "You take it?"

The kid raised his hands in front of his face, chopping them to punctuate his words. "How many times do I have to say it? No."

"Okay, kid, look, here's where we're at," she said. "Ralph is old, and he's a bit of a bastard. He'll push this and it'll turn into a thing and there's a chance you end up with a strike. Or you can send him a couple of credits now and we tell him you paid for it, and we talk him down for you."

"So, you want me to pay for a candy bar I didn't take because this racist old man is loud? That's what you want?"

"No, I want us all to go down the path of least resistance," Dakota said. "Which means this all ends in the next two minutes, nobody gets a strike, and in a month's time you won't even remember how much this cost you. You got me?"

The kid looked at Ralph, who was at the counter. He didn't like it. Neither did Paxton. But he understood where Dakota was coming from. Sometimes you had to look aside on the little things to keep the peace.

What was the exchange rate for a credit?

"This ain't right," the kid said.

"It may not be right, but it's easy on everyone, including you," she said. "There are a million other shops you can go into that aren't run by obnoxious old men. So, c'mon. Do us all a favor. Take the shot on the chin. Live to fight another day."

The kid sighed. His shoulders slumped. Then he walked to the counter, tapped at his watch, and waved it over the disc, which lit up green.

"That's what I thought," Ralph said, triumphant.

The kid had nearly turned all the way around, but at that, he stopped. Balled up his hand. Put his head down and closed his eyes.

Gave serious thought to plowing his fist into the old man's face. Paxton stepped forward. Got close to the kid, so the kid could hear and not Ralph.

"Not worth it," he said. "You know he's not worth it."

The kid opened his eyes. Frowned, and pushed past Paxton hard on his way out of the store.

Dakota turned to Ralph and sighed. "You're a real son of a bitch, you know that?"

He shrugged. Smiled a little smile of victory. "What?"

Dakota left and Paxton followed. When they were out of earshot Paxton said, "The kid wasn't wrong, you know."

"You think he's the only one who would have suffered for that? I bring in Ralph and the kid, you know what happens? Dobbs sits me down and he says"—she dropped her voice a few octaves—" 'All this for a damn candy bar.' " Her voice returned to a normal register. "And he would have been right. It's a lot for a few credits."

"So that's how Dobbs likes things to get done?"

"When an incident gets logged, it turns into a stat. A stat going into a report. Those reports determine a lot. Our job is to keep the numbers low. Think of it like a reverse quota. The fewer things you have to carry upstairs, the better."

They walked some more. Through the second dorm, into the next section of promenade, and finally, to the third. Paxton's watch buzzed.

Your shift has ended. Your next shift begins in 14 hours.

Dakota was looking at her watch, too. Her shoulders relaxed, presumably because she got the same message. "You have good instincts," she said. "Separating them like that. I think you'll be a good fit. Think about what Dobbs said, okay? A lot of this job is walking around, being seen. The oblivion task force is at least interesting."

"I'll think about it," Paxton said.

"Good. I'll see you tomorrow then."

She turned and left, not waiting for a response. As he watched her disappear into the crowd his stomach grumbled at him, so he wandered to Live-Play, not entirely sure what he wanted to eat, until he came across CloudBurger. He'd been wanting to check it out. The CloudBurger was renowned for being one of the best and most affordable fast-food burgers in the country, but you could only get it in a MotherCloud facility.

Burger sounded about right. He'd earned a burger. He couldn't even remember the last time he'd had one. He stepped into the restaurant, greeted by the smell of sizzling meat and fryer oil. It was packed, most of the seats filled up, though at a small table off in the corner, an empty seat across from her, was Zinnia.

ZINNIA

Your shift has ended. Your next shift begins in 12 hours.

Zinnia looked down at her watch with a mix of relief and resentment. Was this how people lived in the real world? She was used to deadlines. Taking jobs as they came. But this, having to punch a clock, or at least having the clock punched for you—she didn't like it. She needed seven and a half hours of sleep to function. That meant four and a half of free time, which did not seem like a lot.

Would you like to proceed to the nearest exit?

Zinnia raised the watch to her mouth, said, "Yes."

The directional vibrations carried her across the warehouse floor. It took twenty minutes to find an exit. She stepped through the door, expecting to see some kind of hallway leading to the tram or an elevator, but instead found herself in a room not unlike the one where she'd queued up to get in. A long, snaking line of people, and at the end, body scanners. Men and women in blue polo shirts and baby-blue latex gloves waved people into the scanners, instructed them to put their hands up, and the machines whirred their giant blades around them.

"Can I get through?"

A young Asian woman stood behind her, and Zinnia realized she was standing in the doorway. "Sure, sorry." As the woman brushed past her, Zinnia said, "This is my first day. Is this the exit?"

The woman nodded gravely. "We go through the scanners on the way out, yeah."

Zinnia sighed. Followed the woman and got in the line. Five minutes passed. Then ten. At the eighteen-minute mark Zinnia made her way into the scanner. Raised her arms over her head. The mechanical blades spun around her. It was a millimeter-wave machine, shooting electromagnetic beams at her to create an animated picture of what was under her clothing. The man on the other side of the scanner looked at a screen, nodded, and waved her through. Zinnia glanced back, saw her outline on the video screen. She could just barely make out the shadow of her nipples, the tuft of hair between her legs. Seeing it, and then the grin on the face of the security officer looking at it, made her want to slap him, a little impulse tickling her fingers like static electricity.

Having proven that she didn't steal anything, she was allowed to leave, through a long hallway that wrapped in a curve until it reached the tram platform. As she waited next to a young man with black hair and a sharp nose, she asked, "Is it always like that?"

"Is what always like what?" he asked, not looking at her.

"The peep show," she said. "Waiting on line for twenty minutes just to get out."

He shrugged. Like, *It is what it is.*

"Do we get paid for that time?"

He laughed, finally looked at her. The band of his watch was rubber, bright orange.

"First day?" he asked.

She nodded.

"Welcome to Cloud," he said as the tram slid into the station. He pushed through to get a spot on board and she followed, not standing near him, because he was a sarcastic little asshole and she didn't want to talk to him anymore. She studied the faces of the people around her. Everyone looked dead on their feet. People were holding themselves up, or people who seemed to be friendly were holding each other up, and as the tram engaged, sliding down the track, a few stumbled from the sudden movement.

Every second Zinnia spent in the stink of this place made her want to finish the job. That's what it felt like—a smell, seeping into her skin. The thick odor of neglected cattle in a pen, and already her feet felt as if they were being sucked into the accumulated piles of shit on the ground.

So of course the tram came to a halt between lines, and a collective groan went up from the crowd. There was a chime, and a male, robotic voice said: "For your safety, there is debris on the tracks that must be removed. The tram will resume momentarily."

The way everyone reacted—annoyed but resigned to their fate—it was like this was a regular occurrence. The woman next to Zinnia looked friendly enough. Blond hair, cute glasses, lots of tattoos. Zinnia asked, "What's that about?"

"Happens a few times a week," the woman said. "It'll be clear in a minute. Don't want to crash, do we?"

Not very friendly, then. But Zinnia remembered a story she'd stumbled on in her research: Ten years ago there'd been a derailment at a MotherCloud because of some ceiling tiles that'd fallen on the tracks. Two people died. The trams were maglev, which meant the car didn't actually touch the rails. It hovered a few millimeters above, which improved speed and cut down on wear and tear. Apparently that left them susceptible to derailment.

A few minutes later they were under way again and she got off at her stop, took the elevator up, stepped into her apartment. Flicked the light. A box sat on the counter. She froze. First, because she'd forgotten, briefly, she had ordered some stuff, and second, because she would have expected the box to be outside the door, or available somewhere else for pickup, not sitting on her kitchen counter, because that meant someone had been inside her apartment.

She swept the place, which didn't take long. She ran her hands over places she couldn't see. Looked into the cupboards and closet, just to make sure nothing else had been left behind. Then she checked her bag. Her makeup kit was intact, and her laptop hadn't been opened, because if it had been opened by anyone but her, the guts would have fried themselves when they registered the wrong fingerprints.

When she was done, she sat on the bed and peeled off her boots. The backs of her feet were raw, bleeding, white layers of dead skin bunched up toward her heels. A few of her toes were scratched at the joints. Taking the boots off, and then exposing the wounds to the air, made them come alive and throb.

She found a thin roll of paper towels in a cupboard. Wet a handful in the sink and washed her feet, the towels coming back pink. She took a first-aid kit out of her bag, applied antibiotic cream to where the skin had been rubbed raw, and placed bandages around her feet.

When she was finished, she inspected her work, found it satisfactory, and unpacked the box, putting everything aside but the sneakers. Pulled on some socks and tried them on for size. Needed a little breaking in, which meant she was looking forward to a week of cracked and beaten feet, but at least they were better than the boots.

She walked down to the lobby, through the promenade to Live-Play, figuring she'd get something to eat. As she walked she made note of the CloudPoints. Their locations, how visible they were. They were mostly embedded into walls, but they all had access panels on the bottom, which took a single specialized, rounded key to open. Unlikely she'd get a copy of the key, but it was the kind of lock she could get past in seconds with the plastic tube of a pen carved into the right shape.

Easy enough.

The real problem was planting the gopher.

Whichever CloudPoint she picked, there'd be a record of her being there thanks to the watch. Which meant she had to plant it while she wasn't wearing her CloudBand.

She figured on good old-fashioned social engineering to get around. She couldn't get on and off the tram without swiping, but as for the elevator, politeness prevailed. When the elevator was crowded and already headed to the first floor, no one swiped.

She just had to get out of her room without the watch.

For that, she needed one more item. She wandered in and out of shops until she found a store with a little display of multi-tools by the register. They looked sturdy enough to do the job.

What she didn't like was the man lurking behind the counter. A toad in a green shirt who gave her the *You're not white so I think you'll steal shit* look. She briefly considered just buying the multi-tool, but she imagined anything she paid for was being logged and tracked. Somewhere, dug into the computer brain at Cloud, was a list of all the stuff she'd bought.

She was alive because she was cautious.

Sometimes caution meant taking the long way around.

Plus, she didn't like the look on the man's face.

So she circled the store as if she were browsing, keeping an eye out for cameras, and finding none, she went to a large display of candy and protein bars in the rear. She glanced back at the man, looking at him in her peripheral vision, and he wasn't even trying to hide the fact that he was staring.

She rooted through the candies, like she were trying to choose, her hand snaking through so she could loosen the bolt on a shelf with her fingertips, just until it was about to go, and then she pulled off a package of sour gummies and brought it to the counter and said, "The shelf over there seems a little loose. Fourth down from the top."

He didn't budge. Eyed the payment disc. She placed the gummies down next to it and swiped. The payment registered and he nodded, impressed, as if she'd proven him wrong about the whole of colored society. She gave him a *Fuck you* smile and he wandered over to the shelf. As soon as he put his hand on it, it crashed to the floor, and the moment it did Zinnia lifted a multi-tool and put it in her back pocket.

He turned to look at her, wanting to blame her even though he wasn't really sure how, and Zinnia just shrugged and said, "Told you."

Having worked up an appetite between a long stretch on the warehouse floor and making that asshole's day worse, she headed to Live-Play and surveyed the various floors and the shiny glowing signs. CloudBurger caught her eye. The draw of cheap beef was strong. Her legs felt like jelly and she could use the protein.

The inside of the restaurant was clean and crowded. White subway tile with red accents, tables that were metal but made to look like wood. She sat at a free table in the back, where she found a tablet inviting her to place her order. She settled on a double CloudBurger with cheese, large fries, a bottle of water. Once the order was confirmed she swiped her watch to pay, and the screen told her it would arrive within seven minutes.

While she waited she fiddled with the watch. Swiping up, down, left, and right through the various screens. Found a screen for health data. She'd walked sixteen thousand steps, or the equivalent of eight miles. It made her wish she'd ordered a milkshake with her meal.

A few minutes later—less than seven—a round Latina woman in a green polo placed a tray in front of her. Zinnia smiled and nodded. The woman didn't acknowledge her, just turned back to the kitchen.

Zinnia picked up the burger, wrapped in a wax-paper sleeve. It was hot. Almost too hot, but she was starving. She took a bite and went cross-eyed. It'd been a long time since she ate beef—it just wasn't worth the expense—but more than that, it was cooked well. Griddled, deep brown, crisp, the cheese melted into the cratered surface. There was a pinkish sauce on it, too, giving it a little vinegary kick that cut through the richness of all the fat. Before she was halfway done she clicked through the tablet, ordered another, as well as a milkshake. Eight miles.

"Zinnia?"

She looked up, mouth crammed with food.

The goof from the bus.

Peter? Pablo?

"Paxton," he said, pressing his hand to his blue polo shirt. "Mind if I join you? There don't seem to be any free seats."

She chewed. Swallowed. Thought.

No, she wanted to be alone.

But that shirt. A beautiful shade of blue. That could be useful.

"Sure," she said, nodding to the empty seat across from her.

He smiled, pulled the tablet toward him, and clicked through the screen, selecting what he wanted. He raised his watch, but before swiping it he nodded at the burger. "How is it?"

"Really good."

He nodded, swiped, and sat back.

"So, you made red," he said.

"I did."

"How is it?"

"My feet are bleeding."

He grimaced. She shoved some fries in her mouth.

"You must be happy," she said. "Former prison guard. This must be a cakewalk. Probably less likely you'll get shanked in a place like this."

"I wanted your job. I left the prison for a reason. I wasn't in love with it."

She laughed. "You're in love with picking items off shelves?"

"No, just . . . this is a temporary stop for me."

"Well, cheers to that," she said, raising her bottle of water, taking a sip.

The woman in green showed up again, hoisting two trays. She placed down Zinnia's, then gave Paxton his. It held two burgers, two fries, and a shake. He hoisted his burger, took a bite. Eyes went wide. He swallowed most of what was in his mouth and said, "Jesus."

"I know, right?"

"Last time I had beef I was celebrating," he said. "Out at a restaurant. Got a steak. Cost an arm and a leg."

"Well, that's what happens when you own the cattle farms and you can cut out the middleman," she said. "There are some perks to working here, I guess."

He nodded. "Right. Perks."

There was a pause in the conversation, so Zinnia filled it with food. Paxton followed. The two of them ate, not looking at each other, but looking around the restaurant. Zinnia ran it through her head. Security guards probably had unlimited access. And she could social-engineer the shit out of him; he was straight and had a penis.

So when Paxton finished his food and wiped his mouth with a napkin, and looked at Zinnia and said, "I don't want to be too forward, but, I don't know anyone here, and I was wondering if you'd be interested in grabbing a drink," Zinnia said, "Sure."

GRACE PERIOD³

GIBSON

The thing about getting toward the end is, you start thinking about legacy. That's a big word.

Legacy.

It means that people will still be thinking about you after you're dead and gone, which is a pretty nice thing, isn't it? I think we all want that.

It's a funny thing, too, in that you don't have any control over it. You can try your best to build a narrative. A story of who you are and what you did. But history decides in the end. Doesn't matter what I write here. It'll be part of a record, but it might not be the deciding factor on how people see me.

I want people to see me well. No one wants to be a villain. Look at poor old Christopher Columbus. The man found America, but then a couple of folks decided they didn't like *how* he found America. People say he and his crew brought all these diseases that devastated native populations. How was he to know that? He didn't launch knowing the folks in the New World wouldn't be able to handle stuff like smallpox and measles.

It's a damn sorry thing. It's never nice when people die, especially getting sick like that. But he didn't do it on purpose, and I think that ought to be taken into account. And there's all this other stuff said about Columbus, about what he did to who, but we ought to focus on the endpoint.

He found America. Not that it was lost! But he changed the face of the world.

Sometimes that means making tough decisions and some people just don't get that. Which is why we got to a point a few years ago when people were tearing down every statue of Columbus they could find. Which capped off with that big demonstration in Columbus,

Ohio, and I don't need to tell you how that ended. I think we're all still haunted by the pictures.

Imagine what that would be like, if we could pluck Columbus off the deck of his ship in 1492, just as he saw land. That promise of a new beginning. And then we whisk him here and we tell him what his legacy will be. That he'll become a villain. Would he keep sailing? Or would he turn back around?

I don't know. And Cloud hasn't cracked time travel yet (though, and I'm being serious here, I had a division looking into this for a couple of years, because why the hell not?). So it ain't gonna happen, and certainly not within the last few months of my life.

Still, it makes me think of my own legacy.

There are two things I'm damn proud of.

I talked a bit about how Cloud created a model aimed at fixing the environment by reducing greenhouse gases, and how a big part of that was cutting down commutes. But that didn't happen in a vacuum. We didn't just build a MotherCloud and say, "Here we go. Now things are different."

The first thing we had to do was rethink the model of how we built things. I know America is supposed to be a country founded on capitalism, but it's sort of incredible how damn hard this country used to make it for businesses to thrive. It's why so many American companies went overseas. If you put up wall after wall in front of me, why would I build here? Why not just go someplace where there were no walls?

Think of an apartment building. Say it's got six floors. A lot of people want to live in this apartment building because it's pretty nice. But more and more people want to move there, and the man who owns the building thinks: why not build another floor or two? So he does, and that's okay. Growth is a good thing. He makes a little more money, he can provide better for his family.

But let's say the city is getting crowded. Say more people are moving there, and it's not just that he wants to build more, he *has* to build more to meet demand. This goes beyond wanting to make money. He has property. That property is valuable. I'd say he has a responsibility to the city as a whole. A city can't grow without people. So he adds another floor or two. But the foundation is only so stable. You've got to deal with the existing infrastructure.

The bigger the building gets, the less stable it becomes.

Build on it too much, it topples to the ground.

And that's because you're trying to graft new needs onto an existing model.

The smarter thing to do would be to tear down the damn building! Start from scratch! Look at the needs you have now, really think about your future needs, and build from there. Put up a thirty-story building. And make the foundation strong enough you can build on more if you need to.

Think about all those cities that got unlivable because the roads were built to support a hundred thousand people, but then they swelled up to more than a million. How sewer systems corrode and collapse because suddenly you've got triple the amount of people flushing their waste away.

Point is, sometimes you've got to rethink how you do things, rather than try to build on unsteady ground. It's why I lobbied so hard for laws that would help businesses grow, rather than hinder them. For example, the Red Tape Elimination Act. Used to be it took years to build a structure and open it as a business. You had to do all these studies and cross off all these boxes, and most of them were pointless. For example, in one state, I think it was Delaware? You had to do an environmental impact study for one agency, which cost a whole bunch of money and took something like six months. And there was *another* agency that wanted an EIS, but you couldn't use the same one for both agencies. You had to do two of the exact same thing—and eat the cost. It was basically just a way to keep people in the government employed.

And God forbid you tried to build it and didn't hire a union. They'd set up a big inflatable rat in front of your building and scream at everyone who tried to walk through the door. Except if you did try to hire them, you'd pay quadruple the going rate, plus the work wouldn't be as good. People don't commit when they've got job security. People earning their wages, they work harder. This is why I championed the Freedom from Harassment in Construction Act. Now you don't see those inflatable rats anymore. Someone puts them up, cops can pull them right down, put them in the trash where they belong.

Or the Paperless Currency Act, which pushed the government to make near-field communication more secure and widespread, so we could stop printing and exchanging so much money.

The most important, by far, was the Freedom from Machinery Act, which mandated hiring quotas, as well as the maximum number of jobs any given business can field out to robots. This was the most controversial thing I ever did, more so than the employee rating systems, because a lot of other business owners got real mad at me for doing it. The reality is, a lot of the things at Cloud could be done cheaper if we had robots doing them. I might be worth another billion or two. But, damn it, I want to see people working! I want to walk across a warehouse floor and see men and women able to support themselves.

That really turned the tide for a lot of things. The year before we got the Freedom from Machinery Act passed, the unemployment rate was somewhere around 28 percent. Two years later? Three percent. That figure keeps me warm at night. Plus, all those business owners eventually came around, when they realized the tax incentives were pretty good.

Each one of these things made my job easier, helped me to grow Cloud, and got people good-paying jobs. I'm proud of this, not just for me, but for all the other businesses I helped.

But it would be a pretty sad thing if that were my only legacy, and I'm happy to say it's not.

My other legacy is my daughter, Claire.

Claire is our only child. I've never really talked about this, but Molly had a hard pregnancy, so we decided one child was enough. I remember when she was born and people would ask me if I was disappointed I had a girl instead of a boy. And I would get so mad at that. Here is this beautiful little thing, the most perfect thing in the world, a physical representation of the love I feel for my wife—how can I feel an ounce of regret anywhere in my heart? What kind of person even asks that?

Claire was a lucky kid. She was born around the time Cloud was really hitting its stride, so she never wanted for anything, but I didn't let her off easy. Soon as she was old enough, I put her to work. In the office, doing odd jobs. Even paid her a little salary. I don't think I was violating child labor laws, but don't hold me to that.

What I wanted to instill in Claire was that no one hands you anything in this life. You have to work for it. And I never wanted her to follow in my footsteps. I wanted her to go out in the world and do her own thing. But she was just so damn smart, and so interested in how everything at Cloud worked. Wasn't long before she got herself hired. Swear to truth, she did it under an assumed name, at a satellite office where nobody knew her. She wanted to show me she could do it. We all had a good laugh over what basically amounted to a minor case of fraud.

After she did that I brought her on in the main branch, and I always held her to the same standard as everyone else. She got rated, just like every employee, and I made sure that nothing I said or did could influence that rating. And she was a consistent four-star employee, year in and year out. She dipped down to three at one point, but that's the year she had her first child and she wasn't around the office that much, and that kind of thing just can't be helped.

Important thing is, I raised a smart, strong woman. The kind of person who will tell me I'm wrong in front of a room full of people. The kind of person who will meet an unwanted advance with a smack in the teeth. The kind of person I'm proud to call mine. She made me a better person in a million different ways. But she made Cloud a better company, too.

PAXTON

Paxton peeked into the open door of Dobbs's office. Empty. That was a relief. He figured he owed Dobbs an answer, on joining the task force, and he wasn't ready to answer yet, even if it seemed Dakota had decided for him.

He was looking for an empty desk, unsure of what to do next, when he turned and an Indian man with a carefully tailored beard anchoring sharp cheekbones appeared in front of him, almost as if he'd materialized out of thin air. His CloudBand strap was the same color blue as his polo shirt. He was a head shorter and cleared his throat the way people do when they're about to make a point. He asked, "Are you Paxton?"

The way the man asked, Paxton wasn't sure if he should admit to it, but he said, "Yeah, I am."

"Vikram," he said, not offering his hand. "You know you shouldn't just be standing around?"

"I know, but no one told me what to do. . . ."

"Someone shouldn't have to tell you what to do," he said, crossing his arms.

Paxton's train of thought hit a boulder before tumbling off the tracks. He didn't know what to say. He stuttered in response. A small smile curled at the corner of Vikram's mouth.

Then he heard a familiar voice. "Pax. Ready to head out?"

He found Dakota standing ten feet away. Her arms were crossed, too. Vikram looked at her and sighed. "I didn't realize new recruits were allowed to stand around all day."

"And I didn't realize you got upgraded to tan," Dakota said. Then she tapped her head and stuck a finger in the air. "Wait, no, that's not a thing that happened. So why don't you leave my new partner alone, Vicky?"

Paxton stepped back, gave room for the tug-of-war. Vikram clenched his fists hard. Then he threw his hands up. "What the hell do you think he's going to accomplish that we couldn't?"

"I guess we'll have to wait and see," Dakota said.

"This is the world's biggest haystack and you're looking for the world's smallest needle," Vikram said, more to Paxton than to Dakota. "Even if you do find it, it won't be with anything more than luck."

"Carry on," Dakota said, shooing him away.

Vikram turned to Paxton. "I'll be watching you."

It was such a bad-movie-dialogue move Paxton had to hold his breath to keep from laughing. Vikram made it worse by turning it into a staring contest, as if he was goading Paxton into responding, so

Paxton pressed his lips together and pushed his shoulders up a little. He'd learned a long time ago that people in an argument will tussle over the last word long enough the point will get lost. The better way to handle it was to act as if the last word wasn't important enough to take.

It worked. Vikram stalked off down the corridor, his footsteps muffled on the gray carpet. A few people who had been watching dove back toward their workstations.

"C'mon," Dakota said.

She led him down to the tram, which they took around to the dorms, not speaking until they were free and clear of prying ears. They started their stroll down the promenade, cutting long, circuitous paths around the benches and the kiosks.

"So," Paxton said. "That was dramatic."

"Dobbs had Vikram working on the oblivion thing for a little while," she said. "Problem was, Vikram promised the moon and stars. Said he'd sort it out in no time, and a few months later he had a little less than nothing. So Dobbs booted him down to the warehouse exit line. Which is among the shittiest of the security details. That and the drone field."

"Yeah, when Dobbs sat me down he said something about people getting out of hand because they were hungry for power."

"Napoleon complex, big-time," Dakota said. "Be careful around him. He thinks you were brought on to replace him. Which is not true at all. It's just you came on at a time that Dobbs needed some fresh blood. But he might rat on you if he thinks it'll bring you down a peg and take him up a notch."

"Lovely."

"He's a pain in the ass but the rank-and-file like him," Dakota said. "He works hard, he's aggressive, he does everything by the book, so Dobbs can't justify kicking him to another section. Not that I know if Dobbs has even thought of doing that. I don't know what that guy is thinking half the time."

"Got it, got it," Paxton said.

By the second dorm it became clear the crowd had thinned. Not much shift change happening. Paxton made note of the time in his head. Trying to build out a flow of the place. It was like looking into a great big machine. He didn't know how any of it worked, but pay attention long enough, you could figure some stuff out.

"Any good prison stories?" Dakota asked.

"No such thing as a good prison story," Paxton said.

They walked in silence for a bit. Then she said, "I'm sorry."

Paxton sighed. "No, it's fine. That's all anyone ever wants to know. Was it a rape-and-shank kind of place? It wasn't. I worked in a minimum-security facility that was mostly for people with civil penalties. The hardest guys in there weren't nearly as hard as they thought. I mean, it taught me a ton about conflict resolution, but at the end of the day, it wasn't like you see on television."

"Ah," Dakota said, not even bothering to hide her disappointment.

Which made Paxton feel like he was letting her down. It was a silly way to feel, but still, he did, so he thought back. There was one story that came to mind instantly. The one that didn't make his stomach twist up.

"Okay," he said. "Okay."

And Dakota perked up.

"So every morning, six on the dot, bell goes off and everyone has to get out of their cell for count," he said. "And we had this pair of prisoners. Titus and Mickey. Older guys, kinda squirrely, mostly kept to themselves. Used to tell stories about how they were going to escape, but no one believed them. We should have. 'Cause one day we do count and they're not lined up. We go into the cell and find Mickey, halfway into the ground, bare ass and legs kicking in the air. He and Titus dug this hole, and he got stuck."

"Wait . . . he was naked?"

"Oh yeah," Paxton said. "They'd been digging at the floor and flushing the dirt. Can't believe no one noticed, but they only ever had one person on guard at night on that block, given everyone was locked in their cells. It was a cost-saving measure. A dumb one. Should have had someone walking the stacks, too. So apparently Titus goes down first, given he's a rail of a guy, and it's narrow so he gets through fine. No one ever saw him again. Mickey, though, he's a bit bigger and he couldn't make it through. So he figures, if he strips down, his clothes won't get caught on anything."

"Not exactly a rocket scientist, was he?"

"It gets better," Paxton said. "So me and another guard go to get him out. We each grab a leg, brace ourselves, and pull. We both went flying. The other guy ended up with a concussion. Turns out, Mickey already thought the hole might be too narrow. He stole a big block of butter from the kitchen and lubed himself up. He didn't want to take any chances."

Dakota let out a deep laugh from the center of her belly. "Good god."

Paxton laughed a little at the memory. "So he's crammed down there, stuck, ass up, covered in butter. We had to wash him down first just to get enough of a grip on him. Which, you know, there were a lot of moments I knew I wanted to get the hell out of that place. Staring at a naked, sobbing man's ass while giving him a sponge bath was right up there."

Dakota laughed again, high and light. "Well, lucky for you we don't get that kind of stuff here."

"That is a lovely thing to hear," Paxton said.

They entered the vaulted space of Live-Play. Dakota seemed to know where she was going, so Paxton followed. Up an escalator, then another, into a darkened arcade full of old-school cabinets that looked beaten to hell but still worked, the cacophony of sound and dim light making the space feel that much more empty.

"What are we doing in here?" Paxton asked.

Dakota didn't answer, just continued toward the back, to a Skee-Ball machine, a little pool of shadow next to it, where Paxton thought he saw movement. Dakota reached into the pool and pulled out a young man in a green polo shirt. Scrawny, mop of blond hair, not happy to be out in the light. He put his arms up to protect his face.

"Hello, Warren," she said.

"I'm not doing anything."

"Just skulking."

"I was playing Skee-Ball. I saw you coming and I knew you were here to hassle me." He looked at Paxton, nodded toward him with his chin. "Who's this goofy asshole?"

"New to the detail," Dakota said. "Former prison guard. I was you, I wouldn't fuck with him. He's seen some shit."

Fear flashed across Warren's eyes. Paxton played along by not saying anything. Let Warren's imagination put in some overtime.

"Warren here is an oblivion dealer," Dakota said to Paxton. "That's what he was doing." She pointed toward the corner. "Not a lot of folks come in here, so he uses it to sling that jank shit."

Warren went hands up, palms out. "I have no idea what you're talking about."

"What would I find if I turned out your pockets?"

"You can't do that."

"Who says I can't? Who's to say it didn't fall out of your pocket? Who's to say I didn't see you with it out in the open?" She looked at Paxton. "Who's to say?"

Paxton's face burned. He shrugged. Gave the distinct impression of *I didn't see nothing*.

Warren nodded. Turned out his pockets. Gave a little smirk.

"Happy?" he asked.

"You know that I'm not," Dakota said. "What if I tear this place apart? What will I find?"

Warren looked around. "Lots of electronics, I guess."

Dakota sucked air through her teeth. Looked like she wanted to do something she'd regret. After a moment she said, "Get the fuck out of here."

Warren turned, disappeared between the gaming cabinets. Paxton and Dakota gave it a minute, exited the arcade, and resumed their stroll, same as before except for the steam coming out of Dakota's ears.

"Why not stick someone on him?" Paxton asked. "Or lean on him harder? There have to be ways to exert pressure."

"Dobbs says no," she said. "Dobbs says use a light touch."

"Why?"

"That's the way he wants it done."

"C'mon, the kid is a twerp. Stick him in a room and turn up the thermostat and he'll melt."

"That's the way Dobbs wants it done," Dakota says.

"Meanwhile, you're knocking out pimps. Nothing light about that."

Her voice whipped at him. "When you're in charge, you call the shots."

"Fine, fine," Paxton said, throwing up his hands. "I'm sure you checked the watch, cross-referenced who met with him, right?"

She nodded. "Whenever he's in the arcade, it's always just him. Whoever he's working with has figured out a way to conceal his movements, or he's wandering around without a watch on at all. Which is part of the reason Dobbs is so intent on nailing this down. Besides blowing open the oblivion distribution, clearly there's some kind of flaw in the tracking."

Paxton looked down at his watch, turned his wrist over.

"You're only supposed to take it off at night," he said.

"Yeah."

"You can't get around without one, with all the doors and elevators and access points."

"Yup."

"So how do you spoof it?"

"That's the question."

"Any thoughts?"

"None," she said. "Try to dismantle it, alert. Take it off for too long without putting it in the cradle, alert. And it's coded to each user so it's not like people can swap them."

"So it would help if we found the weak point."

"It would."

"I imagine you've had tech people on this?"

"Up and down."

Paxton adjusted the watch on his wrist. On one hand, this felt over his pay grade. But on the other, he relished the idea of a mystery to crack. It broke up the monotony of the day, at least.

They walked some more. Back down the promenade. He glanced at the various blues passing them by. Studying faces. No one he recognized. Not from the bullpen or his introductory session. There were a lot of people here. More important, no Vikram.

"How worried should I be about Napoleon?" Paxton asked.

"We'll see if he's even here in a few days."

"How's that?"

"Cut Day soon."

"I don't know what that is."

She stopped. Turned. "Geez, I thought that was part of the intro. Okay, so, on Cut Day, a whole bunch of low-ranked employees are going to get a notification they've been turfed. That day tends to be busy for us. A lot of people don't want to leave. Sometimes a couple of people . . . well." She drifted, came back to it. "It's a busy day for us."

"Got it. Sounds pretty cutthroat."

"It is, but don't worry," she said. "You get a grace period. First month you don't qualify to be cut."

"That's . . . good," Paxton said. He wasn't sure if *good* was the right word, but it was something.

"C'mon, let's head back," Dakota said. "Put some notes down for the task force."

"I still haven't agreed to be on that."

"Yes you have." And she walked, without turning to make sure Paxton was following. He jogged to keep up.

ZINNIA

Turkey baster. Book. Cat food. Christmas lights. Activated-charcoal teeth-whitening powder. Faux-fur slippers. Webcam. Tablet. Toy laser guns. Selfie stick. Markers. Yarn. Vitamin D tablets. Night-lights. Pruning shears. Meat thermometer. Dehumidifier. Coconut oil.

Zinnia ran. The new sneakers were ugly as fuck but they were comfortable, and even with her feet bandaged up and protesting, she was able to work up a head of speed as she danced between the shelves and conveyor belts. As if she were being guided by an unseen hand. The algorithm, keeping her safe, moving the workers and the shelves in tandem. She turned the job into a game. How many times could she make the green bar flash?

Printer ink. Grill cover. Pajamas. Dog chew toy. Sleeping bag. Tablet. Book. Paintbrushes. Wallet. Shoelaces. Micro-USB cable. Airline neck pillow. Protein powder. Power strip. Silicone baking cups. Essential oils. Portable charger. Travel mug. Plush robe. Headphones.

Four. She'd gotten four green flashes since she started and she wasn't even at her first piss break. She hit the wall and pushed through. She could make the bar flash green, but how long could she make it stay green?

Mesh waste basket. Tick-control collar. Colored pencils. USB hub. Tablet. Moisturizer. Forehead thermometer. French press. Patterned socks. Ice cube trays. Leather gloves. Backpack. Book. Camping lantern. Thermos. Sleep mask. Wool cap. Boots.

It only ever stayed green for a couple of seconds, and every second it did felt like an achievement. Like she'd done something good. It was that flash of color, yellow to green, yellow the color of weakness, green the color of power. Money, nature, life. That color in this context was both completely worthless and all she wanted. The running made the time move, which made lunch come up quick. When it did she found herself, mercifully, near a break room, where she ducked inside and got some water and pulled the protein bar from her back pocket, then sat at a free table.

As she chewed on the bar—PowerBuff salted caramel, her favorite, which a bodega on the promenade stocked—her watch buzzed.

We are currently facing a period of increased demand. Would you be interested in volunteering to extend your shift?

She looked at the message. Thought about it. Then held up her wrist and pressed the crown.

"Miguel Velandres."

The watch carried her back onto the warehouse floor. Ten minutes later she caught sight of Miguel, holding a package of pens. She jogged to catch up and fell in step alongside him.

"Hey," she said.

He turned, lingering for a second, trying to remember her name. Then his eyes lit up. "Zinnia. Everything okay?"

"Yeah. Just a quick follow-up."

"Sure."

"The watch asked me to work overtime."

"Oh, yeah. Definitely do that."

"Do they pay us extra?"

Miguel laughed, placed the pens in a bin on a conveyor belt, gave them a nudge to send them away. "It's strictly volunteer. But it keeps you in good standing. Counts toward your employee rating."

"I thought it was an option."

"It is an option," he said, giving a brief glance at his CloudBand and setting off, on the hunt for his next item. "It's an option you want to take." He looked around, made sure there was no one close by, and waved at her, as if he wanted her to lean in. "Builds you a buffer on your rating. The more you refuse, it goes the other way."

Zinnia's watch buzzed again.

We are currently facing a period of increased demand. Would you be interested in volunteering to extend your shift?

She paused, but Miguel kept going.

"Don't rock the boat, *mi amiga*," he said.

He turned a corner and disappeared. Zinnia raised the watch to her lips. Wanted to say, *Fuck off, I'm tired.* Instead she said, "Sure." The watch showed an exaggerated smiley face.

Her lunch break over, she was back on shift, and she lost herself in a whirlwind of books and health care products and pet food and batteries, less interested in the green-bar game, and more interested in getting the hell out of there for the day.

At the end of her extra shift, which only lasted an additional half hour, and then the forty minutes it took to get through the pat-down, she found herself utterly spent, but as if she'd just completed a good workout. She concentrated on that feeling.

Calories burned and muscles worked, rather than dignity surrendered.

As she passed through the promenade, just before she entered the archway that opened onto the lobby of her dorm, she threw a glance through the glass doors that led to a concrete hallway and a series of public bathrooms at the end.

Halfway down, fifty feet or so, dug into the wall, was a CloudPoint.

She'd walked through to wash her hands on the way to her shift. It wasn't a high-traffic bathroom since it was close to the elevators. It seemed people used their floor bathrooms before leaving for work, or preferred the refuge of the same on the way home. Walking past it now, the hallway was empty.

She reached the elevator, swiped her way in. Another woman got on. Young, boxy, in a wheelchair, hair cut in a brown bob. Yellow polo. The strap of her CloudBand featured a repeating series of cartoon cats. She had a pile of boxes on her lap. She smiled at Zinnia and gave a polite "Hello," then looked at the lit-up number on the panel and didn't bother to swipe her own watch—she was going to the same floor.

Zinnia's social-engineering theory was holding up. Which was why the CloudPoint in the hallway was a solid option. She would have preferred to use one farther away from her apartment, even in another building if she could manage it, but it had to be close. Only way she'd get there and back without the CloudBand. The longer she was out of her room without it, the greater her exposure.

The doors opened and Zinnia shot her hand out to hold them open, let the woman slide her wheelchair out. The woman said, "Thanks," and rolled down the hallway. Zinnia followed. She stopped at her door and heard the light thump of boxes falling. To her left, the woman in the wheelchair had dropped what she was carrying in the course of opening her own door. Zinnia let the door close and walked down the hallway. "Need help?"

The woman glanced up. "That'd be great, thank you."

Zinnia picked up the boxes and held them while the woman swiped into the apartment and pulled open the door. She expected to see a living space that was more handicapped accessible, but it was the same as her own. Same narrow pathway, and as the woman rolled her wheelchair in, it barely fit. Zinnia followed behind and put the boxes on the counter, next to the cook plate.

The woman rolled toward the futon, where she had enough room to spin the wheelchair around. She moved quickly, with grace. She was used to it. "I really appreciate it."

"No problem, just . . ." Zinnia looked around. The apartment was small enough for her to manage so it didn't really bother her, but looking at it now, it felt suffocating. "I hope it's not uncouth to bring this up, but they can't offer you something a little more . . . appropriate?"

The woman shrugged. "I don't need a lot of space. I could get a bigger apartment but I'd rather save the money. I'm Cynthia, by the way. . . ."

She stuck out her hand. Zinnia shook it. It was strong, her palms thick and callused.

"New to the floor?" she asked. "I haven't seen you before."

"First week."

"Well," she said, huffing and giving a conspiratorial smile. "Welcome to the neighborhood."

"Thanks," Zinnia said. "Anything else I can give you a hand with?"

Cynthia smiled again. A painful little smile. It took Zinnia a second to figure out what it meant. It was a *Don't pity me* smile, and Zinnia wanted to apologize for it but realized that would just make it worse, so she let the silence linger until the woman said, "No thanks, I'm good."

"Right then. Well, have a nice night."

Zinnia reached the door and the woman said, "Wait."

She turned.

"This place can be a lot, especially when you're new. If you need anything, feel free to knock on my door."

"Thank you," Zinnia said.

She left, returned to her apartment. Stepped inside and marveled at what that poor woman was dealing with. Then realized what an asshole she was for thinking of that woman as poor.

She had some time to kill before drinks with Paxton so she picked up the multi-tool and climbed on the bed, pulled out some of the pushpins holding the tapestries across the ceiling. The corner dropped down, revealing a six-inch-long line she'd been gouging out. She didn't like working in long bursts—it made the room too dusty and she was worried about the noise. At least it was easy. The ceiling was cheap, thin drywall and it cut like a steak. She pushed the knife in and out, gritting her teeth and bunching her shoulders at the sound. White dust rained on the bedspread.

Another day or two and she'd be through. Hopefully there'd be enough room for her to move around up there. Hopefully she wouldn't trip some kind of alarm. Hopefully she wouldn't get stuck.

After she knocked out a few more inches, she folded up the knife, replaced the tapestry, and bunched up the bedspread. She dumped the accumulated dust in the sink and ran the faucet, then went into her bag for the electric trimmer. Opened the battery compartment, slid out the battery, and pulled out her tweezers. Reached in and rooted around, breaking the light glue she had used to fasten the gopher, a USB nub the size of her fingernail.

The most dangerous part of hacking anything was the amount of time you had to sit there doing the work. A big lift job like this could take hours, maybe even days. But a second was enough to get caught.

That was where the gopher came in—a handy, ruinously expensive little device that would sample an organization's internal computer code, but do all the heavy lifting of decrypting and processing later, without being connected to the system.

She could plug it into a terminal—any terminal connected to a company's intranet—and within a few seconds it would carve off a sample of internal code. Then she would place the gopher in her laptop, where it could quietly brute-force its way through as many CPU cycles as it needed, doing all the heavy work from the bottom of a drawer.

It would take some time, and require a little help here and there, but once it was done, it would create a wicked piece of malware she could plug back into the system. It would waltz right in and find what she needed in a matter of moments.

Maps, schematics, energy data, security reports.

The process wasn't fast. She'd used it a few times and it often took weeks to process. Given the density of Cloud's security she wouldn't be surprised if it took a month or more.

But again: the long way around tended to be safer.

The biggest obstacle, really, was a hardware issue. The blue-and-white cloud logo on the top of the CloudPoint, at eye level, was just vaguely translucent. She was sure there was a camera behind it. Even with Cloud's lax stance on cameras, they wouldn't *not* have cameras in the ATMs.

But she had a plan.

As she approached, she would duck down to tie her shoe, or maybe have a bag full of groceries and drop them. It would be an awkward movement—she'd have to get low well before she got in range of the camera, because it was probably a fish-eye lens. Then, boom, into the access panel, gopher in, gopher out, close the panel, up and away.

She pulled a plastic pen from her toiletry kit, yanked the point of the pen and the ink reservoir out with her teeth. Then she took a penknife from her bag and got to carving a swoop in the plastic that would catch the lock and make it a simple matter of jamming it in and turning it hard.

Her favorite part of being a corporate spy was the complete lack of investment by the world at large in new lock technology.

With that done, she took the transmitter and pen and laid them on the counter next to each other. Took out a small glasses case and placed them inside. She'd carry them with her, just in case she stumbled across an opportunity better than the current plan.

She checked her watch, found it was almost time to meet Paxton. They'd agreed on a bar in Live-Play. The place that looked like a British-style pub, which he seemed excited about. She was a vodka girl, and therefore less picky about location. Vodka being the most efficient delivery system of alcohol.

She stripped down. Realized she was covered in funk from work. Dried sweat and pity. She considered taking a brief shower, or even pulling on a clean pair of underwear, but she wasn't planning on fucking him tonight, and even if it ended up that way, she doubted he would protest. Most men were more concerned with the state of play than with the condition of the field. As she pulled on a clean shirt her watch buzzed.

Just a reminder, you still need to review your pension paperwork!

Damn it. She had meant to do this already. Signing up for the pension was part of the plan. Not a hugely important part, but she figured it would make her less of a sore thumb, if she was making moves like she planned to be around for the long haul.

Then:

She picked up the remote control. Turned on the television, which immediately began blaring a commercial for PowerBuff bars, in which a skinny guy ate one and swelled up to comic-book-muscle proportions.

PowerBuff bars. Get buff!

"Well," she said to the empty room. "That's vaguely unsettling."

She picked up the remote, flipped it up so it turned into a keyboard, hit a button that said Browser, and the television launched into the CloudPoint landing page.

At the top it said: *Welcome, Zinnia!*

"Fuck you," Zinnia replied.

PAXTON

Paxton arched his shoulders and the stool wobbled. It wasn't a normal wobble. More like an ass-over-elbow wobble. He hopped off and exchanged it for the stool next to him. Same black-leather-cushioned top and rough-hewn wood legs. He rocked it back and forth and it didn't budge. He climbed on top and took another sip of his beer. Three-quarters done now.

The bartender wandered over. Green shirt, hair slicked back, a nose that'd been broken a few times. His CloudBand strap was thick and leather, wider than the face of the watch. "You want another?" he asked.

No sense in getting drunk before she even showed. "Not yet. Waiting for someone."

The bartender gave a little smile. Paxton couldn't tell if it was an *Okay, sure* or a *Good for you* smile. It was a smile. He glanced down at his black T-shirt and jeans. Felt good to be out of the blue. People didn't look at him with eyes full of caution. He was just another guy.

"Sorry."

Paxton turned, saw Zinnia hustling into the bar. Black sweater, purple leggings, hair bunched up and pulled into a bun at the top of her head. He nodded toward the wobbly seat.

"Don't take that one," he said. "Broken."

Zinnia climbed onto the stool on the other side of him. As she settled, he moved his stool a few inches away from her, not wanting to make her feel crowded.

She looked around. "This is pretty nice."

Paxton thought so, too. Shiny gold pint spouts, lacquered wood. Definitely not built by someone who had ever been in a proper British pub—Paxton had spent some time in the UK on business—but the person who put this place together had at least had the concept explained to them.

The bartender came over, wiping down a pint glass, and nodded toward Zinnia.

"Vodka, ice," she said. "Well is fine."

The bartender nodded, assembled the drink.

"You don't mess around," Paxton said.

"No I do not," she said, accepting the glass, not looking at him. She sounded exhausted. Which made sense, being a red, running around all day. Zinnia leaned forward to swipe her CloudBand against the payment disc set into the bar, which was more in front of Paxton than it was in front of her.

"Let me add you to my tab," he said, throwing his arm forward, his hand brushing against hers in the process.

"You don't have to . . ."

"I want to," he said, tapping his CloudBand against the circle, the light turning green. She smiled, hoisted her glass. He picked up his, clinked it.

"Cheers," she said.

"Cheers."

She took a healthy sip while he drained his beer, put the pint on the edge of the bar so the bartender could see and bring him another. Silence hung in the air a second too long, and then it grew bigger, sucking in the gravity of the room, and Paxton gave up on trying to say something clever and asked, "How are you adjusting?"

Zinnia threw up a little eyebrow. Like, *That the best you got?* "So far so good. It's harder than I thought it would be. They really run you into the ground."

Paxton accepted a fresh beer, took a sip. "How does it work, exactly?"

Zinnia ran through a clipped explanation: the watch, how it moved them around, bringing items to bins. The whole process like a dance. Paxton pictured Zinnia as a cog in a giant machine, spinning around, a small part keeping the whole thing going.

"Were you hoping for red?" he asked.

"Hell no," Zinnia said, taking another sip of the vodka. "I wanted to be on tech. That's my background."

"Thought you said you were a teacher."

That eyebrow again. The kind of eyebrow that could draw blood. "I did. But I put myself through college doing electronics repair. My housing alone was covered fixing cracked screens. Kids getting drunk and smashing their phones."

Paxton laughed. "Well, I'd trade you if I could."

"Really?" she asked. "You don't like being a rent-a-cop?"

Paxton felt the booze soaking into his synapses, neurons unfurling. It felt good to be drinking and talking, because it'd been a while since he'd done either.

"It was never a good fit for me," he said. "I'm not an authoritative kind of person."

"Well, hey, there are worse things. . . ."

She seemed to be drifting. He didn't want to lose her so soon. "So, tell me about yourself. I know you're a teacher. I know you can fix a broken phone. Where are you from?"

"Here, there," she said, staring off at the back of the bar. At herself in the mirror, reflected through a rainbow of glittering liquor bottles. "I moved around a lot as a kid. I don't really feel like I'm from anywhere."

She took a small pull of vodka. Paxton's shoulders sagged. As far as first dates went this was turning into a bit of a bomb. But then she smiled. "I'm sorry, that's a little dreary, isn't it?"

"No, not at all," Paxton said, then he laughed. "Well, I mean, yeah, it is."

She laughed in return, smacked him on the arm. It was light, with the back of her hand, and it only seemed to happen because her hand was already up, on the way to grabbing the glass of vodka, but still, he took it as a good sign.

"What about family?" Paxton asked.

"My mom is still around," Zinnia said. "We talk on Christmas. That's about the most we can manage."

"I've got a brother," he said. "We're like that. Get along okay but don't go out of the way to see each other. Which . . . I don't know. . . ." Paxton trailed a thought but the beer was getting in the way. He wondered if he ought to just drain his glass, apologize, and head back to his place. Cut his losses before he bled to death.

"What?" Zinnia asked.

There was something about the way she asked it, like she didn't need to know but still wanted to. Paxton breathed in, then out, and found it. "Being here, it almost feels like being on another planet, doesn't it? Like, you couldn't even just walk out of here. Where would you go? You'd die of thirst before you found civilization."

"It does feel like that, yeah," Zinnia said. "Where are you from?"

"New York," he said. "Staten Island, originally."

Zinnia shook her head. "Oh, New York. I don't like New York."

Paxton laughed. "Wait, what? Who doesn't like New York? That's like saying you don't like . . . I don't know, Paris."

"It's so big. And filthy. No one has any personal space." She scrunched her shoulders together, like she was walking down a crowded hallway. "Paris isn't so great either."

Paxton swung his arms around. "You think this is better?"

"Now, I didn't say that," Zinnia said, that eyebrow going up, but then coming back down, relaxing. "This . . . it's like . . . I don't know. . . ."

"It's like living in a fucking airport," Paxton said, dropping his tone, as if someone might hear it and admonish him.

Zinnia laughed. It was a fast little laugh and it slipped between her lips like it was coated in oil. Her eyes went wide, like the sound had surprised her. As if she wished she could pull it back. But finally, she said, "Exactly what I thought the first night here. Airport chic."

Zinnia knocked back her vodka, waved over the bartender for another. "If you'll excuse me, I'll be going hard in the paint tonight." She stuck a finger in the air. "And don't give me any of your chivalry bullshit. Next round is on me."

"I like a woman who doesn't fuck around," Paxton said, immediately regretting it, like it was too much, but that eyebrow went up and it suddenly looked completely different. It looked like a check mark, and it framed a big beautiful brown eye; he could see white all around the iris.

"So," Paxton asked, feeling bold. "Any particular reason you're not fucking around?"

"Feet."

"Feet?"

"I made the dumb-ass mistake of wearing boots on my first day." The bartender put down a fresh glass. "Thank you." She took a sip. "Because I didn't have sneakers. I have them now. Wish I would have thought that through. I imagine you're on your feet a lot, too."

Paxton wondered whether he was allowed to talk about the task force. He didn't think it was a secret. Dobbs hadn't told him not to tell anybody. And sometimes talking things out helped. Plus, it might impress her, that he'd gotten pegged for a special assignment as soon as he walked through the door.

"Apparently this place has an oblivion problem," Paxton said. "And they think because I used to work in a prison I might be useful. Like I might be some kind of smuggling and contraband expert. Which isn't really true. But hey . . . it's better than just standing around. I like solving problems."

"Is that why you became an inventor?"

"I don't know if I could call it that," he said, placing his hand around the base of the beer, looking down into the foam. "I only invented one thing. And even that was just taking a bunch of products that came before it and figuring out how to make them better."

"Yeah, but you did it."

He smiled. "And now I'm here."

The words came out cold, brittle. Zinnia tensed. Paxton knew it wasn't in keeping with the vibe he was trying to maintain, but he couldn't help himself. He turned a little, away from Zinnia and toward the beer, the memory lodged in his throat like a hot coal.

A flash in the corner of his vision. Zinnia raised her glass.

"I'm here, too," she said, giving a little smirk, a tilt of the head.

He tapped his glass off hers and they drank.

"So tell me more about this gig," Zinnia said. "Have to figure you get access all over the place."

"I guess? It's been less than a week. I'm sure there are some doors I can't open. But I haven't come across any."

"You should see the warehouse," she said. "You can't even see the end of it. And this isn't even all there is. There's a whole other set of buildings I don't even have access to."

"Right, yeah," he said. "It would be cool to see those."

"I would love to just take a walking tour of this place. See the whole thing, you know? It really is incredible."

The smirk crept onto her lip again. It disappeared when she sipped her drink. Paxton wondered what she was asking. Did she want him to take her on a tour? He didn't even know if he was allowed to do that. Was she angling to get him somewhere alone?

"Not sure I can swing that, but if I can, I'll let you know," he said.

"Fair enough," she said. Disappointed.

"But, who knows. I can ask." He glanced at Zinnia. "So. You said next step from here is teach English in another country, right? Is that what you want to do, full stop?"

She shrugged. "Cost of living is pretty low in other countries. I'm a bit tapped out on America, in a general sense."

"It's not great, but it's better than a lot of other places. We still have clean water."

"That's what fire and iodine tablets are for."

"I didn't mean it like that. Truth is, I'm a little jealous. Might be nice to get away."

"So why not do it?"

"Do what?"

"Get away."

Paxton paused. Thought about it. Sipped his beer. Placed it down. Glanced around the mostly empty bar. At the shiny landscape of Live-Play beyond the entrance. He didn't know how to answer the question. The way she said it made it sound as if it were as easy as picking up the pint glass and placing it to his lips. Like it was a thing you could just do.

"It's not that simple . . . ," he said.

"Usually is."

"How? Say I left here right now, walked out the door. What would I do for money? Where would I go?"

She smiled. "That's the thing about freedom. It's yours until you give it up."

"What does that mean?"

"Think on it."

She took another sip and smiled, the muscles in her face going a little slack. She was feeling the booze, too. And she was testing him. He liked it. So he told her, "All I know is this: I can't get out of here soon enough."

Which was exactly why he'd been ignoring the CloudBand's request that he sign up for the pension system. Soon as he did that, he was admitting that this was the endgame.

"Amen to that," she said, throwing back the last of her drink. "Speaking of, can we walk around a bit? I know I've been on my feet all day, but now it feels like my legs are getting stiff."

"Sure," Paxton said. He pounded his beer, closed his tab, tapped through the pay screen on his watch so he could leave a tip. Zinnia did the same. He followed her out of the bar and she seemed to have a destination in mind.

"Where to?" Paxton asked.

"I'm in the mood for some video games. You like video games?"

"Sure."

They made it to the top level and entered the arcade Paxton had visited with Dakota, where they shook down Warren. She made a beeline for the back and stopped in front of Pac-Man. She took the controls in her hands, but then let them go. "I'm sorry, this is one-player."

She clearly wanted to play. Next to Pac-Man was a deer-hunting game, with big plastic shotguns—one orange, one green. "It's okay. Go ahead." He picked up the green shotgun. "I'll take this one."

"You sure?" she asked, even though she had already started playing.

He swiped his watch across the sensor and cocked the gun. "Sure."

Zinnia jerked at the controls. Paxton turned to the video screen, which displayed a bucolic field. Forest in the distance, babbling brook. A deer bounded out; in real life maybe it would have been a few hundred yards away. He aimed and fired. Missed. The deer made it to the end of the screen untouched and disappeared.

"You like video games?" he asked.

"I like this one," she said. "I think I'm going to try and get the high score."

"And what's that?"

"The highest score ever is over three million," she said. "The high score on this one is a hundred and twenty thousand. It'll take some time but I can beat that. Not tonight. But I figure I may as well get some practice in."

Another deer. Another miss. "Something to do?"

"Something to do."

Paxton focused on the game. Watched another deer come into view. This one stopped at the stream to drink. Almost as if the game felt bad for him and was throwing him a freebie. He aimed, fired. The deer fell over, a small spray of pixelated crimson erupting into the air.

Good Work!, the game said.

Zinnia glanced over. "Nice."

She turned back to the screen, her jaw clamped, the tip of her tongue sticking a little out of the corner of her mouth. She played the game as if she were performing brain surgery.

There was movement in the corner of his eye. Someone moving toward the rear of the arcade. Paxton thought it looked like Warren. He holstered the gun in the machine, and before he even realized he'd committed to it, he told Zinnia, "I'm going to hit the restroom. Be back."

"Sure thing," she said, not looking away from the game.

Paxton did a quick map of the arcade in his head. Went past Zinnia and around a bank of game cabinets that would give him a view of Warren's corner, without making it too obvious that he was standing there.

He leaned around and saw Warren counting something in his

hands, looking up, but in the opposite direction. Paxton waited a little bit, long enough he got nervous Zinnia might think he was taking a shit, which was not an image he wanted to instill on a first date, but then another man appeared. Paxton stepped back to make himself less visible, though the space was dim and the distance was great, so geography was on his side.

It was a short man. Shaved head. Broad shoulders. Thick arms. Weight lifter, for sure. Brown polo. A tech worker. The two of them spoke. The man in brown tugged at the sleeve of the long-sleeved shirt under his polo, pulling it over his wrist. When the man in brown retreated, Paxton ducked behind a game cabinet before Warren could turn and see him.

He remembered what Dakota had said, about people fooling the tracking on the watches, so he moved to the far end of the arcade and tried to circle around to the front, so he could see the face of the man in brown, but he found himself in a dead-end alcove of video game cabinets. He moved back the other way and realized that he'd have to move past Zinnia on his way out the door and explain what he was doing, and even then, the guy would probably be long gone.

Well, at least he had something. A partial description was better than none.

Anyway, why run after him? He wasn't on shift. He had something slightly more important on his plate. Paxton made it to Zinnia as she took her hands off the controls, oblivious to the amount of time that had passed.

"I'm rusty," she said.

"That's okay," he said. "It'll come back to you."

"You hungry?"

"A little."

"How do you feel about ramen?"

"I've never had ramen." She laughed and Paxton fumbled for a save. "I mean, I've had those cheap little packages of ramen that taste like salt."

She put her hand on her hip a little. Cocked it out. More comfortable now. Wanting to take him to a third location. "They got a ramen place here. Want to check it out?"

"Sure," Paxton said.

They exited the arcade and walked toward the restaurant. Paxton glanced down at Zinnia's hand. The way it swung at her side. He thought of taking it. To feel the smoothness of her skin. But that would be presumptuous, and he decided against it, happy at least to spend a little more time with her this evening.

ZINNIA

He was sweet, and eager to please, like a puppy. Worse, he made her laugh. In that brief little burst, the airport thing, it had felt like he'd stolen something from her.

But she liked it a little bit, too.

Zinnia had meant to shut things down after the drink. But the more he talked, the more she felt she could tolerate him. The arcade and the follow-up meal didn't make her regret staying out. The company was better than the food, at least.

The ramen was okay. All the parts were there, but it lacked the alchemy of place. That special touch that came from someone who studied the dish like it was a passion, rather than the reality of it: a small white woman in a hairnet and a green polo scooping out a pre-measured portion into a bowl and sticking it into a microwave.

At the end of dinner Zinnia decided she could use some rest, but she let Paxton walk her to her dorm, and as they lingered in that end-of-date space she decided she wouldn't mind so much if he leaned in to kiss her.

He didn't lean in. He smiled that goofy, bashful smile, and he took her hand and he kissed that, which was just so fucking lame. She blushed, more out of embarrassment for him.

"I had a lovely time tonight," he said.

"Me too."

"Maybe we can do it again sometime?"

"Yeah, I think we should. At the very least, it'd be good to have a drinking buddy."

The word *buddy* made Paxton deflate. She'd chosen it specifically, so as not to let him get too familiar too quickly. This was a delicate balance. She could benefit from a relationship with him. He wasn't repulsive or obnoxious. He smelled nice. Hell, he seemed like the kind of guy who might actually care whether his partner got off.

She left him with a sly smile—the kind that suggested something else might be in the offing—knowing it would blur the lines, and it did, because he smiled back with a very clear sense of relief.

Zinnia made for her room, where she stripped down to her underwear and sprawled out on the bed—as much as she could sprawl on the narrow mattress—and stared at the ceiling, wondering about who exactly it was Paxton had been following in the arcade.

The way he excused himself, something was up. That was obvious from the jump. It wasn't hard to sneak behind him, even though she hated to leave a game half-played.

The arcade was a jumble of shadows and tight spaces. He was watching a handoff of some kind. Drugs, probably. Which meant he was the kind of person who liked to work off-hours.

She wasn't tired enough to sleep so she considered logging into the television, to apply for the Rainbow Coalition, which stood the chance of netting her a promotion at some point, increasing her level of access around the facility. But she had just enough booze in her system that she didn't want to look at words.

She sat up, rubbed her sore quad muscles, then her aching feet. Shower time. Not so much to clean up but to stand underneath the hot spray. She pulled on a clean pair of sweats and a T-shirt—something to change into after the shower—slid into flip-flops, and grabbed a towel. Made her way down the hall, where she found an out-of-order sign on the women's bathroom, so she swiped into the gender-neutral bathroom.

Two of the stalls and one of the urinals were marked off with yellow tape. She made her way to the rear, to a small locker room with a line of two dozen showers, each one with a curtain. All empty. Zinnia picked the last one in the row. She stripped down, folded the clothes and placed them on the bench closest to her, hung her towel from the wall. The cold air raised goose bumps on her skin.

She stepped into the shower and swiped her CloudBand across the sensor next to the faucet, starting the five-minute allotment of water.

An anemic spray erupted from the spout, frigid at first, snapping her muscles tight and snatching her breath, the lingering drunkenness from the night cracked in half like a stone.

It warmed up quick, and as the timer wound down she considered paying the extra few credits to extend the shower time but figured she'd save that luxury for another night.

Thank you for being green! was emblazoned above the sensor, which beeped to notify her she had thirty seconds left.

"Fuck you," Zinnia said.

When she was done she turned off the faucet, which rattled in the handle, and flung the curtain aside to find a man sitting on a bench.

She pulled the shower curtain back and reached for the towel, wrapping it around her torso. She was embarrassed, but that quickly made way for anger, because he was watching her stall. She stepped out. He was wearing a white polo shirt and jeans. Barefoot. His sneakers sitting next to him, socks balled up and placed inside. Pudgy, red face, dark hair. No towel. And still, staring at her. The band of his watch was stainless-steel mesh.

"Can I help you?" Zinnia asked.

"Just waiting for my turn."

She looked down the row of shower stalls, all still empty.

Zinnia's brain went into kill mode, breaking his body down into pressure points. All the locations she could hit to elicit a pain response. But that was a sure way to get herself turfed, so she took her clothes so she could dash for the privacy of her room.

As she picked up the items, he stood.

"You're a red, aren't you?" he asked. "New to the floor, right?"

"Excuse me . . . ," she said, taking the long way around the room, circling it, to keep benches between the two of them.

He figured out what she was going for, so he stepped over to the exit and blocked her path. Glanced out into the bathroom to make sure they were alone.

"I know being a red isn't the most fun job here," he said. "I mean, everyone wants to do it until they actually do it. There are shifts in there that are a bit easier, though."

"Excuse me," she said, trying to move past him.

He shifted to block her path, getting so close now she could smell him. Laundry detergent. Cigarettes? "I'm sorry. We got off to a bad start." He stuck out his hand. "I'm Rick."

She took a step back. "And I'm leaving."

"You can tell me your name," he said. "You're being pretty rude."

Zinnia took another step back and tightened her towel, drawing Rick's eye to the patch of skin below her clavicle, where the towel rested. A look on his face like he wanted to snatch it away and see what was underneath. Which made Zinnia want to snatch his face off to see what was underneath.

She had her watch on. That was what was keeping her from smashing her fist into the soft part of his throat, which would crush his trachea like a beer can, allowing her to sit quietly on a bench and watch as he struggled and failed to get air down his ruined throat into his lungs, until he grew more red and then blue and then dead.

"Look, you're new, so you don't really get the power structure around here," he said. "Managers can help you, or we can be a pain in the ass. For example, I can make it so you never see an overtime notification again, and it won't impact your ranking."

Zinnia didn't respond.

"Or, you know, there are a lot of things that can mess with rankings." He looked around again, dropped his voice. "Listen, I get it. It's a lot to take in." He stepped back, put up his hands. "I won't even touch you. How about you just dry off and get dressed and we'll leave it at that, huh? Call it a wash. You can have a little more time to get . . . acclimated."

Zinnia thought about it. Wanting even more to hurt him. Not just because of what he was doing. But because he had done this before. There was such an ease to his actions. As if he were ordering coffee.

But the long-term goal won out in the end. She took a few more steps back. More for his safety, in case he got handsy. Dropped the towel. Felt the air against her exposed skin. It touched every inch of her, sharing space with his gaze.

He smiled, sat slowly on the bench, near the door.

"Go ahead now," he said softly.

She picked up the towel again, ran it over her body. As she did it she tried to make eye contact with him. Every time his eyes met hers they would dart away. Fucking coward. She stared harder.

After she finished drying herself, she reached down for her under-wear, stepped into them, then her pants.

As she reached for her shirt he put his hand up.

"Just a second more," he said. "I want to remember this for later."

She breathed in hard and pulled the shirt over her head. When she was done she slipped her feet into her flip-flops and stood there and shrugged. Like, *What now, asshole?*

He paused. Like he was thinking. To push for more? Zinnia was afraid. Not of him. He was nothing. But of what this might turn into. He didn't realize how pegged down he had her, how compromised she was simply because she was on a job that depended on subterfuge.

Finally, he stood, said, "That wasn't so hard, was it?"

She didn't say anything.

"Tell me your name."

"Zinnia."

He smiled. "That's a lovely name. Zinnia. I'll remember that. You have a nice night, Zinnia. Welcome to Cloud, okay? I promise you, once you get used to how things are around here, it's pretty easy."

She didn't say anything to that either. He turned and left. As he reached the door he called over his shoulder, "See you around, Zinnia."

After he was gone she sat on a bench and stared at the wall.

She hated herself for not hurting him but she didn't know any other way to handle it. That didn't stop her from running each and every scenario through her brain: Elbow to the eye socket. Foot to the balls. Slam his face into the tiled wall until something broke, the face or the tile, whichever came first.

She sat there for long enough that she forgot where she was. When she worked up the energy to leave she stepped out and found the out-of-order sign was now on the gender-neutral bathroom. The women's room was free.

No wonder they'd had privacy for so long.

She made her way to her room, glancing over her shoulder along the way, and when she reached it she hung her wet towel from the hook on the wall and sat on the futon, her head filled with a chain-saw sound, so she turned on the television and navigated to the screen for the Rainbow Coalition, hoping to drown it out.

RAINBOW COALITION

Our mission at Cloud is to promote an enriching and supportive atmosphere that allows everyone to thrive and succeed. We provide a comprehensive approach to inclusivity, access, and equality, through collaborative, deliberate efforts within our community. The Rainbow Coalition empowers employees to take control of their own destinies.

Humanity is a rich tapestry, and here at Cloud, we know the importance of what each and every person brings to the workforce. In that regard, we've created the Rainbow Coalition to make sure opportunity is available and abundant for anyone who wants it.

According to the genetic record you provided during the interview process, you are eligible under the following tracks:

Female

Black or African-American

Hispanic or Latinx

During the rating process your ranking will be taken into account, as well as your previous work history, and we will reconsider your placement and find a position that is mutually beneficial to both our needs and yours. To start, you must schedule a meeting with a Rainbow Coalition representative in the Admin building.

The next available appointment is in: 102 days.

Do you wish to proceed?

PAXTON

"Are you kidding me with this?"

Dakota's face was twisted into something grotesque, brows heavy and mouth hanging open. She paused like that for a few moments, the coffee pod still in her hand. Paxton was suddenly thankful the break room was empty.

After a moment Dakota sighed, put the coffee pod into the machine, set her mug underneath. She put her hands over her face.

"So you had a lead, right there in front of you, and you just let it walk away?"

"Well, I was off shift, and—"

"Okay, let me stop you right there," she said, holding the flat of her hand up like a blade. "You're on the security team. You are never off shift."

Paxton's skin flushed. "I'm sorry, I didn't think—"

"You're damn right you didn't think." Dakota looked at the coffee machine, realized she hadn't actually started the brewing process, and slapped the top of the machine before she hit the On button. "Damn it. Now I really need this." She crossed her arms, leaned against the counter, looked back at Paxton. "You got me in a not-terrible mood today, so I'm not going to tell Dobbs. It's your first week so I'll give you a pass. But if you want to succeed here, you got to knuckle down, you understand me?"

"I'm sorry," Paxton said, though the apology tasted wrong in his mouth. What exactly was he sorry for? He hadn't wanted this job in the first place.

"You damn well better be," she said. "I'm real disappointed to hear this."

That stung. The kind of shot that made Paxton want to retreat into himself, or disappear into the floor, or float up through the ceiling—be anywhere but here. He turned to leave, figuring he would come back later for a cup of coffee when he could brew it in solitude. But he stopped himself. "Thank you."

Dakota nodded, her face softening. The coffee finished, she plucked the mug, held it under her nose, inhaled the steam. "Look," she said. "I get it. You'll get it, too. Just . . . c'mon. You have to stay on top of this shit."

"I wasn't thinking."

"You weren't."

"I'll do better."

"I know you will." And she curled the corner of her lip a little, threatening a grin, which managed to displace some of the shame pulsing in Paxton's gut. But then the smile disappeared. Her eyes focused on something behind him.

Paxton turned and the bottom fell out of his stomach, like the room had just suddenly dropped ten feet. Vikram was standing in the doorway. Just standing, like he wanted them to know, yeah, he'd heard everything they said. Rather than say anything, he whistled a tuneless tune, moseying over to the coffee machine, giving exaggerated nods to the both of them.

"Hey, Vicky," Dakota said, feeling out the words.

"Good morning, my dear. Just here for the coffee. Coffee is good here."

"The coffee here is shit. We drink it because it's free."

"One man's shit is another man's smorgasbord."

"That is not as clever as you think it is."

Vikram shrugged and smiled as he tossed Dakota's coffee pod in the trash and inserted his own. While it brewed he turned to Paxton and stared. It was an *I got you, motherfucker* stare.

"C'mon, Pax," Dakota said. "Let's go someplace with less dickheads."

"Right behind you," Paxton said, following her from the room. Once they were out of earshot he said, "That doesn't bode well."

"No, it does not," she said. "You might want to clench up, because I suspect your ass is about to get wrecked."

"Thanks."

"I tried."

They made their way down to the promenade. Every step Paxton took, every inch he put between him and Admin, felt like salvation. Maybe Vikram hadn't heard them. Maybe he was just being smug. After a little walking Paxton figured, Hey, I'm in the clear, and maybe this would be a good time to get a cup of coffee.

His CloudBand buzzed. He looked down and found a message that made his stomach twist.

Please report to Admin to see Sheriff Dobbs.

He had stopped walking and Dakota hadn't, so when he looked up, she was twenty steps ahead, looking back. First with confusion, then with realization. Finally, and worst of all, with a touch of pity. She nodded at him. "Good luck."

Ten minutes later Paxton was standing in front of Dobbs's office door wondering why he was even doing this to himself. Why not just turn around and walk away, like Zinnia said? Did he really need this job?

Which, yes, he did. He'd walked into Cloud with the change in his pocket. Roughly enough to set up shop on a street corner somewhere with an empty hat on the ground.

He held his breath, knocked. Dobbs responded with a terse "Come in."

Paxton entered to find Dobbs sitting behind his desk, leaned back, with his hands folded over his stomach. He didn't say anything, so Paxton sat in the chair across from him, folded his hands between his knees, and waited. It didn't even look like Dobbs was breathing and his stare had claws.

The second hand on the clock made nearly a full revolution before Dobbs pointed his chin over Paxton's shoulder and said, "Close the door."

Paxton got up, pushed it closed. He didn't like the way the room felt, like it was filling up with water.

"You mean to tell me you saw a handoff and you didn't pursue, you didn't even try to get a good look at the guy's face?" Dobbs asked. "Is that what you're telling me?"

The way he asked it wasn't sarcastic. It wasn't angry. It was concerned, and sad. Like he thought Paxton might be broken.

"I just figured, I mean . . . I was on a date." He cringed as he said it.

Dobbs smirked. "On a date. Well there's that. Listen, I cannot stress this enough. You work for me, you are always on the clock. I'm not saying you can't live your life. But if you see illegal activity and you're the only one around to stop it, then you have to step up and stop it."

"I know, I just . . ."

Dobbs put his hands behind his head. "Musta been wrong about you. Too bad. Starting tomorrow you'll report to the warehouse for scanner duty. That might be a better fit."

"Sir, I—"

"Thank you, Paxton. That'll be all."

Dobbs spun his chair and squared up to his computer, pecked at the keyboard with two fingers. After a moment, and without looking up, he said again, "That'll be all."

Paxton stood, face hot, shame digging a finger into his ribs.

"I'm sorry, sir," he said. "I'm going to make this right."

More typing. No response.

Paxton wanted to grab him by the shoulders. Shake the old man. Show how sincere he was. But there was only one thing to do: make it right. He left the office, found Dakota leaning against the wall.

"Scanner duty?" she asked.

"Yeah."

"Good luck with that."

"You ran Warren's watch? Tried to find out who was with him last night?"

"Nobody in or out. You and some picker. But no man in brown."

"The watches," he said. "How do they work, exactly? With the tracking?"

Instead of answering Dakota stared at his third eye, boring a hole into his forehead.

"I get it," he said. "I fucked up. I want to fix it. Just give me a chance."

She kept staring.

"I'll do it with or without you," he said.

She rolled her eyes a little. Turned and nodded for him to follow. Brought him to a conference room, where she shut the door and picked up a wireless keyboard. Tapped the keys and one entire wall flickered on, a giant screen filling the dim room with artificial light. Paxton tried to make sense of what he was looking at. Wireframe schematics, and on them, countless tiny dots moving like ants.

"Press a dot," Dakota said.

Paxton picked one at random, pressed the tip of his finger to it. A small box popped up on the screen, with a long mix of letters and numbers.

"Okay, now press and hold," she said.

He did. The box grew, showing a headshot, name, and housing assignment for a middle-aged black woman with a shaved head.

"Watches track you, everywhere you go," she said. "That much is obvious. But we don't have someone sitting in a room, keeping an eye on everything. It's passive monitoring. We can go back and review if we need to. So we reviewed the data from last night. . . ."

Paxton watched a wireframe of the arcade. Two dots entered. Him and Zinnia. They stopped at Pac-Man. Another dot entered. Warren. Paxton broke off to go look at Warren.

Zinnia followed.

Behind him, out of sight.

After a little bit, the Zinnia dot made a quick leap back to Pac-Man. Then he rejoined Zinnia and they left.

No other dots. No man-in-brown dot.

"So he wasn't wearing his watch," Paxton said.

"You can't even leave your room unless you're wearing the watch."

"Then he took it off and left it somewhere."

"We get an alert if a watch is off and not in a charger for more than a few minutes."

Paxton stood and watched the dots floating back and forth. Merging, breaking apart, forming random shapes. Like clouds. It was both oddly satisfying to watch and infuriating, because there was something there, on the screen. Something obvious . . .

"Well, you're on patrol for the rest of the day, so . . . ," Dakota said.

"What does that mean?"

Dakota lifted her watch, tapped the face of it a couple of times. "It means you walk back and forth on the promenade. Transfer to scanner duty will be tomorrow. So head out."

"All right. Well. Sorry, I guess."

"Yup." Dakota spun on her heel and walked away.

Paxton stood there for a minute, watching her leave. Annoyed at himself for being upset. He didn't know why he felt so invested in this, but it felt like a mess he had to fix. Though, as he left Admin and climbed on the tram, rode it around to the promenade, he wondered what exactly he meant by *mess*. How was this a mess? Because he hadn't worked extra, unpaid hours? Hadn't put himself possibly in harm's way?

But the more he walked the less he could think about that, and the more the issue of the Zinnia dot invaded his head. The way she'd followed him, the way she'd jumped back when he turned around.

She had been watching him while he was watching Warren.

CUT DAY ^{4}

GIBSON

Been a while since we talked, huh?

I'm doing my best with this, but it ain't easy. Every day, I can feel it. Takes a little more effort to climb out of bed. Got this throb in my midsection now. I'm drinking coffee like a maniac just to keep myself vertical during the day.

You know what I keep thinking about?

Lasts.

See, the other day, we were rolling through New Jersey, and we're going south on the Garden State, and I tell Jerry, my driver, to pull off for this sandwich shop. Bud's Subs. I swear to you, there is no better sandwich on this green earth. And whenever I'm within thirty miles of that place, I have to stop by. So Jerry pulls off, and the poor guy had to wait on line for an hour and a half just to get inside. That's how popular they are.

So he appears with the Bud Sub Special. Now, this thing is a beast. Two feet long, with salami, provolone, ham, capicola, sweet peppers. Used to be I would get two. One to eat on the spot, one to save for later. But this time I only asked for one, on account of my appetite not being great. Figured I would eat just half. Save the other half for the next day. And I'm about halfway through this thing, about as happy as I can be, when I realize this is the last time I'm probably going to eat this sandwich.

I put it down and got a little emotional. What else had I done for the last time? I'm probably not going to find any time to go hunting or fishing again, which are the only times I ever unplug and refuse to answer my cell phone. Never going to have another Christmas morning with my wife and daughter. That weighed on me pretty hard, so I wasn't really in the mood to write anything for a bit.

But the more I thought about it the more I accepted it. Just like everything else, this is the hand I've been dealt, and I don't like it, but it's my hand to play. I figured this was a good day to pop back on and talk a little bit about today. It's Cut Day at Cloud. We only do this four times a year and yet people get so worked up every time. People call it barbaric. I don't believe it to be. I talked about this a bit earlier: it doesn't do anyone good for you to do a job that's not a good fit, for you or your employer.

Not that I'm happy about it. I don't want to let anyone go. But it's better for them and it's better for me, and it drives me nuts, the way people talk about it, telling all these stories that are untrue, of people getting thrown out on their asses or running in front of trains or something. Simply doesn't happen, and if it does happen, it's pretty rare, and anyway, probably a sign of some underlying issue. It's a rotten thing to make us responsible for people like that, for the way people are on the inside, but it's just another way to advance the narrative of Cloud as some kind of evil empire. I've got a pretty good sense of who does that—those same geniuses who were responsible for the Black Friday Massacres—but I won't get any more specific than that, because I can already hear my lawyers having a collective aneurysm.

Point is, a job has to be something you earn. It's not something that's just going to get handed to you. That's the American imperative: strive for greatness. Not: cry about something that someone else has.

Anyway, sorry. Like I said, lots on my mind lately. I'm trying to stay positive. I'll do a better job of being positive here, because there's no sense in burdening you with that. That's for me to carry.

Important thing, though, is I'm doing pretty well on my trip around the country. After New Jersey we made it over to Pennsylvania, to one of the first MotherClouds I built, and I hadn't been there in years, and it was a hell of a sight to see. Back then, there were two dorms and they were six stories high. Now there are four dorms, and they're all twenty stories, and they're still growing. In fact, the entire thing looks like one giant construction site. I love construction vehicles. The sound of a backhoe is the sound of progress. It was even nicer to see in Pennsylvania. One of their biggest industries, historically, was heavy machinery and construction equipment. I should know. I took over the trade there something like twelve years ago!

I got to walk the floor a bit and meet some real nice people, and it was a good reminder of why I was spending my final few months on the road, rather than sitting in my house, moping the days away. Because of people like Tom Dooley, one of the senior pickers.

The two of us got to talking, and we're both old-timers, so we had a lot in common, and he told me about how he lost his home during the last housing crisis, and he and his wife ended up buying this clunker of an old RV to live in. And how they got to driving around the country, doing odd jobs, until one day they stopped at a gas station to fill up, but they had lost track of their finances—Tom's wife wrote a check for something she forgot to tell Tom about—and their account drew empty. So here they were, stuck in the middle of Pennsylvania, no money, nowhere to go, barely enough food to make it through the week.

That was the same week the Pennsylvania MotherCloud opened. Talk about providence. He and his wife got themselves good-paying jobs and a place to live and they were so grateful, and I felt pretty good about that. He said it was thanks to me, but I told him, no, Tom, that's not true. I told him he and his wife did it because they worked hard and didn't give up. They were survivors.

Me and Tom got to talking for so long, we ended up grabbing a bite to eat in the cafeteria. I talked to a manager and got his wife, Margaret, off her shift in the tech support center and we brought her down and we had a grand old time. I bet they're going to be pretty popular for the next few weeks. You should have seen all the people who wanted to talk to them after we finished up.

Tom and Margaret, thanks for your kindness, and listening to an old man jaw a bit. I'm happy to see you both doing so well, and I wish you happiness for many years to come.

Seeing them truly lifted my spirits.

Something else I wanted to report, too: I'm ready to name my successor.

And it's . . .

. . . going to be announced in my next post!

Sorry, didn't mean to tease you there. But it's out of respect for the fact that this is Cut Day; there's a lot going on and I don't want to distract from what is generally a bit of a hectic day at our Cloud facilities. Point is, the decision has been made. Don't expect any leaks though. I told one person: my wife, Molly. And I'm more likely to spill it before she would ever let anything go. So the secret is safe. You can expect to hear more soon. I think everyone is going to be pleased. It's the most logical choice to my mind.

Anyway, that's all I got for now. Onward, westward, for some more last experiences. I've found it's important for me to think of it like that, because it taught me a real important lesson. To slow down and savor things, because you never know when they'll be gone. Swear to truth, after I collected myself, that Bud Sub Special never tasted better.

I'm going to miss it, but I'm glad I had it.

ZINNIA

The girl fell to her knees and screamed.

Zinnia had been trying to get the yellow bar to turn green when it happened. She was engrossed, actively ignoring a twinge in her knee, but still she stopped to look. So did a dozen other folks in red.

The girl was in her midthirties. Dyed pink hair, her face an explosion of freckles. She was very pretty. Also now very sad. She looked down at her watch and sobbed, staring at it like whatever she was looking at might change if she looked hard enough.

Next to Zinnia was an older woman with silver hair curled into ringlets. She shook her head and tsked. "Poor girl."

"What happened?" Zinnia asked.

The old woman looked at her like *How could you not know?* "Cut Day," she said. Then she glanced down at the package she was carrying—a keyboard case for a tablet computer—and took off at a brisk pace to find the correct conveyor belt. Zinnia watched the girl for a few seconds more, until another woman who seemed to know her came over to console her, and Zinnia turned back to her task of finding a pink tool kit.

Even with the distance between them Zinnia felt the girl's cry deep in her chest. It was primal. The kind of grief that usually didn't surface outside a funeral or physical torture. Zinnia's brain said, *Stop being a baby and buck up,* but she couldn't deny, too, the feeling of a cold little finger poking her in the heart.

As Zinnia moved through the warehouse, she came across more people on their knees, or standing still, staring off at the newfound wreckage of their lives.

As she dropped a tablet computer onto a conveyor belt, she saw a man in red arguing with a man in white. Something about a foot injury slowing him down. The man in white was unmoved and the man in red clenched his fists, holding himself back, and Zinnia could smell the potential for violence in the air. It smelled like blood. Liquid copper. She wanted to stay, just to see what would happen, but glanced at her watch and found the yellow bar creeping down.

Wireless earbuds. Fitness tracker. Book. Sneakers. Shawl. Building blocks. RFID-blocking wallet . . .

As she carried the wallet to the conveyor belt, the plastic clamshell case shifted in her grip. She held it up, found there was a slit in the side. The wallet looked okay, but she wasn't sure what to do with damaged merchandise. She briefly considered going back to get another but the shelves had already repositioned themselves, and she'd forgotten the bin number. She raised the watch and said, "Miguel Velandres."

Miguel Velandres is not currently on shift.

"Manager."

The gentle buzz guided her through the warehouse floor and she walked for nearly a half hour. The bar paused, mercifully. She passed six people in white shirts, but still the watch prompted her onward. Which seemed wasteful, or maybe she was on her way to see a specialist.

She reached a long aisle of housewares and bathroom goods. Mats, shower caddies, curtains, toilet seat covers. The watch buzzed and kept buzzing.

"There you are."

She turned to find Rick.

"Are you fucking kidding me?" she asked.

He smiled, showing off yellow-tinged teeth. "Well, you were just so pretty and nice I added you to my roster. That way I can be your point manager in case you need anything. See, Zinnia, you get treated better around here when you have a relationship like that."

She wanted to punch him. She wanted to vomit on his face. She wanted to run away. She wanted to do anything other than what she did, which was hand him the package. "It's open. I don't know what to do with an open package."

He took it, reaching farther than he needed to so that his hand would touch hers during the exchange. His skin was cold. Reptilian. Or maybe that was Zinnia's imagination manifesting her distaste. She pushed back against the shudder in her shoulders.

"Let's see here," he said, turning it over in his hand. He found the cut in the package. "Might have gotten damaged coming in. But you were right to bring it here. We don't want damaged items going out to customers."

He took a step closer to Zinnia, held up his watch.

"What we do, sweetheart," he said, slowing down, as if he were about to explain something to a child, "is we hold up our watch like so, and we say, 'Damaged goods.' And that'll give you a conveyor belt, just like anything else."

He smiled at her like he'd just shared the secret to eternal life. Zinnia could smell his breath. Tuna fish. She choked on her gag reflex.

"You really should have been told this by your trainer," he said, raising his eyebrow, suddenly upset. "Can you give me his or her name?"

Zinnia thought about it for a moment. Miguel had probably forgotten. She didn't want to get him in trouble so she said, "John something."

Rick scrunched his face and shook his head. "You really need to remember things like that, Zinnia."

"Oops."

"Don't worry, I'm sure you'll make it up." He raised his watch, tapped at the face of it. Her watch buzzed. She glanced down and saw it directing her to get a package of guitar picks.

"Now, you go on," Rick said. "I'll see you around. Off at six?"

Zinnia didn't respond. Just turned and walked off.

She made it through the rest of her shift by focusing hard on the yellow-bar game. She had lost some time watching the people crying their way through the cut notification. No matter how hard she hoofed it, she couldn't get it to green.

Through security and on the way to her dorm, she thought she should at least check into the lobby hallway, see if the coast was clear, if she could plant the gopher. But she knew the thing driving her at that moment was disgust, anger. Not the kind of emotions that should play into decision-making.

She made her way to her floor, which was busier than normal. She was used to seeing one or two people out, headed to the bathrooms, or out to shift, but there were a half dozen people crowded around a tall, elderly man with a buzzed haircut and sagging skin. He was holding a duffel bag over his shoulder and looking down at the floor while people consoled him, Cynthia included. Two security officers—a black man and an Indian woman—stood nearby, watching. The girl with the cartoon eyes was there, too. Harriet? Hadley.

Hadley the nice girl.

Zinnia watched the scene, which was taking place about a dozen doors down. It was a good-bye ceremony. Hugs and cheek kisses and back slaps. Clearly the man had been around for a while. There was a warmth to the interaction that made Zinnia feel that cold finger in the heart again.

The crowd lingered, as if they didn't want to move on to the next thing, like maybe they could get stuck in that moment, until Cynthia clapped her hands, bringing everyone to attention. It was time to go. The good-byes said, the man left, the security officers trailing behind. Not close enough to be escorting him, just close enough to watch. As the man crossed her path, Zinnia saw his CloudBand was decorated with glittery dice. The crowd made for their rooms. Cynthia lingered, caught Zinnia's eye, shook her head, like, *Can you believe this?* She turned her chair toward her room.

Zinnia stood with her hand on her knob. But instead of going in she made for Cynthia's room.

At the door, Zinnia knocked. A few moments later the door swung inward. Cynthia smiled. "What can I do for you, dear?"

"I was hoping I could talk to you about something," she said. "Confidentially."

Cynthia nodded. Zinnia took the door and allowed her to roll backward into the apartment. She stepped inside and shut it. Cynthia rolled all the way to the back, against the wall, giving Zinnia some space to sit on the futon.

"Quite a thing, isn't it?" Cynthia asked. "The cut."

"Who was that?"

"Bill," she said. "But everyone called him Dollar Bill, on account of he liked to spend all his time in the casino. Been here eight years."

"What happened that he got cut?"

"He made it to the pension, to the adjusted work assignment," she said. "Bill was still pretty spry and he liked to walk, so he elected to stay as a picker, and he got put on the senior pick rate." She sighed, stared off, like she was looking after him, still trudging down the hallway. "But he was getting on in years, and he couldn't even keep up with that, but he thought he could, and well . . . here we are." Cynthia looked back at Zinnia. "Damn shame. He should have just taken reassignment."

"How do you get reassignment?"

"If you get injured or can't handle something anymore, you get moved into something else," she said. "I used to be a picker, but I fell off one of the spinners. Paralyzed below the waist."

"Jesus," Zinnia said, cringing.

Cynthia shrugged. "I didn't hook myself in, so it was my fault. I was lucky, though. Cloud kept me on and moved me down to customer support. I can still talk on the phone and use a computer. Anyway, point is, Bill should have accepted reassignment to someplace more his speed, and he wouldn't."

Zinnia sat back on the futon, the cold finger really digging in now. "I'm sorry to hear that."

Cynthia shrugged again, gave a painful little smile. "At least I have a job, you know?" She leaned forward and patted Zinnia's knee. "I'm sorry, dear, you said you had something to ask me and I made it all about me. Now, what's up?"

"Well, I . . ."

"Oh god." Cynthia put her hand to her mouth. "I am so rude.

Would you like something to drink? I'm afraid you'll have to help yourself, but still, I should have offered."

Zinnia shook her head. "No, I'm good, thank you. I just . . . this will stay between us, right? I just wanted to take a temperature on something."

Cynthia nodded gravely, like they were about to be bound by a blood oath.

"I came across this guy," she said. "A manager. Rick . . ."

Cynthia huffed. Rolled her eyes. "Rick."

"So it's like that?"

"It's like that," she said. "He lives down on the other end. Let me guess. He played the bathroom switcheroo on you when you went to take a shower?"

"How is he still working here?"

Cynthia's chin dropped to her chest. "I have no idea. I figure he's related to someone important. Or else upper management just doesn't want to deal. All I know is a woman complained about him to HR— real sweet girl, Constance—and next Cut Day she was gone. Constance was in support, with me, and she was real smart." Cynthia sighed. "I know this isn't the most pleasant thing. I know it's not the answer you were looking for. Just . . . you see him, walk the other way. Only use the ladies'. With any luck he'll focus on someone else."

The sympathy Zinnia had felt evaporated.

Luck. The word sounded malformed, the way she said it.

"I asked for a manager today for something and got brought right to him," Zinnia said.

"He's really taken an interest in you," she said. "That's not good."

"How far is this going to go?"

"He's not stupid," Cynthia said. "He's not going to force you into bed or anything. He's just a creep. He likes to watch. My advice? Just . . ." She sighed again. "Deal with it."

For a moment, Zinnia couldn't decide who she was angrier with, Cynthia or Rick. But her anger was bigger than that. It was like a person, standing beside her, prodding her to do something.

She thanked Cynthia for her time, got out of the apartment before she could say anything she might regret. Stalked down the hall, swiped into her room, and plopped onto the futon, turning on the television, hoping the sound of it would drown out the noise in her head.

Struck by an idle thought, she raised the CloudBand and asked, "What's my rating?" Wondering if that was even a legitimate command.

The CloudBand flashed four stars.

"Fuck you," she said.

She pulled the multi-tool out of the back of the kitchen drawer, climbed on the bed, undid the tapestry, and got to work. Only a couple of inches left to go, and this time she didn't stop until she was done, jamming the blade into the ceiling the way she wished she could jam it into Rick's throat, the square of drywall coming free in a final hiccup of dust, opening into darkness.

She dropped it to the bed and ran her hands around the opening, looking for the strongest place of purchase, and pulled herself into the ceiling. She used the flashlight on her phone to illuminate the space. It was a mess—wiring and ducts everywhere, and a smell, like something was rotting. But there were a couple of feet of clearance, so it would be easy enough to move, and she could make out the placement of the support walls, so she wouldn't crash into someone's room.

From here it was approximately 122 feet to the women's bathroom. She'd been counting.

PAXTON

The man with the unibrow threw a hard shoulder into Paxton, nearly taking him off his feet. He caught himself from falling and looked at the man, expecting some kind of apology, but the man just grumbled.

"Fucking bullshit," he said. "Been on line for an hour."

The man stood in the millimeter-wave scanner and raised his arms, let the metal blades spin around him. Paxton glanced over to Robinson, the woman on the screen, who gave a slight nod—no contraband.

No one had any contraband. No one was stupid enough to steal from this place. They knew what it meant. Immediate termination. Not even the opportunity to collect their belongings; they'd be led outside and left there.

Three days now he'd been doing this dance, and Paxton counted unibrow's shoulder among the pleasant interactions. No one was happy about queuing up to stand on line after a long day on their feet. So Paxton did what he did best: smiled and pretended like everything was okay and hoped he might see Zinnia, but of the thousands of people who had passed him in the last three days, he hadn't. This might not even be her section of the warehouse.

To pass the time between the whirring blades and the slight dips of Robinson's chin, he chewed on the three-star rating he'd discovered on his CloudBand after he left Dobbs's office.

That, and the dots.

It was probably nothing. Maybe Zinnia had been looking for him. It could have been any of the other million possible explanations, rather than that she was following him.

Thinking about stars and dots was a distraction from the screens surrounding them that played Cloud videos on a loop. At the end of his first day, he'd had the scripts memorized. By the second day, they'd bored into his head like a drill. By the third day, they'd become the soundscape to his own personal hell.

> Cloud is the solution to every need.
> I work for you.
> Thank you, Cloud.

At the end of his shift he wandered slowly to Live-Play, where he found Dakota jogging toward him from the direction of an elevator bank.

"What's the story, kiddo?" Paxton asked.

"Don't call me kiddo. I think I'm older than you. You and me are on patrol."

"I just finished my shift," he said.

"And today is Cut Day. That means every hand on deck. If you don't want to get back into anyone's good graces, by all means, say no."

Paxton shrugged, fell in line with Dakota. "Where to, boss?"

"That's better. Promenade. We do a circuit. Mostly keeping an eye on the trams."

"Why the trams?" Paxton asked.

"Lots of people in and out today," she said. "Stop asking so many questions and move your ass."

"Fine, fine, fine," Paxton said under his breath. He tried to out-pace his annoyance but found he couldn't, so he asked, "If Dobbs is done with me, why aren't you?"

Dakota threw him a sideways glance. "Because you have half a brain in your head, which is three-quarters more than most of the mooks who come through here. You fucked up but I think he was too hard on you. I tried to get you back on the task force but he wouldn't budge."

"You mean the task force that isn't a task force."

"That's the one."

"Well, thanks for trying."

Dakota shrugged. "At least I got you for the day."

They reached the promenade, where people passed in tears, carrying duffel bags or roller suitcases, headed for the tram, for Incoming, which, for them, would now be Outgoing.

Dakota's watch gave a chime. She brought it up.

"Got a code J in engineering," a voice said.

She pressed the crown to respond. "Copy that."

"Code J?" Paxton asked.

Dakota offered a stone grin. "You'll find out soon enough."

They walked some more. In the space of two hours they didn't see much. More sad people shuffling away. They took a break to get lunch. Paxton suggested CloudBurger but Dakota wrinkled her nose, insisted on tacos. Not the worst trade-off. They ate in silence, watching the crowds. Two more code J's came in. Dakota didn't seem to be logging them or very interested. She just responded in the affirmative and carried on.

After a long stretch of silence, Paxton voiced a stray thought that had been rattling around his head, in the interest of promoting some conversation. "What if it's like a Faraday cage?"

"What's that?"

"It's an enclosure used to block electromagnetic fields. It's named after the scientist who invented it, back in the 1800s. It's why your phone doesn't work so well in an elevator. Metal enclosure."

Dakota nodded. "Signal blocking."

"We had this thing in the prison. You're not supposed to have cell phones, right? Big-time contraband. We had these sensors that could detect cell phone signals. So a couple of the skells, they figured out to carry their phones in baggies lined with aluminum foil."

"Did that work?"

Paxton shrugged. "Depended on the carrier, how well they lined the bag. Apparently they got the idea from booster bags, which is a shoplifting thing. Take a bag lined with foil, go into a store, put stuff in the bag; it blocks the sensors that would go off if you tried to leave without paying. Anyway, a new cell phone tower went up right next to the prison, and it stopped working. Signal was too strong."

Dakota finished the final bite of her last taco, wiped her mouth with a napkin, and dropped it on a tray. They got up and dumped the empty wrappers and napkins into the trash, made their way into the hallway. Dakota was nodding her head like she was listening to music.

"So you think these geniuses are wrapping their arms in foil?" she asked.

"I doubt it," he said. "It worked okay. It wasn't foolproof. But maybe it's something like that."

Paxton's and Dakota's watches crackled to life. "Code S, code S, Maple lobby."

"Party time," Dakota said.

"What's a code S?"

"Squatter. Someone who won't accept a cut."

"What do we do?"

"Figure it out."

They took off at a half jog. As they approached the Maple lobby, the crowds grew thick with people stopping to watch the commotion. It didn't take long for them to find it: a group of six people—two reds, two greens, a brown, and a blue—lying on the ground, playing dead, letting their bodies go limp as a brigade of blues tried to drag them toward the tram. The area was strewn with bags, some of them torn open, clothes and personal items flung about. Paxton kicked a pink tube of deodorant out of his path. From the scrum, he could hear the people on the floor yelling.

"Please!"

"No!"

"Just give us another chance!"

"Christ," Dakota said. She dashed toward the fray as Paxton caught sight of Zinnia making her way to a hallway leading to a set of bathrooms. The sight of her made his brain short-circuit a minute, until Dakota yelled at him, "C'mon!"

He snapped out of it, ran over, found Dakota taking the arm of a middle-aged woman, dragging her toward the tram.

"What exactly are we doing here?" Paxton asked.

"Get them on the damn tram car and let the team at Incoming sort them out," she said.

"Is that really the best use of our time?" He dropped to a knee next to a middle-aged blond woman and said, "Miss, I'm Paxton. Can you tell me your name?"

She looked at him, her eyes welling with tears. She began to work her mouth, like she was going to speak, but instead spit a wad of saliva onto his face. Paxton closed his eyes as the warm spray splattered his cheek.

"Fuck you, pig," she said.

They were surrounded by security officers now, a wall of blue that kept anyone on the outskirts from seeing what was happening on the floor. Dakota looked around to verify this, then pressed her thumb into the woman's neck, just above the clavicle, and pressed hard. The woman screeched and tried to jerk away, but Dakota had a good grip.

"Get the hell up," she said. "Game's over."

"Please stop . . . ," the woman said.

"Dakota," Paxton said.

"What?" she asked, looking up at Paxton, increasing the pressure. "They don't work here anymore. Doesn't matter what we do to them. And the sooner we get this done, the better, because—"

From behind them, there was a scream.

Paxton leapt to his feet and sprinted in the direction of the sound. It had come from the tram tracks. There was a bigger crowd now, standing around the steps leading to the platform, a tram pulled halfway into the station. Paxton pushed his way through until he made it to the edge.

The tram conductor, an older man with a bald head, was leaning out and looking at the space of track in front of him, his face slack. About fifty feet down was a jumble of something that, as Paxton drew closer, he realized had been a man.

Paxton hopped onto the track and made his way in the man's direction. He didn't have to get close to know he was dead. Too much blood. He was completely still, one leg bent at an inhuman angle, like the knee had pivoted completely the other way. Something at his wrist caught the light. His CloudBand was decorated with glittery dice.

Paxton stood over him, his head giving a little spin. There was a scratch and shuffle next to him. He turned to find Dakota, staring down at the body.

"That's a code J," she said.

"J is for 'jumper,'" Paxton said.

Dakota nodded. "Was hoping you'd make it through your first cut without having to deal with one. But I guess that was wishful thinking." She raised her watch. "We got a code J, Maple track. DOA."

Paxton dropped into a crouch, put his hand to his mouth. It was not the first dead body he'd seen—the prison hadn't been a nightmare, but there had still been a few ODs and assaults that went too far. And just because he'd seen some didn't mean he wanted to see any more.

"C'mon," Dakota said. "We got to clear the area." She paused. "Better him than us, right?"

Paxton tried to speak, but found all he could muster was a single word, and even that got caught in his throat.

No.

ZINNIA

Zinnia spent fifteen minutes waiting in the ceiling, peering through a crack between the tiles, waiting for the bathroom to be empty. This, after two jolts from loose wiring and a nice scratch on her knee from some shoddy masonry.

The air had settled, but Zinnia's lungs still felt heavy with the debris she'd kicked up dragging herself through the narrow space. She'd watched people come in to shower or use the toilets in waves, but finally, there was one woman left. She washed her hands and then made her way out the door.

Zinnia moved the ceiling tile aside and dropped to the floor. Climbed on a bench and replaced it. The ceiling was low enough she should be able to get back up. It wasn't fun, but it worked, because when she stepped into the hallway, there was not a team of blue shirts standing outside the door, which was what she half-expected to find.

She checked her pocket for the eyeglass case and pulled down the sleeve of her sweater, so that it wasn't obvious she wasn't wearing the watch.

People were distracted by Cut Day. If there was a time to do something, it was now. It wasn't just that she wanted to get the fuck out of there. Though, after finishing her assignment, she might come back to beat the shit out of Rick. Just for fun.

A few people were heading toward the elevator bank. She followed. When they got onto the elevator, there was a jumble as everyone reached forward to swipe their wrists past the sensors. Plenty of cover. Zinnia pushed toward the back, held her arms behind her.

The elevator made a stop on the next floor—two more people got on—then on the next. Zinnia rolled her eyes, stopped herself from audibly sighing. Of course. Now's the time for a parade.

As the doors opened on the lobby, she briefly considered finding a lighter and setting something, somewhere, on fire. That was always a tried-and-true way to create cover. Her mind always went to fire, ever since that little blaze in a police station trash bin saved her from the death penalty in Singapore. But as soon as she stepped onto the shiny floor of the lobby she realized she didn't have to worry. A group of people were mounting some kind of protest, lying on the ground, refusing to be moved, as security officers tried to pull them to their feet.

Perfect. Zinnia made for the hallway. Everyone was watching the altercation.

She glanced behind her to make sure the coast was clear, and as she reached the CloudPoint she dropped into a duckwalk, which would take her under the eye of the camera. When she was clear, she went to the bathrooms. Neither of them had doors, just an entrance with a tight turn, so that if you leaned forward, you could see inside. She peeked into the men's room, which appeared empty, then went into the women's bathroom. A pair of wedge sandals was visible under one of the stalls. Great. She picked a stall and sat on a toilet, counting her breaths while she waited for the other woman to finish, flush, wash her hands, leave. It took longer than she would have liked, but at least no one else came in.

On the way out she gave another glance into the men's room. Still empty. She made her way down the hallway, walking quickly, watching for movement, eyes on the end of the corridor in case someone popped up. A few people flashed past, but they were all on their way to watch the scene by the tram.

She stuck close to the wall and dropped into a crouch, then fell to her knee at the base of the CloudPoint and stuck out her foot. She undid her shoe with one hand, letting the laces flop onto the floor, as she reached for the eyeglasses case with the other. She thumbed it open and took out the pen, jammed it into the lock cylinder. Gave it a hard twist. The thin metal panel popped open.

Inside was a tangle of wires and computer chips. She rooted around, looking for a free slot, running her fingers along the surfaces she couldn't see, her heart picking up pace now, wondering what she would do if there wasn't one.

More people walked by the doorway. No one turned in.

But eventually someone would.

She felt a recess. Empty space under her finger. Risked a glance down.

No, not right.

Kept searching.

She was about to give up when she felt it, a small rectangular gap, and she slid the gopher in, counting to ten in her head, then went to eleven, just to be safe, and pulled it back out.

Step one.

She tied her shoes and shoved the panel closed, as her heart went full jitterbug. She walked a few feet forward on her hands and knees, then stood up to full height and hustled out of the hallway, back into the lobby. She moved over to the elevators and was shifting from one foot to the next, waiting for the crowds to disperse, for a large group of people to get on, which would increase the likelihood of someone going to her floor, when Paxton came walking from the tram, headed to the hallway.

It was actually less a walk and more a shuffle. His hands hung down limp at his sides. Twice he stopped and looked at them, but from this distance Zinnia couldn't tell why. She moved behind a map kiosk, so he wouldn't turn around and see her standing there.

PAXTON

Paxton waved his hands under the sensor for the sink, wanting more than anything to get the sticky, drying blood off his skin.

Nothing happened. He cupped his hands and moved them up and down, then in a circle. Still nothing. He waved. Saw his face reflected in the flat silver fixture.

He balled up his fist and hit it. Once, twice. Leaving smudges of blood on it, so he couldn't see himself anymore.

He had checked the man's pulse even though he knew he was dead, even though there was so much blood. One of the paramedics who showed up vomited at the sight of the crumpled body and ran off, so Paxton helped the other paramedic load the jumper's body into a bag. It was like handling a sack of loose change.

He closed his eyes. Breathed in through his nose. Stuck his hands repeatedly under the faucet. Finally, a weak stream of water dribbled out. He wet his hands, covered them with soap from the dispenser, and scrubbed. The water was lukewarm and he wanted it to be scalding. He wanted to take off the top layer of skin. Even when his hands were pink and clean, they didn't feel that way.

He left the bathroom and passed the CloudPoint, the bottom panel of which was swung out. He leaned down and closed it, but the door wouldn't close all the way because the lock wouldn't engage. He ran his finger along the lock, found a small piece of white plastic wedged inside.

He'd seen Zinnia come into the hallway. She must have been coming in to use the bathroom. Paxton wondered if she'd noticed the door open. If someone could trip on it. He walked back to the lobby and waved over Dakota, who was talking to another blue.

She jogged over. "What?"

Paxton led her to the door. Gave it a little kick. She dropped into a crouch and looked at the lock. "Piece of plastic in here."

"What do you think?"

Dakota stood. Put her hands on her hips. Looked down the hallway, then at the CloudPoint. "Could be vermin. I'll run the watch data."

"Vermin did that?"

"Special kind of vermin we get. Good catch."

"Didn't take a whole lot of skill to spot that," he said.

"Don't shit on a compliment, bro."

"Fair enough."

Dakota pressed the crown of her CloudBand. "Can I get a tech team down to the bathroom hallway in the lobby of Maple? Got a CloudPoint issue I need someone to look at." Then she looked up at Paxton. "Shift is over."

"Already?" he asked.

"Talked to Dobbs," she said. "We can call it. You see something like that . . . you can call it for the day."

Paxton surveyed the crowd. Even from their vantage point in the hallway he could tell the lobby was filling up.

"Let's help get the area cleared," he said. "Then we'll call it."

Dakota nodded. "Sure."

They made their way over and spoke to the assembled groupings, asked them to return to their rooms, or to clear the area, and not everyone listened, but most did. Dakota seemed to carry some extra weight of authority on her slight frame because people recognized her. After a bit, some folks in green with cleaning supplies came trudging through, carrying themselves like they were headed to wipe up a grocery aisle spill.

Paxton waited for Dakota to finish speaking to a woman, then slid up beside her. "This happen every Cut Day?"

"A handful." She paused, like she was going to say something else, then seemed to change her mind. "Listen, at this point I think we're in the clear. Why don't you head back?"

"Okay," Paxton said. "Thanks."

He lingered for a moment, wondering if he should do something. If this was a test and he should stick around. But Dakota turned away, worried about something else.

He made his way to his apartment, then the bathroom, got a shower well up to scalding and stood underneath, letting the spray scratch at his skin. He paid the credits for an extra five minutes. Back in his room, he pulled out the futon and loaded up the pillows and blanket so he could both sit up and spread out, pulled out the keyboard, and fired up the television.

It played an ad for a really nice thermos, which made Paxton want coffee, so he hit a button to drop him into the Cloud store. He bought the thermos, and then it offered to sell him a coffee maker and coffee pods. He realized he hadn't bought anything for the apartment yet, which he was loath to do. The more settled he got, the longer he would be here. But coffee was a necessity, so he ordered those, too, and the screen told him everything would be there within an hour.

He could use a cup before going out.

He was still unsure of how to handle Zinnia. Maybe best to leave it alone.

She was pretty and she seemed interested in him and couldn't that be enough? Did he have to complicate it by being weird?

Still a few hours until he was due to meet her for drinks, so he figured the sudden off-time would be a good opportunity to get some work done. He went to the small pile of books he had brought with him, found an empty notebook. He sat down with it and opened it up to the first page. Blank, crisp, full of promise.

At the top he wrote: *NEW IDEA.*

And he stared at the page until the coffee maker arrived. The knock at the door startled him so that he dropped the notebook. At the door a small pale man, wearing a red polo and a neon-yellow CloudBand strap, handed him a box. The man nodded and ran off.

Paxton ripped it open on the counter, took out the coffee maker and the pods. The box he put aside to deal with later. The pods came in an assortment of flavors. He selected cinnamon bun and set it to brew into an old mug he found in a cabinet. The mug said HOT STUFF on the side. With that going, he sat down and fired up the internet browser on his television and searched "revolutionary kitchen gadgets." Maybe browsing through ideas other people had had would spark one of his own. He used the touchpad to scroll through lists and blogs, about digital scales that were Bluetooth connected, a countertop machine that made craft cocktails from packets, a butter mill you could use to ground frozen sticks to make them more spreadable.

Homemade ramen noodle maker.

Self-regulating temperature pan.

Instant pancake machine.

His brain remained a barren wasteland. No flashes of insight. He lost himself in the clicks until he remembered the coffee. He pulled it off the brewer and sat with the mug cradled on his stomach, softly blowing off the steam as he clicked around the television, looking for something interesting to watch. He found more commercials than actual programming. He lingered on the Cloud News Network for a few moments, which was reporting the strong stock performance of the company, as Ray Carson was expected to be named CEO.

As the time to meet Zinnia approached he threw on a clean shirt; downed the last of the coffee, which had gone cold; and left the apartment. Made his way to the pub, early by about ten minutes, but Zinnia was already sitting on a stool, halfway through a glass of vodka. He went to the stool next to her, gave it a shake to make sure it was stable, and climbed aboard.

Zinnia waved over the bartender, the same one from the other night, who went to pour the same beer Paxton had previously had, which made him happy. It made him feel like a regular, and it was nice to feel like a regular anywhere, even here.

More than that, too, he felt the way the smell of the coffee in his room had made him feel. Sitting next to Zinnia made this giant waiting room feel like an actual place, for people to live.

Zinnia waved her arm over the payment sensor. "On me tonight."

"That's not terribly chivalrous of me."

"It's also reductive and sexist to think I need your money." Zinnia turned, frowning, and Paxton froze. But then she smiled. "I'm a modern kind of gal."

"Fair enough," Paxton said, accepting his beer. They clinked glasses and he took a sip. They sat in silence for a few minutes.

Finally, Zinnia spoke. "Heard someone got killed by a train downstairs in Maple."

"Yeah."

"Accident?"

"No."

She huffed. "Terrible."

Paxton nodded. "Terrible." He took a sip of beer, put the pint glass down. "Want to tell me about your day? Something that wasn't terrible?"

For example, dots. Can we talk about dots?

"I picked stuff up and dropped it off," she said. "Nothing even remotely interesting."

Zinnia didn't speak for a few moments, and Paxton tried to get a read off her and couldn't.

This was not the day to be doing this. After a few sips and a little more silence he was ready to call it a night and try again in a few days, when she asked, "How's the task force thing going?"

"I think that's done," Paxton said. "They decided to go in a different direction. I'm going to be working the exit line at the warehouse."

"That's too bad," Zinnia said.

"Yeah, I guess I didn't have some amazing insight or, you know, move heaven and earth during my first week. The problem is, somehow, people are moving around without being tracked by the watches, right? Nobody can figure out how, and I just get here and I don't have some kind of answer for them, and they're all bent out of shape." Paxton exhaled. "Sorry."

Zinnia sat up a little straighter. Her face brightened. "No, it's fine. This is really interesting."

Paxton fed off her enthusiasm. "Yeah, so, there are a couple of problems with blocking the signal. If you take the watch off for too long and it's not on a charging mat, an alert is supposed to go off. And you can't leave your room without it on."

Zinnia's gaze drifted to the concourse of Live-Play. The crowds outside were thick. A rainbow of polo shirts filtering past the front of the bar in both directions. "So how the hell are they beating it?"

"Planning on running some oblivion?"

"Maybe."

Paxton laughed. A real laugh, the kind that hurts your ribs.

"No," she said, picking up her glass, holding it aloft. "No. Just, it's fascinating."

Paxton nodded, took a sip of beer. Thought about the dot. About asking. How easy it would be just to say the words.

But the longer he sat there the less he cared about it.

Then she slid her hand across the bar, touched his elbow. It was a glancing, almost friendly touch. Sort of a getting-your-attention thing. She said, "I run around all day picking things up and putting them down. It's interesting to hear about something else."

And she smiled again. It was the kind of smile a person could get lost in, and for a moment he thought it was her inviting him to lean in for a kiss, but before he could, he heard someone mutter, "The fuck . . ."

The bartender was looking at his watch, so Paxton looked down at his. On the display was an unlit match. Same on Zinnia's. Paxton tapped the screen but nothing happened. The image remained the same.

"What do you think this is?" Zinnia asked.

Almost in response, the match caught fire, orange flame curling off the tip. The image dissolved and it seemed like words were forming, little squares sliding into place, when the screen went blank and returned to the home screen, which showed both the current time and a small countdown in the corner—hours until his next shift.

The two of them looked at the bartender, like maybe he'd been there longer and would have a better sense. He just shrugged. "I got nothin'."

Paxton made a note to ask Dakota about it tomorrow. Maybe it was a glitch. Anyway. The warm-and-fuzzies he was feeling for Zinnia disappeared in a puff, and his mind snapped back to the man on the tracks, as if the thought itself were intent on ruining his night.

The blood. His face. The slackness of it. The way the body seemed to collapse on itself in death.

It made the dot thing and the door thing seem so much smaller in comparison.

Paxton weighed it all. Like flies buzzing around him. He needed to swat it, or at least try.

"Got a weird question for you," he said.

"Shoot."

"I saw you today."

Zinnia didn't answer, so Paxton turned to her. Her eyes were wide. She seemed frozen on her barstool, like he could give her a little nudge and she'd tumble off, shatter like glass.

"You were going into the bathroom hallway, down in the lobby."

"Okay . . ."

"Nothing weird, I just wanted to know—I had to go into the bathroom later on to wash my hands and the CloudPoint door was open. Did you see anyone messing around with it?"

Zinnia let out a long stream of air, then nodded. "I noticed that, too. I mean, half the shit around here is broken, isn't it?"

"Yeah," Paxton said. "Maybe that's it. It's weird. Seemed like there was a piece of plastic wedged in there or something. I let my supervisor know."

Zinnia's hand, which had been lying on the bar, tightened into a fist, and she slowly spun her knees away from him, toward the exit. He suddenly wished he hadn't said anything. It felt invasive.

"I'm sorry," Paxton said. "I wasn't spying on you or anything. Just . . . I'm sorry. I shouldn't have asked." He put his head in his hands. "It's been a day."

"Hey," Zinnia said.

"Yeah."

"You okay?"

"No."

Zinnia nodded. "Want to walk around a bit?"

"Sure," he said.

They knocked back their drinks, walked out in silence. Zinnia took the lead, seemed to know where she was taking them, so Paxton followed, down the promenade, toward the elevator bank of Maple, and he felt a twinge shoot through his body as she led him onto an empty elevator car and swiped her wrist, her floor appearing on the flat panel. She leaned against the wall, looking forward, her face set like she was marching off to war.

Paxton wasn't the kind of guy who liked to assume, but at this point he figured it was safe to assume.

They made it to her door and she swiped it open. They entered, the light off, fading sun streaming through the frosted window so the room was barely lit. The ceiling layered with tapestries, overlapping each other, every color of the rainbow, and it made Paxton happy to see this part of Zinnia that she kept hidden away in her room.

He was a good six inches taller than her, but briefly he felt shorter, like she was growing to fill the space, and then he reached out his hand and took hers, leaned in and pressed his lips to hers. She kissed him back. Soft, then hard, then she put both hands on his chest and shoved him back. He landed on the futon, which was already folded down into a bed.

ZINNIA

The good news, at least, was the sex was solid. Paxton didn't make her go cross-eyed, but he gave it an honest effort. He didn't give up. He even got close. And close was better than she'd had in recent memory. She gave him a little pity shudder-and-gasp. He'd earned that much.

They even had a few laughs when they both found themselves in those awkward first-time places, where you're feeling each other out, crashing into each other in stops and starts, not used to each other's bodies or rhythms.

When it was done they cuddled on the thin mattress, trying to find a comfortable position, until Paxton sat up on the edge of the bed, naked, looking away from her but trying to twist around.

"I'm sorry," he said. "I think I'm going to go back to my own room. Nothing against you, nothing against you at all, but I can't usually sleep next to other people. I sleep too light. Not that this mattress is even big enough . . ."

Zinnia felt a little jolt of sadness. She did like to sleep next to someone. That proximity, the warmth. It made her feel safe. Which was funny, in the sense that Zinnia could kill him a dozen different ways just from that angle. But still, she wished the bed were a little bit bigger.

She watched him dress, found he was in better shape than he appeared from outside his clothes, which didn't really fit him right, doing too good a job at hiding the muscles between his shoulder blades that bunched up and caught the light.

After he got dressed he leaned over and pressed his face to hers, and said, "I liked this a lot. I'd like to do it again."

Zinnia smiled with his lips still pressed to hers. "Me, too."

After he left, she wanted to linger a bit in the after-sex glow but found she couldn't. She couldn't stop her brain from spinning.

Someone had figured out how to block the watch signal.

She was climbing through the ceiling like a goddamn amateur, and a bunch of dumb-ass drug dealers had come up with a more elegant solution.

Which, one, pissed her off because they'd figured it out and she hadn't, and, two, made her want to know their secret.

Her solution was workable but not preferable. It would be so much better to block the signal when needed, rather than leave the watch behind entirely. Because not wearing it left her vulnerable; if someone caught on, if her sleeve went up too far or she found a door she couldn't get through, she'd be screwed.

She would have to find a way to pump Paxton for information, without coming off as too probing or eager. If someone figured it out, she wanted to know as soon as possible.

That was why she wanted to see him again.

That was what she told herself, and after a few tries she believed it.

She got dressed. Checked the hallway to make sure it was clear. Found the out-of-order sign on the women's bathroom but went inside anyway. It was in working order. And as she set herself up a shower, she decided to track down a bottle of wine, and then drink it while she reread the watch manual. Something to keep busy while the laptop, under a pile of clothes, chewed on Cloud's internal code.

PAXTON

Paxton floated down the hallway, like his feet weren't even touching the floor. This felt like the start of something. Something real.

He got to his apartment and fell into his futon and didn't even bother removing his shoes. When the faded yellow glow of the sun cut through the window and woke him, he realized it was the best he'd slept in weeks.

The CloudBand beeped at him, like it knew he was awake, reminding him he had three hours to shift and only 40 percent battery, so he placed it on the charging mat and brewed some coffee, the small space filling with the smell of roasted beans. The sense-memory section of his brain flared, and he replayed the previous evening in his head.

He'd made her climax. He was sure of it. You couldn't fake that, the way she dug her nails into the back of his head, bucking her hips forward so hard it nearly unhinged his jaw.

He flicked on the television—"Hello, Paxton!"—and it launched into a commercial for a new model of the CloudPhone, this one with 4 percent more battery life and two millimeters thinner, and Paxton considered whether he should put himself on the waiting list to get one but figured he could wait a bit. He'd heard the next generation, the one after this, was going to be even better.

Then the Cloud News Network showed video of border crossings into Europe. Tear gas canisters arced through the air. Police in riot gear slammed into families. Refugees from cities like Dubai and Abu Dhabi and Cairo, now uninhabitable due to the temperature swings.

Except, no one wanted to take them in and risk the additional strain on local resources. Too depressing.

Paxton turned it off and sipped his coffee, staring at the blank wall.

Someone had been messing with the CloudPoint, so Dakota was going to pull watch data, to see who was there. It might show no one, because clearly people were wandering around without their watches on. He thought about dots. The way people moved around the Cloud floor like ants. Or like clouds. Big, thick clouds of people, breaking apart, re-forming. Masses of them that blended together . . .

Huh.

He pulled out his phone and sent a text to Dakota: *Had an idea I wanted to run by you. If you're willing to hear it.*

After clicking around the television for a few minutes and being unable to settle on anything, he strapped his watch back on, now at 92 percent, and made his way out to the shower.

He almost didn't want to shower. Wanted that smell of Zinnia on his skin to linger all day. But he knew he needed it, probably reeked of booze and sex, which was no way to go into work, and anyway, as he turned on the water he thought about the sink in the bathroom and washing his hands and the blood that was on them after the man got hit by the tram, and that erased any residual good memories of the previous night.

Showered and changed, he felt a little more comfortable, and he felt even better when he checked his phone and Dakota had written back: *Report to Admin. Let's hear it.*

He found Dakota sitting in a cubicle. She glanced up from a piece of paper she was scanning and said, "Geez, someone got laid last night."

Paxton stuttered, searching for words.

"You reek of it," she said.

"Well . . . I mean, I showered. . . ."

Dakota slapped down the paper. "Don't admit to it. That's even worse."

"I'm sorry, I—"

"C'mon, out with it."

Paxton put his hands together like he was praying, to center himself. "Okay, we know people are somehow blocking the signal. And this morning I had this thought. We can't track these people. But shouldn't we be able to see them disappear off the map? Like, when their signal drops off. Shouldn't we be able to at least see that?"

Dakota stared at him, her face revealing nothing. After a few moments she stood up and stalked off. Over her shoulder she said, "Wait here."

Paxton watched her disappear into a conference room. He sat in her seat, still warm from her, and stared at the empty cubicle across from him. He spun back and forth in the seat until he heard footsteps. Dakota was standing above him.

"Come with me," she said.

The conference room was dim, the screen on the wall lit up with the same view as the other day—Live-Play and the swarms of orange dots. Dobbs was seated at the head of the table, and three people— two women, one man, all in tech brown polos—were seated against the wall.

Dobbs nodded at Paxton as he entered. Dakota sat and Paxton followed, leaving an empty seat between them. He smiled at the three people across from him, who looked like animals caught in the headlights of a speeding semi.

Dobbs cleared his throat. The techies jolted. "We were just having a conversation about a few things. CloudPoints and CloudBand signals and such." He nodded toward Paxton. "And Dakota comes in, tells me about this theory of yours." He looked at the tech workers. "Siobhan. Go ahead."

One of the girls—strawberry hair and button nose—perked up. "Okay," she said. Then again. "Okay." She took a deep breath, looked at Dakota and Paxton. "We never really . . . um, I mean . . . the problem is the signals all sort of . . . merge when there are too many people."

Dobbs exhaled hard through his nose.

Siobhan kept an eye on him, like she was afraid he might pounce. "There's too much data. Too many people. Too many signals. That . . ." She pointed to the orange dots. "In many ways those are an approximation. Your CloudBand marks position based on a few things: Wi-Fi, GPS, cellular. But we can't track you down to within an inch of where you're standing. Those dots could be ten, twenty feet off. Sometimes more. Sometimes they'll just randomly jump a bit. It's a lot for the system to process."

Paxton thought of Zinnia, of her little dot following his dot.

That must've been it. A glitch.

"What you're saying is, you hadn't thought to look for signal drops?" Dobbs asked.

Siobhan mumbled something that sounded like "No."

Dobbs exhaled. "Thought this place had its own damn satellite."

"Six," Siobhan said. "But until the moonshot team cracks quantum computing, there's only so much data we can process at a time. In fact, it gets harder as we go along, because there's more and more. . . ."

Dobbs stared.

"I mean . . . we could try," Siobhan said. "We would have to look manually, and it would take a lot of time. . . ."

"Try," Dobbs said, smiling. "All I ask. But still no idea what they could be using to block the signal?"

The three techies looked among themselves, the two lackeys terrified of answering, of opening their mouths, so they defaulted to Siobhan, who whispered, "No."

"Great," Dobbs said. "Just great. Since we've got nothing there, can you tell me what the hell was with that match yesterday?"

"I was thinking the same thing," Paxton said, eager to show Dobbs he was on the ball, but Dobbs shot him a hard glance. Paxton shut up, turned his attention to Siobhan.

"The usual," Siobhan said. "Hackers. This is the first they've gotten through in, what . . ." She looked at the woman to her left. "A year and a half? More?"

"More," the woman said.

"More," Siobhan said. "Honestly, we're not even sure what it meant. All we know is, it was an outside attack and they didn't leave anything behind in the system."

Dobbs sighed. Put his hands on the table. Stared at them, hard, like they might turn into something more interesting than hands.

"We found the weakness they exploited," Siobhan said. "It was a little glitch of code left by the last system update. It's already been patched. But we do have to prep a bigger software update now. To address this, but also, we think we might be able to do a better pinpoint on the location data. We just need . . . time."

Dobbs raised an eyebrow and looked at her.

"How much time?"

"Two months?" she said. "Maybe more."

"Faster than that," Dobbs said, not a suggestion. "And I want a team assigned specifically to looking for signal drops. Even if it means a bunch of people sitting in a room and staring at a screen."

Her mouth fell open, like a protest was forming, but she thought better of it.

"Good," Dobbs said. "That'll be all."

The three techies got up and filed out of the room, nearly tripping over themselves to get into the light beyond the doorway. They left the door open, so Dakota got up and closed it and returned to her seat.

Dobbs tented his fingers and did that damn thing where he took his time before speaking, but when he did, he said, "Sometimes you need a new set of eyes on something. Can't believe we didn't think to look for signal drops. And that was a good catch with someone tampering with the CloudPoint." He nodded at Paxton. "I guess I wasn't wrong about you."

Paxton didn't know how to respond. He just basked in the approval, which felt a little like sunlight on a cold day.

"Forget scanner duty," Dobbs said. "You keep making observations like that, that's exactly what I need on this team. I want you and Dakota out, talking to more people. Look around. Gonna take old-fashioned shoe leather to shake this one out. You can both go. Try and bring me something I can use, okay?"

Dakota stood straight up, pushing out her chair, and turned to the door. Paxton lingered, thought there'd be at least one more thing on the agenda. Dobbs's face was planted firmly south and he knew he was making a mistake by bringing it up, but he did anyway. "What about the man who got hit by the train yesterday. And the others?"

"Damn shame," Dobbs said. "What about it?"

"Shouldn't we do something? Like, you ever see those subways with the partitions? It's like a glass cube, and the doors don't open until the train pulls in. That way no one can fall. Or, you know . . ."

Dobbs stood, put his hands on his chair. Leaned down. "You know how much that would cost? We looked into it. Millions, to do all the stations. And that's just here. Men upstairs don't want to spend it. That's why we increase patrols. We do the best we can. Maybe next time you'll be a little more aware of your surroundings and we can avoid things like that."

Paxton's voice caught in his throat. He hadn't thought of it like that. As his fault. And for a moment he wasn't sure Dobbs did either, but that didn't make it any better or worse. He kicked himself mentally, realized he should have stuck with the good part.

"What are you waiting for, son?" Dobbs asked. He raised his hand toward the door. "Back on patrol."

Paxton nodded, found Dakota lingering outside, listening. They walked in silence to the lobby and took the tram to the promenade and completed almost an entire circuit before Dakota said, "It's not your fault."

"Feels like it."

"Dobbs is in a mood," she said. "But you're on his good side right now, and that's all that matters."

"Right," Paxton said. "Right. All that matters."

As he stepped off the elevator he made a mental note to check his star rating at the end of his shift.

GIBSON

The time has come. Time to tell you who's taking over for me when I'm gone.

I want y'all to know, right up front, that this was a difficult decision to make. I had a lot of factors to weigh. A lot of things that kept me up at night, and I've already been having trouble sleeping so this wasn't exactly a pleasant few weeks now.

And I thought: I'm going to have a hell of a time explaining this. Because there's a lot about this decision that makes sense on paper, but there's also a lot that makes sense in my head. The stuff in my head, every time I try to say it, it gets all jumbled up.

But at the end of the day, the decision is mine. This isn't about any one person. This is about the good of the company. It's about building on the promise I made to myself with Cloud—that we wouldn't just concern ourselves with getting goods from one place to another. That we'd do our best to make the world a better place. By providing jobs, and health care, and housing. By reducing the greenhouse gases suffocating our planet, with the dream that one day people will be able to go outside again all year round.

I want to thank Ray Carson for his years of service to Cloud. Man has been there since the beginning. He's been like a brother to me. And I will never forget the kindness he showed me on our first night, that night where all I wanted was a celebratory drink and I couldn't afford it. That's a true measure of character. The man has it in spades. I know he's the one you all expect me to name. Every news network on earth, even all the ones I own, has been reporting it like that.

But my daughter, Claire, will replace me as the president and CEO of Cloud.

I've already asked Ray to stay on in his position as vice president and COO, and I'm awaiting his response. I truly hope he stays on. Claire needs it. The company needs it. We're at our best with him. That's all for now. I just really want to make this clear. It wasn't easy. But it was the right decision to make.

GRIND ^{5}

ZINNIA

Zinnia woke to the gentle buzz of her CloudBand. Checked the time. One hour to shift. Climbed out of bed and threw on a robe. Walked down the hallway, watching for Rick. Not there. Went into the ladies'. Showered. Returned to her room. Checked her laptop. Still working. Dressed. Stopped in a bodega to get a PowerBuff salted caramel protein bar. Took the tram to the warehouse floor. Picked tablets and books and phone chargers. Stopped for a piss. Picked flashlights and markers and sunglasses. Ate her protein bar. Picked welcome mats and backpacks and charcoal scrubs. Another piss. Picked shower radios and wineglasses and more books. Picked headphones and dolls and baking sheets. Left, feet aching. Passed the arcade and considered some Pac-Man. Passed the bar and considered some vodka. But her feet protested. She made her way to her apartment and read until she fell asleep.

PAXTON

Paxton woke a few minutes before his CloudBand was meant to wake him up. Checked his rating. Still three stars. Stumbled to the bathroom, showered, shaved, dressed in blue, and made his way to Admin, where he met Dakota. The two of them walked back and forth on the promenade, the stroll broken up by the occasional intervention. Two people arguing. A young man accused of shoplifting. Belligerent drunk. Then: more walking. Eyes peeled for handoffs, of which none were apparent. Some small talk with Dakota. Lunch at the ramen shop. More walking. More interventions. Passed-out oblivion user on a bench in Live-Play. Fistfight in a bar. Kids skateboarding in the rec zone. At the end of shift, Paxton turned toward his apartment, considered texting Zinnia, decided against it. Too tired. He went home, didn't bother unfolding the futon, and fell asleep watching television.

ZINNIA

Zinnia woke to the gentle buzz of her CloudBand. One hour to shift. Walked down the hallway, watching for Rick. Not there. Went into the ladies'. Showered. Stopped in a bodega to get a PowerBuff salted caramel protein bar. Took the tram to the warehouse floor. Picked fish oil pills and knitting needles and spatulas. Stopped for a piss. Picked stools and measuring tapes and activity trackers. Picked grill covers and night-lights and showerheads. Left, feet aching. Passed the arcade and made it to the bar, where she ordered a vodka. Paxton entered shortly thereafter. They talked. No movement on the signals. They went back to her place and fucked. He left. She went to take a shower but the ladies' room was locked, and in the gender-neutral bathroom Rick cornered her and watched her change. She went back to her room, but before she entered she watched as a team of people removed a body bag from the apartment two doors down, one of them saying something about an oblivion overdose. She went inside and picked up a book, considered it, put it back down, went to sleep.

PAXTON

Paxton woke to the soft beep of his CloudBand. Showered, shaved, dressed in blue, and made his way to Admin. He and Dakota walked back and forth on the promenade, the stroll broken up by a search for Warren at the arcade, to see if there was anything worth seeing, but there wasn't. Then: More walking. Eyes peeled for handoffs. Some small talk with Dakota. Lunch at the taco shop. More walking. Some interventions. Drunks fighting in a bar. Kids being loud. At the end of shift, Paxton turned toward his apartment, texted Zinnia, didn't hear back right away. Stopped in a store that sold CloudBands, found a nice brown leather strap in a vintage style, with rivets and raised stitching. He bought that and went home, where he swapped out the standard band. He didn't bother unfolding the futon. Sat with his journal open, to *NEW IDEA,* and fell asleep watching television.

ZINNIA

Zinnia woke. One hour to shift. Walked down the hallway, watching for Rick. Not there. Showered. Stopped in a bodega to get a PowerBuff salted caramel protein bar. Picked shawls and energy drinks and weight-lifting gloves. Picked pillows and wool hats and scissors. Passed the arcade. Stopped in for Pac-Man. Met Paxton for a movie. Fell asleep during it and told him they couldn't fuck afterward; she had her period. She liked his new CloudBand strap so he walked her over to the store, where she found a nice fabric fuchsia band. Afterward she made her way to her apartment and read until she fell asleep.

PAXTON

Paxton woke. Three stars. Uttered a string of curses. Showered, shaved, dressed in blue. He and Dakota walked back and forth on the promenade. Looked for Warren. Lunch at the arepa shop. More walking. Got a call about a red who hadn't shown up for his shift or reported in sick, and it turned out to be an oblivion OD. They kept the area clear while the medical team removed the body, then knocked on every door of the hallway, trying to find out more about the dead employee. His name was Sal. They turned up no new leads. At the end of shift, Paxton turned toward his apartment, considered texting Zinnia, didn't, went home. Fell asleep watching television.

ZINNIA

Zinnia woke. Went to work. Picked scales and books and ratchet sets. Wandered for two hours, wondering about the source of the electricity, the thing that kept this place moving, as her laptop translated the Cloud code into something she could use. Went to sleep.

PAXTON

Paxton woke. Went to work. Walked back and forth on the promenade, wondering what it would take to finally get him to four stars. Made love to Zinnia. Fell asleep watching television.

ZINNIA

Zinnia woke. Worked. Fell asleep.

PAXTON

Paxton woke. Worked. Fell asleep.

SOFTWARE UPDATE 6

GIBSON

Here we go. Once again, I have to set the record straight on some things.

It's been a while since I've written. And that's because after I announced that Claire would be taking over the company, things got a little nutty. First off, the press went and started reporting all these stories about Ray being mad at me, because he thought he was next in line, and that couldn't be further from the truth. Anyone who watches the Cloud News Network would know that, but it seems like some people can't be bothered to do their research.

Worse than that, some people have been reporting that Ray got hired away by one of the last few big-box retailers, which seems to spend more time trying to knock me down than doing any actual work (which, if they focused on their own business, maybe they wouldn't be in so much trouble). That ain't true either. Ray is still my VP.

In fact, I just got off the phone with him and he told me how excited he was to work with Claire. I didn't have any brothers and sisters growing up, but Ray was so close to me that Claire called him "Uncle Ray." Fact was, she thought he was my brother until she got a little older and could understand that calling him "uncle" was just a sign of respect.

Here's what I want to say about Ray: Like I told you, he was there at the beginning, when I was a kid looking to make a buck. And he stuck with me and fought with me and helped make Cloud into the company that it is. I trust Ray more than I trust anyone. And Ray trusts me. Even though I don't have a brother, he's the next best thing. And sure, like brothers, sometimes we fight and sometimes we argue, but that's why this relationship works so well.

I want to tell you a story. This is a good one. It's the story Ray told at my wedding, because of course he was my best man.

Molly was a waitress at this diner near the Cloud offices. I liked going there because they did breakfast all day, and it was pretty good, but also, I liked Molly. I would always sit in her section, and I would try to say something smart or clever to her, which I'm sure never sounded as good as I thought, but still, she always had a smile for us. A lot of the time I was there with Ray and he could see how much I liked her, and one day, we're sitting there, tucking into our eggs and bacon, and he says, "Why don't you ask her out?"

And I just sort of froze up. I figured, woman as pretty as Molly isn't going to go for a guy like me. This was back in the very early days of Cloud, when I had an idea and two pairs of trousers and not much else. At that point it wasn't even that I was broke; I was in debt, and I was worried I'd made a huge mistake. But Ray pressed me. Said a girl that pretty and sweet doesn't come along every day. But, swear to truth, I was scared, so I didn't. Just tipped my hat to her like I always did and we finished our breakfast and left.

Two hours later, I get a phone call. It was Molly. And she says, "Sure, Gibson, I'd love for you to take me out to dinner."

Now, I am dumbstruck. I snapped out of it long enough to tell her I would get back to her with some concrete plans, and I turned, and Ray is sitting there at his big old metal desk, feet up, hands behind his head, smiling that smile, like it was going to reach all the way around the back of his skull and his head was going to fall off.

He had written her a note on the bill, pretending to be me.

So me and Molly make plans for a few nights later, and I figure on picking her up after leaving work. It was a busy day but Ray made sure I got off on time. I'm in my office and I'm getting ready, and I got this bow tie. Now, this is a hell of a bow tie, or so I thought. Red and blue sort of paisley design. I still have it. I put it on and I step into Ray's office and I ask, "How do I look?"

Now, me and Ray have been pals a long time, but still, I was his boss. And a lot of men would have looked at their boss and just said, "Oh, yes, sir, you look great."

But not Ray. He looked me up and down and said, "Buddy, you do know the point of the first date is to get yourself a second date, right?"

What are friends for? I ditched the bow tie and borrowed one of his regular ties—a nice little black number. Which Molly told me that night over dinner looked "distinguished." Couple of years later I told her this story and showed her the bow tie and she cringed in horror.

I thought it was nice. Anyway, point is, the reason Ray means so much to me isn't just that he was there from the beginning. It's because the man is a straight shooter. He's honest with me. There've been a lot of times where I wanted to do this or that and Ray has told me not what I wanted to hear, but what I needed to hear. That's a special sort of thing.

But this is the thing about the press, isn't it? This is why the newspaper model collapsed all those years ago. It's not that people don't want news. Of course they want to know what's going on in the world. But they don't want to be lied to. And people know when they're being lied to. Put up a story about how me and Ray are at each other's throats, maybe they get enough clicks their advertising revenue pays for a few cups of coffee. It's sad. It's why I started the Cloud News Network in the first place. I got tired of having to set the record straight.

Now, the stock price thing, that much is true. Yes, our value took a bit of a tumble after I named Claire. That had nothing to do with her. That's the way stocks work, folks. It was just the market acknowledging that my time is almost up and things are going to change hands. That aside, everything will continue on as it always has, and the market will right itself. In the meantime I'm down a little less than a billion dollars. Boo-hoo.

So that's where we are. This is a good reminder that if you want the straight dirt, tune in to the Cloud News Network. Anything else is just fake news, driven by some kind of agenda, and the whole thing is sad. But that's what happens on the internet. No regulation, no standards, people can say whatever they want. Let 'em have it. I'll be over here, doing real work.

Phew.

So like I said, it's been a while since I wrote anything. I'm feeling pretty good, actually. I'm taking six different kinds of new medications because my doctor figures at this point there's not much else I can do to hurt myself, and one of them might even give me a little more time. I take so many pills during the day I've lost count. Molly helps me portion them out.

The bus tour is going pretty good. We're getting close to the holidays, which is good and bad. Good because it's Cloud at its best, delivering happiness and convenience to people around the country. Bad because it's also another year for us to reflect on the Black Friday Massacres, though it's important we don't ever forget them either.

But I gotta tell you, based on what my doctor is saying, my expiration date ought to fall sometime after the New Year. So I might get one more Christmas on this earth. Which means one more opportunity to watch Cloud pumping and thriving. That'll be nice. I always loved walking around Cloud facilities during Christmastime. So much good work going on.

Keep your eyes on the road, folks. You never know when I might roll by. . . .

ZINNIA

The laptop chimed.

Zinnia thought it might be a phantom chime. She'd heard it a dozen times in the past week. She would be reading or napping and she'd hear that soft little ding, so she would pull open the drawer below her bed, dig underneath the clothing and the books, and find it was her mind messing with her.

Teasing: *not done yet, asshole.*

But it sounded real enough so she checked, digging the laptop out, and found it was true. The gopher's work was complete. She removed the plastic nub from the USB drive and held it in her palm. All she had to do was plug it into a computer terminal somewhere, and in about a minute, she'd have what she needed.

She slipped the gopher into the coin pocket of her jeans. Her pants slipped a little and she tugged at the waistband. It pulled out a half inch. The only upside to running around the warehouse.

Downside was the twinge in her left knee. The concrete floor was unforgiving—she'd already gone through a pair of sneakers. She stood on her left foot, raised her right knee in the air. Put her hands out. Lowered herself into a single-leg squat. Her leg wobbled. She nearly fell, and she threw out her other foot to keep from toppling over.

She sighed. Turned on the television, which showed her an ad for a topical menthol rub, which was close to what she needed, but not close enough. She signed in to the Cloud store and ordered herself a fabric knee brace. Just something to keep it stable. It wasn't good to mess around with knees. Knees were stupid. Like a ball and two sticks held together with rubber bands. It took way less torque than most people thought to screw up a knee. Last thing she wanted was to dump the money from this gig into surgery.

While she was at it, she ordered another pair of jeans, one size down. That, at least, felt nice. When she was done she left the apartment, sharing nods with her neighbors, people she recognized but mostly avoided.

Too-Tall Bald Guy.

Human Bear.

Nice Hadley.

She had Cynthia and Paxton and Miguel. That was enough friends. It seemed to be the way of the place anyway. People brushed up against each other but didn't engage. There were no gatherings, no group activities, other than rushed conversations in break rooms. She had a theory about that, that the more time you spent with people, the more the algorithm responsible for work shifts drove you apart. She and Paxton had started on roughly the same schedule but they'd been creeping apart, so that he was getting off four or five hours earlier than her. Same with Miguel—the few times she'd tried to raise him on the watch, he never seemed to be working. She'd just see him in passing out on the promenade.

Still, people talked. In the bathrooms, on the line to get in and out of the warehouse. Mostly in hushed tones. Lately it was about the coming regime change. People wondered if things would be different under the daughter. Better or worse. Zinnia didn't think there was much room for things to be worse, but corporate America was always good at finding "worse."

She made her way out of her dorm and onto the promenade, taking a long, looping walk around, like she did every day before shift.

Specifically, she was looking for anything resembling a terminal. Not a CloudPoint—those were too risky, and she was worried that after Paxton caught that little bit of plastic she left in the lock, security measures may have been stepped up. She needed someplace where she could sit for a minute or more and not get caught.

But none of the stores had computers. At least none that seemed accessible. She'd gone on some errands in Admin and thought she might be able to sneak into an office, but if an office door was open, there was a person inside. She had yet to pass one that was obviously vacant.

Op like this was delicate. Push too hard, and people saw you pushing.

Sometimes a good op played out when inspiration crashed into opportunity. Lucky for her, the deadline was six months. She still had time. Not a ton, but enough.

On her way to shift she stopped into the convenience store, the shelves shiny and backlit so the colorful packages on them seemed to glow. She made her way back and to the left, to where she always went, to the box of PowerBuff bars. She was thankful that after years of searching, she'd discovered a protein bar that was low in fat, low in carbs, high in protein, and didn't taste like a block of Styrofoam smeared with stale peanut butter.

She found that, during the hardest moments of her shift, she could look forward to when she'd unwrap the salted caramel PowerBuff bar, which could be eaten in four bites but she stretched it out to five so that she could really enjoy it.

But when she reached the back, the box was empty. They had other PowerBuff flavors, which she had flirted with and found to be wanting. The chocolate peanut butter was too thick and slightly bitter, and the birthday cake bar tasted like the waste pipe at an artificial sugar factory.

She looked at the empty box for a few moments, wondering how long it had been empty, how long ago someone had taken the last one, or if it had been her, yesterday, and she wasn't paying any mind.

Yesterday had been her last salted caramel PowerBuff bar and she hadn't even known it. It made her sad. And she grew sadder the more she thought about how sad it made her.

A heavyset Latino man in a green polo appeared at her side. He had a fresh box. Zinnia smiled. The man smiled back, took the empty box, replaced it, pushed in the perforated cardboard to open it up. "I noticed we were running low. I was surprised at first 'cause they're the least popular. No one likes 'em. But then I noticed you taking 'em and figured you might be disappointed if I didn't keep them in stock."

He took out a bar and offered it to her. She stood there, held it in her hands, the cellophane crinkling. He waited, like maybe he expected a parade or a high five or a blow job or something. Zinnia muttered, "Thank you."

He nodded, turned around, and walked back toward the front of the store.

As sad as she had been before, she was sadder now. She'd set a routine. Become a regular. Been here long enough that a complete stranger recognized her eating habits. This wasn't about the mission. It wasn't about being compromised or staying out of sight. It was just a shitty feeling because it reminded her she'd been in this place for months, and nothing had changed. She'd just gotten more comfortable with it.

She made her way to the warehouse, where she stepped onto the hard concrete floor, her knee grumbling in protest.

Tablet. Leather passport cover. Bow tie. Wool cap. Tampons. Markers. Headphones. Phone charger. Lightbulbs. Belt. Humidifier. Makeup mirror. Socks. Marshmallow-roasting sticks . . .

PAXTON

The conference room was packed. It made Paxton think of a tram car at rush hour. Bodies pressed together, so you could smell who hadn't brushed their teeth, who'd gone too heavy on the cologne, who'd had eggs for breakfast.

Most of the people he recognized. A few he didn't. Dakota was up near the front, next to Dobbs. Vikram had pushed himself that way, too. Paxton was glad to be in the room. In the past two months he'd felt like he'd fallen out of favor.

It used to be Dobbs would ask for oblivion updates, but those requests happened less and less often, because every time they came, all Paxton could do was say he was working on it. Which was true. He thought about it all the time. But he couldn't crack it either. The folks in tech had been no help with the signals, surveilling Warren hadn't been useful, and Paxton was still in the process of learning the facility and the people.

All he knew was that stuff wasn't getting in through the delivery bay. He'd been up and down the place with nothing to show.

This light-touch approach that Dakota kept reminding him about didn't seem very effective, but he didn't want to question Dobbs either. Those three stars taunted him. He'd hoped to be useful, to do something that would set him apart. But between the lack of movement there and the first page of his notebook, which was still blank, he'd gone from feeling sort of hopeful to just treading water, which was beginning to tickle at his nose.

At least he had Zinnia. It was the sole bright spot that allowed him to convince himself it wasn't as bad as the prison.

"Okay, everyone, listen up," Dobbs said, snapping the room to attention. "Tomorrow is software update day. You all know what that means. . . ."

Paxton didn't know, but he knew better than to raise his hand and say that. Dakota nudged Dobbs. "Got some new recruits here, boss."

"Do we, now? Well." He looked around. "Software update is getting sent out on the CloudBand. Which means the facility goes into lockdown. Everyone reports to his or her room for the duration of the update."

A hand. A young black guy with a tattoo on his neck of a lotus blossom.

"Why not do it at night when everyone is sleeping?"

Dobbs shook his head. "There are shifts running here twenty-four/seven; at no point is everyone sleeping. At eight a.m. the day of, everyone is to report to their rooms. Except us, hospital workers, and a few tech people."

Murmuring around the room. Paxton couldn't suss out what kind of murmuring it was. Excited or frustrated or just vaguely curious. But it seemed like an interesting opportunity. See this place when it wasn't completely packed with people. It was almost unbelievable to think about, like seeing Times Square suddenly evacuated.

"Now I'll turn it over to Dakota," Dobbs said, tossing her a little grin. "She'll be running point this year. Her number two will be Vikram. So you all listen up, because I have something to attend to."

Paxton breathed in sharp enough that a few people turned to look at him. Not Dobbs, thankfully. Dakota looked over, not because she'd heard him but because it was the natural thing to do. She had a funny look in her eye. Paxton let his face fall flat, like *This is no big deal*, except it was, because Vikram was an asshole, and this pretty much confirmed his star had faded and he was, once again, another warm body in blue.

"Okay, listen up," Dakota said. "If you're in this room, means you're a section leader. Which is exactly how it sounds. Each one of you gets a section and the blues in that section report to you. This is pretty easy. No one's supposed to be out. Tram is shut down. Ambulance trams still run. There'll be emergency medical staff at Care and some tech folks out and that is it. So we stay sharp. Our watches will be updating, too, so we'll be out of communication with each other. That means we'll be creating a text message chain using our personal cell phones. But there'll be so many of us out it won't matter. Safer that way."

The black guy again. "Safer?"

"Mostly people like to fuck around when we do software updates. Run around the facility. See how far they can get. We have to unlock all the doors when we do an update. Otherwise, it's a fire hazard because people can't swipe. We don't advertise that, but some people figured it out. Fucking around during software update means you lose a full star on your ranking, but people do it anyway. You'll get your section assignment to your CloudBand pretty soon. Come to me or Vikram with questions." Dakota turned, seemed to speak through gritted teeth. "Vik, anything to add?"

"Just be sure to follow directions, watch each other's backs, and stay vigilant," Vikram said, surveying the room, his eyes settling on Paxton for a moment and lingering longer than Paxton was comfortable with.

After the meeting, after Paxton had run through some paperwork he needed to check, he tracked Dakota down in the break room, where she was digging a small knife into the top of a coffee pod, before knocking some salt into it. She looked up as Paxton entered. "Makes it less bitter," she said.

"What does?"

"The salt."

"So I'm off the team?"

"What team?"

"I dunno. The you-and-Dobbs team."

"This is a different thing," Dakota said. "Vikram may be a prick but he's pretty good at organizing. Dobbs can't just shut him out entirely. Anyway, he wants you to concentrate on the oblivion."

"I feel like that's not entirely true."

Dakota stared at him for a few moments, then placed the pod into the coffee maker, closed it, and pressed the On button. "That's where things are right now."

"Fine," he said. "The software update, is that related to the match thing?"

"It's a software update," she said, not looking at him.

Paxton sighed. "Fine. When do we head out?"

"We're not," she said.

"What?"

"You're patrolling solo for a little while," she said. "I've got to work on the update scheduling. And after that . . ." The coffee machine sputtered and beeped. She picked up the mug, inhaled the steam. "I think Dobbs might be putting me in tan soon. Anyway, I think you know enough of the ropes to handle yourself."

"Okay," Paxton said. "Okay."

"I promise you," she said. "Business as usual."

The way she held his gaze while she said it, trying real hard to make it clear she wasn't lying, meant she wasn't telling the truth. Paxton nodded, said, "Let me know if you need a hand with anything on the update stuff."

She took a sip of coffee and turned away to the fridge, opened it, said, "Will do."

Paxton left. Made his way to the promenade. Walked a bit. Stopped to eat, picking CloudBurger because Dakota wasn't there to veto it. After he ate he walked some more. Broke up an argument. Gave a newcomer directions. Wondered why he felt so jealous of Vikram. Why he wanted so bad to be the one up there. He hated this. He didn't want this life. He wanted to be done with it.

But he was here, and this was what he had. If he was going to do it, he wanted to do it well. He wanted recognition. He didn't want to be a nameless blue wandering the promenade.

At the end of his shift he changed and went to the bar, texted Zinnia to let her know he'd be there, not caring if she showed up, but also hoping she would. She didn't respond but she did climb onto the stool next to him, still wearing her red polo, as he was ordering his third beer.

"You have some catching up to do," Paxton said, tilting his pint toward her.

"Rough day?"

"Could say that."

She paused. It was a long pause, like she had gotten distracted by something else. Then she asked, "Want to talk about it?"

"No." Paxton drained the glass and picked up the fresh pint, took a sip, put it back down. "Yeah. So, big new thing at work. Software update day. And that asshole . . . Vikram. Did I tell you about Vikram?"

"You told me about Vikram."

"He's Dobbs's new favorite. Dakota's, too, I think. I just feel like . . ." He picked up his beer, put it back down without taking a sip. "I don't know how I feel."

"You feel like you worked hard and when the time came to get a little recognition it went elsewhere."

"I feel like that."

"It's weird. . . ."

"What's weird?"

Zinnia took a pull of her drink. "If this guy Vikram is such a dick, why do they keep him around? Like, do you ever feel like Dobbs is pitting you two against each other?"

Paxton sat back. Stared into the mirror behind the bar. "I don't know. No. Why would he even do that?"

Zinnia dropped her voice. "Classic abuser tactic. Make you work harder for his affection."

"No." Paxton shook his head. "No. That's too much. C'mon."

"Okay," Zinnia said. "So what's the deal with the software update?"

Paxton sat back, took a deep breath. "It's this thing, all the Cloud-Bands need to get updated. Remember when we saw the match? I think it was that. Anyway, everyone gets locked down to their rooms. It doesn't take long, but we have to be out in force. Make sure no one is outside."

Zinnia leaned forward. "If everyone is locked down, then what's the need for so much security?"

Fuck, shouldn't have said that. He looked around. The bar was mostly empty. The bartender was off on the other end, serving a woman a complicated mixed drink. "Every door is unlocked. Fire codes. So it's just us and hospital staff out, and everyone else is in their rooms."

"Huh," Zinnia said, taking a big swig of her vodka. "Huh."

Well, Paxton thought. At least he'd impressed someone today.

ZINNIA

Zinnia passed on a second vodka. She wanted to keep her head clear. As the night wound down, Paxton's hand snaked onto her thigh, and she didn't brush it off but she didn't wiggle into its path either. And when he ducked his head in, his breath heavy with the yeasty smell of beer, to ask if they could head upstairs, she told him she had her period.

Which was a lie. It wasn't going to start for another week. By now he should have known that, but men never seemed to retain period-related information. He was disappointed but gracious, even walked her to her dorm, where he kissed her and bid her adieu, and then she practically ran up to her apartment.

Software update. Everyone on lockdown, but not really a lockdown because nothing would be locked.

That was good.

Army of security officers out.

That was bad.

She dropped onto the futon, leaning forward, elbows on knees.

Think it out.

Everyone would be in their rooms because the CloudBands would be down and couldn't provide tracking data. Security officers used the watches to communicate with each other. Presumably they'd be down too, so there would be a lot of security officers out in case something required a rapid response.

The hospital would be open. She hadn't been to the hospital yet, but that would have to be her point of access.

Zinnia liked hospitals. They tended to not have the same kind of security as other facilities. Disinterested guards retired from something else, mostly focused on protecting stockpiles of drugs.

The plan knitted itself together in her head faster than she could keep up. She'd feign some sort of injury or illness right before the software update. Something that'd get her placed in the hospital facility. She'd figure it out from there. The security officers would likely be focused on the dorms, keeping everyone under control. There'd probably be a skeleton staff at the hospital. Some nurses? She could dance circles around them.

A shower. She needed a shower. She did her best thinking in the shower.

She stripped, threw on her robe and flip-flops, grabbed her toiletry bag, stepped into the hallway, and barely made it ten feet before she saw Rick coming out of the gender-neutral bathroom, which had an out-of-order sign hung on the door. Anger ripped through Zinnia's body like water rushing into a tight space. It got worse when she saw the figure behind him: a young girl, also in a robe, her hair wet, face, too, but not from the shower. She was holding the robe tight to herself like it might protect her.

Hadley.

Rick looked over and smiled. "Long time no see. I was beginning to think you didn't like me or something."

Zinnia didn't acknowledge him, couldn't take her eyes off Hadley, who was staring at the floor, wishing herself anywhere but there. Rick looked over his shoulder at the girl and said, "Now run on back, Hadley. And remember what I said."

The girl took off in the opposite direction. Zinnia watched over Rick's shoulder as she stopped and swiped her watch in front of her room. Rick shrugged. "Why don't we head on in?"

A storm raged in Zinnia's head, waves crashing against the inside of her skull. She could handle Rick. She didn't like it, but she could handle it.

Hadley, though . . .

The job beckoned. With a great deal of effort, Zinnia relaxed her muscles. She pushed a smile onto her face. "Sure," she said, the remainder of the vodka working through her system but maintaining just enough of a fingerhold that she still felt warm in the middle.

He looked around to make sure they were alone and pushed the door open. Zinnia stepped past him, careful not to touch him, like his skin was poisonous, and entered the bathroom, walking back toward the shower area.

She was so high on the possibility of getting a real crack at this that it was easy to ignore the lech who wanted to stare at her tits for a couple of minutes. She walled Hadley off into a corner. She could come back to that. She could come back for Rick when this was over.

She turned as he entered and was about to drop her robe when he said, "Software update coming soon."

Zinnia nodded, grasping the tie around her waist.

"Maybe you can come give me a private show, since we're going to be on lockdown," he said. "Make up for all that time you've been avoiding me. I'm in apartment S."

Zinnia paused, the tie of the robe half-pulled from the knot. She looked up at him. He wasn't smiling. Wasn't winking. He was serious.

"It'd be a nice thing for you to do, Zinnia," he said. "Smart, too."

"No," she said, the word leaping from her mouth. "I won't be doing that."

Rick's face went dark. "I'm sorry, this wasn't an either-or type of thing."

Another hot flash. After two months of day-in-day-out nonsense, she would not tolerate this sick fuck derailing her opportunity.

But more than that, as much as she didn't want to, she couldn't stop thinking of Hadley's face.

Usually Zinnia had no time for soft people. The world was a tough place, and you either learned to take the shot or you bought a helmet. But the look on her face, the way Rick lorded over her, it was like watching someone crush a baby bird in the palm of their hand.

"How about this," Zinnia said, letting the robe drop, allowing Rick's eyes to roll over her skin. "How about I give you a special show right now? An extra-special show?"

Rick smiled but stepped back, afraid of the sudden burst of sexual aggression. Coward. Zinnia moved in and he grew bold, stood his ground, preparing himself for what was coming.

He wasn't expecting it to be a hard, fast elbow to his eye socket.

Her adrenaline surged as her elbow connected. He yelled and went down hard, cracking his head on the bench on the way. She knelt next to him as he writhed on the floor, trying to crawl away, blocked by a bench.

"It's a sad and sorry thing you fell down and hurt your face," Zinnia said.

Rick spat, "You fucking cunt—"

Zinnia grabbed his throat. "Can you not appreciate the peril of making me angrier than I already am?"

That shut him up. Zinnia got in close.

"This is the last time you're going to play your little sign-swap game," she said. "This is the last time you're going to be a creepy-ass fuck with the women who live in this dorm. And you can get me fired, but you better believe on my way out I will find you and fucking end you. It's not like you can get someone to protect you from me, because then you'll have to tell them why, and it'll be a thing. You feel me?"

Rick mumbled something, the sound cut off by the lack of oxygen getting through his trachea. Zinnia let off a little.

"You feel me?" she asked.

"Yeah."

"Make me believe it."

"I do. No more."

"Good."

She let go. Considered giving him a jab or a kick. Some kind of parting shot. But then she figured she'd done enough, so she put her robe back on, exited the bathroom, took the out-of-order sign, and tossed it over her shoulder.

That was stupid.

So stupid.

She also did not care one inch.

She went into the ladies' room. It was slightly more crowded than usual. Two stalls occupied, and in the back, all of the showers. Two women Zinnia barely recognized were sitting and waiting their turn, along with Cynthia. The room was thick with steam and whispered conversations.

Cynthia waved her over and Zinnia sat next to her. "How you doing today, sweetheart?"

"Walking on sunshine," Zinnia said.

"You must be," she said. "No offense, dear, but that's the biggest smile I've ever seen on your face since you got here."

"Some days are special."

"Are they, now?"

Zinnia nodded, warmed by the thought of the give she felt when her elbow connected. There was a very real chance Rick's orbital socket was broken.

A shower curtain pulled aside. An older, lithe woman with gray hair stepped out, grabbed a towel, wrapped herself up. One of the other girls who was waiting got up and took her place.

"Honestly, though, I think I'm coming down with something," Zinnia said. "Stomach bug."

"That's too bad, dear."

"Might check myself into the hospital for a day or two. Just to be safe."

"Oh, no no no," Cynthia said. "You don't want to do that."

"Why not?"

Cynthia looked around, leaned forward in her wheelchair. "Calling out sick affects our ranking."

"Are you serious?"

"If you're injured, they have to send you to the hospital," she said. "But if you just have a tummy ache, or a cold, or something like that, you're expected to come in and work through it. Sometimes the ambulance trams won't even take you if they don't think it's serious enough."

Zinnia laughed, because it sounded like a joke. "That's ridiculous."

Cynthia didn't smile, didn't laugh back. "You don't want to mess around with that stuff."

"God, this fucking place."

This time, Cynthia did smile. "Here's my advice. Avoid the hospital the best you can. The care is pretty good. The problem is they don't want you to actually use it. It costs a ton of credits, too."

The curtain of the handicapped shower at the end of the row opened. A woman came out, nude and on crutches, a robe clutched under her arm, toiletry bag hanging around her neck. She made her way to a bench while Cynthia grasped the wheels of her chair and propelled herself forward.

"Sorry about your stomach," she said. "Feel better."

Zinnia sat back. Watched Cynthia pull the curtain closed. She sat there for a couple of minutes, her thoughts drifting back to Hadley.

She could imagine the girl sitting on the corner of her bed, holding herself, sobbing still over whatever violation Rick had subjected her to. She considered walking over to her room, knocking on her door. Checking on her. But she wasn't emotionally equipped for that, so she went to Cynthia's stall and called through the curtain, "Hey."

"Yes, dear?"

"You know that girl Hadley? Looks like a cartoon bunny?"

"Of course."

"Can you check on her? I saw her earlier. She seemed upset. But I don't know her well enough. . . ."

"Say no more," Cynthia said. "I'll pay her a visit after."

Zinnia smiled. She was still frustrated but that helped a little. And as she walked back to her room, she got another idea.

It wasn't an idea that she liked, but it probably would work.

SOFTWARE UPDATE ANNOUNCEMENT

At eight a.m. tomorrow, Cloud will issue a software update to your CloudBands. This update will repair a few minor bugs, as well as improve heart rate tracking and battery life. At six thirty a.m., all work at Cloud will cease, and unless otherwise instructed, you are to report immediately to your rooms, where you will stay until the software update is completed.

After the update is complete, anyone on shift will report back to work immediately to finish the remainder of their shift. Anyone due to work will report to work immediately.

Please be advised that only essential security and medical staff are allowed out of their rooms at the time of the update. Anyone who is found outside of his or her room during the update will be docked one full star. For those of you with two-star ratings, that will mean immediate termination.

Thank you for your understanding and cooperation in this matter. We know it's an inconvenience, and as always, we will work to make it as smooth as possible. We appreciate your assistance in this.

PAXTON

Paxton skipped his preferred breakfast—two fried eggs and toast—in favor of a protein bar, lingering over a single thought as he chewed: today would be a four-star day.

His assignment was the lobby of Oak, and he was the section leader, so mostly he just had to be sure everyone was spread out enough that there were eyes and ears where they needed to be. He'd have twenty people to assign and that was more than enough. He didn't want Vikram to have an opportunity to shit-talk him to Dobbs any more than he already had.

The lobby was slightly less crowded than usual. People probably taking the day to stay inside, since they'd have to be there soon anyway. He did a few circuits, found some good vantage points he hadn't thought of, then made his way to Admin, where he was due to meet with Vikram for final checks.

Same conference room. Same lack of space, though the atmosphere was lighter without Dobbs in the room. Vikram stood at the front and waited as people filtered in, and when the room was finally at capacity, he stared at people, waiting for them to end their conversations. As if they should have known better than to speak when it was his turn.

"Good," he said when the room finally fell quiet. "So today's the big day. I cannot make this more clear to you. If you fuck up, it's my ass. Which means I'll make sure it's your ass, too. I've got all your personal cell phones on a text blast. I'll be sending out updates as they happen. Everyone will get them, just ignore the ones that don't pertain to you. Someone is out of containment—"

Someone snickered in the back, at the way he leaned on the word *containment*, like they were in a science fiction film, acid-spitting aliens banging on the other side of the door, and Vikram paused.

"If anyone is out of containment, you report and detain. I'll be around to answer questions for the next few minutes."

He clapped his hands to signify the end of the meeting. Someone pushed the door open to get air in the room. People filed out. Paxton nodded at Vikram, trying to convey *I'm a team player* without having to actually talk to him. Vikram just scowled.

Halfway to Oak his CloudBand buzzed.

One hour until software update. Unless instructed otherwise, please report to your room.

ZINNIA

One hour until software update. Unless instructed otherwise, please report to your room.

Then:

Please make your final delivery.

The shelf in front of Zinnia slid to a halt. At the top of it, her task, was a puzzle box. She climbed up, not bothering to engage her safety harness. She wondered what the trade-off would be here, whether she would be penalized.

Not that it mattered as much as landing right.

At the top of the shelf she found the bin with the puzzles, took one out, let it register with the CloudBand.

Then she held her breath, turned, and launched herself into the air.

Her stomach lurched. She tucked her chin to her chest and put her arm out. One, to brace the fall, and two, to make sure her shoulder popped out of the socket. It'd been loose ever since that job in Guadalajara.

The second she landed, she felt it shift and pop. She exhaled, hard, pushing the air out of her lungs, like that might move out some of the pain. It didn't. She rolled onto her back, her left arm like a dead piece of meat tied to her torso. Pain blared through her body like an out-of-tune orchestra.

She breathed in. Breathed out. Got in the middle of the pain, the cacophony of it. Let it fill her up. That was the thing about pain. People tore themselves up fighting against it. The secret was to accept it as a temporary reality and focus on something else. Like standing.

A few people had stopped. Not many. Too many people making final deliveries. Zinnia picked up the puzzle box with her good arm and shuffled to the conveyor belt, which was, mercifully, nearby, then raised her CloudBand but found she couldn't press the crown with her free arm flopped at her side, so she pushed it against her chin until it registered, and said, "Emergency. Manager."

She got a set of walking directions and followed them, quickly coming across a blond soccer mom in a white polo who took one look at Zinnia, arm flopping against her side, and said, "You need help or something?"

"That'd be nice, yeah," she said. "I fell."

"Were you using your safety harness?"

"No."

The woman pursed her lips, held up her tablet. Came near Zinnia and held it by her wrist until it paired with her CloudBand. Tapped at the glass surface and turned it to face Zinnia. "I need a quick signature asserting that you weren't wearing your safety harness."

Zinnia exhaled. A new thing to focus on. Asshole bureaucracy. She took her good hand—not her dominant hand—and made a few whirls in the empty space. The woman nodded and typed for what seemed like a very long time while working with someone who had an injury.

"I think I might have a concussion," Zinnia said, hoping to speed things along. "I hit my head, too."

"I guess you'll be wanting to go to Care?"

"That's what it's there for."

The woman gave her a harsh look. Like, *Now is not the time for jokes.*

Yeah, no shit, Zinnia thought. But, flies with honey, or whatever the fuck.

"Please," Zinnia said.

"Can you walk, or do you need to be escorted?" the woman asked.

Zinnia rolled her eyes. "I can walk."

"Good." She tapped at the tablet. Walking directions popped up on her CloudBand. "Follow that to the emergency shuttle."

Zinnia didn't think the woman deserved it, but anyway, she said thanks. It didn't take long to get to the shuttle bay, nestled into a port next to a break room and some bathrooms. It was about the size of a tram car, but outfitted with beds and medical equipment, on a dedicated track to the hospital facility. Zinnia climbed on to find a young man, rugged and handsome with that just-enough stubble, playing on his phone. He saw Zinnia and shoved the phone in his pocket, nearly leaping a bed to meet her at the mouth of the car.

"You okay?" he asked.

"Fell," she said. "Shoulder popped out."

The man tried to ease Zinnia onto a bed. She resisted. Not easy with the shoulder. But it defeated the purpose of doing it in the first place if he fixed it now.

"You have to let me set this," he said. "The muscle will spasm. Longer it stays out, harder it is to get back in."

"No, I'd really rather—" But as she spoke he dug his fingers in, and while she hadn't even thought it would be that easy, he gave her shoulder a good squeeze and twist, and click, it was back. Just like that. The pain changed, growing oddly pleasant for a moment, then quieting down until it was a din in the background. Zinnia leaned against the bed, raised her arm perpendicular, turned her forearm in and out.

"That was good," she said, impressed.

"We deal with these a lot," he said. "Let me guess, you weren't wearing your safety harness."

Zinnia laughed. "Of course not."

"Go home, take some ibuprofen, ice it. You'll be fine." He looked around. "Or, if you're looking for something a little more . . . comforting . . ."

Zinnia was open to trying anything twice, but now was not the time. "I hit my head."

He took a pen from his breast pocket, and when he clicked it, a light erupted from the end. He waved it back and forth across Zinnia's eyes, the brightness of it making her cringe. He shook his head. "I don't think you have a concussion."

"I think it's safer if I go to the hospital," she said. "Just in case."

He looked around. Like he was making sure they were alone. "You sure about that? 'Cause, look, I'm not trying to mess around on something serious. But this is the kind of thing you're better off trying to walk off." He leaned forward, dropped his voice. "I'm trying to help you here."

"I get it," she said. "But my head is killing me, and I want to be careful."

He nodded. Sighed. Like he got it but felt bad she wasn't taking his advice. He patted the bed. "Climb on. Strap in."

Zinnia did as told, and the man disappeared to the front of the tram, to an enclosed compartment. She found a seat belt hanging down from the bed. Climbed on, looped it over herself, did the clasp. The tram took off, the ride so smooth it was like they were barely moving.

PAXTON

The lines for the elevator were long, the final wave of workers ready to tuck in for however long the update would take. It was like a rainbow had been smashed up and pushed into a pile. Paxton looped the lobby area again, making sure all the blues were in position.

He found Masamba, whom Paxton had made his unofficial second-in-command, on account of the fact that he seemed to give a shit about doing a good job. People were constantly asking Masamba to repeat himself, given his accent, but Paxton understood him just fine. He nodded to the tall, heavy man and asked, "You good?"

Masamba saluted. "Yes sir, captain sir."

Paxton laughed. "Please don't do that."

He went to salute again, to indicate he understood, but then stopped himself. "Okay."

Paxton's phone buzzed in his pocket with a text from Vikram.

Testing the mass text. Please ignore.

He didn't like Vikram having his personal cell. But fine, whatever, at least Paxton was a team leader, not one of the plebs just randomly assigned to stand in a spot, or worse, sent to their room.

The crowd wound down, only two elevator trips left, tops, before the lobby was cleared. Another text went out.

One ambulance tram en route to hospital. Otherwise, all trams stopped and accounted for. Blues, please make final sweep.

After a few moments another message popped up.

That chick headed to the hospital is fuckin' hot, man. I should go check on her. Give
her a little of my tender love and care.

Then:

Another text, with an employee-profile picture of Zinnia.

Paxton blinked. That couldn't be right. Why the hell was Vikram
sharing Zinnia's picture?

Then:

The systm has been haced. Hacked. ignore ignore ignore last message. That was
not Vikram repeat that was NOT VIKRAM WHO SENT THAT.

Paxton glanced around the lobby, like someone there might be
able to answer his questions: Zinnia was in an ambulance? Was she
hurt? How bad? He looked at his CloudBand, thinking he could radio
into Admin or Care to check, but wasn't sure who to call.

The last elevators were going up. The lobby was empty, save for
the blues. Paxton's leg shook. His body wanted to move and it was
manifesting through involuntary twitching.

The tram was down. But the emergency trams were still manned
and running. He went to Masamba. "You're in charge. You know the
drill?"

Masamba shook his head. "I don't know—"

"My friend just got transported to the hospital. I need to know
she's okay."

He saluted, stopped himself, then shrugged, committed to it. "I
got you. Go do what you have to do."

"Thanks," Paxton said, slapping him on the arm and taking off in
the direction of the closest emergency shuttle bay.

A MESSAGE FROM CLAIRE WELLS

A woman sits at a desk. Brilliant red hair, like flame. The desk is big, heavy, shiny. A statement desk. The desk is free of items. Behind the desk is a window looking onto a wooded setting. The trees are bare.

The woman has her hands folded on the desk. She smiles the smile of someone who doesn't understand the way a smile can be interpreted. She speaks as if speaking to children, carefully enunciating her words, in a downward trajectory.

Hello. My name is Claire Wells. And I want to start off by apologizing that you can't turn this off. I know you were all looking forward to a couple of minutes of free time during the software update, but frankly, I can't meet you all, and I thought this was the quickest and most efficient way to introduce myself. I promise, I won't be long.

You all know my dad, and what a great man he is. And you all know this is an incredibly tough time for my family. But my dad raised me to push on, even when things got hard, so I'm just here to tell you that even though my father will be passing along the torch, I plan to run Cloud just the way he did.

Like a family.

Just like my dad liked to visit MotherCloud facilities, I hope to do the same in the coming months. In fact, I'll be joining him for some of his farewell tour. So if you see me, feel free to say hello!

Claire raises her hand and gives an exaggerated and awkward wave.

Thank you for your time. Again, sorry for the interruption.

ZINNIA

The tram came to a stop at a small station and as Zinnia climbed off she asked, "You said something about comfort?"

Oblivion could be helpful. As a bargaining tool, or as a way to ingratiate herself with the dealers, or just a way to check out for the night. Didn't hurt to have on hand.

The tram driver looked around, made sure they were alone. Reached into his pocket and pressed something small and square into her palm. "My name is Jonathan. Look for me on Tuesdays around Live-Play."

"How much?" Zinnia asked, sticking her hand in her pocket.

"First one is free."

She wanted to ask him about the CloudBand exploit, but, time and place. She could always follow up. "Thanks."

Jonathan gave a little smile. "Follow the red line."

On the polished concrete floor was a red strip. Zinnia followed it down a long corridor, to a large room with a maze of roped stanchions and a series of teller windows. Only one of them was manned, and just a few people were waiting on line. Zinnia made her way along the circuitous path until she reached the end of it.

There were three people ahead of her. One, an older man, was bleeding from a head wound, holding a soaked-through wad of paper towels to his forehead. The second, a girl, was holding her stomach and doubled over in pain. At the window, speaking to the teller, was a man who looked like a detox case, a jumble of sweats and twitching.

A cave troll of a man sat behind the window and worked through everyone quickly. He got to Zinnia, at which point he sighed and rolled his eyes, shocked and appalled that he had another person to deal with.

"Malady?" he asked.

"Dislocated shoulder," Zinnia said. "Hit my head. Maybe a concussion."

Zinnia raised her arm to the scanner disc but saw her watch screen had gone blank. A gray line appeared, slowly crawling a path from left to right.

The man shook his head. "Guess we'll have to do this the old-fashioned way. Employee ID?"

Zinnia recited it and watched as he typed it into the computer. The hospital computers were still online, like she suspected. Score.

The man behind the glass shook his head. "You weren't wearing the harness."

"I know," she said. "Can I go in now? My head hurts."

He went back to typing, his hands flying across the keyboard. After a few moments he said, "Please proceed to room six, bed seventeen, and someone will be by to see you shortly."

The way he said *shortly* made it pretty clear the wait would be anything but. Zinnia walked through the swinging doors at the end of the row of windows and proceeded down a long hallway that smelled of spilled cleaning supplies. The floor was so shiny her sneakers squeaked. There was a series of gray doors with large blue numbers painted on them.

Door six opened into a long room of beds and curtains, most of the curtains pulled back, most of the beds empty. The room turned to the right at the end. There were two other people: the doubled-over girl, who seemed a little better now that she was on her side, and a young guy, feet crossed, playing on his phone.

Zinnia made for bed seventeen and climbed aboard. It was narrow and felt like a stone slab covered by a piece of thin foam padding. She looked around, saw a computer embedded into the wall across from her, with a little station underneath—roller desk and keyboard. Not bad, but also right across from her assigned bed, which was too close for her to be comfortable.

The man playing on his phone had his head shaved, the stubble dyed bright green, splotches of forest green on his scalp. She called over to him. "Hey."

He didn't look up from his phone.

"Hey!"

He didn't turn, didn't stop playing on his phone, but he did raise an eyebrow in response.

"How long since a nurse has been through here?" she asked.

"Hour at least," he said. "I doubt we'll be seen until the update is over and the full staff is back."

"Good," Zinnia said. "Going to take a nap if I have to wait, then."

The guy shrugged a little. Like, *Do whatever.*

Zinnia pulled the curtains around the bed and dropped to the floor, military-crawled underneath the beds and deeper down the corridor, taking it extra slow as she passed under the bed of the girl with the stomach issue. The longer she crawled the more her shoulder rasped in the joint, but she ignored it.

She stopped at the corner, looked down the hallway. No feet. She couldn't tell if any of the beds were occupied from down on the floor, and she didn't really like that, so she pushed herself up against the wall where it turned.

There was one nurse, tapping at a tablet computer. One bed, occupied, the person on it in the fetal position, curled up in a blanket, looking away.

Zinnia jerked back. Closed her eyes. Took a deep breath, then turned the corner and strode down the hallway. The nurse, a Latina with brown frizzy hair, looked up and said, "Sorry honey. I'll be over in a second."

"Actually, I'm headed in there," Zinnia said, pointing at the women's room. "But you ought to know, girl around the corner is in a lot of pain."

The nurse nodded, put down the tablet. "Sure. You okay?"

"I'm fine," she said. "But maybe you can check on her?"

The nurse took off, feet squeaking on the floor. Zinnia watched her disappear and reached into her pocket, took out the gopher. Hustled down the hallway until she found a circular desk full of computers. All of them still on. She selected the one closest to her, put the gopher into a free USB slot on the back.

She couldn't hear it, couldn't see it, but she could almost feel it— her little custom malware sliding through the system, pulling out the information she needed.

She turned toward the bathroom, counting in her head.

1:00

:59

:58

:57 . . .

The numbers broke apart as something heavy was laid across the back of her skull.

She hit the ground hard, barely getting her hands up in time to stop her face from smacking into the ground teeth first. She rolled, one foot planted, one foot up, ready.

Rick stood over her, his face red and swollen and bandaged, wielding an IV pole like a baseball bat.

Zinnia pushed herself back, tried to get away, stopped against a hard surface. He must have been the one lying on the bed next to the nurse.

"You fucking bitch," he said, raising the pole over his head, preparing to swing it down.

Zinnia shot her foot into his nuts. They gave under her heel. He doubled over and she struggled to her feet, falling over herself in the tight, awkward space. But he'd already gotten enough of his bearings back to shoot out his foot and catch her in the jaw.

That one made her see stars. She rolled, crawled, did anything she could to increase the space between them, and it was all going to shit, and worse, it was her fault.

She channeled that anger away from herself. She'd give it back to him.

She got to a knee, just as Rick was getting to his feet. Grabbed a bedpan and winged it at him. It caught him in the face, and while it wasn't heavy it surprised him, which was enough to knock him off his feet. Zinnia wanted to make a grab for the gopher but wasn't sure if enough time had passed yet. Most likely no, adrenaline dilating time. She should have looked at the clock on the wall when she planted it.

Back on her feet. Rick was a chump. A weak piece of shit. But he'd gotten in a good sucker shot—she might actually have a concussion now, the way it felt like she was standing on a rocking boat.

She looked behind her. No nurse. Maybe the sound didn't carry. Maybe she'd stepped away. Maybe she was afraid. She turned and found Rick getting up, so she charged, led with her knee into his face, and his head snapped back. He crashed to the floor, knocking a bed aside, and Zinnia looked for something, anything, she could use to restrain him, but came up empty.

Her belt. That'd have to do. She pulled it out, gave it a snap, but Rick stuck his foot out, making her trip and fall. She was still woozy from the head shot. Not making smart choices. She rolled onto her side, caught herself on a bed again, the space really and truly not designed for a goddamn fight, and Rick was standing, this time with the stool the nurse had been sitting on.

As the stool arced down toward her, Zinnia put her arms up. Sacrificed her forearms to protect her head.

This was going to hurt.

"Hey!"

She knew the voice. She knew it before she saw him. Paxton slammed into Rick, and the two of them tumbled to the floor. Zinnia pushed herself back, watched as Paxton straddled Rick, facing away from her, raised his fist and slammed it into Rick's face. There was a thud like a pumpkin hitting the floor.

This was about to end, after which Paxton wouldn't let her out of his sight. The nurse would come back. So Zinnia ignored the feeling of her brain rattling around her head, pushed herself up, and ran for the computer station, praying enough time had elapsed that the gopher had gone out and done its thing and come back.

She grabbed it.

Turned to see Paxton, twisted part of the way around, Rick prone underneath him.

He was staring at her.

PAXTON

Paxton stopped at the teller window. The old man behind it was looking down at something in his lap. Paxton slapped his palm on the glass so hard it shook. The man jerked up, nearly fell off his chair.

"Did a woman named Zinnia come through here?"

The man replied with a look of confusion.

Paxton held his hand up by his chin. "Yea tall. Bronze skin. Pretty."

The man nodded. Pointed toward the doors. "Sent her in a little while ago. Room six, I think?"

"Thanks."

Paxton hoofed it through the double doors, came onto a long corridor of beds. On one was a sullen teen staring at his phone and nothing short of a nuclear blast was going to get his attention. A little farther down was a girl on a bed, writhing in pain, and a nurse, ducking down next to it, like she was hiding from something. The nurse looked at Paxton and nearly passed out from relief. "Thank god you're here. Something's happening over there."

"Where?" Paxton asked.

There was a crash at the end of the corridor and around the corner. He ran down the aisle and made the turn, found a man holding a stool, ready to bring it down on someone. And on the floor, blood smeared on her face, was Zinnia.

Paxton saw red. He charged the man, put his full weight into him. It hurt Paxton but hurt the other guy more, as they tangled and rolled over each other, until Paxton was able to straddle him.

Situations like these, the best thing to do was restrain the person and wait for help to arrive.

As if that was even an option.

He balled up his fist and slammed it into the man's face. His eyes went wide, then flicked, like a light being turned out. After a moment Paxton recognized the feeling in his hand. The pain, radiating from the bones of his knuckles up to his elbow. Might have broken something.

He turned to check on Zinnia, found her on her feet, by a bank of computers fiddling with something on one of the monitors.

"What are you doing?" Paxton asked.

Zinnia turned. Looked at him. Confused. Upset? In pain? He couldn't tell. He was about to ask again.

And then she passed out.

ZINNIA

Zinnia folded to the floor in such a way as to protect her head. Let Paxton rush over to her, let him grab her and shake her, let him be worried and upset. It would distract, she hoped, from the chip she'd planted in her cheek, high up next to her teeth, where it raked against her gums.

She thought about pocketing it but feared that if he searched her, if she was admitted and had to surrender her clothes, or any number of a million reasons, she would lose it, and then she might as well just walk off the job because at this point it was getting to be a bit much.

This was exactly the reason she made her chipsets waterproof. A little more expensive, always worth it. She still had the oblivion in her pocket, but that she was okay parting with.

Paxton ran off to look for help. Zinnia stole a glance at Rick. Still on the floor.

He must have seen her plant the tracker. But things were about to get very uncomfortable for him, on an administrative level. A security guard had witnessed him assaulting a woman. You don't just walk away from that.

Though the way Cynthia described it, he was a known abuser. Did he have some kind of entrée with the company? Something that would protect him during this process?

Would he try to trade information on her?

There was a pair of scissors on the desk. She could see them now, in her head. She'd seen them during the scuffle, had tried to reach for them, but things were moving too quick. They had bright yellow plastic handles. They looked dull, like they might easily break, but the skin of the throat was a delicate membrane. She could claim he came to, tried to attack her again.

Before she could stand, Paxton came around the corner with the nurse and another man in blue, a rangy guy with a buzz cut. She shut her eyes, playing at being passed out again.

"Where the hell were you?" Paxton asked.

"I was just . . . I just . . ." The other blue.

"You were just what?" Paxton asked. "Napping on the job?"

"Please . . ."

"Don't 'please' me. You're ten different kinds of fucked. She could have gotten killed."

Zinnia felt Paxton's hands on her again, then another, smaller set, the nurse. Probing, checking for breaks, pulling her eyelid. Zinnia placed her palm against her forehead, blinked her eyes. They helped her to her feet, put her on a bed. Paxton asked, "Are you okay?"

She couldn't tell what he was thinking. He was concerned. That much she knew. It was a good start. "Yes," she said. "Just . . . I'm okay."

Paxton looked down at his watch at the same time Zinnia's buzzed. The update was complete, the smiley face now on the CloudBand, then dissolving into the usual watch face.

Zinnia's said: *Please report back for your shift.*

Paxton looked at it, too. "Ignore that." He turned to the nurse. "Keep an eye on her." Then he stepped to the side and began speaking into his CloudBand. He was walking away so Zinnia couldn't make out what he was saying.

The nurse shone a penlight in Zinnia's eyes. "Are you sure you're okay?"

"I don't know."

"Do you need something for the pain?"

"No." Of course she wanted something for the pain. She wanted to pop a tab of what was in her pocket. But now was not the time for med-head.

Paxton appeared back at her side. "My boss is going to be here in a few minutes. According to him a lot of shit has hit a lot of fans. But first, before that, do you know why this guy attacked you?"

Zinnia considered saying no. That it was random. Unexpected. She preferred that because it meant spending less time going through those shower interludes, and her acquiescing to Rick's demands, as if she were some weak little thing that didn't have a choice otherwise.

But that chip was still in her cheek and she didn't want Paxton to think about it.

So she told him what had happened.

She left out the part about putting Rick here in the first place, but the story worked, because both Paxton and the nurse, their faces fell further and further. Paxton, in particular, kept glancing at Rick, lying there on the floor, on his back staring at the ceiling, just knowing he was done for. It seemed like a struggle for Paxton to not go over and lay his boot across the man's face.

At the end of it, Paxton said, "You should have told me."

The way he said it, it was like a scold, which Zinnia did not like.

"Sometimes it's best to leave well enough alone," she said.

He shook his head. "You should have told me."

Except this time, it sounded sadder. It raised complicated feelings in Zinnia's gut. Feelings she couldn't describe to herself but knew she didn't like.

From there, the room turned into an explosion of people. Lots of questions. Rick was put on a bed and strapped to it. An old man with a face like a meteorite and a tan uniform—the infamous Dobbs—quizzed her on what happened. No judgment, no nothing, just wanted the story. She ran through the version that worked best for her, and in the interim, put together bits and pieces from the questions he asked, as well as the conversations happening around her.

The security officer assigned to the ward, Goransson, had been goofing off or maybe napping in another room. Dobbs admitted that the officer in charge of the update process had accessed her employee profile, which was flagged when she came to Care, and sent out a text saying something crude about her. He'd meant to send it to a single person and instead blasted it out on a security-wide chain.

Which was why Paxton was able to arrive at the right time.

They seemed to be taking her complaint against Rick seriously. She hated to have to play the victim role, but at least he'd pay for it. She was about to mark this down in the win column when she heard Rick yelling from the bed that was being wheeled out of the ward. "Ask her. *Ask her!*"

Dobbs, from where he was standing across the room, talking to Rick, put his head down and his hands on his hips, shook it back and forth, and strolled over to Zinnia's bedside.

"Sorry to have to ask this," he said. "He says you were messing around with one of the computers when he found you. I'm not inclined to believe a shitbird, but I have to at least ask the question."

Zinnia felt the sharp edges of the chip against her gum.

"I was heading to the bathroom when he hit me," she said. "I have no idea what he's talking about."

Dobbs nodded, happy with the response. Over his shoulder, Paxton stared. She didn't like the way Paxton was staring.

PAXTON

Dobbs put his hands on his hips, digging his fists in, almost like he wanted to put his hands inside himself.

"Vikram, that dumb son of a bitch," Dobbs said. "I'll bust him down after this. Goransson, too." He sighed, surveyed the commotion in the medical ward. "You, I'm not so sure about."

"Sir?" Paxton asked.

"You abandoned your post," he said. "Be straight with me now. You got a thing with this woman?"

"We've been seeing each other, yes," he said.

Dobbs nodded. "Pretty."

Paxton flushed at the mark of approval.

"So you left your post during an important assignment," Dobbs said. "And if you hadn't, that shitbird would have bashed that poor woman's skull in."

"About him," Paxton said. "Zinnia said he did this a lot. Were there any complaints lodged against him? Anything like that?"

"None that I know of," he said. "Got to look into it a little further. System only just came back up."

"Well, that's a problem. Because if this is something he made a habit of, then you better believe I'm going to make as much noise as it takes to get him turfed and put in prison."

Dobbs nodded slowly, chewing something over. Paxton wasn't sure what. Mandarin was easier to read than Dobbs. After a few moments Dobbs spoke again, moving in and lowering his voice. "Here's what I need from you. Are you listening?"

"I'm listening."

"I need you to be a team player. Can you be a team player?"

"How?"

"I need you to tell your woman that this is going to be handled," he said. "That this asshole will be expelled from Cloud and within the next ten minutes or so, he'll be completely unhireable anywhere else in the country. Vikram will pay a price, too. But I'm going to need something in return."

"What's that?"

"She doesn't kick up a fuss. I know she's probably a little rattled right now, a bit knocked around, which is where you come in." Dobbs put his hand on Paxton's shoulder. "I need you to convey to her how much of a pain in the ass this would be, taking it to the mat the way she might want to. Important thing is that justice will get served, just in a way that makes everyone's life easier."

Paxton's mouth filled with sand. His first instinct was to tell Dobbs to fuck off. He took a deep breath, thought about it rationally.

Divorcing himself from the personal connection, it made sense. Keep things contained.

But he felt like he was betraying Zinnia. Telling her to sit and fold her hands, to stay quiet. What if she didn't want to? What if a fuss was exactly what she wanted to kick up? It wasn't right for him to stand in the way of that.

"Think you can handle that?" Dobbs asked.

"I'll do what I can."

Dobbs squeezed his shoulder. "Thanks, son. I won't forget that. Now you go be with your woman. Make sure she's okay. You two can have the day off, rest of today and tomorrow, all right?"

"Are you sure?"

"Absolutely. Consider it my gift to you. You've both been through a lot."

Paxton didn't know what he had been through, but he was happy to have the day off. He smiled, without realizing he was smiling, and then wiped the expression from his face. Dobbs nodded and sauntered off to put out another fire.

Zinnia was standing against the bed by the time he reached her. She was holding herself in the manner of injured people: delicately, as though if she moved too fast, she would shatter. A bruise was building steam under her eye and there was a scratch on her cheek. Her knuckles were bandaged, which made Paxton think about his own throbbing fist. He flexed it. Still hurt, but probably not broken.

"So," Paxton said. "It's been a day, huh?"

Zinnia's lip curled. A laugh rattled her chest even though no sound came out of her mouth, just little bursts of air. "You could say that."

"So everything's taken care of," he said. "You're off shift today and tomorrow. Me, too. I heard the doc say you're in the clear. You want to get the hell out of here?"

"Yeah," Zinnia said. "That'd be nice."

Paxton ignored the urge to kiss her, to put his arm around her, to do any of a million things that might be deemed inappropriate in that setting, but he did stick out his arm and let her take it, thinking that offering a little support, at least, was within the bounds of reason. Paxton cut a path through the people milling about.

They made their way onto the tram. The bruise on Zinnia's face wasn't easy to hide. A bruised woman escorted by a security guard. Of course people were looking.

They reached Maple and made their way up to Zinnia's room. She stepped inside and Paxton thought for a second about leaving, letting her have some time to herself, but she held the door for him so he could follow. She leaned against the counter as she stripped off her shirt and bra, ran her hands down her body, looking for bruises or other injuries. Paxton looked away. Not that he thought he had to. It just felt rude, given the current state of things.

After a few moments he asked, "Do you need anything?"

"A hundred vodkas and a pint of ice cream."

"The ice cream I can handle." Paxton paused. "That might be too much vodka."

"Vodka and ice cream would make me the happiest person in the world."

"On it," Paxton said, leaving the apartment, hitting the promenade, happy to be out of that small space. There were conversations he didn't want to have. Not yet, at least. He went to the liquor store first, to get the vodka, wishing he had asked if she had a preferred brand, but then remembered what she usually ordered in the bar, so he got that, and then to a convenience store, for a pint of ice cream—that was easy, she liked chocolate chip cookie dough—and a prepackaged deli sandwich for himself.

The whole time his head buzzed. Because he had to now try to convince her to trust that Dobbs would handle it and drop any kind of idea she had about pursuing this asshole through official channels.

But more than that, something else about this didn't add up right.

The guy, Rick, had claimed Zinnia was messing with a computer before he attacked her. And Paxton couldn't deny that after he'd hit Rick, when he turned, Zinnia was definitely standing at the computer bank, doing something. He wasn't sure what.

The look on her face, like he'd interrupted her.

The dot. The CloudPoint door.

Little things, like fingers, poking at his brain.

ZINNIA

Zinnia pulled the gopher out of her cheek and dove for her laptop. The closest place to get booze was toward the middle of the promenade, so she had at least ten minutes before Paxton would get back up, and she couldn't wait. She needed to know. She needed something to push back against the shame and anger of Rick getting one up on her with that sucker shot.

She dried the chip off and slid it into her laptop, let the machine work for a couple of seconds. She'd designed the bug to drop similar types of files into different folders so they were easier to sort.

Zinnia was most interested in the folder with the maps. She opened it and flipped through, breathless, her fingers slipping on the screen. Electrical schematics. Waterworks. Vaguely helpful. Finally, she came across the tram system. There was something off about it. Something different from the maps that were plastered all over Cloud.

The water, waste, and energy processing facilities were tucked into the southeast corner of the campus, a tight cluster of buildings served by a tram that left from Incoming but didn't connect with the rest of the system.

Which was the entire problem. She couldn't get on that tram. No access for reds.

But in the tangle of tram lines, she spotted one that wasn't accounted for on the official map. It went from the waste processing facility directly to Live-Play. A garbage chute, maybe?

She'd wandered all over Live-Play. She'd seen no tram entrance other than the main one on the lower level that connected into the entire system, plus the emergency lines. She zoomed in on the termination of the line, tried to guess where in Live-Play it might be, but the stores weren't marked. Somewhere on the northwest side.

She would find it. Just seeing it made this entire stupid day worth it.

PAXTON

Paxton handed over the ice cream and vodka and Zinnia poured two glasses, offered one to him. He took it even though he didn't want it. Zinnia put on the television, which first blared a commercial about a new low-fat brand of ice cream that apparently tasted just like real ice cream, and then Zinnia flipped to a music channel. Some sort of orchestral electronic music, from a band Paxton both didn't recognize and could barely pronounce. But he liked it. It was blood-pressure-lowering music.

She flopped onto the futon, put her vodka on the bedside table, and pulled the top off the ice cream, tossing it next to the glass. She stuck in a spoon, carved off a large chunk, crammed it in her mouth. Paxton sat next to her and she held the ice cream toward him, the spoon sticking out of it. He waved it off, went at his sandwich instead.

"I'm sorry I didn't get there sooner," Paxton said.

"I'm glad you got there at all."

"I wish you would have told me."

"Let's not talk about that."

"Okay."

"So." She put down the ice cream, picked up the glass. Downed it. Got up to pour another. "What's next?"

"Well." Paxton leaned forward, put his arms on his knees. Tried to fold inward, away from the conversation he didn't want to have. "Dobbs thinks it would be better to avoid going through official channels. Said it'll be a whole big thing. But he promised the guy who attacked you would be fired, and Vikram, he would get demoted."

Zinnia reached into the mini-fridge, pulled out a handful of crushed ice, and dropped it into the glass, the frozen water clinking.

"I want you to know, we'll do this the way you want to do it," Paxton said. "I don't care what Dobbs thinks. I have your back."

Zinnia cracked the vodka and poured a few fingers into the glass. Placed the bottle back down and took a sip.

"But I can see his point," Paxton said, wincing. "Path of least resistance and all that. The important thing is, they'll suffer. No need for us to suffer, too. Or, at least, for you to suffer more."

Zinnia turned. Her face was a blank stretch of beach. Paxton had no sense of how to interpret it. What she might be thinking. How big of a mistake he'd just made. He was considering standing, speaking, doing anything other than sitting and staring, when Zinnia nodded. She returned to the futon, slid over until her head was on his shoulder.

"Path of least resistance," she said, before digging the spoon into the ice cream again.

Tension rolled off Paxton's shoulders. He told himself it was the best thing, for himself, for her, for Dobbs, for everyone. And he considered asking her about the computer bank but then thought he'd done enough talking, and he was tired, so he put down the sandwich and took the pint of ice cream from Zinnia, his fingers clasping around hers for a moment.

"Hey," she said.

"Yeah."

She looked up, into his eyes. The way you do when you really want someone to hear. "Thank you." And she reached her lips to his, and he forgot about everything else except for the beat of his heart in his chest.

GIBSON

Earlier today the employees of Cloud got to meet my daughter, Claire, in a special video that played during a routine software update (you know, so they might actually pay attention to it!).

I wanted to share that video with you all here, so you could meet her, too. I think she does a real fine job of introducing herself. Makes me proud like I can't even explain, to see her like this, taking a leadership role in the company.

And I want to say, to anyone who thinks a woman can't run a company the size of Cloud: to hell with you. I wish I were being facetious but I've had a few folks say to me that maybe she might not be up to the challenge. I don't know what kind of people y'all spend your time around, but the women in my life are strong as hell. Claire and Molly don't need me standing behind them, fighting their fights for them.

Since the day I built Cloud, I promised no more of the good-old-boy atmosphere that'd been so prevalent in the workforce for such a long time. Men and women would be paid the same, and I'm pretty sure Cloud forced the end of the wage gap, another legacy I'm incredibly proud to have.

It is very important to me that we support and respect the women in our lives. Because, let's be honest—without them, where would we be? Without Molly I'd be living in a ditch somewhere. Without Claire to push me to want to build a better world for her, and then her children, Cloud might not be the company it is today.

Anyway, here's that video. I'm proud of you, kiddo.

(Oh, and just ignore that little bit at the beginning. Like I said, it ran during the software update.)

Hello. My name is Claire Wells. And I want to start off by apologizing that you can't turn this off. . . .

ZINNIA

Zinnia's cell phone buzzed.

It woke her from half sleep—her head throbbing—and she thought it might be Paxton's, because her cell phone never buzzed, but then she remembered Paxton had left, apologizing profusely but reminding her he couldn't sleep on the thin bed, that he was too light a sleeper, just like he did every night.

And just like every night, she hated how much she wanted him to stay, but tonight most especially. She didn't need protecting, but sometimes it was nice to end the day with an arm around you.

When she realized the buzzing was real and it was actually her phone, her heart froze in her chest. She scrambled for the table by her feet, where her phone was plugged in next to her CloudBand, and found a text message from "Mom."

When are you coming home, honey? We miss you.

Zinnia fell back into a sitting position, staring at the phone. A coded message from her employer.

It meant someone wanted to meet her, in person, off campus.

Zinnia put the phone down and placed her head in her hands and sighed, that feeling of victory from having discovered the secret tram line now completely evaporated.

DAY TRIP 7

CLOUDBAND NOTIFICATION

Please be advised that two weeks from today, Gibson Wells is scheduled to visit
our MotherCloud. This visit will coincide with our yearly remembrance of the
Black Friday Massacres. More information to follow. . . .

ZINNIA

Zinnia didn't bother turning on the overhead. Pale yellow light
streamed through the window. She glanced at the near-empty bottle
of vodka on the counter. Her brain felt twisted up in cling wrap that
was slowly being cinched tighter. She wasn't sure if it was the vodka
or yesterday's blow to the head. Maybe a little from each column.

The lack of sleep didn't help.

She'd drifted off a few times, when her body couldn't handle the
pressure of being awake anymore, but mostly she stared at the tapestries hanging over the bed and wondered why in the holy fuck her
employer wanted to meet with her.

That had never happened before. Not once. Not before a job was
done. Even an assignment change could be done through encrypted
message. This meant what had to be said was too sensitive to transmit.

Or it was something else.

Zinnia didn't like something else.

There were cars available for rental in Incoming. She logged in to
the system on the television and clicked through, found the wait to be
three months, unless you paid a premium, and the premium would
wipe out her account. She considered what it would take to just walk
out of the facility, get far enough away to safely make contact with

her employer and agree on a meeting spot. But there wasn't any cover that would provide shade for miles around this place.

Which was why she had a Paxton in her life.

She pulled out her phone, fired off a text.

Day trip? Would love to get the hell out of here for the day. But car rental waiting list is too long. Any strings you can pull?

She didn't have to wait long.

I'll do my best. More soon.

Zinnia smiled. She threw on a robe and made her way to the women's room so she could shower. She'd probably need a shower when she got back, too, because she felt as if she still had Rick on her and that feeling probably wouldn't go away any time soon. She wanted to stand under the hot water until her skin stripped off.

Two shower stalls were taken, and sitting on a bench was Hadley, a white fuzzy towel wrapped around her torso, pink neon flip-flops on her feet. Cynthia was sitting next to her, in her wheelchair, naked but for a towel, rubbing Hadley's bare shoulder. She was whispering something to the girl, who was nodding along.

Cynthia looked up as Zinnia stepped into the room and did an exaggerated double take. It took Zinnia a second to remember why: her own banged-up face. Cynthia frowned and took her hand off Hadley's shoulder.

"What happened to you?" she asked.

Zinnia shrugged. "Got in a fight."

"Lord . . ."

Hadley peeked up. Zinnia gave her a little smile. "You should see the other guy."

Zinnia held Hadley's glance. She wanted to say it without saying it, but Hadley dropped her eyes to her lap. Zinnia walked over to a far bench, opened a locker, put the clothes she would change into inside. Cynthia gave Hadley another reassuring pat on the shoulder and rolled off to the far end of the bathroom, to the handicapped shower stall.

Zinnia walked to a free shower stall, was about to pull her towel off and place it on the hook on the wall, when she looked back at Hadley, still curled up on herself, like a cat, staring at the floor. Zinnia walked over and sat across from her, their knees almost touching.

Hadley didn't look up. Didn't say anything. She seemed to shrink away.

"Stop that," Zinnia said, her voice quiet, afraid Cynthia would overhear and try to intervene.

Hadley looked up, one eye visible through the hair hanging limp over her face.

"Don't be afraid of him," she said. "Then he wins. And what's going to happen is, the idea of him will grow into a monster you can't kill. You'll lie in bed every night until exhaustion takes over. And he's not worth it. He's not invincible." Zinnia leaned in, dropped her voice even more. "Like I said, you should see him right now."

Hadley paused, as if she were shocked by the words, but then some life came to her spine. She revealed a little more of her other eye through the veil of hair.

"Quit it with that whiny baby bullshit."

Hadley jerked a little, the strength she had developed in that moment fading, and Zinnia felt a little bad, finishing that with such a strong forward thrust. But the girl needed to hear it. One day she'd even be thankful.

Zinnia went to a free stall, where she stepped under the blast of water. It spread warmth over her skin. She pressed the soap dispenser in the wall and lathered up and realized she felt a different kind of warmth, this one spreading through her from the inside, and it seemed to start somewhere in the region between her lungs, on the left side of her chest.

PAXTON

Paxton knocked on the open door, peeked his head in. "Got a second, boss?"

Dobbs looked up from the tablet on his desk. "Thought I told you to take the day off, son."

"Got a favor to ask."

Dobbs nodded. "Shut the door."

Paxton closed the door and leaned against it, arms crossed. Wondering if he should lead with the request or if he should tell Dobbs how the talk had gone last night. Probably the latter. That would put him in the man's good graces. He hoped. But then Dobbs made the decision easy. He sat back in his chair, the plastic joints creaking, and asked, "Did you talk to your woman?"

"I did," Paxton said. "She'll be leaving well enough alone."

"Good," Dobbs said, his face flat. "That's good. I'm real happy to hear that."

"But he's gone, right? And Vikram is somewhere else?"

"All done."

"Great."

"So . . ."

"Right." Paxton stepped forward, arms still wrapped around himself. He was a little afraid to ask, because it meant asking for special treatment, which he wasn't sure he had earned. And anyway, special treatment always came with some kind of caveat. It was a promise you'd eventually have to make good on. But it was for Zinnia, and not him, which was enough to press on. "My wom— Zinnia wants to get off campus for the day. Drive around a bit. But the rentals, there's a long wait for them. Any chance—"

"Consider it done," Dobbs said, waving his hand. "Head on over to Incoming, they'll have a car waiting for you. Security gets a discounted rate. Where you headed?"

"No idea. All I know is, she wants to take a little road trip, we both have the day off, and considering the day she had yesterday, I ought to accommodate, right?"

"Smart man," Dobbs said. Then he raised his wrist and tapped his watch. "See the news this morning?"

Paxton's heart gave a little skip. "I did. The man himself, coming here."

"That he is. As I'm sure you can imagine, that's going to be a hell of a time for us."

"I bet."

"Dakota will be taking point among the blues, naturally," he said, looking out to the bullpen, like she might be standing over Paxton's shoulder. "Going to need a few good people backing her up."

Paxton considered the question. It sounded silly to ask but he asked it anyway. "Am I good people?"

Dobbs got up from his seat, walked to the window overlooking the office. Behind the glass, blues went to and fro, oblivious to the two of them looking out. He stood close to Paxton, close enough Paxton could smell the man's aftershave. Woodsy and astringent. "I'm still not thrilled you abandoned your post yesterday. But at the end of the day, I'm not a process guy. I'm a results guy." Dobbs looked at Paxton. "I like to think I get a good read on people and I got a good read on you. You get up and move when a lot of people are inclined to just sit there."

"Thank you, sir," he said. "I want to do a good job."

Dobbs nodded and returned to his seat. "Talk to Dakota when you come in tomorrow. Tell her I suggested it. But it's her team, her call."

"Okay," Paxton said. "I will. And thank you."

Dobbs dropped his chin, returned his attention to the tablet. "Welcome. Now go have fun on your day off. You know how rare those are around here."

Paxton closed the door behind him and smiled. Completely involuntary. But the feeling had built up in him so much he had to let it out somewhere, and he couldn't hoot and holler, so he just wore it on his face like that fourth star he maybe hadn't earned yet but might have been closer to achieving.

It was more than that, too. The human brain did not have the capacity to count the number of times he had wished he could give Gibson Wells a piece of his mind. Tell him about how Cloud had shut him down.

And now it looked like he might have that chance.

Which of course would piss away all his stars.

But it wasn't like he wanted to make a career of this place anyway.

ZINNIA

The dash of the electric car breathed a steady stream of cool air. Outside, the parched earth glowed with radiated heat. Zinnia glanced in her mirrors, watched the drones filling up the sky, like a swarm of insects. The boxy protuberances of the MotherCloud disappeared under the horizon. Ahead of them, a blank stretch of road, flat land on either side, nothing but straight as far as she could see.

It felt good to be out of her polo shirt. It made the day even more special, getting a break from the uniform. She'd found an airy romper at the bottom of her drawer that she'd forgotten she'd packed. Paxton was in blue shorts and a white T-shirt that went a little high on his arms, showing off the curve of his triceps.

"So where we headed?" Paxton asked, fiddling with the incline of the passenger seat, searching for a comfortable position.

"Not sure," Zinnia said. "I just need some sky."

They were clear enough of the facility that she felt comfortable keying in a response, tapping at the phone with her left hand, her right on the wheel. *Soon, I hope.*

Zinnia put down her phone and realized it had been more than two months since they'd arrived and this was the first she was stepping foot outside. Or as outside as you can get in the relatively safe environs of a climate-controlled vehicle.

"Do we have water?" he asked.

"Plenty in the trunk."

"Should have brought my sunglasses."

Zinnia touched a button next to the rearview mirror. A small compartment yawned open, with a row of sunglasses. "Rental guy said we might need them. While you were in the bathroom. You certainly got us the VIP treatment."

"It seems like I'm back in with the brass."

"Because you got me to agree to not press charges?"

Paxton took a couple of seconds before answering, "Yes." After another few: "Is that . . . okay?"

Zinnia shrugged. "It would have been too much trouble." She didn't want to tell him it was her preference, but also, she saw nothing wrong with letting Paxton stew a little bit. Because in most other situations, no, that would not have been okay. It did sour his heroism a tad.

Zinnia reached into the compartment and pulled out a pair of sunglasses. Thick, plastic, bright blue frames. Paxton followed. The other pair was white, feminine, pointed in the corners like cat eyes, but he shrugged and put them on. Turned to her and gave a big grin, showing off all his teeth.

"They look good," Zinnia said, letting out a deep laugh after she tried to hold it in, found she couldn't, and then realized she didn't care.

"They fit my style."

"They go with the shirt, at least."

The sky cleared, the drones thinning out. The sun shone in the car, raising the temperature. Paxton nodded up at them. "Kind of incredible, isn't it?"

"What? The drones?"

"Yeah, I mean, look at them all up there. Back and forth all day, they don't crash into each other. At least I don't think they do. Carrying all that stuff . . ."

"You sound very wistful. Did you have a pet drone as a kid?"

"No, just . . ." He trailed off, then shrugged. "They're cool. That was the thing that put Cloud over the top, right? Once they were able to pull off drone delivery, that was the end of online retail. No one could compete. I wonder what that must be like. To come up with something world-changing like that."

"Eggs are cool, too."

Paxton's voice dropped. "C'mon. That's not nice."

Zinnia's scalp burned. She looked at Paxton, who was looking out the window, his head turned as far from her as he could get it.

"I'm sorry," she said. "Bad joke."

When he didn't answer, she thumbed the dial on the air conditioner, trying to find a balance between tepid and frigid. She clicked on the radio, not so loud as to discourage conversation, though she wasn't really looking for it either.

She checked her phone. No response.

"So how are you doing, with everything?" Paxton asked.

Zinnia thought about apologizing again but figured this meant he wanted to drop it. "Car handles nice. Seat is pretty comfortable. I don't like the gas pedal. It's sticky."

"You know what I mean."

Zinnia did. Would have preferred it if he had gotten the hint and left it. She watched as the odometer increased a tenth of a mile at a time. "It happened and it's over."

"If you want to talk . . ."

Zinnia waited for more. Nothing came. "I'm fine." She turned to Paxton and gave him a brief *It's cool* smile.

"So now that we're out of that damn building . . . what do you think about all this?" Zinnia asked.

"All what?"

"Cloud. Living at your job. Being rated on a damn star system. It's not really what I expected."

"What did you expect?"

Zinnia thought about it. After a moment she went chasing after an analogy she thought might fit. "You know how when you go to a fast-food restaurant? And you've got this idea in your head of what it's going to be like? From the commercials. Like, the burger looks perfect on television, but when you open the wrapper, it's just a mess? Everything is smashed and smeared and gray. It looks like someone sat on it."

"Yeah."

"Kinda like that. I thought it would be nicer. But it just feels like a fast-food burger. I can eat it but I sort of wish I didn't have to."

"Interesting way to put it."

"What do you think?"

"I don't think CloudBurgers deserve to be the subject of your derision."

"Oh, so you got jokes now?"

A bus passed on the other side, headed toward Cloud. Fresh grist. Zinnia tried to see inside, see how many people were aboard, what they looked like, but the sun glared off the side of the bus so bright it hurt her eyes, even with the sunglasses on.

Paxton leaned back in his seat. Stretched his arms over his head, arched his lower back. "I miss my company. I miss being in charge and running something. But this is better than the alternative. It's better than nothing."

"You going to have words with the big man?"

"Wells?"

"He's going to visit, isn't he?"

Paxton laughed. "I've been thinking about it. Dobbs even wants me involved with the protection detail. It would still have to be approved by Dakota, because she's in charge of that, but I've been thinking about it."

"So, you tell him off, and how long is it before they send you packing?"

"Seconds, probably. Maybe less."

Zinnia laughed. "I'd love to see that."

"You want to see me lose my job?"

"You know what I mean."

The phone buzzed.

Great! Let's try to sort something out soon. Here's a picture of me and Dad to hold you over until we get to see you again.

Attached was a stock photo of a black couple who were clearly not her parents, their skin tone being so much darker than hers, but whatever. She clicked the photo and saved it, eyes darting between the phone and the wheel, and dropped it into an encrypted app.

"Who's that?" Paxton asked.

"Mom. Checking in."

"Tell her I said hi."

Zinnia laughed. "Sure."

As she suspected, there was a string of code embedded in the photo, which the app revealed to be a map, displaying a pulsing blue dot about twenty miles east. It looked like there was a highway system coming up, and as if on cue, something jutted on the horizon. A blip on the flat landscape. Zinnia pressed the pedal a little, sped up toward it.

Highways were dicey, a lot of them so poorly maintained they were crumbling, but it didn't look too bad, so she turned onto the entrance ramp.

"So how's your plan going?" Paxton asked.

Zinnia stopped breathing for a moment. But then she remembered her cover story, and she let the feeling of panic settle. "So far so good. Saving my money."

"Right, right," Paxton said, trailing off like there was something else he wanted to ask. Zinnia wondered if she should push it, but then she didn't need to. "Can I ask you something?"

"You just did."

"Ha, ha. Yesterday. That guy, Rick. He said you were messing with one of the computer terminals."

"I wasn't."

"But after I got there . . . I thought I saw . . ."

"Saw what?"

"It looked like you were back at it. At the computers. After I got him off you."

Zinnia breathed in deep, breathed out deeper. Tried to make this sound painful so maybe he would drop it. But he didn't. He held on to that silence like it was a weapon. She lowered her voice when she answered, hoped it would make her sound vulnerable. Hoped if she sounded that way, he would take a few steps back. "I was panicked. I was looking for a pair of scissors or something. Anything I could use to defend myself. He tried to kill me." She threw him a little glance, dropped her voice. "I was worried he might kill you."

"Okay," Paxton said, processing. Then again, "Okay."

"What would I be doing at the computers?"

"I have no idea," Paxton said. "Truly, I don't. But he said it, and then what I saw . . . I'm sorry. And there was this other thing . . . it's been bugging me."

She tightened her grip on the wheel. "What other thing?"

"I mean, it's probably nothing. . . ."

"No, it's not nothing, or else you wouldn't have mentioned it."

Another stretch of silence, during which Zinnia's heart tried to climb up her throat and out her mouth. Paxton said, "I shouldn't have said anything."

"But you did."

"That first night we went out," he said. "In the arcade. I was sur-veilling someone. For work. And when we were reviewing the location tracking data later . . ." He looked out the window again. "You followed me."

Again, Zinnia didn't know what to say. It was as if her brain were a record and it had suddenly come off the track, just spinning. Fuck. How long had he been sitting on that?

"Your ass," she said.

"What?"

She dropped her hand into his lap. Rubbed his thigh, her fingertips coming within an inch of the bulge at the front of his shorts. The fabric stretched. "I was checking out that fine ass. There. You've embarrassed me. Are you happy?"

Paxton put his hand on Zinnia's, and she thought he might pull it onto his dick, but he just held it. "I'm sorry. And you shouldn't be embarrassed. I was checking out your ass all night."

Zinnia laughed as he leaned over and kissed her shoulder, wet lips pressing to her bare skin, and it felt cool when he pulled away. The way she laughed probably sounded to him like a playful, sexy reaction, but the truth was, she couldn't believe how easy that was.

"I'm sorry, I wasn't trying to spy on you," she said. "It was just there. Are you mad?"

"It's a little weird, but it's fine."

A sign appeared over the highway. Sun-bleached to sea-mist green, the words indecipherable. Another two miles and they saw evidence of civilization. A crumbling gas station on the side of the highway. A row of low-slung buildings, old businesses now empty, the signs faded or fallen, the parking lots full of weeds. She checked her phone. The dot was in this town.

Zinnia clicked her blinker, then giggled to herself, wondering why she even needed to, as they hadn't seen a car in the twenty minutes since they'd gotten on the highway. She drifted into the exit lane and then down the ramp. A couple of turns later, they were traveling down a wide street, the buildings on either side no more than two stories tall.

Zinnia craned her neck, looking for the address. And she was thrilled when she found it.

A bookshop. She always looked for bookshops in towns like these. The ghost town they'd trudged through on the day of the interview, it didn't have one, and it had made her sad. This was a corner spot, big dusty bay windows, the sign over the door: FOREST AVENUE BOOKS.

She saw something else, too.

Something in the corner of her eye. A mote of dust, maybe, or a furtive bit of movement on the roof of the building. An animal? She stopped the car, looked at the edge of the building, where it fell off to blue sky. Waiting for something to break that straight line.

"What?" Paxton asked.

Her eyes playing tricks. Reflected sunlight. Her brain overloaded, being out in the wide-open world. She still had a headache. Low-level concussion for sure.

"Nothing," she said. "Can we check out the bookstore?"

Paxton shrugged. "Sure."

Zinnia nosed the car into an alleyway a few storefronts down, between buildings where there was some shade, noon still a few hours off. She turned off the car and climbed into the choking heat. Her skin erupted in sweat immediately. Paxton groaned. "What a day to be outside."

"Are there good days to be outside?"

"Fair."

They walked up the alley, back to the main strip, sticking to the shadows at the edges of the buildings, past an antique shop and a deli and a hardware store until finally, they got to the bookshop. The space was bigger than the outside indicated, narrow but headed so far back she couldn't see the end of it in the gloom. She jiggled the knob.

"Sure we should be doing this?" Paxton asked.

"C'mon," she said. "Live dangerously."

Zinnia dropped to her knee, pulled a set of hairpins out of her hair, and got to work on the lock.

"Are you kidding?" Paxton asked.

"What?" Zinnia asked, working the first pin into the mechanism, all the way to the back, then giving it a bend down, so she had some leverage to turn the tumbler.

"This is illegal."

"Is it?" she asked, using the other hairpin to move the lock's pins into place. "No one's been in this place in years. Who's going to bust me, you? I don't think your jurisdiction extends this far."

Paxton leaned down to get a closer look. "Have you done this before?"

"You never know what you might find," Zinnia said, struggling with old, cranky metal. "Old books. Out-of-print stuff you can't get anymore. Think of it as urban spelunking."

"What do you do?" he asked. "Sell them?"

"No, dummy. I read them."

"Oh."

When the last pin clicked, Zinnia gave the bent hairpin a hard turn, and the lock screeched as it twisted. The door sprung open. She stood and put out her hand. "Ta-da."

"I'm impressed," Paxton said. "Though I'm not sure what Dobbs would think, knowing I'm spending time around a criminal."

Ha ha, yeah, thought Zinnia.

She picked an aisle and wandered down it, found the shelves were half-full. She was trying to put some space between her and Paxton and figured on hanging around the store long enough that he would get bored and wander off. Her contact would be smart enough to wait for the right opportunity.

A lot of the books toward the front held no interest for her: cookbooks, nonfiction, kid stuff. But as she got farther back, toward the fiction section, she found things that spoke to her. Covers that jumped through the layers of dust. She felt like an archaeologist. She made a small pile of books, anything that looked interesting, to bring back.

As she approached the rear of the store, the air grew thick. That old bookstore smell—the must and old paper, amplified by endless heating cycles from the sun. Paxton called from the front of the store. "I'm going to poke around outside a bit. Get some air. See what else there is around town."

Perfect. "Okay," Zinnia said. "I'll be done in a few."

She listened to him walk to the front, open and close the door. She jogged to the rear of the store, where she found a desk and a dusty cash register, the cash tray pulled out and upended, empty save for a few pennies scattered across the floor. Her phone buzzed, another text message coming in, which pulled her attention away for a moment, so she didn't react in time to the creak of the floorboards behind her.

And then there was a hard click. Metal on metal.

Not that she needed the verification, but something cold and hard pressed to the base of her skull. Pointing up, so whoever it was, they were shorter than she was.

A female voice. "Are you with them?"

PAXTON

"Mr. Paxton, I'm Gibson Wells—"

Wrong, damn it. Breathe.

"Mr. Wells. My name is Paxton. And before I worked here at Cloud, I was the owner . . . no . . . I was the CEO of a company called the Perfect Egg. It was a small American business that I worked very hard to build, and Cloud's constant demand for deeper and deeper discounts . . ."

Too long. The words felt like marbles in his mouth. Open with a strong statement. Keep it direct.

"Mr. Wells, you say you're for the American worker, but you destroyed my business."

Paxton nodded to himself. That ought to make Wells take notice. He wiped the sweat from his brow. Stepped out of the sun and into the shade. It was getting toward noon so the supply was running low. He considered stepping into the bookstore again, but that place gave him a bad feeling. There was a scuttling sound in there, somewhere. Rats maybe.

He went back to the car, circled around it, and continued down the alley, wondering where it would lead. Another block, maybe. Instead he found a loading bay and parking lot and the bare backs of the buildings. Weeds everywhere, huge stalks shooting out of the pavement like fireworks.

There was a sound behind him, footsteps crunching gravel. He turned to find three people standing in the blazing sunlight, their eyes hidden behind sunglasses, mouths by bandanas, their clothes rugged and worn. Two men and a woman.

The men were white, tall, and skinny, like they'd been stretched out. They might have been twins, but it was hard to tell with their faces obscured. The woman was strong and stout, dark skin and gray dreadlocks piled on her head. She was holding an ancient rifle, the barrel of it pointed at his chest. It was a .22, barely a BB gun, and so rusted it might not even fire, but Paxton didn't want to gamble on that.

He stopped and put his hands in the air. The three people stood, staring at him. Waiting. Not in a rush. Paxton had never heard of something like this happening. This was America, not a shitty late-night movie. Bands of thugs didn't roam the outlands waiting for distracted travelers.

The woman pulled down her bandana to free her mouth. "Who are you with?"

He almost mentioned Zinnia and then realized if they didn't know about her, she might be safe, so he said, "Nobody. By myself."

The woman gave a little smirk. "We know about your friend in the store. We've got her covered. Who are you *with*?"

"Where's my friend?" Paxton asked.

"Answer us first."

Paxton puffed out his chest a little.

"We have a gun," she said.

"That has been established, yes."

The woman stepped forward, punctuating her words with jabs of the rifle. "Who sent you all the way out here?"

Paxton took a step back. "No one sent us. We're out for a ride. Day trip. Urban spelunking."

"Urban spelunking?"

Paxton shrugged. "It's a thing."

The woman waved the gun in the direction of the store. "C'mon. Inside."

"How about you put the gun down?"

"Not yet."

"We're not here to hurt anyone."

"Do you have water?"

Paxton pointed. "In the trunk."

"Keys."

Paxton took the keys out of his pocket and threw them in the dirt at her feet. She reached down to get them. He could have charged. Should have. He waited a second too long, and then she was back up. She handed the keys to one of the skinny men, who went to the back and opened the trunk, pulled out the jugs of water.

"Great," she said. "Now let's go."

The three of them backed up, giving Paxton plenty of space to walk along the brick wall toward the front of the store. They were smart. Not getting too close. Another few feet, Paxton could have grabbed the barrel of the gun, pointed it at the sky, reached underneath, pulled it away. It was an easy disarm he had practiced once every three months during the mandatory weapons defense training at the prison.

At least it was supposed to be easy. A rubber rifle was pretty different from a real one.

He didn't feel like they wanted to hurt him. They put up a strong front, but for the woman at least, there was a slight quiver to her voice. Her shoulders were too tense. The harder Paxton looked, the more they seemed like scared little animals whose hidey-hole had been found, who were now baring their teeth in hope the predator might back away and pick another fight.

He stepped inside the store and called out, "Zin. You okay?"

She answered from somewhere in the back of the store. "I'm fine."

Paxton heard the others enter behind him. He kept his hands up, moved slow. No sudden movements. If he was smart, if he and Zinnia could play this cool, they could be out of here within a couple of minutes. Back to the comfort of Cloud.

Zinnia was sitting against the wall, back pressed to it, hands on the floor. A small woman with her hair in braids, skin like milk, was twenty feet away, pointing a tiny black revolver in Zinnia's direction.

Zinnia looked at Paxton, confused, and then the three other folks moved into the open space between the shelves and the desks.

"They got you too, huh?" she asked. Paxton took some comfort in the fact that she didn't seem panicked.

"Are you hurt?" he asked.

"No."

Paxton threw a sharp-eyed glance at the girl with the revolver. "Good."

"Shut up," said the woman with the rifle. She moved around, flanking Paxton, holding Zinnia at gunpoint. Zinnia kept her hands on the floor.

Paxton could feel it. The temperature in the room rising. He knew this feeling. Best to knock it down before the thermometer popped. Loud and clear he said, "Hey."

Everyone looked at him.

"This is all a misunderstanding," Paxton said. "No one is here to hurt anyone. No one wants to get hurt. We all just want to go home." He reached his hand toward the girl with the rifle, to get her attention. "You can keep the water. So how about we all just put down the guns and turn around and walk away? The best part is, no one gets shot."

The woman tightened her grip on the rifle, but she was looking at the girl with the revolver. Which meant revolver girl was in charge.

"What's your name?" Paxton asked, turning to her. "Let's start with that." He touched his hand to his chest. "I'm Paxton. My friend on the floor is Zinnia. What's your name?"

"Ember."

"Amber?"

"Ember. With an E."

"Okay, Ember. Now we're pals. So how about you both put the guns down, and we walk out, and everyone goes home."

"Your car has a Cloud logo on it," she said.

"We work there."

Ember nodded. She held his stare. Something about her face was familiar. He couldn't place it. He had seen it. Maybe at Cloud? There were so many faces.

"You're the girl from processing," Zinnia said. Everyone turned to her. Zinnia was staring at Ember and nodded. "You're the girl they took away. In the theater."

The hard-ass look on Ember's face softened. "You were there? You remember that?"

Zinnia shrugged. "I've got a thing for faces."

Now that she said it, Paxton remembered, too. The girl in the secondhand lavender pantsuit, with the orange tag. As they were all being led to the bus, there'd been some kind of commotion.

"What is this?" Paxton asked.

Ember smiled. "This is the resistance."

"To what?" Zinnia asked.

"To Cloud. And I think you can help us."

ZINNIA

What a stupid bunch of bullshit this was.

They couldn't be her employers. Their bones were pressing out of their skin at odd angles, their teeth tinted yellow and covered in grime. They could barely afford to care for themselves, let alone drop eight figures on her tab.

She hadn't been able to check her phone, so she didn't know if her contact was here, or waiting, or gone. The best she could do was play dumb and wait for an opportunity. She worked the angles of the room. No way she could disarm two people over such a wide space without someone getting shot. She didn't want to get shot, and it was her preference that Paxton didn't get shot either.

Not that she cared. She didn't. But she also didn't think he deserved to go out like that.

Paxton joined her against the wall, slid down into a sitting position.

"If we could just—" Paxton started.

"Stop," Ember said. "Stop talking. Right now, you listen. Do you understand? You listen and then you can talk. We better like what you say, or this ends poorly for everyone."

The woman with the rifle spoke, quietly, turned away from Paxton and Zinnia, like maybe that meant they wouldn't hear. "Do you think this is who we were following?"

"Couldn't be," Ember said. "That signal stopped before they arrived. And their car is a beater anyway."

Fuck. They'd been tailing her contact.

But why? She didn't want to ask. Didn't want to appear interested. She was relieved when Paxton did it for her.

"Wait, you were following someone? I thought you lived here."

Ember looked down at him. She spun the handgun in her hand, so that it was hanging from the trigger guard by her finger, barrel pointed at the floor. One of the beanpole men took it. "We picked up the signal of a luxury car traveling through the area. Rare they come so far out. We were planning to rob it."

Yup, Zinnia thought. Definitely her contact.

"Like Robin Hood?" Paxton asked. "Does that make you the princess of thieves?"

"I'm sure they're long gone at this point." She clapped her hands. "We just found ourselves a bigger prize."

The beanpoles and the gray-haired woman moved off toward the shelves and sat like children, cross-legged, looking up at Ember with excitement on their dusty faces. Ember reached into her back pocket and took something out, held tight in her fist. Lowered herself to the floor without taking her eyes off Zinnia and Paxton. There was a slight scuff, and she stood back up. At her feet was a plastic thumb drive.

"This is the match that is going to burn down all of Cloud," she said.

She said it like she was on a stage, addressing a theater full of people.

The match on the CloudBand. Was it them? She wanted to ask how they'd broken into the system, because that was actually really impressive, but it wasn't the time for questions.

"What are your jobs?" Ember asked. "What do you do there?"

"We're both pickers," Zinnia said, just as Paxton said, "Security."

Zinnia turned to Paxton and gave him an *Are you fucking kidding me?* eyebrow.

Ember nodded and turned to Paxton. "Perfect. Here's what you're going to do. You're going to take this to Cloud. You're going to plug this into a software port and follow the prompts until you execute the program. We'll hold her until you get back and it's done."

Zinnia laughed. She made it sound so easy, like she hadn't just wasted months of her life on this thing. But then a burst of cold air expanded in her chest. Their gig sounded similar to hers. Were they competition? Was that the message from her employers? Was she being frozen out?

"No," Paxton said.

"What do you mean, no?" Ember asked.

"I mean exactly what I said. I'm not going to leave her here. And I'm not going to do anything until you explain to us what the hell is happening."

Ember turned to her compatriots. Gave a little side-eye to Paxton and Zinnia. Said, "If you need it explained to you why Cloud needs to be destroyed, then I'm not sure where to even start."

"What is your problem with them, exactly?" Paxton asked, his voice taking on a condescending, sarcastic tone, and it was in that moment Zinnia was most attracted to him. "Please. Enlighten me."

Ember laughed. "Do you know what the average American work-week used to be? Forty hours. You got Saturday and Sunday off. And you got paid for overtime. Health care was included in your salary. Did you know that? You got paid in money, not a bizarre credit system. You owned a home. You maintained a life separate from work. Now?" She huffed. "You're a disposable good packaging disposable goods."

"And?" Paxton asked.

Ember froze, like her words should have had some greater effect on them. "Doesn't that infuriate you?"

Paxton looked around the room, dragging his eyes off her, and her cronies, seated on the floor behind them. "Things sure are going great for you, aren't they? Robbing cars in the middle of nowhere. What other choice do we have?"

"There's always a choice," Ember said. "You have the choice to walk away."

Paxton's voice rose in the dim space. For Zinnia, it was taking a sharp turn away from self-assured and attractive, and into something else. Ember seemed to have hit a vein running deep below the surface of his skin, accessing emotions he maybe didn't know were there. "Is there a choice? Really? Because I spent years working a job I hated so I could own a business. And you know what happened? The market made its choice. It chose Cloud. I can kick my feet and scream all I want. What good will it do? I can either buck up and do my work, or go live in squalor and starve to death. Thanks but no thanks. I choose a roof over my head and food in my stomach."

"So that's it?" she asked. "You'll accept the status quo? Take things the way they are? Isn't it worth fighting for something better?"

"What's better?" Paxton asked.

"Anything other than this," Ember said, her voice rising.

Paxton's voice was rising, too. And the muscles in his neck were tightening, his face growing red. "This is the best of a bad situation. So you can play your games all you want, it's not going to change anything."

"Whoa," Zinnia said, and the two of them turned to look at her. She nudged Paxton. "What happened to keeping calm?"

Ember sighed and took a few steps forward. "Let me tell you something about Cloud. They are the choice we made. We gave them control. When they decided to buy up the grocery stores, we let them. When they decided to take over farming operations, we let them. When they decided to take over media outlets, and the internet providers, and the cell phone companies, we let them. We were told it would mean better prices, because Cloud only cared about the customer. That the customer was family. But we're not family. We are the food that big businesses eat to grow bigger. It seemed like the only thing that kept them in check was the last of the big-box retailers. And then Black Friday happened, and people were too afraid to leave their house to go shopping. You think that was an accident? A coincidence?"

"Okay," Paxton said, nodding slowly, his voice back to normal. "Now you're being ridiculous. Now you're spouting conspiracy theory nonsense."

"It's not nonsense."

"So you're nuts, is what you are."

She stamped her foot. Her friends jerked where they were sitting. "How can you not see this? How can you not be angry at the stranglehold they have on you and your life? How can you be content to be one of the people of Omelas?"

"Omelas? What?"

Ember pressed her hands against her face. "This is the problem. It's not that we've lost the ability to care. We've lost the ability to think." She removed her hands, looked back at Paxton. "We live in a state of entropy. We buy things because we are falling apart and the newness makes us feel whole. We are addicted to that feeling. That is how Cloud controls us. The worst part is, we should have seen it coming. For years we lived with stories about this. *Brave New World* and *1984* and *Fight Club*. We celebrated these stories while ignoring the message. And now, how come you can order anything in the world and it'll show up at your door within a day, but if you try to order a copy of *Fahrenheit 451* or *The Handmaid's Tale*, it takes weeks, or it doesn't show up at all? It's because they don't want us to read these stories anymore. They don't want us to get ideas. Ideas are dangerous."

Paxton didn't answer. Zinnia wondered what he was thinking. She knew what she was thinking: Ember was a hell of a speaker. She had the kind of voice that snaked itself around you, caressed your cheek, convinced you to hand over your credit card number.

It also helped that she wasn't wrong.

"This is the system we have," Paxton said. "The world is falling apart. At least Cloud is trying to put it back together."

"Oh, with their 'green initiatives'?" Ember asked. "Like that excuses them?" She shook her head, took another few steps forward. She reached into her pocket again. Pulled out something small. It took a second for Zinnia to focus and see what it was, held aloft between two pinched fingers.

A black match with a white head.

"Do you see this?" she asked, looking at Paxton and Zinnia in turn, not relenting until they both nodded. "It is so small, and so fragile. In time it'll get old and worn out. It won't even work if it's wet. It's so easily lost, so easily misplaced. And yet, the spark contained within this could burn down a forest. It could light a stick of dynamite capable of destroying a building."

Paxton laughed. "So that was your plan, with the CloudBands? You thought showing people a picture of a match would change things? No one even understood what it meant."

"We were laying the groundwork," she said, her voice sharp. She was not used to verbal parrying. She was used to people who hung on her words like rocks at the edge of a cliff. "We're easing people in slow." She pointed behind her, to the thumb drive, still on the floor, sitting like a sacred object. "But with that, we're going to get there. That's our answer. That's our match."

"And then what?" Paxton asked. "Take down Cloud, then what? Where will people work? What will they do? You're talking about completely rewriting the American economy. And the housing market."

"People will adapt," she said. "We can't allow one company to have complete control over everything. You know there used to be laws against that? Until governments found themselves with less and less, and companies found themselves with more and more. Soon the companies were the ones writing the laws. Do you think your salary pays for your food? For your housing? Because it doesn't. The government pays for them. It subsidizes that, along with your health care. It pays money to keep you employed, because then you pay votes to keep them employed. This is too broke to fix. It is time to pull this system down and smash it to pieces."

"Damn straight," muttered one of the skinny men.

"That's awful cavalier," Paxton said.

Zinnia was surprised at the passion with which Paxton was defending Cloud. The company that ruined him. He had always seemed prickly about it. Maybe he had been converted. Become a true believer. Maybe in the face of violence or death he needed to justify it to himself, because the truth was too hard to accept. Zinnia sat back, watched it unfold, waiting for a free moment.

But there was something Ember had said that was scratching at the back of Zinnia's head. Omelas. It was a story. She'd read it. She knew she had. A long time ago. It was a story she didn't like. . . .

"Hey," Ember said. "You."

Zinnia looked up.

"You stay," she said. "He goes. He does the thing we want him to do and he comes back. We won't hurt you. Not unless something goes wrong. Not unless he comes back anything other than alone. I'm sorry for this, okay? But it has to be done. We've been trying for years. This is our best hope."

"Sure," she said, and turned to Paxton. "Go ahead."

"Wait, what?"

She peppered a little fear onto her voice. "I think it's best to do what they say."

"I won't leave you here like this."

Goddamn chivalry. She put on her brave face. "Please. It seems like the only way."

Paxton sat back, getting comfortable. "No."

Ember took her gun back and pointed it at Zinnia's forehead but looked at Paxton. "Go, now."

Paxton put his hands in the air and stood, using the wall as leverage. Every step he took, Ember lowered the gun a little. He picked up the thumb drive and turned toward Zinnia. "I'll be back soon."

"Thank you," Zinnia said.

Paxton made it a dozen steps and turned. "You hurt her—"

"Yeah yeah, I get it," Ember said, cutting him off. "No one's getting hurt. Just do it."

Zinnia watched the group head toward the front of the store, leaving her and Ember. This was the first flat-stupid move they'd made, leaving the two of them alone together. They probably figured Paxton was the dangerous one. Undone by ingrained sexism. She looked up at Ember, asked, "You going to tie me up or something?"

"Do I need to?"

"I thought you were cautious."

She pointed with the gun. "Stand up."

Zinnia stood, hands out, moving toward Ember, slow enough that maybe she wouldn't notice. Funny thing about guns was, they were way less dangerous than knives. She'd rather have defended against a gun than a knife. Minimum safe distance to keep someone covered with a gun was twenty-one feet. Anything less than that, they could turn the tables. Adrenaline fucked with your fine motor skills. The sudden increase in blood pressure made you dizzy.

Took years of training to get over that kind of thing. Zinnia figured Ember didn't have the same kind of training she did. And the girl was less than ten feet away now.

"I don't need to tie you up," she said. "There's a storeroom in the back. You can wait there. It's hot, but lucky for you, you brought water."

Zinnia took another step in. Eight feet. Seven. Zinnia made it like she was walking past Ember toward the storeroom, and Ember seemed preoccupied with Paxton and the rest, so when the front door chimed and her eyes flicked in that direction, in that fraction of a second she had been waiting for, Zinnia threw herself forward.

She grabbed for the gun, locking her hand around the cylinder and squeezing hard. It rattled against her palm as Ember pulled the trigger, but it wouldn't budge. Zinnia pushed it away from them, off line, in case she lost her grip and it fired.

At the same time, she threw her elbow into the side of Ember's head. It sent a shock up Zinnia's arm and the girl hit the floor hard, collapsing to the ground like a sack of rocks. As her body fell Zinnia twisted the gun and yanked hard, claiming it for herself.

Zinnia stepped back to approximately twenty-one feet, popped out the cylinder to make sure it still had bullets, and finding two left, aimed the gun between Ember's eyes. "What's on the drive?" she asked.

Ember spat, "You fucking shill. You fucking drone. You're going to fight for them?"

"Who hired you?"

"No one hired us," she said. "We resist."

"Yeah yeah, blah blah revolution," she said. "I get it. Wait here."

It tracked that they were independent. Their plan was smash-and-grab bullshit. They just wanted to get in and make a mess and run away. It annoyed Zinnia that they made it all sound so simple. Like she hadn't been jammed up for months and wasn't popping her arm out and shit just to get this job done.

She made for the front but stopped. She felt an overwhelming urge to hurt Ember. Not to hit her. Not to cause her physical pain. But to show her some of the pain of the world. The pain that was the background noise to her every day in that damn building.

"Take your match," Zinnia said. "March over to Cloud. Strike it and place it against the side of the concrete wall. Tell me how long it takes to burn down."

The girl's eyes dimmed. A little of the fight left her.

Zinnia made for the front, pressed herself to the window. No one in sight. They couldn't have left yet. Must be in the alley. She jumped up to yank the bell off the wall so it wouldn't chime as she exited, then stepped out the door, doing her best to stay quiet. Cringing at every scratch of her sneakers on the dry pavement. She moved slowly against the brick wall, the stone scorching her skin.

At the corner, voices. She stopped at the edge of the alleyway and listened. She caught the end of something Paxton was saying. ". . . and I swear if you hurt her there'll be hell to pay."

Aww.

His voice was clear, which made her think she was facing him, which made her also think the three captors were looking at him, away from the mouth of the alley. She ducked down, below eye line, poked her head around the corner. Saw six legs. The one with the rifle was in the rear.

Easy enough.

She stepped out. Paxton's eyes went wide when he saw her. She held the gun to the head of the woman with the rifle. It was risky to be this close, but they weren't good enough to take the gun from her. Most they'd manage to do was get shot in the process. They turned as one and looked at her, confused at first, then afraid.

"The rifle," Zinnia said. "Toss it to him."

The woman's shoulders bunched. She looked at Paxton, who was smiling. He took a few steps forward and she held out the rifle, tossed it with both hands. He caught it and trained it on one of the skinny men.

Zinnia fired the gun in the air. They all nearly leapt off their feet, including Paxton.

"Now run," she said.

The three of them bolted, pushing past Paxton, down to the end of the alley, and then they were gone. Zinnia let the gun dangle from her hand and fall to the dirt. Paxton lunged forward and grabbed her around her shoulders, then pulled her in tight. Zinnia let him do it. They stayed that way for a bit, giving their hearts a chance to slow down.

"Are you okay?" he asked.

She spoke into his shoulder. "I am."

He pulled back, looked in her eyes. Frantic, sweating. "What the hell happened?"

"I worked in the Detroit school system. You think this is the first time I saw someone waving a gun?"

"Stop that."

"She underestimated me and I got lucky," Zinnia said. "I've been taking Krav Maga since I was a kid."

"You never told me that."

Zinnia shrugged. "It never came up."

Paxton shook his head. Reached down and picked up the rifle. Pointed it into the sky and fired. Nothing.

"So much for a relaxing day trip," Paxton said.

"Yeah. I guess we should head back."

"They took the water inside."

Zinnia held the gun aloft. "I'll go in and get it. I want to get my books anyway."

"You sure?"

"I am," she said, and nodded toward the car. "Get in there and get that air-conditioning charged up and ready. I want to freeze my ass off when I sit down."

"I can come in with you."

Zinnia smiled. "I can handle myself. Seriously, I could use a minute, too. That was . . . a lot."

Paxton put his hands up. "Okay. Go ahead."

"Going to look for a bathroom, too," she said over her shoulder. "I might be a few minutes. Sorry."

Zinnia made for the bookstore, ran to the back, which was now empty. She pulled out her phone, and before she could even check the text she had received there was a creak behind her and a voice said, "Don't turn around."

It was a man's voice. Deep, and old. Raspy. A smoker. Zinnia gripped the gun, making sure it was in full view but not raising it. She wondered where he had been. Maybe in the back. Maybe watching.

"You are to continue with the previous task."

Zinnia nodded, unsure if she should respond.

"There is one additional task. Compensation will be doubled if you're successful."

Zinnia held her breath.

"Kill Gibson Wells."

The words rang in her ears.

"Count to thirty, and then turn around."

Zinnia made it to a hundred and twenty before she found that she could even move.

PAXTON

Paxton rested his head against the steering wheel, the air coming out of the vents cool, getting cooler. He could feel every flutter of his heart.

What a bunch of lunatics. What was their plan? What would they even accomplish? That world, the one they were fighting for, it was a dream. It didn't work like that anymore.

He thought back to the theater, sitting in that hard seat, interviewing for the job. The way he felt, like he wanted to puke on himself. Not even just puke, but literally do it on himself. Befoul himself just for sitting there.

For them to be right, Paxton had to be wrong. Two months wrong and growing wronger, as he found himself invested in people like Dobbs and Dakota, and how they felt about him. Their approval a currency now.

Plus, he'd found Zinnia. Being at Cloud meant being with Zinnia and maybe when she left he'd find the strength to go with her.

After yesterday, after today, it was like she looked different. Her skin glowed more. Her eyes were brighter. The L-word teased him. He was getting to a place where he thought he could say it. But he didn't want to push it, because Zinnia didn't seem like the kind of woman who stood on formality or romanticism. He could see himself putting his hands on her shoulders, looking deep into her eyes, telling her. And she might respond with a little eye roll, or a giggle, and that'd be that. And he would have to live with it.

Be happy with what you have, he told himself. You have a job, a place to live, and a beautiful woman. Everything else is icing.

He shifted in his seat, felt something in his pocket bite hard into his skin. The thumb drive. He went to crack the window and toss it just as Zinnia opened the passenger-side door. She sat, put her hands in her lap, staring at them. The way her body sagged, it was like the weight of the last few days had caught up to her. Paxton tried to think of something comforting to say but couldn't, so he put his hand on her knee, feeling the smoothness of her skin, the hardness of the bone, and asked, "You okay?"

"We should go."

He put the car in drive, backing out of the alley, and turned in the direction they had come from.

They made it back to the highway before he said, "Bunch of crazy hippies."

"Hippies," she said, her voice low.

"I mean, what do they think they're going to do? It doesn't make sense."

"Doesn't make any sense."

"Hey," he said, putting his hand on her thigh. "Are you okay?"

For a moment he thought she might recoil, but she didn't. She put her hand on his. Her thigh was warm but her hand was cold. "Yes, I am. I'm sorry. It's been a lot."

"Yeah, it has."

"So what do we do now?"

"What do you mean?"

"Do we tell someone?" Zinnia asked. "Do you think you should report all this to your boss?"

Paxton wasn't sure it was worth it. They were miles away. Anyway, what would four hippies do against Cloud? Dobbs liked to keep things simple. Piling this on top of Gibson Wells's visit might be too much.

"More trouble than it's worth, probably," Paxton said.

"Yeah," Zinnia said. "That makes sense."

They made it to the highway and then halfway back in silence. Paxton realized that without mile markers, he wasn't sure what exit to get off at, but then he saw the swarm in the distance, the sky darkening as the drones sped toward MotherCloud.

Paxton remembered what Ember had said about the books. Could that be true? The idea of censorship was a hard one to let go, like a seed stuck between his teeth. There would be a public outcry if Cloud was actually withholding books. People would fight that. Wouldn't they?

Thinking about the books made him think about the blank journal pages. He was burning the daylight of his life while they remained empty. If he was going to be at Cloud, he should make the best of it. Maybe he could get promoted. Make it to tan.

He got off the highway, drove a bit. Watched the sky. There wasn't much else to watch. The sun was blotted out by the black swarms.

"Remember when these things were just toys?" he asked, desperate to fill up the void inside the car.

He glanced at Zinnia, who nodded.

"I remember this one time," he said. "At the prison, this guy got the brilliant idea to have his buddy smuggle stuff to him by having a drone carry it into the yard. It worked for a little while, too. Except, this one time, it was windy, and I guess they got impatient. Me and this other guard, we were doing our rounds, walking the yard, watching everyone, and suddenly this thing crashes at our feet. Full up of comic books. Can you believe it? Apparently he didn't like the books in the library, and it was illegal to send prisoners anything, so that's what he had his friend smuggling in."

"That's funny," Zinnia said, her voice flat and empty.

"Just funny the way people will adapt to things," he said.

And as he said it, something dinged in his head.

GIBSON

Do you know the story of Lazarus and the rich man? It's from the book of Luke. It goes like this: There once was a rich man who dressed in fine linen and lived in luxury. At the gate of his palace was a beggar named Lazarus. Now, Lazarus was in a pretty sorry state. Covered in sores, starving, filthy. Desperate just for the crumbs that would fall from the rich man's table.

Time came when Lazarus died, and the angels carried him to the gates of heaven. The rich man died, too, but no angels showed up for him. He went down to hell, where he was tortured and maimed. And he looked up and he saw God and Lazarus by his side, and he asked, "Please have pity on me and send Lazarus to dip the tip of his finger in water and cool my tongue."

And God replied: "Remember in your life, you received good things, while Lazarus received bad things. Now he is comforted and you are in agony. There is a great chasm between the two of you that cannot be crossed."

The rich man, then, asked that Lazarus go to his brothers, to warn them about their eventual fate, so that they might avoid it. And God said, "They should know to listen to the prophets."

So the rich man suffered for the rest of eternity while Lazarus had a front-row seat to the wonders of the universe.

I want to tell you about why I don't like this story. Simply: it casts the simple act of having wealth and ambition as a sin. There's so much about Lazarus and the rich man we don't know. Why was the rich man rich? Did he come to his money through crime? Did he hurt people in the course of his life? Or did he build a business? Was he providing for his family and his community? Why was Lazarus poor? Why was he covered in sores? Was he cast out from society because of some injustice? Or did he make bad choices in his life? Did he do something to deserve it?

We don't know. All we know is that the most basic quality of being wealthy is wrong, and the most basic quality of being poor is a virtue, with no sense of how these people came to where they are.

Most folks judge me by what I've done: built a business, provided for my family, created a new live-work paradigm aimed at making a better world for the American worker. But there are still some folks out there who think I'm a greedy bastard. That after I'm dead and gone—which will not be long now—I'll be headed down to hell, to sit next to the rich man, looking up at Lazarus, wondering where exactly I went wrong.

And I want to say, first and foremost, it is not a sin to want to make the world a better place. It is not a sin to want to provide for your family. It is not a sin to derive some enjoyment out of your life. So I have a boat. I like to fish. Does that damn me to hell? I've never raised my hands in violence. Should I be made to suffer for that?

Look at the sorry state of this world. Small towns collapsed. Coastal villages underwater. Cities packed to capacity. Beyond capacity. Some third-world countries are practically wastelands.

The world is in a sorry state, and I'm trying to help. Has everything I've done been perfect? Hell no. That's the price of progress. Making Cloud was like making an omelet, just like any business. Some eggs had to be broken along the way. Not that I ever felt good about breaking eggs. It's never something I took pleasure in. But the end result is the thing that matters. You know what I've always said, what I've been saying for years: the market dictates. Nearly had that tattooed on my shoulder at one point, during a period of youthful folly. I never went through with it—I'm not too proud to admit I'm afraid of needles—but it is on a piece of paper that I stuck above my desk on that first day that I started Cloud.

That same piece of paper is still there. A small slip, yellowed, cracked, the words barely legible. But I had that phrase put on mugs and hung around our offices. I have lived and breathed it. Succeeded and failed by it.

The market dictates.

If the market says: this thing can be cheaper for the consumer, it can be delivered more efficiently, it can make a difference in people's lives, I say, let's do it!

You know, I remember, years ago, we were dealing with this pickle company. Molly can tell you, I love pickles. And I loved the pickles this company made, but they were pretty expensive, and our customers weren't really too hot on paying as much as the company was charging, which I think was something like five dollars for a jar.

So we went to them and we said, "Let us work with you." We helped them change their packaging. We helped them better source their ingredients. We got them to switch from glass to plastic and that alone saved them a ton of money on shipping, because then the trucks leaving their warehouses were lighter and they could spend less money on gas.

The ultimate goal was to get them down to two dollars a jar, which is what our customers wanted to pay. But they insisted on three fifty. And we told them, look at the amount of money you're saving now. You could easily do two. And they said no, they couldn't, and gave me this song and dance about what it would mean for their back end and having to change their internal structure, and I said, great, you should do that, and let us know if you need a hand with it.

Anyway, long story short, they wouldn't budge, so I said fine. I'll give my customers what they're asking for: pickles for two dollars a jar. That's what led to the creation of Cloud Pickles. I don't care what anyone says, I like our brand of pickles more than theirs.

They eventually went out of business. And I never want to see someone out of a job, but that was on them. All they had to do was meet us in the middle, and we would have been able to do great things together. You would be amazed to find out how many pickles we sell. People really like them and they keep pretty well and that works out pretty good for everyone.

The market dictates.

I remember when that happened a couple of people got mad at me, but you know what? If I can provide a product or a service for people, and it's cheaper, and just as good, and it lets them put the money they saved toward something else—more food, housing, health care, even a night on the town—I will gladly do that. The whole point of Cloud was to make people's lives easier. There are plenty of companies that worked with us to cut costs and now they're thriving. They don't work with us because they have to, they do it because they want to.

I'm sorry, I'm veering a little off topic here. Haven't been sleeping so good lately. There's this pain in my gut now, like a slow-burning fire. Like coals at the bottom of a barbecue. You don't think they're hot, but they are. That heat is reaching up to my head. I've been getting real annoyed at things lately and I've been working on not being so annoyed, because I want to meet my maker with a smile on my face, not a sneer.

Point is, I won't apologize for being rich. And I am sure that when my time comes, when I cross that line, I won't be sent down to hell for the simple fact of the work that I did. Man has to be judged on more than that.

Twenty years ago the United States was responsible for 5.4 million tons of carbon dioxide. This past year it was less than a million. That's it! A lot of that can be attributed to what we did at Cloud, and you better believe the mandate I've given Claire is to get that even lower. I don't want Cloud to be carbon neutral. I want it to be carbon negative. I want us sucking carbon out of the air. I want those rising sea levels to recede. I want people in coastal cities to return to their homes. I want a Miami that doesn't look so much like Venice did. I want Venice back.

Should I be condemned to eternal damnation for that?

PAXTON

"Put these on," Dakota said, handing Paxton a pair of sunglasses.

They cut down on the glare significantly and made it easier to focus on the utter chaos of the roof. He couldn't see the edges, so standing on it gave the feel of standing in the middle of a busy field. The sun shone off solar panels embedded in the ground, and dotted around the landscape were shed-sized bays, where boxes rose through a lift system and could be attached to waiting drones.

The workers wore orange. Many of them wore long-sleeved white shirts under their polos, and wide floppy hats, water canteens hanging from their belts. The docking bays provided some shade, but not much, especially now, at the height of the day.

"They don't have orange in the introductory video," Paxton said.

"This is one of the shittier details," Dakota said. "They don't show the shitty colors."

Paxton was overwhelmed by the scene, by the sound of it, or really, the lack thereof. The drones were nearly silent. There was an electric buzz all around him, like an insect that was close but darting around the edge of his vision. He could feel it on his skin.

"You really think this is it?" she asked.

He had told her the story about the drone at the prison. He verified with her and Dobbs that there weren't many security officers up here, because they weren't really needed. Everything that came up was boxed and recorded by the CloudBands so nobody could steal anything. The workers had their own exit where they queued up at the end of shift. More important than security officers was having a med team up here, because of the constant danger of heatstroke and dehydration. Every loading bay included signage reminding workers to stay hydrated, and there were fountains everywhere, with two spigots—one for water, one for sunscreen.

"Where do we even start?" Dakota asked, looking over the field, at thousands of workers, and miles of flat space, and swarms of drones that blotted out the sun like a passing cloud, delivering moments of relief that never lasted long enough.

"At the beginning," Paxton said, taking a few steps, making sure Dakota was following, and then continuing on, walking down the striped paths where workers could safely travel, marked off with yellow reflective tape so it was easy to see, so that nobody crossed onto the dark surfaces of the solar panels, which looked like perfectly square pools of still water.

Every station was the same: a flurry of workers, drones moving up and down through the air, oddly shaped packages sprayed in weatherproof cardboard foam. No one paid them any mind. Which was what Paxton was counting on. He wasn't interested in the people who weren't interested in him.

One of the lessons he'd learned in prison was: You don't look for the handoff. You look for the side-eye. That frightened glance, the tension that builds up in muscles. The badge reflecting off frightened eyes. Prisoners were professionals at subterfuge. You had to become an expert not on seeing the hidden things, but on seeing the people who were doing the hiding.

They walked for an hour. It was more of a stroll. They got a few looks, but more *What are they doing here?* looks, not *Oh shit, it's the fuzz* looks. Paxton knew the difference. So he walked, watching faces, watching hands, watching shoulders, as Dakota grew more anxious. Audibly sighing, stopping to drink water, stopping to pump out globs of sunscreen that she rubbed on her neck and face, until her skin was pasty white and the black void of her sunglasses made her look like a skeleton roaming the blazing-hot roof.

At one point, Paxton saw a familiar figure and turned a little in that direction, just to be sure. It was Vikram, in a wide-brimmed hat and sunglasses, a canteen of water dangling from his belt. His shirt gone from blue to navy because it was soaked with sweat. He was slightly turned away, watching a group of men and women in brown servicing a drone that was sitting on the ground. Paxton wanted to get closer, so Vikram could see him, be reminded of who had won, but decided against it. It was petty. He rejoined Dakota, who was taking a long slug from her bottle of water.

And then he saw it. A skinny white guy, stick-and-poke tattoos from elbow to fingertip. The kind you get in prison, or from an idiot friend with a sewing needle and some printer ink. He froze as Paxton and Dakota wandered into his field of vision. He moved himself so that someone would be situated between him and them, like a child hiding behind a tree that was too narrow. He pushed his hands into his pockets, like there was something he wanted to make sure was still there but also wished it wasn't.

"Him," Paxton said, nodding in the skell's direction.

Dakota tipped up her sunglasses, looked at the guy, sweating now, maybe not from the sun. "You sure about this? We turn him out and he's got nothing on him, Dobbs is going to be pissed. Maybe reassign-you-up-here pissed. We call this the skin cancer beat."

"Trust me," Paxton said as the skell took a few steps backward.

"Okay," Dakota said. Then she waved at him. "Yo. You. Over here. *Ándale.*"

The guy looked around, like someone might help him. No one did. Rather, the people closest to him took a few steps away, like they knew what was coming. He wandered over from the docking station, forcing a smile onto his face, trying to play it cool. Like, *Who, me?*

"Inside-out those pockets," Dakota said.

The guy looked around a little. Shrugged. "For what?"

"Because it'll make me fucking happy," Dakota said.

The guy sagged. Reached into his pocket and held out his fist. Opened it. Nestled in his palm were more than a dozen oblivion containers. Dakota stuck out her hand and he put them in hers.

She turned to Paxton and smiled. "Nice."

Paxton smiled back. "Now the real fun starts."

It took a full half hour to make it to an exit point, then down to a tram and over to Admin, where they brought the skell—Lucas—to an interrogation room, so small the table and two chairs facing each other could barely fit in the space. Paxton sat Lucas down and left him in there for a bit, to think about the shit spot he was in.

Dobbs came across the bullpen at Paxton, Dakota trailing behind him, clapping his hands in a slow, deliberate motion. When he reached Paxton he smacked him on the shoulder. "Knew I was right about you. How'd you do it?"

"Just a hunch," Paxton said.

"Well, it paid off," he said. "So the next step, I guess, is to get him to explain to us how the smuggling operation works, who else is involved, etcetera, etcetera."

"Mind if I take a run at him, boss?" Paxton asked.

Dobbs gave him a hard stare. Chewed on it. Finally said, "Sure thing, kid. You earned it. We'll be listening in though. No sense having to go through the whole thing twice."

"What do I offer him?" Paxton asked.

"Reassignment. We'll stick him in one of the processing facilities. He may want to leave, and that's on him, but we don't have to fire him outright."

"Okay then." Paxton nodded to Dobbs and Dakota, went back to the room. Entered it and sat across from Lucas. Got comfortable in his seat as Lucas fidgeted in his. After a few seconds of staring Paxton said, "Let's talk."

"About what?"

"The oblivion in your pocket."

Lucas shrugged, looking at everything in the room—ceiling tile, tabletop, dust in the corners, obvious two-way mirror. Everything except Paxton. "For personal use."

"This is what I've guessed so far," Paxton said. "I'm sure it's more complicated than this, but, someone orders something from Cloud; when the drone drops it off, they stick some oblivion on for the return trip." Lucas narrowed his eyes, indicating that Paxton was right. "Now, the complication is, how do you know which drones to check? Maybe the same drones always come back to the same spot. Maybe there's something about the coding, the way they move around, some kind of pattern you guys have cracked. Surely there are a lot of people in on this. Probably some of the managers and security guards. Maybe a lot of those drones are flying around with little stashes of oblivion on them, but only certain people know to look for it. I don't know. What I do know is this: You were carrying more than a hundred hits. That is grounds for immediate expulsion. And you know what that means." Lucas's eyes went wide. "But I can help."

"How?"

"We'll stick you in a new dorm," he said. "Put you in processing, way on the other side of the campus."

"What do you want?"

"An explanation of exactly how the operation works," Paxton said. "And as many names as you can give me. People in charge. Security, especially. You give me those things, and if I am suitably impressed, then you get what you want."

Lucas looked at his hands in his lap. Mumbled something.

"What was that?" Paxton asked.

"I want a lawyer."

Paxton had no idea how to proceed, and he didn't want to say the wrong thing, so he simply nodded, stood, pushed in his chair, and left the room. Worst-case scenario, it would scare the life out of Lucas.

That was the best-case scenario, too. When he closed the door Dobbs appeared.

"Good first attempt," he said. "But now I'll talk to him."

"Does he get a lawyer?"

"Hell no," Dobbs said, laughing under his breath. "But don't worry. You gave him a little of the good cop. Now it's time for the bad." He reached down for the knob, then looked back up. "I'm damn proud of you, son."

Dobbs went in, and Paxton watched as he pulled out the chair and sat down across from Lucas. Dobbs started talking but Paxton couldn't hear what he was saying. Must have been someplace else to listen in. He stood there for a minute, lathering his skin with the word *son*.

After a little while he went looking for Dakota, and one of the other blues—a blond surfer bro whose name he'd forgotten—told him she was running an errand but to wait for her to get back, so he sat at a desk and logged in to a tablet.

All day long, in the back of his head, he'd been thinking about what Ember had said. About Cloud hiding books. He had noticed, in the first few days, that his login gave him access to the inventory system, so with nothing better to do he jumped in, clicked around a bit, hitting walls, going down paths blindly until finally, he found a way to access how much of every item was available in this MotherCloud.

He picked *Fahrenheit 451*, because he remembered that was a Ray Bradbury book. He had read it in grammar school and he liked it. There were two copies available. Which didn't seem like a lot. He looked up the top-selling book in the Cloud store—a remake of an erotic novel originally based on a young adult series—and found they had 22,502 copies on hand. That seemed like a pretty big swing, but at the same time, Paxton understood the principle of demand. Of course they'd have more copies of the top-selling book, whereas Bradbury's book had been published in, according to the database, 1953. Next he looked up *The Handmaid's Tale* by Margaret Atwood, and found there were no copies on site. That was slightly more recent, at 1985, but still. No copies?

A little more clicking around and he found something called

"order metrics." In that section he could look up search and order histories for items in this MotherCloud's delivery radius. He looked around, suddenly worried he might be doing something wrong. That information ought to have been more private. But then again, he was a security officer, and if he had the access, it was probably for a reason. He clicked through the history for *Fahrenheit 451*. In the past year, two searches, one order. For *The Handmaid's Tale*, one search, no orders.

Ember was wrong. The books weren't being hidden from people. It was just that people didn't want to read them. And what kind of business stayed afloat by giving customers things they didn't want?

It was almost a relief.

Still, there was something about the things Ember had said that prodded parts of Paxton, parts that still felt raw and tender, even after a night's sleep.

But if she was wrong about this, what else could she be wrong about?

"Good news," Dobbs said, his hand landing on Paxton's shoulder, which made Paxton jump and spin around.

"Sir?"

"We got it," he said, leaning on the desk. "Sounds like a couple of the tech guys were able to hack the flight algorithm so certain drones always returned to the same docking bays. Drone would drop a package, dealer would put the oblivion on, boom." Dobbs clapped his hands. "Nice work, son. Nice work."

"Thanks, boss."

He stepped away and a few moments later Dakota appeared, her face still streaked with sunscreen. She was smiling, too.

"So," she said. "You want on the Gibson detail?"

"Hell yes I do," Paxton said.

He floated through the rest of his shift, and when he finished, he walked to the lobby of his dorm, slowly, drawing it out, not wanting to dive in too fast and disappoint himself, because maybe the system took time to update, but when he got to the elevator bank he couldn't help himself, so he checked his rating and found that he was now at four stars.

ZINNIA

Zinnia tapped at the order screen, selected two CloudBurgers, small fries, and a vanilla shake. Sat back and looked toward the kitchen. There wasn't much to see. A swinging door, and every time someone came out of it, she caught a flash of a clean, tiled space behind it.

This was it. The terminus of the tram line. Had to be. The line led to this side of Live-Play, and the businesses above and below it extended to an outer wall, whereas CloudBurger wasn't deep at all. Plenty of space behind that swinging door for a kitchen and then some.

The question was why. Could have been a maintenance or supply tunnel. Could have been something else. Some quirk of the facility.

It was fun to speculate. It distracted her from the particulars of her new assignment: killing Gibson Wells. She was afraid to even think the words in this place, like the CloudBand might pick up on the particular pattern of her brain waves, and a bunch of men and women in blue would come storming in to drag her off to a blank room.

She wished there was more information. She wished she could make contact with her employers, but of course, it didn't work that way. She still didn't know who they were. All she knew was she was tasked with assassinating the richest, most powerful man on the planet, on his home turf, when he was surrounded by a metric fuck-ton of security.

So now she had two assignments. And she had to do both things at the same time. There was a good chance she'd run afoul of security when she breached the processing facility. Which would mean a lock-down. Surely there'd be one if Wells was killed.

They had to happen simultaneously.

His visit coincided with the Black Friday Massacres ceremony, which meant a whole lot of things would be happening at once. It would be a day of chaos, which was a warm blanket in her line of work.

Paxton would be a big help. Not that he would do it willingly. She hoped he would get on the detail. At the very least she'd be able to tease some intel out of him.

Her food arrived and she ate, chewing the burger slowly, savoring the brown-crusted meat. While she ate she thought about killing. It was something she well and truly had been trying to get away from, but Wells would be dead soon anyway. Did it even really count? He'd be in more and more pain as time went on. Maybe this was a kindness. If she focused on that really hard while eating her French fries she could almost accept that as a reasonable answer.

She hoped that, however she did it, she wouldn't have to look in his eyes. The one thing she hoped to never do again was look in someone's eyes as the life left them. It was the only moment where the work felt unbearable, and even though it was over in a flash, those moments always seemed to last an eternity.

Switching between the cold of the shake and the heat of the fries made her teeth ache. She watched the doors some more, as the order runners moved in and out. If she had a green shirt, a food-service shirt, she could get inside, no problem. Probably not a good idea to order one—there probably wasn't even a reliable mechanism to order a shirt for a job that wasn't yours. She could steal one. Better that than buy one off an employee, because employees had memories, and morals, and mouths from which to squeal. Had to be stealing.

Which left the damn CloudBand. The issue that had vexed her since she moved here. Zinnia picked up her second burger, feeling slightly full but not wanting to waste food, and ate. The tracking wasn't even the problem anymore. If it was going to be her last day, blowing her cover would be no big deal. But her watch didn't have enough access—she needed blue- or brown-level access. Hadley was a brown. If she could take Hadley's watch, that would be great. But the damn thing would know it wasn't Hadley wearing it.

And *then* she needed an exit strategy.

First, she needed a shirt. That was the easiest. Blue or brown—security and tech had the most access and she was leaning toward tech. The tech workers were like wallpaper. They did their job and no one paid them much attention. At least she would look the part.

Her phone buzzed. Text from Paxton.

Drinks?

She finished the last of her fries and wrote back: *Two minutes.*

She found him at the pub, already with a pint of beer in front of him, a couple of sips pulled off the top, and a fresh vodka rocks for her. A huge smile on his face. She sat and he raised his glass. "I made the Gibson detail."

"That's great," she said, clinking her glass against his, really and truly happy for him, but also for herself. "So what does that entail, exactly?"

"Not sure yet. I mean, roughly . . ." He looked around. There was no one in earshot. He leaned forward, lowered his voice. "Roughly, he'll come into Incoming, where they're going to do the reading of the names for Black Friday. Then he'll get on a tram car and take it around to Live-Play. He'll walk around here a bit. Apparently this is the first MotherCloud where they built a separate sort of entertainment facility for the workers, so he wants to see how it's grown. Then it's back on a tram car, back to Incoming, and gone. I have no idea what I'll be doing. I'll be in the mix."

"You must be proud."

He opened his mouth, then shut it. Picked up the beer and took a sip.

"You look proud, at least," she said.

"It's weird. The day I got here I wanted to tell him off. But now, I don't know. It feels like I accomplished something, that they would trust me with this kind of responsibility. There should be a word for that, for when you're frustrated with someone but you sort of like them, too."

"Yeah," Zinnia said. "There should be a word for that."

A fissure opened in her heart. A tiny one, the slightest bit of light leaking through. She drank some vodka.

The most important detail here was the tram.

Gibson would be on the tram.

The trams that were susceptible to derailment.

A tram crash would be a hell of a thing. The only downside was she'd have to kill way more people than Wells for it to work.

Including Paxton, if he was riding next to him.

WELLS PROTECTION DETAIL MEMO

Welcome to the detail responsible for protecting Gibson Wells during his visit to our MotherCloud. Please review and internalize the following notes. Violating any of the guidelines will likely result in serious repercussions. You'll get kicked down a full star *at least*. This is not a joke.

- Do not address Wells directly.
- I say again, do not address Wells directly.
- If he addresses you, you may engage in conversation, but please don't expand much beyond pleasantries or answering questions he may pose to you.
- Do not lodge complaints or grievances with him. This is not the time or the place.
- If something needs to be brought to his attention, tell me or a member of his team. Do so discreetly.
- Maintain a perimeter around him at all times. Employees are not allowed near Wells unless he initiates or approves of contact.
- Your shirt is to be clean and tucked in. Sneakers are fine but jeans are not acceptable. Wear slacks or khakis.
- Do not, do not, use your personal phone in Wells's presence. You must appear to be focused on your task, not distracted. Even if you're passively surveilling a crowd, do not look like you're not doing anything.
- Things will be extra chaotic because this will coincide with the Remembrance Day ceremony, which, on top of everything else, is the start of our busiest season. Which means when you are given the rest of your material—routes, timing, etc.— you are to memorize it down to the last detail. We will be conducting a series of practice runs, off shift. Attendance is mandatory.

You fuck up, it's my ass on the line, so you better believe that I will make your life a literal living hell. I am using literal correctly.
—Dakota

PAXTON

On Paxton's first day at MotherCloud, the Incoming building had been filled with buses. Today they'd been moved outside, to make room for the Black Friday ceremony, so besides the steady stream of trucks driving through the sensors at the far side of the facility, the place was empty and cavernous.

Paxton watched as a team of workers in green and brown polos erected a raised platform, servicing speakers the size of SUVs, creating the framework that would hold the humongous 360-degree projection screen. They moved with an incredible amount of speed and precision. This was the setup they used every year apparently, for the reading of the names.

The sight of work crews had grown familiar over the last couple of days. The hallways and the bathrooms were full of them. Even though there were no plans for Gibson to visit other parts of the facility, management seemed to be treating it like he'd be inspecting every square inch. Which meant every imperfection—every loose faucet, every busted urinal, every out-of-order escalator—was being fixed.

"You ready, comrade?"

Paxton turned to find Dakota had deep bags under her eyes—he doubted she'd slept in the last few days. But she was buzzing with energy, a large thermos on her belt loaded with her custom red-eye coffee, so dark it absorbed light. Paxton had tried it once and spent three hours worried his heart might explode. Though he figured by this time tomorrow, he might be asking to chug it.

"Think so," he said.

Dakota nodded. "Going to be a team of five with him at all times. You, me, then Jenkins, Cheema, and Masamba. You know them?"

"Cheema and Masamba."

"I'll introduce you to Jenkins later. She's good. This is a good team."

"Listen, thanks again for trusting me with this."

"Hey," she said, balling her fist and jabbing it into his arm. It hurt more than he'd expected but he didn't want to show it. "You earned it. Can't believe you finally cracked that damn thing."

Paxton laughed. "You want to know something? It was a momentary epiphany, and it could have hit anyone. I think it did me good just to get out for the day. I don't know. It doesn't feel that special."

"Hey," Dakota said, her voice sharp. "Do not sell yourself short. We don't have much of a hierarchy at Cloud, but I've been Dobbs's right hand for a little while now. With him maybe moving me up to tan— there's going to be room for someone who distinguishes himself."

A lump formed in Paxton's throat. He didn't know what to think of that. On one hand, it meant another rope tying him to this facility. But the more he thought about it, the more it felt like this place was the whole world, and everything else on the planet had withered away and died.

Being in that town, held at gunpoint, had been more than terrifying. It had been heartbreaking. As if he'd seen the world after sobering up and found out what it really looked like in the harsh light of day. Here he had safety, and cool air, and fresh water, and a place to sleep. Here was a job and a life, and maybe it wasn't the life he wanted, but if he worked on it for a bit, maybe it could be one that he would grow to appreciate.

"You don't have to decide now," Dakota said, taking a swig of coffee and grimacing. "But keep an open mind. Job like that comes with perks."

"Yeah, I'll think about it," Paxton said. "How you holding up?"

"Best I can," said Dakota. "Hardest part is my mom is sitting up in my room right now watching television. She's here for our yearly Thanksgiving dinner. I was going to take her to CloudBurger. They have a special turkey burger. But I just don't think I'm going to have the time."

"What do you think we're in for tomorrow?" Paxton asked.

Dakota took another pull from the thermos, looked around. "No idea. I spoke to some people at the other MotherClouds who hosted him. Seems he gets around okay on his own. Looks like a zombie but I guess that's to be expected. Question is the crowds. At the New Hampshire site, people couldn't be bothered. Kentucky? They treated him like a messiah. People rushing barriers just to touch him."

"Has he ever been here before?" Paxton asked.

"Not in my time," she said. "Dobbs said once, yeah, but not for anything major. Meeting. Not a meet-and-greet like this. You get the memo?"

"I got the memo," he said.

"Good," she said. "Dobbs said if things run smoothly tomorrow he'll give me two days off in a row." She paused, thought about it. "Fuck, I wouldn't even know what to do with myself."

"Sleep," Paxton said. "Please."

"Sleep is for people who lack ambition." Sip. "How much longer you got on shift?"

"Hour."

"Good. Give the route another walk. Remember, soon as he's done speaking, ceremony over, we go to the tram, there'll be a car waiting. The system will be shut down for everyone but us. We go to Live-Play, he walks around, back to Incoming, he's out. Nice and simple. Bunch of monkeys couldn't fuck this up."

"I'm sure we'll find a way."

Dakota leaned forward, put the sharp point of her finger toward Paxton's nose. "Do not even joke."

"Sorry."

"All right, skedaddle, comrade," she said.

"Sure thing, boss."

Paxton walked away and had made it about ten feet when Dakota yelled, "Hey."

He turned. She approached, a hop in her step. "Forgot. My brain is like pudding right now. The guy you got? Dobbs has been working him over. He gave up names. Then Dobbs worked *them* over. And we found out how people were beating the bands."

"Holy shit, really?"

"You'll never guess."

"I didn't guess. That was exactly the problem."

Dakota smiled, enjoying drawing it out, making it dramatic. Then she said, "So you know how the watches are coded to the user? Seems that functionality broke, like two software updates ago. The nerds in tech didn't notice. A lot of folks are getting fired over this one. Someone could take off their band and put it on a partner. Since all the watch needed to do was register a warm body, the alarm didn't go off. The person without the watch would run their errand and come back. You were right about another thing, too—they would do it in crowds, because they thought no one would notice the signal dropping out for a couple of seconds."

Paxton shook his head. "That's . . . ridiculous. I can't believe it was that simple."

"They're working on a fix," Dakota said. "Might need more than a software update. Might need a hardware update. Expensive one, too. But hey, at least now we know."

Paxton laughed. "Well, damn."

"And this," Dakota said, "is why Dobbs is so happy with you. Keep it up, idea man."

ZINNIA

As Zinnia tipped the bottom of the vodka bottle toward the ceiling, draining the last of the stinging liquid down her throat, she wondered if she should walk.

She didn't see any way through multiple layers of security, into the bowels of a restricted area, and then all the way back to kill someone who would be surrounded by a heavy guard. Not when she couldn't open a single door between here and there.

It didn't compute. It had nothing to do with killing Paxton. Nothing. The more she said it, the more she believed it.

She shook the empty bottle of vodka and set it on the bedside table. Called up the Cloud site on the television to see if she could order some more. And no, as it happened, you couldn't order alcohol on Cloud. What terrible bullshit that was.

She wanted to drink more, but that was being overruled by her lack of any desire to get up, or put on pants, or see other people. So she sat, figured it was best to leave soon. She wasn't sure how, exactly. Maybe rent a car again and ditch it somewhere. But that would mean getting Paxton to intervene, again, and it might be suspicious to ask.

She could hike it. Nearest city was maybe a hundred miles? It would take a couple of days. She might be able to flag down a ride at some point. She'd need to pack a lot of water, to be safe. Maybe a weapon, to be safer, after her little dance with Ember and her hippie brigade.

As for her employers' maybe coming to kill her—she'd figure it out. She was too drunk to care at the moment.

Her phone buzzed. She stared at the wall.

It buzzed again. She rolled her eyes.

Hey, what are you up to?

Then: *Fancy a drink?*

Zinnia stared at the text bubbles for a few moments. Tonight was likely her last chance to see Paxton. She had a funny little feeling in her tummy that could have been gas but also could have been approaching something close to regret. Whatever. She could get him to bring more vodka and then he'd go down on her. Those were the reasons and the reasons alone, she told herself, as she wrote back: *Come by. Bring vodka.*

Twenty minutes later there was a knock at the door. Paxton was all smiles, first because of something else, something that had happened that day, and then he looked down and saw she wasn't wearing pants, and he smiled even wider. He leaned down and kissed her and she stepped back into the apartment, made her way to the futon, and fell into it while Paxton prepared two rocks glasses with ice from the mini-fridge.

"Wow," Zinnia said. "You're joining me?"

"It was a good day," Paxton said. "I'm a fucking rock star."

Zinnia nodded, reclined on the futon, her head swimming. Paxton handed her a glass. They clinked them together and drank and Paxton pushed his head down toward her crotch, and she went a little breathless until he dropped his head in her lap and rolled over, looking up at her, wanting to cuddle like some girlfriend-boyfriend nonsense. She wanted to admonish him, tell him to get to work, but he was still smiling, and that smile really was the thing she liked best about him.

It was an honest smile.

"It feels good," he said.

"What?"

"Being in their good graces again. Does that make me a bad person?"

Zinnia shrugged. "We're hardwired for approval. It's all anyone wants."

"Yeah, but these are the people who destroyed my company," he said. He was silent for a bit, and said, "Well, Dakota didn't. Dobbs didn't. I guess when it comes down to it, Gibson didn't either. He didn't come and personally . . ." He waved the glass around. "Smash up my shit. The market did. I tried my best. But the market dictates."

"It does tend to do that," Zinnia said, sipping at her vodka.

Paxton furrowed his brow, looked at her a little harder. "You okay?"

No.

"Yeah," she said. "Tired."

"Ever hear anything back from the Rainbow Coalition?" he asked.

"Not a peep."

"Well, things are working out with Dobbs, so maybe I can put in a good word with him, get you onto security." He put his feet up on the counter, trying to find room in the cramped space. "Way you handled yourself back in that town with those loony toons, you're well suited for it."

Zinnia huff-laughed. Sure. Can you get me on by tomorrow afternoon?

"Maybe," she said. "That wouldn't be so bad."

"I keep thinking about them," Paxton said. "How sad that must be. Living in squalor. Squatting in broken towns. They'd been doing it for a while, right? You could tell. The way they smelled. They hadn't seen a shower or a clean piece of clothing in a long time. I know what we have here. . . ." He paused, looked at his vodka, lifted his head a little so he could sip from the glass. "I know what we have here isn't perfect, but it's something, right? We have jobs."

Zinnia didn't know who he was trying to convince. But she'd take the wasteland. She was sick of this place. The brutalist surfaces and the cramped spaces and the digital scales and scarves and books and flypaper and flashlights and staplers and tablets. The mini-marathon she ran every day at work so that when she came home her knees ached. And worst of all: the prospect of doing that every single day.

She'd take the wasteland.

"I was thinking," Paxton said.

Zinnia thought he was going to go on from there but he didn't. "What were you thinking?" she asked.

"I was looking into it, and if it's weird, we can just drop it," he said. "It was just an idea. But, if we were to get a two-person apartment, it would be a little pricey, but we'd get a little more space, and I just thought . . ." He looked at his feet, the only way to hide his eyes that didn't involve completely covering his face. "I thought it might be nice. You know. Bigger bed, especially."

Zinnia took a big chug of vodka, and as the alcohol poured down her throat she felt her heart crack in two. Maybe years of trying to make it hard had made it brittle. Maybe that was all it would take, one solid smack of a hammer.

Every day the monkey job, then coming home to, what, read books? Watch television? Sit around and wait to run the marathon again? How was that supposed to be "nice"?

Zinnia sipped her vodka, thought about it.

About whether it was nice.

She'd worked hard for a very long time. Like, very hard. Her body carried the memories of her work. Scars Paxton's fingertips would linger on, but he would never ask about, and she liked that about him. That and his smile. And he was funny sometimes, too.

She thought about the wasteland. The hot sun and the fight for water. The emptiness outside the cities and the cool air circulating in this room, and she would give this to Cloud, there were a great many things about this place she didn't like, but at least it was quiet. Tomb quiet, and after years of the kinds of things she'd gotten used to—from the crack of gunfire to the raspy voices of interrogators to the deep thrum of explosions—she found that quiet was another thing she liked.

If she stayed, tomorrow she would wake up and report to the warehouse floor and pick shit out and put it on conveyor belts and send it off to whoever.

Could she even stay without finishing the job?

"I'm sorry," Paxton said, his voice heavy. "I shouldn't have brought it up."

"No, it's not that," she said. "I've never lived with anyone before." She leaned down and kissed him on the forehead. "I thought it was expensive."

Paxton shrugged. "I'm still waiting for my patent on the egg to come through. Once it does . . . I'll make some money selling it to Cloud."

"You really want to do that?"

Another shrug. "Not like I can afford to start another company."

"Okay," Zinnia said. "Let me think about it for a bit."

Paxton smiled; reached his arm to the floor, where he put down his glass of vodka; and then put his face where Zinnia had wanted it to go in the first place, and as she dug her nails into his scalp and arched her back, pushing herself into him, she thought, well, maybe this kind of life wasn't so bad. Maybe it was like a kind of retirement.

PAXTON

Paxton returned from the bathroom to find Zinnia sprawled on the futon, half-tangled in the top sheet. He closed the door; dropped her robe, which had just barely fit him for the walk down the hall; and climbed onto the futon beside her.

That feeling reared up in his stomach again. Like he wanted to tell her that he loved her. So easy to say, but also a bell that couldn't be unrung. He rolled onto his back and looked up at the tapestries hanging from the ceiling. Told himself: Be happy she's thinking of moving in with you. Leave it at that.

He thought about an apartment that was full with the two of them together, and that made him think of the emptiness of his notebook. Moving in with Zinnia wasn't just about his feelings for her. It was an acceptance that the notebook would likely stay empty. That this would be a good enough future. And who knew, maybe inspiration would strike, and he'd have the opportunity to try again, but Cloud was where he belonged, because it was where he was with her.

Zinnia stirred, climbed over him, her body radiating heat, and padded to the sink. Pulled a clean glass out of the cupboard and filled it with water, downed it in one large gulp. "Want one?" she asked.

"Nope," he said, admiring the curve of her back in the dim light. Hoping she would notice his admiring and want to go for round two. Instead she bent down to pick up her robe and threw it over her shoulders, cinching it tight at the waist. She nodded toward the nightstand.

"Can you hand me my watch? Need to hit the restroom."

Paxton reached back blindly, grabbed the first one off the charging mat that he felt. It was his. He shrugged and handed it to her.

"C'mon," she said. "Our bands aren't even close."

"Doesn't matter," he said. "Use mine."

"I thought the watches were coded to the user."

Paxton laughed. "Funny story. Turns out they're not. That feature is broken. Remember when there was that issue with people fooling the tracking? Turns out all you had to do was give your watch to someone else to wear for a bit, then go do what you had to do and come back. Which is crazy, right? They're working on a fix, but apparently that's going to take some time."

"Huh," Zinnia said.

After a few moments she said it again. "Huh."

And she smiled.

"Keep that on the down-low," Paxton said. "Actually maybe you better take your own watch. . . ." He reached back to grab hers, but when he turned, she was already out the door.

REMEMBRANCE 9

GIBSON

This is a tough thing to write about. Must have gone through six or seven versions of this. I've never talked a lot about the Black Friday Massacres, mostly because I felt like it wasn't my place to say anything, but I figure since I'm getting near the end of the road here, I ought to weigh in.

What a terrible day that was. I know, a real controversial stance to take, isn't it? America always had this uncomfortable relationship with firearms. And, I get it. I was born in a family with a proud hunting tradition. I knew how to strip and clean a rifle before I was ten, and I was always taught to treat guns with the utmost respect. Same goes for anything I shot. I was never one of these idiots out in the Serengeti shooting a lion so that I could prove something.

No, we would hunt moose and elk and squirrel, and we'd eat them and tan the hides. My dad would even whittle tools out of the bones, because it felt important to use as much of the animal as we could. You don't want to waste.

But at the same time, I know the way I feel about guns is very different from how someone might feel if they live in Detroit or Chicago.

Everyone has an opinion and every opinion is different. That's the problem. Here's my opinion: it was a damn stupid mistake to make firearms part of a doorbuster sale. Honestly, and I remember this exactly, I was drinking my coffee and reading the paper and I saw that get announced, and my first thought was, Some poor fool is liable to get shot.

It was a dark thought and I pushed it away. I like to think better of people than that. I hate that I was right. I hate even more how right I was. Who knew that it would happen, and at so many stores? Who knew so many would end up dead?

That's when I put my foot down and said we weren't selling guns anymore. Which I had spent years negotiating for the right to do, and they were the only item in our entire store that had to be delivered by a person and signed for by a person.

But I was sick, to my stomach and my heart, and I knew something had to change. Sometimes you got to take the lead. And look what happened. With the brick-and-mortar chains circling the drain and Cloud handling everything else and small shops unable to compete—used to be something like twenty million guns were manufactured a year in the United States and that number is down to less than a hundred thousand. And even then, guns are really expensive, putting them out of reach for most folks, and if there's one industry I don't feel bad about hurting, it's that one.

The Black Friday Massacres were the last mass shooting in America and I am happy to have played a role in that.

The market dictated. By that I mean, Americans voted with their wallets, accepting us as their main retail point, knowing full well we wouldn't be flying guns out to their front doors.

I'll say it again, because I know how easy it can be to misrepresent what people say: I mourn those people more than you might think, but I am glad, at least, that America finally came to its senses on this difficult issue.

So, there we go. I'd encourage you all to take a couple of minutes to yourselves, have a good long think. At Cloud, as usual, we will hold a ceremony, and a moment of silence for workers who can't get off shift. We'll read the names of the deceased, and we will continue to honor their memory the best we can, by working hard, and by showing compassion for each other.

The other thing I wanted to say, and this is a hard reality to admit but I can't avoid it any longer, is today will probably be my last visit to a MotherCloud facility. I just can't do it anymore. I'm barely sleeping. It's tough to keep food down. I'm trying my best but there are days where I need my nurse—big fella named Raoul—to carry me around a bit. And that's no way to live.

So today is going to be very special for me. It'll be another last.

My last tour of a MotherCloud. Claire and Ray are going to join me for it, and we're going to have a nice little walk around, and then it's back on the bus, and home. I'll keep on trying to write, though it might not all make it onto the blog. Not yet. I had to have Molly look this one over for me, and she even took over typing for me halfway through. Say hello, Molly.

Let the record show that Molly just smacked me in the arm. She wants me to take this seriously.

So, in case this is it, I want to thank you all for tuning in. I wish I was able to meet every Cloud employee before I went. I am just full of wishes right now. Things that'll have to be left undone, but that's life, isn't it?

I guess at this point I should try to leave you all with some words of wisdom. As if anything I said could be considered wisdom. But you know, I always lived by a pretty basic principle: work gets done or it doesn't, and I like when the work gets done.

If you can focus on that, and your family, everything will probably be all right.

Swear to truth, from the bottom of my heart, thank you.

It has been an honor to live this life.

ZINNIA

The tram line is officially shut down for Remembrance Day ceremony.

Zinnia put her CloudBand on the charging mat and dressed quickly, pulling on workout clothes—sweatpants and a thick hoodie, something that would conceal her empty wrist. As she dressed she ran through the plan in her head. There were a lot of moving parts. It relied too much on intel she didn't have. But it would have to be enough.

She pulled down the tapestry in the corner, climbed into the ceiling, and shuffled across to the bathroom. Empty. She dropped to the floor and stepped outside, found a woman at the elevator already, so she jogged to get on before it closed.

Once inside, the woman swiped her wrist and Zinnia stepped to the back and waited. She got off at the lobby and made her way to the gym. She lingered until someone else was coming in—a dudebro with beautifully sculpted arms who opened the door for her so he could very obviously scope her ass.

Inside the gym she threw some light weights around until she was sure there was no one looking, and stuck a ten-pound rubber plate in the front pocket of her hoodie. She exited the gym, keeping one hand on the plate so it didn't sag, and made her way down the hallway, to the lobby, where she could get a look at the tram entrance.

The place had been emptied out. There was only one blue, an older man who looked bored. Probably everyone else was over at Incoming preparing for Wells and the ceremony. She pressed herself against the wall, out of sight of him, and waited.

He made a long loop of the place, not really letting the tram out of his sight. Which was not great.

She thought about the matches in her pocket, of lighting something on fire in one of the trash bins, which would draw his attention away, but also might attract too much attention. Not the best option, but it would work. Before she could reach for the matches, the guard looked around like he was afraid of being caught and made a beeline for the bathroom.

As soon as he was out of sight, Zinnia popped out and made her way to the tram and slid underneath the arm of the gate. She flattened herself on the platform and reached down, and placed the plate between the wall and the track, careful not to touch the actual lines. It was an octagon, with a flat edge, so she was able to balance it on its side. She paused, waiting for a sensor to go off, but nothing happened. The lines were most likely weight-sensitive to detect debris. Being able to stand up the plate without touching any of the lines—it should go undetected. And it should work to jam up the train.

Should should should. This was sloppy, and she hated sloppy, but sloppy was better than the alternative.

She slid under the gate arm and made her way back to the elevator. As she was waiting, the guard came out, so she busied herself looking at the Cloud map, bouncing from foot to foot like she might go for a jog, not wanting him to wonder why she was standing there.

This stretch of track was a straight shot, and it was where the trams usually picked up a little speed. Since it wasn't stopping until Live-Play, it ought to be going pretty fast.

Zinnia thought about Paxton. About his standing next to Wells, and the car hitting the plate, and the derailment. Broken bodies and mangled limbs. Lots of blood. She put it out of her head. Concentrated on the money she'd get. The freedom it would give her. All the things she could leave behind.

A man approached the elevator and Zinnia got on behind him. He swiped, but for the wrong floor. Zinnia yelped, "Oh, damn it, forgot something," and leapt off. She had to do that two more times over the space of fifteen minutes until finally, someone got on who was going to her floor.

She stopped in front of a door a few doors down from her own and knocked. Her chest buzzed with anticipation. She had seen Hadley earlier this morning, in the bathroom, and Zinnia had asked if she was going to the ceremony, and the girl had said no. After a moment she heard a shuffle and the door opened, and Hadley's big cartoon eyes peered out from the darkness, from beneath a tangle of hair. She stared at Zinnia like a cat would stare at anything, betraying no particular emotion.

"Can I come in?" Zinnia asked.

Hadley nodded, took a step back. The air in the apartment was thick. Unwashed body and old food. The walls were strung up with Christmas lights but they were turned off and there was a heavy shade over the window, so only a little filtered sunlight made it through. The countertop was piled with paper takeout bags, crumpled up around empty containers. Hadley retreated to the rear of the apartment and sat on the futon, looking up at Zinnia, her hands clasped together. Zinnia leaned against the counter and was about to speak when Hadley cleared her throat.

"I've been thinking a lot about what you said, in the bathroom," she said, her voice barely above a whisper. "And you're right. It was my fault."

"No, no, honey, that's not what I said at all," Zinnia said, the bottom dropping out of her stomach. "It's not your fault, what he did. That's on him. But you have to swing back. That's all I meant."

"I'm having such a hard time sleeping. Sometimes I wake up and I feel like he's in here with me." She put her arms around herself, shivered despite the warmth. "I just . . . I need to sleep." She looked up. "I want to be strong. Like you."

Zinnia went temporarily speechless. She hadn't expected this feeling, of wanting to put her arm around the girl and pull her close and stroke her head and tell her everything was going to be all right. She couldn't remember the last time she'd felt that way with anyone, which made it all the more appalling. She tried to think of Hadley as a toy doll that said things when you pulled its string but otherwise was a lump of plastic.

Zinnia brushed her hand against the little case in her pocket. "I have something that might help."

Hadley looked up, eyes wide, expectant. Zinnia knelt down next to her, held the oblivion container in her outstretched palm.

"Is that—" Hadley said, cutting herself off, like she couldn't say the word.

"You'll sleep like a baby," Zinnia said.

"I have to work. After the ceremony."

"You need to sleep. Punch out sick."

"But my rating—"

"Fuck your rating," Zinnia said. "It's a number. It'll go down a little and then you'll work hard and it'll go back up. You'll be fine. You need some mindless, empty sleep. Trust me. You look like you're about to come apart at the seams."

Hadley stared at the container for a long time. Zinnia was worried she'd have to hold the girl down and shove it in her mouth, but then Hadley nodded her head. "How do you take it?"

Zinnia opened the little plastic case and regarded the thin strips of film. She told herself: The girl needs this. She needs to detach her brain stem and float for a little while.

Zinnia said it to herself in such a way that she almost believed it.

"You just put it on your tongue," she said.

"Okay," Hadley said. "Okay."

She stuck out her tongue, then sheepishly tucked it back in, like she was embarrassed to assume that Zinnia would feed it to her. Zinnia knew a girl her size, never having taken the drug before, would get knocked for a loop by one. She thumbed out four tabs, held them together, and nodded toward her mouth. Hadley opened it and Zinnia placed the green-tinted squares on her tongue. The girl closed her eyes, as if she were deep in thought. Zinnia eased her back onto the futon.

Hadley's breathing faded, her muscles went slack. Her head rolled to the side. Zinnia pressed her fingers to the girl's carotid artery, just to make sure she was still alive. Her pulse felt like it was taking deep, purposeful breaths.

Then she got to work. Stripped out of her shirt, picked up Hadley's brown polo. It was snug but manageable. She considered swapping out the straps on the CloudBand but realized they were similar enough— Zinnia's fuchsia band was close enough to Hadley's pink. She rooted through the rest of Hadley's clothes and found an old, beaten baseball cap. She fought her hair into a ponytail, put on the hat. Looked in the mirror hanging from the rear of the door. She strapped on Hadley's watch and it prompted her for a fingerprint, so Zinnia took Hadley's hand and pressed her thumb to the screen. The smiley face appeared.

Good to go.

PAXTON

The crowd was impossible to count. A rainbow of colors stretched around the entirety of Incoming. There were wide tracks of empty floor space: from outside, leading to behind the stage, where Gibson's bus would travel, and then leading down the stage and snaking around to the tram line, where he'd take his ride to Live-Play.

Paxton walked across the stage. Eyes peeled, like Dakota said. Blues were worming their way through the crowd, but it was good to have landscape eyes, too. Paxton wasn't sure what exactly he was looking for. Everyone was all smiles and jittery anticipation.

Cloud videos blared on the mammoth screen behind him. The video that showed during orientation mixed with customer testimonials. An ethnically diverse group talking about how much easier their lives had been made by the people watching them. This close to the speakers, the dialogue crackled.

> Thank you, Cloud.
> We love you, Cloud.
> You saved my life, Cloud.

Every few minutes he glanced toward the gaping maw of the entranceway, a rectangle of blinding white light, where the bus would enter. It was due soon. It would pull up behind the stage and Gibson Wells, the man himself, would get out and walk up the stairs. Paxton would be among a dozen people surrounding him. So close they could touch.

Paxton's stomach twisted on itself, pushing in both directions. He thought again of confronting the man. He would surely lose his job, on the spot, but that raw feeling of walking through that broken town to his interview, that feeling of applying for a job that felt so far below where he had climbed, it made him want, even if not an answer or an apology, recognition. For Gibson to see him, to know it happened.

"You ready?" Dakota asked, suddenly at his side, yelling over the speakers.

Paxton nodded, even though he wasn't sure exactly what the nod meant.

"Good," Dakota said, clapping him on the back. "Because here he comes."

The bus entered, first a dark spot in the white light, then pulling into the facility, rolling slowly through the crowd. People stacked twenty deep on either side of the barricades, shouting and cheering and waving.

The bus was big and maroon with gold trim. Blacked-out windows, so you couldn't see what was inside. It looked like it had just been polished. Even inside it seemed to gleam with eternally reflected sunlight. Paxton watched it pull slowly to the designated spot behind the stage, among a dozen tans and two dozen blues, and his head felt like it was filled with helium and might come off his shoulders.

Zinnia pushed her way through the swinging doors at the back of CloudBurger. There were a few workers in green, buzzing about, even though no one was out front eating, everyone gone for the ceremonies. The greens worked the immaculate stainless-steel machinery in a choreographed dance of clacking tools and fryer oil, prepping for the rush that would come later. A few of them glanced at her but didn't budge beyond that.

It was always funny to her, how people thought this line of work was all gadgets and shit. The most basic rule of subterfuge was to pretend like you belonged, and it was exceedingly rare that anyone would challenge you.

That didn't mean she could linger. She slid her eyes over every surface, not sure what she was looking for but hoping she would find it. The kitchen was larger than she would have imagined, with a few twists and turns that eventually led her to a heavy sliding door. Which looked more out of place than anything in the kitchen, which meant that was where she needed to be.

There was a camera here. She caught it too late, just visible from under the brim of her hat. She didn't look up, so as not to give it too clear a look at her face. There was an entry pad next to the door and she swiped the CloudBand, whispering a silent prayer in her head.

That ding. The disc turned green. She pushed the door to the side. It was big and heavy and she had to put a good bit of muscle into it. It opened onto a small subway station with a tram car, maybe about half the size of a regular car.

And it had a smell. Bleach, and under that, the sweet smell of rot. Like someone had tried to beat it back but couldn't win. On the tram were uncoupled nylon straps. These were for shipping pallets, not people. She slid the door closed behind her, walked to the front of the tram car, found the controls. She didn't even need to examine the panel. There were a couple of buttons, one of them marked Go. They really did like to make things simple around here.

She hit the button and the tram moved forward, slowly at first, but then faster, whizzing through dark corridors, rattling like a service elevator. She grabbed a handle on the wall, to keep from getting thrown from her feet. The nylon straps whipped around and a few times she had to dodge a stray buckle threatening to slap her in the leg. It wasn't a maglev track. It was older. Metal on metal, the squeal piercing her eardrums in the dark tunnel.

The ride took about five minutes, during which she went over the endgame. Even with the confusion of the train crash there would still be trucks moving in and out. There had to be. They couldn't shut down deliveries for too long. And the delivery trucks were automated, so all she had to do was stow away on one and there would be a pretty low chance of someone stumbling across her.

But she felt like she was forgetting something.

Then she realized: Hadley. She wanted to make sure Hadley was okay.

Maybe she could text Paxton. Tell him to go to her room.

But it was risky to keep an open line of communication. And what would she say then?

Bye! See ya never!

"C'mon, asshole," she said to herself. "Don't get soft now."

When the car stopped, before the door opened, Zinnia's skin grew tight and her breath bloomed in front of her. She exited into a refrigerated room full of boxes stacked on wooden pallets, the walls smooth metal and covered with layers of frost, thick in the corners like snow. She wished she was wearing something thicker.

No cameras in here. She wandered among the pallets, looking for a way out, and saw a door at the far end. On the way there, she opened a box. Inside were round balls of ground beef laid out on wax paper. CloudBurgers.

Which was strange. Everything, including food, came in through Incoming. Paxton had said something about that. If she was in the processing facilities, why were they storing the ground beef here? Her understanding was Cloud owned the means of production, which was why the beef was affordable. Maybe they had grazing land beyond the campus. Something where cows could still eat and roam safely, and this was the closest access point. She hadn't seen it on the satellite images, but she hadn't been looking for it either.

Not important. Zinnia made for the door, opened it, found an empty hallway. At the far end was another large sliding door.

She made for that, swiped her wrist. It turned green and she opened it, and a stench hit her like an ocean wave. It filled her nose, clawed down her throat, overcame her, like she'd been shoved head-first into a clogged toilet.

PAXTON

The bus sat, the engine off. The crowd, which was pushed back and didn't have a good vantage point, began to chant, slow at first, scattered, but growing in strength. It grew until Paxton could feel the vibration of it in his chest.

Gib-son.

Gib-son.

GIB-SON!

Signs dotted the crowd—hand-lettered in thick black marker.

> We love you, Gibson!
> Thank you for everything!
> Don't leave us!

Paxton stood at his post, at the top of the stage, watching behind him, to make sure the space was clear. From where he was standing, the door of the bus was on the other side, facing away from him, but there seemed to be movement and activity. People disappearing and reappearing. Moving back and forth.

Paxton had to look down to make sure his feet were still on the floor. That he hadn't floated away.

They were planted. He was still there. Right there.

He looked up and saw the face of the person he'd been waiting for.

Gibson Wells.

The man was flanked by a thick entourage. People who walked with their hands out like they might need to catch him. He was smaller than Paxton would have imagined. A man who had changed so much, who had shaped the world as much as he had, ought to have been bigger.

An image of Gibson appeared on the video screen above them, from the orientation video, and he barely looked like the same person, looked as though the cancer had cored him out. His hair had been thinning, but now it was nearly gone, his bald head shiny under the lights. Skin collected around his neck; lines dug across his face. He walked with shuffle steps. He smiled and waved to the people around him and it seemed to take a titanic amount of effort. Like at any moment he might disintegrate into dust, and the only thing keeping him together was sheer force of will.

Behind him was a handful of people. A tall, muscled Latino man who hovered close. Claire, whom Paxton recognized from the video, though her hair wasn't the same brilliant shade of crimson, it was more of a washed-out red. And the man he suspected was Ray Carson. Dakota had told him to look out for the linebacker. It was an apt description. Carson had a thick brow scrunched under a bald head. Wide shoulders and the beginnings of a gut. He wasn't currently happy, but also seemed like the kind of person who wouldn't be happy anywhere.

Gibson Wells, the richest and most powerful man in the world, reached the bottom of the stairs, placed his hand on the railing for support, and looked up, locking eyes with Paxton.

ZINNIA

Zinnia heaved, emptying the contents of her stomach onto the grated metal floor; it fell in clumps to the ductwork underneath. She forced herself to stand. When she got to her feet, she threw up again. She saw a series of oxygen masks hanging from hooks on the wall, snatched one off, placed it on, breathed in deep. The inside of the mask smelled like shit and rubber and her own vomit, but also candy canes. Which made it worse. She hated candy canes.

The eyepieces of the mask warped her vision a little but she found another doorway at the end of the corridor. As she neared it, a skinny woman in a pink polo came through. Zinnia paused for a moment but then pressed on, not wanting to look like she'd been caught at something. They passed in the hallway, Zinnia stepping to the side a little bit to give her some clearance. The woman nodded at her and kept on walking.

Pink. She'd never seen a pink shirt before.

She made it through a few more corridors, and it felt like she was traveling through the bowels of a ship. Circular hallways, no windows, bundles of pipes running along the walls. She found another door and figured if it led to another hallway, she would double back and look for a better entry point, but on the other side of the door she found a large laboratory. Workstations, buzzing machines, lights. Lights everywhere. There was a second level within the room—a large glass box, a staircase leading up to it. Inside the box were tables, where men and woman in lab coats and oxygen masks fussed with tubes and containers of liquid.

Down on the floor, where Zinnia was, the few workers milling about weren't wearing masks, so she took off hers, hung it on an empty peg on the wall. Her mouth still tasted like vomit but it smelled sweet in here. Artificial, like the air was filtered and treated. She made her way through the room. A few people—some whites but mostly pinks—glanced at her briefly, some of them lingering for a moment on her face, wondering if they recognized it, but then quickly returned to whatever it was they were working on.

The eyes made her nervous. She spied a doorway and hoped it would take her into another hallway, but it didn't. Instead, it opened into a small room where a slight Asian man with jet-black parted hair leaned over a microscope. He looked up, registered the color of her polo, and shook his head. "I didn't call tech." After a moment he turned to her. "You know, you're not even supposed to be in here."

Zinnia didn't like his tone. Like he wanted to report this. Instinct took over and she leapt forward and pushed him down onto the table, knocking the microscope to the side. She looked around to make sure they were alone, that there were no cameras in the room.

"What the hell are you doing?" the man asked, his voice shaking.

Zinnia didn't know how to respond. She was still sick from the hallway. The man struggled beneath her but she had both leverage and strength, so after a few moments he gave up.

"Where is here?" Zinnia asked. "What is this?"

The man twisted his neck, to look up at her. "You . . . you don't know?"

"Know what?"

"Nothing. It's nothing. It's just a . . . this is processing. You're not supposed to be here."

"Processing. Processing what?"

The man paused, so Zinnia applied a little pressure to his throat. He croaked out, "Waste."

She thought of the first room. The burger patties. Her mind went blank, then filled with a silent scream. "What?"

"Listen, they swore to us, okay? They swore to us you'd never be able to taste it. They're perfectly safe."

An image was coming together in Zinnia's mind. "Taste what?"

"We extract the protein," he said, rambling, like maybe that might save him. "Bacteria make protein, and we just pull that out and treat it with ammonia to sterilize it. It gets reconstituted with wheat and soy and beets for coloring. I swear, it's low-fat protein. Totally clean."

She knew the answer but she asked it anyway. "What is low-fat protein?"

Silence. Then, in a whisper, "The CloudBurgers."

Zinnia had thought she had emptied the entirety of her stomach, but she found more, turned to the side and puked a thin stream of bile on the floor. She thought of the countless CloudBurgers she had shoved down her throat since she got here, and she wanted to puke until there was nothing left in her stomach. Until she didn't have a stomach.

"You mean to tell me the beef is just repurposed human shit?" she asked.

"When you get into the science of it, it's not that bad," he said. "I . . . I eat them myself. I swear."

He was lying about the last part. Zinnia, meanwhile, was trying to breathe through her nose, not think about the sizzling brown meat. How often did she eat there? Twice a week? Three times? She wanted to throw her fist into the back of the man's head but didn't. It wasn't his fault.

Or was it? He was facilitating.

She pushed the thought away. "The pink shirts. What is that? I've never seen pink shirts in the dorms."

"We . . . waste processing has its own dorm."

"So like a whole separate workforce?"

"There are only a few hundred of us. We're kept away from most of the facilities here, yes. We get paid better. Nicer . . . nicer apartments. It's a sacrifice."

She let him go and made sure to block his path to the door. He put his hands up and moved toward the rear of the room, looking for protection, for a place to hide, finding none. Zinnia looked around the room for something to tie him up with, her brain spinning, trying to make sense of it.

She forced herself to look on the bright side: if her employers wanted Cloud taken down, this was worth a hefty bonus. This would probably do the job all by itself. Whatever hoodoo was powering this place could not be nearly as bad as human shit burgers.

She had to think of it like that, as a bargaining chip potentially worth something. It helped her to not think about how many Cloud-Burgers she'd eaten.

About the greasiness of them.

She shuddered.

"Tell me exactly how to get to the energy processing facility from this room," she said to the man, who had his hands up to protect his face.

PAXTON

Gibson paused, like he was mentally preparing himself for the journey up the eight steps to where Paxton stood. No one between them now. Everyone had moved behind him, letting him go first, and Paxton was the welcome party.

In a flash, a memory of his first day as CEO of the Perfect Egg came back to him. Filling out reams of paperwork for the patent, for the business, sitting at his desk, alone and afraid, but also free. No more waking up at six fifteen a.m., driving an hour and a half to wander cell blocks while criminals screamed and wept and gnashed their teeth.

Gibson lifted his foot onto the first step, his head down, concentrating. Someone reached out a hand to help—Paxton couldn't see whose hand in the scrum—but Gibson batted it away.

That first official product-ready cast of the Perfect Egg, the first one he was supposed to sell, broke the 3-D printer. The tests had all come out fine, but he changed a calibration and suddenly the whole thing seized up, so that it was stuck, a third of the way down a block of plastic, only the top of the egg-shaped device finished. In that moment, he was convinced he'd made a mistake.

Gibson was halfway up the stairs now. The most powerful man in the world. His arms shook. From this close his skin had a yellowish tinge. His neck and the back of his hands and the parts of his arms that were showing were covered in brown liver spots.

Paxton's feet twitched. He wanted to run. Wanted to throw his foot out and trip the man. Wanted to grab him and shake him and ask, *Do you know who I am? Do you see me?*

Gibson reached the top step, breathing in hard, then exhaling, his head down. Paxton took a step back, to allow him some room, and then Gibson looked up. His eyes were the eyes of a young man. In them, independent of anything else, there was vibrancy. Energy. That way you look at someone and see wheels turning ceaselessly, and you wonder how they sleep.

Gibson smiled and nodded and said, "And what's your name, young man?"

He stuck out his gnarled hand.

Paxton grasped it. Involuntary reflex. The polite thing to do. They shook and Gibson's hand felt cold and sweaty at the same time.

"Paxton . . . sir."

"Please, Paxton, call me Gibson. Tell me, how do you like working here?"

"I . . ." His heart stopped beating for an instant. He was sure of it. It actually stopped. But then it started again. He tried to say what he wanted to say but the words were glued to the inside of this mouth.

Finally, he said, "I like it just fine, sir."

"Attaboy," Gibson said, nodding, stepping around Paxton, heading toward the stage, and a great roar went up from the crowd, so loud it sounded like water crashing into rocks, and Dakota was alongside Paxton, leaning close to him, her breath hot on his ear, screaming, barely audible, "I can't believe he shook your hand."

And Paxton just stood, staring at his feet. Frozen in the spot. In time. The scream in his head louder than the scream of the crowd.

ZINNIA

Zinnia stepped off the tram car that ran between the three processing buildings, into the energy processing facility, still trying to not think about the CloudBurgers, which would pretty much be impossible for the rest of her entire life.

The lobby had the same polished concrete and sharp angles of all the other lobbies and entranceways at Cloud, with video monitors playing ads and customer testimonials, branching into hallways that led into the bowels of the building.

It was also empty.

Most of the places she had gone today were empty, on account of the ceremony, but this one felt different. There was something off about it. She couldn't figure out what, but it might have had to do with her nervousness over finally being here, on the precipice.

After a moment she realized it wasn't completely devoid of life.

There was a small table set up at the far end, and sitting at the table was a zaftig young woman in a blue shirt, her brown hair done up in a beehive, her glasses a pair of thick red plastic frames. She didn't look up from the paperback she was reading.

Zinnia walked through the lobby toward the table, sneakers squeaking on the floor, the sound echoing off the walls, and as she got closer the woman looked up, and Zinnia could see she was reading a worn and beaten copy of *A Is for Alibi* by Sue Grafton.

"That's a good one," Zinnia said.

The woman squinted, like she was confused, like Zinnia wasn't supposed to be there. It made Zinnia nervous, and she was flipping through her head for viable excuses when the woman gave a little grin. "Read 'em all five or six times. I'm starting back at the beginning of the alphabet. The advantage of there being so many is I always forget who did it by the time I get back to the start."

"That's good though, right?" Zinnia asked. "You get to be surprised all over again."

"Hmm." She held the paperback open against her ample chest. "Can I help you, dear?"

"Yeah, just have to head in and talk to someone."

Her eyes narrowed, in a way that made Zinnia feel like she'd said the wrong thing. "Talk to who?"

"Tim."

"Tim . . ."

Uh-oh. "I forget his last name. Something Polish. No vowels."

The woman stared at Zinnia for a moment, the corners of her mouth pushing downward. She placed the paperback on the table, raised her wrist, and pressed the button on the side of her watch. "We have a situation in energy processing."

Zinnia leapt forward, grabbed the woman's arm. She yelled out, "Hey!," the paperback tumbling to the floor. Zinnia maintained her grip while she scurried over the table, then brought the woman down to the ground.

"What do you think you're doing?" she asked.

"Sorry," Zinnia said as she thumbed the oblivion container out of her pocket. She had enough leverage that she could hold the woman down with one arm, and with the other she opened the container and slid out a tab, then, as the woman was yelling for help, shoved it in her mouth. The woman bit down hard on Zinnia's finger and she had to yank hard to free her hand, but after a moment, the woman sagged.

She waited for some kind of reply to come through on the woman's CloudBand. None did. Good. Probably everyone was still wrapped up with the day's festivities.

But then it crackled to life.

"What kind of situation?"

Zinnia stood and bolted.

PAXTON

"Thank you, thank you."

Gibson said it a dozen times, trying to get the crowd to quiet down so he could speak. When he'd spoken to Paxton his voice had wavered, but standing up there onstage, in front of all those people, he'd found a hidden store of energy. There was a bass note to his voice. He drew on the energy of the crowd.

"Thank you so much for that warm welcome," he said as the applause died down. "Now, look, I have to be honest with you. I can't speak for long. But I just wanted to come up here and say thank you. From the bottom of my heart. It has been my great pleasure and honor to build this place, to see so many smiling faces out there. It's . . ." He paused, his voice growing thick. "It's humbling. It truly is humbling. Now, I'm going to sit over there"—he motioned to a series of chairs set up for him and his entourage—"for the reading of the names. And then I want to walk around a bit before we head out. This is a very special and important time for us to remember how lucky we are to be here, with each other." He glanced over at Carson and his daughter when he said this. "How lucky we are to be alive."

He put his hand up and the crowd roared again. He walked to the seats, where he was joined by the rest, and no one sat until he sat first, heavily, dropping his weight onto the chair. A woman in a white polo went up to the microphone and a hush fell over the crowd, and she began to read names.

> Josephine Aguerro
> Fred Arneson
> Patty Azar

Paxton felt his heart tug a little. It always did on this day. The Black Friday Massacres felt like a real thing and a fake thing at the same time. It was easy to forget, even though people were always saying you shouldn't forget. And it wasn't that you forgot it, not really, it just became a part of the background noise of your life. Like, Paxton could remember seeing it on the news when it happened. All those bodies. Blood gleaming red on white linoleum floors under fluorescent lights. But it became part of the landscape. It was a piece of history, and just like everything else in history, after a time it began to gather dust.

Days like today were a chance to run your hand over it, wipe off that dust, take a good look at it. Remember what it was that made it stand out so much in the first place. He wished he could turn it off. Think about something else. But he couldn't. So he stood there, hands folded, head bowed.

After all this time, some of the names he still recognized.

When it was over, Gibson and his small group stood and milled about, before making their way down the staircase on the other side of the stage, toward the tram car that would take them on the ride around campus. This time, Gibson let Claire help him down the stairs.

Carson, though, stood back, letting everyone get ahead of him. He looked around, surveying the crowd, curling and uncurling his fist. It got to the point where he was lagging so far behind Paxton was worried it would hold up the tram, so he came up behind Carson and asked, "Sir?"

Carson shook his head, snapped out of a trance. "Nothing, nothing." He waved his hand without looking Paxton in the eye and followed along with the rest.

Paxton took up a rear position as Gibson walked down the empty lane that had been cordoned off. He stopped every few feet, walked over to the divider, shook hands and smiled. Leaned in and cupped a hand to his ear so he could hear what the people were saying. His people were made nervous by this, like Gibson was approaching a pack of wild dogs while holding a dripping steak. They glanced at each other, getting closer, some of them moving like they were going to get between Gibson and the crowd, but then stepping back, unsure of the right answer in this scenario.

A few times Gibson turned toward Claire and waved her over. Claire seemed more content to stand off to the side, left arm limp, right hand over her elbow, hugging herself. The first few times, Gibson smiled, but soon he grew annoyed. Not that he betrayed it on his face. It was his hand. It started with friendly waves but soon his hand turned into a blade, slicing the air.

When Claire finally joined him, she would shake hands and bug out her eyes and smile and nod in that way people did when they wanted to be extra sure you knew they were listening. Every chance she got, she would hug herself again, while Gibson was nearly subsumed by the crowd, reaching in deeper to find as many of the hands offered to him as he could, the whole time a smile on his face that lit it up like the sun.

As they approached the platform for the tram, Paxton's phone buzzed. He reached for it on instinct, realized he shouldn't be checking it. Whatever it was, it wasn't important.

But then it buzzed again.

By this point he was at the rear of the pack and all eyes were forward. Even Dakota's and Dobbs's. Since no one was looking at him he turned his body away, slid the phone out of his pocket, just enough to see the screen, and found a message from Zinnia.

Don't get on the tram.

Then:

Please.

ZINNIA

Zinnia ran down hallways and ducked into offices and checked in bathrooms and examined server rooms and found no people. Not a single one in the entire facility, and more than that, it was quiet the way she expected the surface of the moon to be quiet.

No wonder the woman out front had pegged her down. Zinnia had asked to see someone when there was no one to see.

More than its being empty, nothing seemed to be turned on. A few times she stopped, at a computer, or at a bank of servers, looking for blinking lights, and found none. She put her hands on them, feeling for heat or vibration, but everything was dead and cold.

She'd expected a lot of people would be at the ceremony, but they had to leave some workers behind. MotherCloud wasn't a coffee maker; you couldn't turn around and walk away and let it do its thing. But it was like everyone had been raptured away from their spots. Everything was open, some of the doors she encountered even sitting ajar. The farther she went, the faster she ran, hoping to outrace the dread bubbling in her stomach.

Yet, despite the fallow nature of the building, she felt something. A static field in the air, like ants crawling on her skin. It pulled her deeper into the facility. Faced with a wide staircase, she went down. The pull felt like it was coming from below her.

As she went, she thought of Paxton.

If all went to plan, they'd be on the tram soon. The tram would hit the plate and it would derail and a lot of people would be hurt or killed. Paxton maybe included. She pictured it in her head. The bodies. The blood. Him, all twisted up in the middle of it, with his goofy face ripped open.

She pushed the image aside. Ignored the gentle *eeeeeeeeeeeeeeeee* that was ringing in her ear. Who was Paxton? Some guy. Who cared? People died. That was what they did. People were just sacks of meat with stuff inside. Some of that stuff made them move and talk. But in the end, it was just meat.

And anyway, the world had too many people. Overpopulation had gotten them into this mess, where you couldn't even go outside, so maybe some depopulation was a good thing. A couple fewer meat-sacks expelling carbon dioxide, sucking up resources.

The buzz on her skin picked up. She stopped. The hairs on her arms were standing. She was close. She didn't know to what, but she could feel it. A thrum.

Ahead of her was a metal door with a big spinning wheel in the center. She ran over, flashed her wrist across the access panel.

Red.

She tried again. Red.

Was she locked out because browns didn't have access or because security was barreling toward her? In what specific way was she fucked? She wasn't sure, but no matter what it was, time was short, so she leaned back and threw her heel into the panel, so hard it sent a shock up her leg. Once, twice. On the fifth try, the disc popped out of the wall, hanging limp from a trail of colored wires.

Good-bye subtlety. She mixed and matched the wires, trying to trip the circuit for the door, and after three shocks, the disc turned green. She spun the wheel, opening the door. Got it halfway. Thought about Paxton again.

The way he put his arm around her.

The way he asked about her day and cared.

The way he was there, like a pair of slippers and a warm blanket.

"Fuck," she said. "Fucking fuck."

She slapped the flat of her hand against the door.

Took out her phone. Pulled up her last text exchange with him.

Don't get on the tram.

Send.
Then:

Please.

Send.

Her phone made a little whoosh noise, and she felt a great relief come over her, like she'd been carrying a bag of sand on her shoulder and just set it down. That was probably a mistake, but on the sliding scale of mistakes, hopefully a good one. She turned the wheel and opened the door.

PAXTON

Paxton stared at his phone, then looked up and watched as Gibson and his entourage filed onto the tram. By the time everyone was on it, it was nearly packed. Everyone was laughing, like it was a big game. How many people could they squeeze on? No matter how full it got, the people crowded at the door were inviting stragglers to join them.

Dakota looked back at him, standing on the platform, and frowned. Then her eyebrows went up and her lip curled when she noticed the phone in his hand. She turned toward him, fists clenched.

What the hell did that mean?

Why would Zinnia not want him to get on the tram?

Dakota waved her hand, down by her hip, so no one would see her make the gesture. Whether she wanted him to come over or stash the phone, he couldn't tell.

It was silly to think, but he thought it anyway: the text message had a tone. Desperation? Fear? He didn't know how a text could have a tone, but it did. Zinnia was worried about him. Why would she be worried about him?

She would only tell him to stay off the tram if there was something wrong with the tram.

Dakota was getting closer now, raising her hands, as if to take the phone away from him. He considered asking her about it, but it looked like the people on the tram were just about done, satisfied with the amount of people they'd gotten aboard, and they were ready to depart.

"Wait," Paxton said.

Dakota asked, "The fuck is wrong with you?"

"Wait!" Paxton said, pushing past her, waving at the open mouth of the car, at the people bowed out of it.

Everyone on the car looked at each other in confusion.

Everyone except Carson. He locked eyes with Paxton and his face scrunched up, like he was trying to sort out a calculus problem in his head. Then his eyes went wide and his jaw drifted open, and he came barreling out of the scrum, face flushed, screaming at people to get out of his way, like he was trying to get off a sinking ship.

ZINNIA

Zinnia was struck by a blast of cold. Colder than the refrigerator room. Sinus-scorching cold. Beyond the door was a massive, square room—four stories at least, the concrete walls zigzagged with staircases and walkways.

And it was completely empty. Except for a box, the size and shape of a refrigerator, centered almost perfectly in the middle of the floor.

She stepped inside and the thrum filled her head. The walls seemed to pulse. The floor underneath her was chipped and uneven. There'd been machinery in this room—big machines. The concrete was discolored from oil spills. There were grooves and bolt holes and gouges where things had been dragged away.

Whatever this was, it was important, and the room was being repurposed for it. In a corner there were piles of scaffolding, bundles of wire, metal brackets, waiting to be assembled.

The refrigerator was gunmetal gray. She moved toward it, slowly, waiting for alarm bells, or for something to fall on her, or to pass out, but nothing happened. The air temperature changed. It seemed to get colder but also, oddly, humid.

She reached the box and pressed her fingers to it and it was so cold it burned her skin. There was a window on the side, but she couldn't see anything due to the frost that had accumulated on the inside.

Was this the thing powering Cloud?

Zinnia's head spun. There was no way—no way. This place was a city and this entire apparatus could fit into the back of a pickup truck.

Hands shaking, she removed her phone from her pocket and began to snap pictures. Every angle, every side of the thing. The walls and the floors. The construction material in the corner. The walls and the ceiling. She shot pictures through the window of the box even though there wasn't anything to see. A few times her shaking hands slipped and her thumb slid in front of the lens and she had to reshoot them. She clicked and clicked and clicked and hoped it was enough.

When she was done she backed out of the room and saw, at the end of the long hallway, an opening door and a flash of pink. She made sure the phone was secure in her pocket and took off down another hallway, searching for anything that looked like an exit.

Zinnia found herself in a long, curved room. Cubicles hugging the right wall, with panes of frosted glass on the left. She was along an outer wall. She considered picking up a chair and throwing it through a window, but then she'd be in wide-open space, an easy target. And that was if she was even close enough to the ground to drop safely.

No, she had to find her way back to a tram car. But they knew she was here. They would be at the cars, or would know she was headed that way. She tried to recall the map in her head, whether there was anything else that might be useful, might be utilized as an exit.

Maybe the medical tram. If this place was empty, maybe the Care tram wasn't staffed. Except she didn't know where that was.

So she ran. Down hallways, through doors, past an empty cafeteria, and another office, and a room that looked like the inside of an alien spaceship. She ran hard, trying to make that yellow line green.

She reached an empty hallway, gray carpet and white walls leading to a T-juncture. At the end of the hallway were six hard-looking men in black polo shirts. Men with bent noses and cauliflower ears and wild eyes. The kind of men who liked to hit and be hit.

Zinnia stopped, her guts twisting.

These guys weren't security. They were something else—something much worse than the goobers in blue roaming the promenade.

She considered retreating, but they were close enough they would catch her. Close enough she could see the glee on their faces, the way they looked at her like something to be savored.

Only one way out now.

And to get there she dug deep into the anger and frustration and resentment that had been building since she'd sat in that theater taking her stupid interview. At first she had been sad for the people who came to work here, thought they were somehow lacking, or weaker, but being here this long had made her realize: This place was designed to take away choice. It was designed to beat you into submission.

She suddenly wished she could see Ember, to tell her she was sorry. For all that was worth.

The men at the end of the hall were impatient and one at the front, a lean guy with his gray hair in a buzz cut and a military tattoo on his forearm, broke off from the pack, moving toward her with an easy confidence.

"Okay, darling, game's up," he said.

She sighed. It wouldn't be ladylike to give up without a fight.

"Well then, motherfucker," she said to buzz cut. "I guess you're first."

The men looked between each other, a few of them smiling, one of them actually snickering. Buzz cut got close enough to put his hands up and make a grab for her, so Zinnia leaned back, putting her torso out of reach, and brought up her foot, snapping it into his nuts. She felt them mash under the toe of her sneaker and he leaned forward, so she stepped back and threw a hard cross, stepping off line at the same time, knocking him to the floor.

The rest of them were surprised but still undaunted, because it was five against one, so the next one to approach her did so alone, which was a mistake. He was a beefy bald guy who looked as if he got into bar fights to pass the time, so Zinnia dove in close and dropped into a crouch, hammering her fists into his gut and liver. One-two. As he attempted to retreat, she put every ounce of her body into an uppercut that landed so hard she was pretty sure she broke something in her hand, from the shock that traveled down her arm.

As he dropped backward, the other four charged, and Zinnia ran at them, moving to the left, toward the wall, trying to keep them in a line, not letting them get behind her, arms up to protect her head, throwing jabs so she could create distance, using her fist like a whip, letting them trip over themselves and run into each other. Playing chess while they played checkers.

By the time she'd whittled them down to two, she figured she might have a chance, but then a stream of black-shirted men and women were running from the other end of the hallway.

She looked away long enough that someone caught her on the chin and she spun, then tripped, then went to a knee, and after that it was just a pile-on. It was all she could do to breathe.

THE MAN 10

PAXTON

Zinnia sat, ramrod straight, staring at the wall. Bleary-eyed, hair unkempt, in a brown polo shirt. Her eye was bruised and there was a smear of blood near her hairline. A few items were neatly arranged on the table in front of her: a CloudBand, her cell phone, a paper cup. Dobbs sat on the other side of the table, facing her, away from Paxton, so he couldn't see anything about the man's face. His arms were crossed and his shoulders were tense and they were rising and falling like he was talking.

Zinnia stared at a fixed point on the wall. A few times, she clenched and unclenched her fist, grimacing while she did.

"She's in a lot of trouble," Dakota said.

"What happened to her?" Paxton asked, fighting to keep his voice level, to keep from punching his fist through the glass.

"She put up a fight."

Paxton turned and looked at the bullpen, which was a flurry of activity. Blues and tans everywhere. Carson and Wells and his daughter had come in, too, but had been spirited away.

"We pulled the tracking data," Dakota said, her voice low. "You were with her last night. You were with her a lot of nights."

Paxton crossed his own arms as Zinnia mumbled something to Dobbs without moving her eyes from the spot on the wall.

"There are going to be questions," Dakota said.

"I know," Paxton said.

"Anything you want to tell me?"

"I have no idea what's happening. And I swear to you . . ."

He trailed off. Dakota leaned into his field of vision, looked him in the eye.

"What?" she asked. "What are you possibly going to do? I'll give you a pass on that, but I would be careful about what you say next."

Paxton clamped his jaw shut. Dakota stared at him, like she was trying to look through his skin, for some kind of evidence of the lie underneath.

Paxton didn't give a damn whether she believed him or not. He still didn't know what he wanted more: for Dobbs to come out and pat him on the head and tell him to go home, or to go crashing in and pick Zinnia up in his arms and run her off to safety.

After another few moments Dobbs came out and waved at Paxton. He followed, as did Dakota. Dobbs put up his hand at her. "Not you."

Dakota backed off. Paxton followed, head bowed, looking at the gray carpet, not wanting to look up because he assumed everyone in the place was staring at him. Dobbs led him to his office and walked inside, closed the door.

Paxton sat without being asked. Dobbs sat too, and watched him for a long time, hands folded on his lap, doing the same thing Dakota was doing. Trying to read Paxton like he had an answer for all this written on his face.

Paxton just waited.

"She says you have nothing to do with anything," Dobbs said, giving a little tilt of his head, like he was considering the prospect. "She told me she was using you to crack our security and that's it. Won't say anything other than that she duped you good."

Paxton opened his mouth to talk but the words tumbled back down his throat.

"She's a corporate spy," Dobbs said, the words landing like a fist on his ribs. "Gets hired to root into companies, steal their secrets. We've been able to piece together some of who she is, and let me tell you, you ought to count yourself lucky to be alive. That woman in there is a cold-blooded killer."

"No, she can't . . . ," Paxton started.

"Now, personally, I don't know what to believe about what you did know and didn't know," Dobbs said. "Maybe you were an accomplice, maybe not. All I know is this: Someone shoved a weight plate down into the tracks in Maple, and the sensors missed it. Had we gotten on that train, it could have derailed. Lot of people might have gotten hurt. Killed probably. So you need to be honest with me when you tell me, why did you tell everyone to stay off the tram?"

"I . . ." He paused.

"Because if you were in on this . . ."

Paxton took out his phone, opened the text message app, his fingers fumbling on the screen, and handed it over. Dobbs looked down on it, holding it far away, trying to focus.

"She texted me," Paxton said. "I figured if she didn't want me on the tram, there was something wrong. It was a gut thing."

Dobbs nodded, put the phone on the desk behind him, out of reach, and folded his arms. Paxton wondered if he'd be getting his phone back.

"What do you know about her?" he asked.

"What she told me," Paxton said. "Her name is Zinnia. She was a teacher. She wanted to move away, teach English. . . ."

Paxton stopped and realized how little he knew about her. He knew she liked ice cream, and she snored a little when she slept, but he couldn't say whether she was actually a teacher, or her name was actually Zinnia. Just the things she had told him.

"What happens now?" Paxton asked.

"We get to the bottom of this," Dobbs said. "And once again, we find ourselves in the position of you having done a good thing under troubling circumstances. However it goes down, you saved lives. I won't forget that."

There was a funereal quality to that statement, which Paxton did not like.

"I loved her," he said.

Paxton's face flushed. He felt embarrassed for saying it. He felt even more embarrassed for how Dobbs was looking at him now, like a child who'd messed himself. Dobbs put his hand to his chin, then said, "Listen, son, we're going to need you to retrace your steps for the last couple of days, okay?"

Paxton wondered how bad things would get when he refused. Surely, he'd be fired. But that was the worst they could do. Fire him. There was still work out there in the world. Not a lot that wasn't Cloud related but it didn't matter. He'd find a way to survive.

Was it worth protecting Zinnia?

She'd used him.

He'd asked her to move in with him. Had almost told her that he loved her. Was she laughing at him? Did she even feel bad about it?

Sure, she'd saved his life, from a trap she'd laid herself. Which meant earlier in the day she had weighed the possibility of his dying and decided it was worth it.

"It's real important that you cooperate, Paxton," Dobbs said.

Paxton shook his head, slowly, side to side.

"Do you know who it is you're protecting?"

Paxton shrugged.

"Look at me, son."

Paxton didn't want to, but he felt compelled to glance up at Dobbs, whose face was flat and impenetrable.

"How about this," Dobbs said. "How about you go in and talk to her?"

"Are you sure that's a good idea?"

Dobbs stood, arched his back like it took some effort, and came around the side of his desk. He leaned against it, his knee touching Paxton's knee, and Paxton shrank away from it. Dobbs loomed over him, looking down his nose.

"Help us help you, son," he said.

ZINNIA

Finger was definitely broken. Every time she clenched her fist, it created a shock. Her insides felt like a sack of potatoes that had been beaten on with lead pipes.

The door opened and Zinnia saw the last person she expected to see, or else maybe she shouldn't have been surprised at all. Paxton stood in the doorway, staring at her as if she were a wild animal in a flimsy cage. As if she might smash herself through the bars and swipe at him.

Those sons of bitches.

Paxton walked to the table, pulled out the chair, the legs squealing on the floor. He sat down carefully, like he still might set her off.

"I'm sorry," Zinnia said.

"They want me to ask you how you did it. They weren't really clear with me what 'it' is. But they said they want a rundown of everything you've done since you've gotten here, so they can figure out how you did it."

He spoke mechanically, like a computer dictating text. Zinnia wondered who he was protecting by doing that. She gave a little shrug.

"They told me you used me, for access." He looked up at her. "Is that true?"

Zinnia breathed in, thought about what to say. She couldn't think of anything that would sound even close to right.

Paxton dropped his voice. "They think I helped you."

Zinnia sighed. "I'm sorry for this. I really am."

And she wasn't even lying.

"What's your real name?" Paxton asked.

"I don't remember."

"Don't be cute."

She sighed. "It doesn't matter."

"To me it does."

Zinnia looked away.

"Fine," Paxton asked. "What are you doing here?"

"I was hired."

"For what?"

"A job."

"Stop this, please," Paxton said, his eyes welling. "They said you're a killer."

"They'll say whatever they need to say, to get you to turn on me," Zinnia said.

"So it's not true."

She was about to say no, but she hesitated. Paxton saw it, his face falling, and she realized it wasn't even worth it. The hesitation was answer enough.

"I couldn't let you get on the train," she said.

"You almost did."

"But I didn't."

"Why?"

"Because . . ." She paused. Looked around the room. Gave a long look at the window, at the people on the other side. She looked at them as she said: "I care about you." Then she turned and looked at him. "That's the truth. I do. Not everything I've told you is the truth, but that is."

"You care about me," Paxton said, feeling the words out in his mouth like there was something sharp hidden inside. "You care about me."

"I promise."

"They want to know how you did it," he said. "Whatever you did. Dobbs says you won't tell them. They think I can get you to tell them." Paxton raised his shoulders, let them drop. "I don't even know what the hell it is you did."

Zinnia threw a raised eyebrow at the glass. "It's better that you don't know."

"What does that mean?"

"Because I think I know what's going on." Zinnia sighed deeply. "And if what I think is true, there is no way in this world I am leaving this place alive."

Paxton froze. The stakes of the game changed and for a moment the anger dropped away. "No," he said. "No. I wouldn't . . . I . . ."

"You had nothing to do with this, and I will say that as long and as loud as I have to," she said, looking at the window.

Paxton seemed to want to say something else but didn't know what. His face contracted and expanded. Anger, fear, sadness, and something else that came up from the inside of him and turned his skin red and made him look like a child, every contortion twisting in Zinnia's heart. In her lifetime she had been shot, stabbed, and tortured. Fallen from great heights and broken multiple bones in multiple places. She had come to know pain as if it were a good friend, learned to internalize it, to get inside the middle of it and accept it.

But this felt like being hurt for the first time.

Paxton was about to say something when he stood. He lingered for a moment before turning toward the door.

Zinnia wanted to tell him. Everything. Why she was here, what she was doing, even her real name. But Paxton was protected by his ignorance. She couldn't drag him down with her. He didn't deserve that.

She couldn't let that be the last exchange between them either. So she said, "Wait."

"Why?"

"Please." She nodded at the chair. "There's just something I want to say. After that, do what you need."

He fell back onto the chair. Raised a hand, prodding her to proceed.

"You know what I keep thinking about?" she asked. "Something Ember said in the bookstore."

"What's that?" he asked, his voice a whisper.

"She referenced this story I read when I was a kid," she said, shifting in the chair. "It was about this place. A utopia. No war, no hunger. Everything was just perfect. Except, in order to maintain that status quo, one child had to be held in a dark room, in a constant state of neglect. I don't know why. It's just . . . that's how it worked. No light, no warmth, no kindness. Even the people who brought him his food were instructed to ignore him. And people accepted it, because it was how things worked. It was like this magical rule to maintain the way things were. Everyone who lived there got all this great stuff, in return for this one kid suffering, and what's one life against a few billion, you know?"

Paxton shook his head. "What's the point of this?"

"That story always made me angry. I thought, there's no way people could live like this. Why would no one help that kid? I always imagined rewriting it with a new ending, where some brave person barged in and picked the kid up and gave him the love he'd been denied." She labored over the last few words, like the earth underneath them had been turned up, revealing the thing buried below. "In the story, the people who found out about the kid and couldn't live with it, they just walked away. They didn't try to save the kid. They just walked away." She laughed. "That's what the story was called. 'The Ones Who Walk Away from Omelas.' By Ursula K. Le Guin. You should look it up."

"I don't care about a story," Paxton said. "You lied to me."

"That's the problem. Don't you see? No one cares."

"Stop it."

"You've never lied to anyone?"

"Not like this."

"You've never fucked up?"

He enunciated each word. "Not like this."

She sighed. Nodded. "I hope you have a good life."

"I will," he said. "I'll have a nice life. Right here."

Zinnia's mouth went dry. "You're taking their side?"

"They're not perfect, but at least here I have a job, and a place to live. Maybe this is the best way to do things. Maybe the market has dictated, huh?"

Zinnia smiled. "Or you could just walk away."

"And go where?"

She opened her mouth, as if to say: *Don't you see? Don't you get it?* She wanted to tell him about what she'd seen, and what she'd found, and what she felt, and what this place had done to him, and to her, and to everyone. To the entire goddamn world.

But she wanted him to live, too, so she said, "Remember, freedom is yours until you give it up," and she hoped that would be enough.

Paxton pushed his chair out, got up, went to the door, and Zinnia said, "Do me a favor, too?"

"Are you joking?"

"Two, actually," she said. "There's a brown named Hadley. She lives on my floor. Room Q. Check on her. And take care of yourself." She shrugged, smiled. "That's it. That's all I got."

PAXTON

Paxton stumbled out of the room, his lungs and heart and skin ready to burst from the pressure, right into a crowd of people pressed up against the window, watching. He pushed his way through and went into the next interrogation room, which was empty. Sat on the chair and put his head in his hands.

The door cracked open. Paxton heard a shuffle of footsteps but he didn't want to look up. He wanted to scream for whoever it was to leave him alone. Figured it was Dobbs or Dakota.

The chair across from him screeched.

He raised his eyes from the table and saw Gibson Wells.

The smile he had worn on the stage, the one that seemed a permanent fixture on his face, was gone. His shoulders were hunched, giving him the look of a bird of prey. He sat and breathed in deep, then out. Still, despite everything—the illness, the stress of the day—there was a strength to him. That cancer must have been some strong stuff to take out a man like this.

Gibson folded his hands in his lap, looked Paxton up and down. "Dobbs tells me you're a good man. Reliable."

Paxton just looked at him. He had no idea what to say. He forgot words. He was afraid of what he would say if he even dared open his mouth. Talking to Gibson Wells was like being given an audience with God. What do you say to God?

Hey, how are ya?

"I know Dobbs a little," Gibson said. "Every year or two I bring the MotherCloud sheriffs out to my ranch. Get to know 'em, since they're really the linchpin keeping these places together. I like Dobbs a lot. He's old-school, like me. Takes his job seriously. Doesn't screw around. Keeps his numbers real low. I think this might be the safest MotherCloud we have. Now, him telling me you're reliable, that's pretty much enough for me to believe it. But I wanted to sit with you for a moment myself. Get a feel for you. So, son, tell me. Are you reliable?"

Paxton nodded his head.

"Speak up, now," Gibson said.

"I am reliable, sir."

Gibson smiled again. It was all sharp points. "Good. Now, I'm going to tell you what's happening. And I'm going to trust that it will stay among friends."

The way he said the word *friends* made Paxton warm and cold at the same time.

"What happened was," Gibson said, "all those big-box retailers, the ones that are still doing business? You might not know this, but they're all owned by the same company. Red Brick Holdings. After Black Friday, when in-person retail started to go down the tubes, a lot of businesses ended up liquidating. So Red Brick comes in, saves 'em all, lumps 'em all together under one umbrella. You follow me so far?"

"Yes," Paxton said, loudly, clearly.

"Good. So, the people who own this company, they do not like me. You seem like a smart kid, and I bet you can understand why. What they did was, they hired that girl out there to break into our energy processing facility to see how it is we generate our power. Do you know how we generate our power?"

"I do not," Paxton said.

"Well, let's just say, it's cutting-edge and real special, and it's going to fix this world," he said. "You don't have kids, do you?"

"No."

Gibson gave a solemn nod. "If you have kids—and you're young, you have time—by the time they have their own kids, those kids, your grandkids? They'll be able to play outside again. Even during the summer. That's where we're going with this. Pretty nice, right?"

Paxton almost couldn't believe it. It sounded too absurd to be true. For years people had been throwing out ideas for how to fix the planet, but none of them had stuck. "Yes, sir, it is."

"Of course it is. So, this girl was hired to steal proprietary information from us. And, much to my chagrin, someone paid her to take me out on top of it. As if that's not going to happen in the next few weeks anyway. So she's tried to kill me, and she's working for the enemy." Gibson leaned forward. "I know this is difficult. I just want you to understand. How this whole thing fits together. It's important for you to have the full picture."

"Okay," Paxton said.

"That it? 'Okay?'" Gibson asked, his tone incredulous, like a parent who couldn't fathom a dose of back talk.

"Well, no, it's not okay. I know it's not okay, it's just—"

Gibson put his hand up. "It's a lot. Listen, I want you to understand something. You saved my life. I don't take that lightly and you will be rewarded. Guaranteed employment. Your star ranking? Doesn't matter. You now have life status at Cloud. The way Dobbs has been talking about you, I get the sense he has big things planned. Your life will be a little easier after this." He put his hand on the table. "But in return, I'm going to need something from you."

Paxton held his breath.

"All this, you put it out of your head," Gibson said. "What happened here, you forget it. You walk out that door and into a comfortable life. You never speak of this again. Not even to Dobbs." He lowered his voice, to just above a growl. "I need you to understand how important it is to me that none of this ever happened."

Gibson said it with a smile on his face. The smile did not extend to his voice.

"What happens to her?" Paxton asked.

Gibson sneered. "You really care? After what she put you through? Son, that is the wrong question to be asking me right now."

Paxton thought about last night. Nearly telling her that he loved her. Of the way her skin felt warm, and soft, and the way she put her hands on him, her lips, and, meanwhile, the whole time she was planning to betray him.

They wouldn't kill her. They couldn't kill her. It was ludicrous to think that.

"So, that's where we are," Gibson said. "I'm going to head out this door and deal with that, and I'm going to take it that you're on board with my proposal. Before I leave, is there anything else you want to say or ask?" He looked around the empty room and smiled. "Not a lot of folks get this kind of chance."

I'm the CEO of the Perfect Egg. It was my life's dream to own my own company, and I did, but Cloud drove me out of business. I had to give up on my dream and come work for you. I was a CEO and now I'm a glorified security guard. The woman I love betrayed me, and all I have to look forward to in the future is a lonely life of wandering the promenade of MotherCloud. That's my reward.

"No, sir," Paxton said, folding his hands so tight he squeezed the blood out of them.

Gibson nodded. "Good boy."

ZINNIA

Gibson Wells walked in and Zinnia felt as though if she squinted she could see the shadow of Death following behind. He reeked of it—the papery skin, the dimming glow in his eyes. He was hanging on by a fingerhold. She was amazed he was standing on his own two feet.

"Where's Paxton?" she asked.

Gibson looked her up and down, an animal glint in his eye, like he was wondering, in this moment, what he could get away with. After a moment he sat across from her, going slow, as though if he weren't careful he might shatter, and folded his hands in his lap and said, "Paxton is fine."

Zinnia had a lot of questions, but the first, the most important, was, "Do we have an audience right now?"

Gibson shook his head. "Watching, not listening."

Her stomach flopped. She was in the middle of a huge, dark ocean. No shores visible, and something was nipping at her heels. So she went paddling around for a life preserver.

"You hired me, didn't you?" Zinnia asked.

Gibson's lip twitched. And then he shifted in the chair, like he was trying to get comfortable.

"How'd you figure it out?"

"I should have guessed it right off, the amount of money you were paying me." She laughed. "Who else could afford that?"

He nodded. "Do you know the name Jeremy Bentham?"

"Sounds familiar."

Gibson sat back and, with a great deal of effort, brought his leg onto his knee. "Bentham was an English philosopher. Died in 1832. Smart fella. He was famous for the concept of the panopticon. Do you know what that is?"

Another familiar sound, dug deep somewhere in Zinnia's memory, but she shook her head.

Gibson held up his hands, like he was outlining something. "Imagine a prison. In this prison, one single guard can watch every prisoner. But the prisoners don't know whether they're being watched at any given moment. The best way to imagine this is, think of standing in a great circular room, where all the cells face inward, like a honeycomb. And in the center is a guard tower. From inside the guard tower, you could see into every cell, because the tower has a three-hundred-and-sixty-degree view. But when the prisoners look up at the guard tower, all they see is a tower. They can't see the guard, they just know he might be there. Do you follow?"

"I think so," Zinnia said. "Sounds more like a thought experiment than a blueprint."

"In Bentham's day, it was exactly that. An idea about a way to get people to behave. If people were always under surveillance, they would figure, well, I could do this bad thing, but I might not get away with it, so better not do it. It was a pretty good idea, but not really possible in that day and age." Gibson smiled and waved a finger in the air, like a bored magician. "But today, it's much different. We have CCTV and GPS. You look at the population of a MotherCloud, it's bigger than some cities. It would cost a fortune to staff this place with a police department worthy of this many citizens."

Gibson sat back, took a deep breath, like he was trying to replenish his energy.

"Thing is, I don't have to," he said. "When you look at the numbers here—murder, rape, assault, larceny—they are so much lower than those of a city of comparable size. Do you know what an achievement that is? I ought to get the goddamn Nobel Peace Prize."

"You are very much a humanitarian."

He raised an eyebrow but ignored the dig. "I created something here." He waved his hands around the small, meager room. "A better model than what we had. I built cities from the ground up." His face curled into a hideous smile, then dropped. "That said, time to time, you need to kick the tires and check the oil. It's true, I don't like CCTV. It really is unpleasant to see a camera every time you look up. It's expensive, too. And I got to thinking, if people are wearing a tracking watch everywhere, then even subconsciously, they know there's not much they can get away with. It's like a built-in security system. Why spend money twice?" He shrugged. "That's my job. Take something, streamline it, make it work better. But that means I have to test the system every now and again. What you found, that's the first of its kind. And I needed to know it was safe until I was ready to reveal it."

"You didn't make it easy, I'll give you that. Until I got to the chick in the processing lobby. That was a real misfire."

"We let too many people go to the Black Friday ceremony, which was a mistake. But we were taking bets, too. I never thought you'd even make it that far. However did you find out about the tram line running from CloudBurger?"

"I'll tell you, but it's a little complicated." She leaned forward, and he leaned in, too, excited to find out. But instead she said, "Fuck you. And your human shit burgers."

"Please," he said, air bursting from his nose in the facsimile of a laugh. "That's language unbecoming of such a pretty lady. You did very excellent work. Very excellent." He waved his hand. He liked to wave his hand, as if a wave of his hand were enough to make anything that bothered him dissipate. Like everything in the world was nothing more than a tuft of smoke to him. "As for the burgers, well, people wouldn't understand. The amount we save, environmentally, from recycling waste, it's huge. We made a massive reduction in methane by cutting down on the cow population. And not a single person has complained. More people eat at CloudBurger than any other restaurant at Cloud."

Zinnia's stomach gurgled. She was sure she'd puked up everything she had inside her but would have been happy to spew a bit more on the table in front of them, just to watch the old man leap back.

"Now we're at the really important question," Gibson said. "Why did you try to kill me? Because that certainly wasn't part of the deal I laid out."

"I'll trade you," Zinnia said. "The box. In the energy processing facility. What is it?"

Gibson tilted his head, put his foot back on the floor. Smoothed out his pants. Zinnia thought maybe he was going to refuse, but then he looked at her and said, "I guess it doesn't matter."

Which pushed her heart up into her throat and lodged it there.

"Cold fusion," he said. "Do you know what that is?"

"Only in a very general sense."

"Fusion," Gibson said, leaning forward, putting his elbows on the table, "is a nuclear reaction. Usually takes place in stars, under immense pressure. Millions of degrees of heat. But it creates a brilliant amount of energy. Now, for a very long time, scientists have been trying to crack cold fusion. Which is the same process, but at or near room temperature. This facility"—he picked up his hand and waved it around—"this entire facility is run on the equivalent of a few hundred gallons of fuel a year. We're about to move into mass production."

"That . . . would change the world," she said, a little spark of hope flaring at her center, before dying out when she realized that even if the world were fixed, she wouldn't live to see it.

"It will change the world," Gibson said. "As good as we've done with green energy, there are still pockets of gas and coal. And this is the magic bullet that'll kill those industries dead. I've never been so happy to put people out of jobs."

"Then why keep it secret?"

He sat back in his chair, gave her an *Are you kidding me?* look. "Because it's nearly limitless energy. How do you monetize that? Though the truth is, I'm thinking bigger. I think it's time to put the lumbering old beast of government out of its misery. And this is how I'm going to do it."

"This is some supervillain bullshit," Zinnia said. "You're going to take over the world?"

"No, dear, I'm going to offer it to any country that wants it, free and clear, in exchange for privatizing the majority of their services and letting us run them. I proved with the FAA we can do a better job. I mean, honestly, do you want to put world-changing technology in the hands of those clowns in Congress? What'll they do with it? They'll sit on it. They'll regulate it to death. Or they'll try to kill it, because it interferes with the gas and oil lobbies. No. I'm the one to do this."

"Why?"

His face stretched into a smile so wide she thought his skin might crack. "Because I am exceptional."

He said it with pride, but with his eyes darting around the room, like it was a kink he had hidden from the world, had kept from everyone for too long, and finally, he'd found someone he could say it to, exactly as he wanted to say it. Zinnia saw everything she needed to know about him in those four words.

"Look what I built," he said. "I am fixing this world, and I am tired of sitting by while other people try to beat back my best efforts. All this nonsense and contradictory rules and regulations, standing in the way of real progress, in the way of salvation . . ." His voice rose and his face grew red. "My one regret is that I won't live to see it. But Claire will. Claire is going to oversee the biggest expansion of Cloud yet. We found the model that worked. It's time for everyone else to adopt it. We're going to take the last thing in this world that just does not work, and we are going to fix it."

He closed his eyes, took a breath. Put a hand on his chest.

"Sorry, this is an area where I can get a bit passionate," he said. "But it's only natural. Do you know we provide more medical services than hospitals at this point? There are more kids enrolling in Cloud schools than there are in regular schools. Hell, the CIA stores their data on our servers. This was the natural next step."

"Are you fucking kidding?" Zinnia asked, her voice rising, and Gibson slid back a little in his seat. "Have you been outside lately? People are dying, all around the world. Kids are dying, at this moment, and you have a chance to fix that, and you're going to hold it hostage until you get something in return?"

Gibson gave a happy, impish little shrug. "We'll get what we need and this world will be a better place. Now, I believe you owe me an answer. Who tried to have me killed?"

Zinnia nodded, happy she could lob a good one back at him. "You did."

Gibson's face went dark.

"I got updated instructions about a week ago to take you out," she said. "Of course I didn't question them, because at that point I didn't know it was you. I figured it was a rival company. So I guess if you want to know who wants you dead, you just need to ask my handler." Zinnia paused for effect. "You must not be as loved as you thought."

Gibson's face fell. He looked at his hands in his lap, piles of bones wrapped in papery, vein-streaked skin, and he sighed with his entire body. "That son of a bitch . . ." After a moment he shook it off, looked up at Zinnia with that glint in his eye, and said, "Thank you for that, and good-bye."

"Wait," Zinnia said. "What happens now?"

Gibson laughed, stood, and stepped to the door.

"What happens to me?"

Gibson paused. Turned to her. Gave her another look, up and down. "When elephant trainers catch a baby elephant in the wild, they tie it to a tree. That baby elephant fights and thrashes to break free, but it's not strong enough. Within a couple of days, it gives up. So even as the elephant gets bigger, it doesn't believe it can break the rope. And then you get a full-grown elephant tied to a tree with a piece of rope it could snap with a simple swing of its leg. It's called learned helplessness. Everything here is built on people who don't think the rope will break. Which means the most dangerous thing in the world for my business model is someone who recognizes how fragile the rope really is."

He gave a little wink and the door snapped shut behind him. A presence remained, and after a few moments Zinnia realized it was that shadow of Death. It had followed him in, but it hadn't left.

PAXTON

"Where is he?!"

The roar came from so deep within Gibson it seemed like it might shatter his frail body. Paxton leapt up from the empty cubicle where Dobbs had told him to wait and followed the shouting. So did nearly everyone else in the office, and soon Paxton was fighting through a crowd, catching elbows in the ribs, trying to reach the source.

What they found was Gibson standing over Carson, who had his hands over his head. It was a comical sight, this wide man cowering under the gaze of someone who looked like he could blow away on a stiff wind.

Though at the same time, Paxton understood. Having sat across from the man, having spoken to him, he understood. And in that moment something clicked in his head. The way Carson had panicked when Paxton said to get off the tram. The way he knocked people down to get off. The way it seemed like he knew what was coming.

"It was you, wasn't it?" Gibson asked.

"I don't know what you're talking about," Carson said.

"You're a liar. What was this supposed to be? Revenge or something?"

Carson stood up, but slowly, carefully, looking around as if someone might come to his aid, but no one did. "Don't you realize that what you're trying to do is insane? You're not the god you think you are, Gib."

Gibson took a step forward, got right up to Carson's nose. "And Claire? What were you going to do? Kill her, too?"

"She's a child. I would have managed her."

"Hey!"

A woman's voice. Claire appeared out of the crowd and slapped Carson, hard, across the face. He absorbed the blow, taking a few steps back, and turned to Gibson. "Not another word. Not here."

"Fine." Gibson turned to Dobbs. "Get him the hell out of here. Put him with her."

Two blues appeared from the crowd and grabbed Carson under the arms. They dragged him away. He fought back, but Dobbs stepped out and threw a hard fist into the man's gut. He doubled over and groaned, then looked up. "You know I'm right, Dobbs. You know I'm right!"

Dobbs drew the heavy-duty flashlight from his belt and smashed the butt into Carson's face. It made a wet *thunk,* and nearly everyone in the crowd jerked at the sound of the impact. Not Gibson. He smiled. Carson's head rolled around on his neck like something had been disconnected, blood pouring from his ruined nose.

The blues dragged him away as Dobbs turned to the audience. "Conference room B. Now." Everyone looked at each other as if they hadn't understood the order, and Dobbs yelled out louder, "Now!"

The crowd broke up and moved toward the hallway that would

bring them to the conference room, but Paxton lingered toward the back of the crowd and grabbed Dobbs by the arm.

"Before we go in there, we have to talk," Paxton said.

Dobbs shook his hand off and seemed ready to refuse, but then he led Paxton to the empty interrogation room, the closest place they could get a quiet word in. They stepped inside and Dobbs said, "Make it quick."

"She thinks you're going to kill her."

"Who thinks what now?"

"Zinnia. She thinks you're going to kill her to keep her quiet."

Dobbs narrowed his eyes and looked at Paxton as if he couldn't believe what he was hearing. Then he laughed. "This isn't a movie. We're not in the killing business."

Paxton had known it wasn't true, that Zinnia was being unreasonable, but still, it helped to hear. He wondered if there was something else he should say, something else he should do.

"I know this is hard, son," Dobbs said. "We got some damage control to do, but everything is going to be fine, you hear? You're squared right now, so why don't you head back home. Get some rest."

Paxton took a deep breath, building up the courage to ask the question he knew he shouldn't ask. "Can I see her? One last time?"

Dobbs shook his head. "Not gonna happen, son."

Paxton felt planted to the spot. He wanted to fight but was angry at himself for wanting to fight. He was angry at himself for even asking in the first place. He was angry at himself for too much, so he said, "I understand," and turned and left.

Out of Admin, to the elevators, across the promenade, to the lobby of Oak, the whole time his head like a big empty room, like it should have been filled with things, but it wasn't. As he swiped his way onto the elevator he remembered what Zinnia had said and doubled back to Maple, where he took the car up to her floor and stood outside room Q and wondered what, exactly, he owed her.

This woman who'd lied to him and manipulated him. Who'd taken advantage of his stature.

Like you've never fucked up.

No, not like that.

Everyone makes mistakes. Paxton had made plenty.

But not that big.

He said it like a mantra.

He reached out and knocked. Heard nothing on the other side of the door. Considered turning around. But something in Zinnia's voice had made him worried, so he knocked again. He looked up and down the hallway, and when he verified the hallway was clear, he swiped the pad. It turned green and he entered.

The apartment was rank with old food. There was a figure curled up under the blankets on the futon and Paxton thought he should leave, like the person was sleeping, but that person also hadn't stirred when he entered, when the light from the hallway fell across the bed. He watched the lump, willing it to move, hoping it would, but it didn't. He crossed the room and found a pretty girl with long hair, curled up under her blanket, and he didn't need to touch her, didn't need to check her pulse, to know that she was dead.

He raised his watch to call it in, pressed the crown, and he should have said something but didn't. He was done. He had nothing left. Not on this day.

The balloon burst, everything about him, everything inside just spilling to the floor in one slippery mess. So he turned around and left, went back to Oak, went to his room, fell onto his futon, and stared up at the ceiling.

And he thought about the other thing Zinnia had said.

The thing about freedom.

LIFE STATUS 11

A SPECIAL ANNOUNCEMENT FROM CLAIRE WELLS

It is with an incredible amount of sadness and regret I announce that this morning, at 9:14 a.m., my father passed away at his home in Arkansas, surrounded by friends, family, and his beloved dogs. I'm pleased to report he died with a smile on his face, in a room full of love. There is, at least, some comfort to take in that.

My father was considered one of the great minds of his generation, an unparalleled thinker and innovator. His influence touched every corner of this planet.

But he was also my dad.

There is a lot to process right now, not least of which is the incredible responsibility of taking over Cloud. I feel like I've been preparing for this moment my entire life, and at the same time, I don't feel that I'm ready. But in a job like this, there is no such thing as "ready." You dive in and do the best you can.

I'm excited to announce that the first major appointment of my tenure will be Leah Morgan as my VP. She has a master's in business from Harvard, is a respected member of her community, and most important, she's a longtime friend. I am positive my father would have wholeheartedly supported this decision, as he always thought very fondly of Leah.

I've got one more announcement to make. And it's a big one.

I wish we could have made it a little sooner, but the project was still in its final stages. It was the last project my father worked on, and it was the one he was most proud of: CloudPower. For years Cloud has invested hundreds of millions of dollars into researching new forms of clean energy, and we're happy to say we've developed a zero-emission process for producing humongous amounts of energy. By the end of the year, all MotherCloud facilities will be up and running under this new system, at which point we'll be implementing a partnership with the

U.S. government—the first of many world governments, we hope—to bring this technology to every corner of the country.

We vow to offer our customers competitive rates and assistance in building processing facilities, and we believe that within the next few decades, we could have the entire planet up and running through CloudPower—a significant step in healing our ravaged environment.

This is my father's legacy, and I could not be more proud.

At this point I know I should say something inspirational, but my father always had the gift of gab in my family, whereas I was happier to listen. I figured that's always the best way to learn. So that's what I'll be doing. I'll be listening and learning while sticking to the values that made this company a success.

Those are the values my father instilled in me.

PAXTON

Paxton downed the last of the vodka, the ice clacking against his teeth. His third. Or his fourth; he didn't care enough to count. He took out his phone and opened his text messages, as if maybe there was already one waiting for him. He found nothing so he waved over the bartender for another round.

In his peripheral vision he saw Dakota appear, backlit at the mouth of the bar. She was looking around for something. Him, he figured. He could have raised his hand to get her attention, but he didn't because there weren't enough people in the bar that it would matter. And a small part of him hoped she wouldn't see him. But after a moment her gaze fixed on him and she strode over, sat on the seat next to him. It wobbled and she held on to the bar top to steady herself.

She ordered a gin and tonic and took three slow sips of it before she asked, "How you holding up?"

Paxton shrugged.

They filled the silence with alcohol, staring at the mirror behind the row of liquor bottles.

"Dobbs wanted me to talk to you," she said. "Make sure things were square."

Another shrug. Paxton decided from now on he would communicate in shrugs.

"He cut that woman loose," she said, turning away, looking toward the rear of the bar, not even risking catching his eye in the mirror. "I know you had a thing for her, and no joke, she was a tight piece. I'm proud of you. But she's turfed. Do you really want to follow her?"

Paxton turned a little toward Dakota. "That a threat?"

"That's not from Dobbs," she said. "That's from me. That's me being a friend. This whole thing." She picked up her glass, took a long swig. She still had more to go but flagged the bartender for another. As he prepared it she leaned close. "This whole thing is big. But they want more than anything to keep it quiet. I'm just saying, as your friend, keep your head down, life stays good, you know?"

"You call this good?" Paxton asked.

"You been outside lately? Hell of a lot better than what they got out there."

Paxton nodded, wanting to disagree, unable to do so. He downed his vodka and ordered another. As if by drinking too many he might be able to conjure her. It was a stupid thing to think but it was better than the things he didn't want to think about.

"I have something for you," Dakota said.

She put her hand on the bar, slid it close to Paxton. Looked around to make sure they were alone, and raised it to reveal a plastic oblivion container. She clamped her hand back over it and waited, like he might take it, but when he didn't she slid it into his pants pocket.

Paxton let her do it, but he asked, "Are you fucking kidding me? After all that."

"This is brand-new," she said. "Oblivion two-point-oh."

"What the hell does that mean?"

"Engineered to shit so you can't OD." Paxton turned toward Dakota, and she was smiling. "Doesn't matter how much you take. Body hits a saturation point and pisses out the rest. No such thing as too much."

"Seriously, is this a trick?" Paxton asked, wanting to take the container out of his pocket and hand it back, but afraid of who might see. "Are you trying to get me fired? Plant drugs on me?"

"That's the beauty of it," Dakota said. "It's ours. We run it."

Paxton put his head in his hands, the pieces falling together.

The task force that wasn't a task force. Keeping an eye on Warren but not rattling him too hard. Looking for the supply but leaving the dealers alone. "We weren't shutting them down. We were just replacing the product."

"Don't act all high and fucking mighty on me now, Paxton. People would be using whether it's our stuff or theirs. We're keeping the network in place and fulfilling the demand while keeping Cloud safe. Lives are saved, and we make a little scratch in the process. Everyone wins."

"Is Dobbs in on this?"

She curled her lip. "What do you think?"

Paxton picked up his vodka, downed it, the alcohol stinging on the way down, but it didn't hurt as much as he wanted it to.

"Why are you telling me this?" he asked.

Dakota accepted her new drink, finished the first one and placed it down for the bartender to take away. When he was out of earshot, she leaned in and lowered her voice. "Because now we know we can trust you. You made the right choice. You chose us. I told you there were perks. Now, don't make me second-guess myself, okay, Paxy?"

Paxton wanted to take the container out of his pocket. He wanted to throw it at her. He wanted to scream. He wanted to run and leap off the balcony on Live-Play, swan-dive the three stories to the hard ground, where he would no doubt break his neck. He wanted to do anything except for what he chose to do, which was get up and leave the bar, and as he reached the front Dakota called after him, "You just keep on doing the right thing, mister model employee!"

PAXTON

Paxton woke up, pulled on his blue polo, checked his phone, and, finding no messages from Zinnia, shuffled to Admin, where he checked in, then went on patrol, walking the length of the promenade, back and forth, until he was tired, and he sat for a little while, and then continued on until the end of his shift, at which point he sat in the pub and drank beer, and then he went back to his room and tried to fall asleep, trying to not think about the little container of oblivion in the drawer next to the sink, typing and deleting text messages for Zinnia that he never sent.

PAXTON

Paxton woke up, pulled on his blue polo, checked his phone, and, finding no messages from Zinnia, shuffled to Admin, where he checked in, then went on patrol, walking the length of the promenade, back and forth, until he was tired, and then he stopped to eat at Cloud-Burger, and then continued on until the end of his shift, at which point he went back and watched television and tried to work up the energy to stand and walk to the drawer next to the sink, to take out the oblivion container and dump it down the sink, but instead he fell asleep.

PAXTON

Paxton woke up, pulled on his blue polo, checked his phone, and, finding no messages from Zinnia, shuffled to Admin, where he checked in, then went on patrol, walking the length of the promenade, back and forth, until he was tired, sat for a bit, then continued on until the end of his shift, at which point he went to see a movie and pretended Zinnia sat in the empty seat next to him, and since he was looking forward the whole time he could almost believe it, and he went back to his room and called her number but it was disconnected.

NOTIFICATION FROM THE US PATENT OFFICE

In accordance with Rule 16-A of US Patent Office regulations, please find herewith a copy of notification of provisional refusal concerning the Perfect Egg, on grounds of claim by another corporate entity, which has introduced and is marketing a similar product, CloudEgg. In order to object to this office action, please be advised that you must hire a patent attorney, who can file a claim through appropriate legal channels.

CLOUDEGG!

A young woman stands in her kitchen, in black and white. Subway-tile backsplash, marble countertops, copper pots hang overhead.

In front of her is a bowl. She's cracking and peeling hard-boiled eggs, but doing it roughly, jabbing her fingers in, tearing them apart, chunks flying, eggshell everywhere.

She looks up at the camera, flustered.

Woman: There has to be a better way!

The screen flashes from black and white to brilliant color. Freeze frame.

Voice-over: There is!

An ovoid device spins on a pedestal. Bigger than an egg, with a seam running down the middle.

VO: **Introducing CloudEgg!**

The woman takes the device, opens it, puts an egg inside, and puts it in the microwave.

VO: **The CloudEgg cooks your egg to the perfect doneness, every time.**

Cut to a pot of boiling water. A buzzer sounds, and a red circle with a slash across it appears.

VO: **No more messing around with imprecise cooking methods. And when the egg is done . . .**

Cut to the woman taking the device out of the microwave and opening it up, the shell coming off perfectly, the shiny, naked white albumen gleaming like something precious.

VO: **Cleanup is a breeze!**

Cut to a long row of the ovoid devices in an array of primary colors.

VO: **Available in the Cloud store now!**

PAXTON

Paxton woke up, pulled on his blue polo, and shuffled to Admin, where he checked in, then went on patrol, walking the length of the promenade, back and forth, until he was tired, and then he went to his apartment and opened the drawer next to the sink and took out the container of oblivion and placed a single postage-stamp slice of it on his tongue, then a second, and then a third, and then another, until his mouth tasted like chemical cherries and he stumbled to the bed, where he fell into the warm embrace and continued to fall like there was no bottom.

PAXTON

Paxton woke up, his head full of wet cotton. He stumbled to the sink, where he found the oblivion container, now empty; he hadn't realized he had taken that much. For a moment he counted himself lucky to be alive and then remembered this was the non-OD version, and he wondered if he'd known that when he crammed them down his throat last night.

He washed the taste of cherries out of his mouth and felt good the oblivion was gone but also wondered if he should get some more. Thinking about that made it easier to not think about the letter from the patent office.

Before he could settle on a course of action regarding the oblivion, his watch pinged, letting him know that he was about to be late for his shift. He pulled on his blue polo, muscles aching, and made his way to Admin.

In the bullpen Dakota called out, "Hey."

Paxton turned to find her striding toward him, in her new tan uniform. It made her seem a few inches taller. Paxton wondered if the smile went with the uniform. He'd never seen her smile like that. He waited for her to catch up with him. "Can you do me a favor?"

He shrugged. "Sure."

She held out a small white envelope. "Bring this to waste processing. Ever been to that side of the world?"

"No."

"I queued up your watch to take you there." Dakota smacked him on the arm. "Thanks, partner. Listen, how about you and me grab a drink at some point soon, huh?" She smiled, thumbed her uniform. "You keep up with what you're doing, and you'll be next."

"Sure, that'd be great," Paxton said, with no intent to follow up on the offer.

He turned and made his way to the elevator, glad to be away from her, away from the bullpen, looking forward to some mindless wandering, because at least when he did that, he could be alone. Surrounded by hundreds of people, he could be alone.

He took the tram to Incoming and made his way to the processing tram, which was empty, and rode that to the waste stop, where he stepped into a plain concrete lobby where a young Asian man in a blue polo sat at a desk and nodded to him. Paxton waved the envelope. "Delivery."

"You're in the system," the man said, glancing down at his watch. "Go right ahead."

Paxton looked at his own watch. *Second floor, room 2B.* He took the elevator up and followed the winding hallways until he found a room with an old man sitting at a desk, who grunted as Paxton dropped the envelope on his desk, and then he was out, down the hallway, and back to the elevator.

At the other end of the hallway was a man in a green polo, slowly pushing a broom across the shiny floor.

There was something familiar about the man.

The elevator door yawned open and Paxton considered stepping on, but he let the doors close and turned. The man looked up. It took a second. His hair was longer, and he'd grown a patchy beard, but then Paxton recognized him.

Rick, the man who had attacked Zinnia in the hospital.

The man recognized Paxton, too, because he dropped the broom and took off down the hall. Paxton threw himself after him, making a hard left at the corner, and he saw Rick look back in fear before swiping his way into a stairwell. Paxton made it up to the entry pad and swiped but it turned red.

He swiped again. Still red. He yanked the handle of the door before slamming the flat of his palm against it. Once, twice, three times, until it went numb. When he realized he wasn't getting through the door he took his anger and balled it up, holding it tightly to his chest, and marched to Admin, where he didn't even bother knocking on Dobbs's door.

Dobbs was talking to a young blue and was straight-up pissed at being interrupted, but when he saw the look on Paxton's face, he softened, like he knew what was coming. He waved the new recruit off.

Paxton waited until he was gone and shut the door.

"You told me you fired him," he said.

Dobbs inhaled, exhaled, tented his fingers. "You agreed to have your woman look the other way. We did the same. Neater that way."

"Neater," he said. "You gave me your word."

Dobbs stood and Paxton took a step back. "Now, listen here. He's off in a shit job and mostly separated from the rest of the population. It's done."

"Why?"

"Paxton . . ."

"You owe me that."

"I don't owe you—"

"I'm not leaving until you tell me."

Dobbs sighed. Looked around the room, like he was hoping for an exit to appear. When one didn't he said, "Because to fire him, I have to give cause. If I list the cause as an assault, I have to file a report, and then I have to answer for why there was another incident in my facility. It's been a busy few months here and the stats are not in my favor. We can't afford to pile more shit on top of the shit pile we already have."

"So, what, we cover it up? We just let it go?"

"Now, listen here," Dobbs said, stepping around the desk and moving toward Paxton, until he was so close Paxton could smell that aftershave. "I get that you've got some kind of shining status here now, but that don't mean much to me. I can't fire you but I can move you to permanent scanner duty. Hell, I can put you on the skin cancer beat. You've been a team player so far, son. Don't let me down now, okay?"

Paxton wanted to be angry. He wanted to admonish Dobbs, to say something that would jab his thumb in the old man's eye.

That was what he wanted but that wasn't how he felt. The way he felt was desperate, for Dobbs to soften, for the man to call him "son" again, the way he did before, because the way he said it now, it had a sharp point on the end.

He left, his hands squeezed into fists so tight his nails cut into his palms, and he looked for Dakota, for more cherry-flavored bliss.

PAXTON

Paxton wandered the promenade, thinking about all the things that vexed him, but mostly he thought about the taste of cherries that lingered on his tongue. The taste didn't wash away, nor did it wash away the things he wanted it to.

He wondered what day it was and guessed Sunday, but checked his watch and found it was Wednesday. He walked, but then forgot where he had walked. A new arrival asked him for directions to Live-Play, and only after he sent the young man on his way did Paxton realize he'd sent him in the wrong direction. As the end of his shift neared he stopped at CloudBurger, and as he ate he figured this would be the highlight of this day. Which he realized he had already forgotten again.

Wednesday.

As he left the restaurant a small figure crossed his path. Her bald head and alabaster skin and short stature made her look like an alien. She was wearing a red polo, and the way she walked, it was nervous. Eyes darting, muscles clenched. He thought it might be the drugs eating a hole in his brain, but as he watched the woman walk away he realized, no, you don't soon forget a person who holds you at gunpoint.

Ember was oblivious to him and it bothered him that she hadn't seen him. That now she couldn't spare him a glance. How little did he matter? It wasn't the right response but it was how he felt, so he followed her, touching the item in his pocket to make sure it was there.

She got on the tram and he did, too, on the other side, standing in the middle of the crowd, as if to say, *See me*, but she kept her head down, hiding her face.

She got off at Admin, queued up at a kiosk, a dozen people ahead of her in line. Paxton stood alongside her. She glanced at him and froze, staring forward. Closed her eyes, like she was trying to wish him away.

"Hello," Paxton said.

It was a ridiculous thing to say, but it was all he could think of.

She sighed, long and hard. Her body drooped.

"Of course," she said. "Of fucking course."

"Finally made it through the interview process," Paxton said.

"Of all fucking people. All the resources we devoted to this . . ."

Paxton put his hand on her arm, digging his fingers in to maintain a grip, but not so hard or tight as to cause a scene. "Let's go," he said.

He thought she might struggle, but she didn't. He recognized the look on her face. It was the same look he saw on his own face in the mirror each morning: complete, whole-bodied defeat. She let him lead her around like a doll, over to the elevator, where he swiped in, and they rode up to the security bullpen.

Paxton stepped off, still holding her arm. At the long end of the hallway was the open door of the bullpen, blues strolling back and forth beyond the frame.

There were six offices between the bullpen and the elevator. One of which was currently empty, as it was often used by other departments coming in to liaise with the security team.

Third door down on the left.

Ember shuffled next to him. "Well?"

Paxton thought of bringing her to the bullpen. The look Dakota and Dobbs would give him when they'd realized what he'd done. Captured some vermin. Maybe Dobbs would call him "son" again. Maybe he'd mean it.

They walked halfway down the hallway and Paxton stopped in front of the empty office and swiped them in. He held the door for her and she moved into the room—a desk with a tablet bolted to it and chairs on either side.

A sign on the wall said in cursive script: YOU MAKE ALL THINGS POSSIBLE!

Ember took in her surroundings, and as Paxton closed the door and flicked on the light switch, she moved into the corner, hands up to protect herself, suddenly more concerned about being cornered in a windowless room with a man she didn't know. A man she'd previously threatened.

"Sit," Paxton said.

She shuffled toward the desk, not taking her eyes off him, and sat like the seat might contain a pressure-sensitive bomb. Paxton sat across from her. Fear morphed into confusion and she looked at him like he was an abstract painting. Something to be figured out.

"You look different," she said. "Not good-different."

Paxton responded with a shrug.

Ember looked around. "The woman you were with. Where is she?"

"You were wrong," Paxton said.

"What?"

"About the books. We have copies of *Fahrenheit 451*. We have *The Handmaid's Tale*. Cloud hasn't suppressed them. No one orders them. They don't stock stuff that people don't want. That's just . . . that's good business, right? That's the market dictating."

Ember started to say something, then stopped. Like, *What would it matter?*

"I guess it doesn't make a difference, whether you were right or wrong," he said. "The point is people didn't listen. It's not because it was kept from them. It's because they didn't want to know."

Ember shifted in the chair.

"Why this facility?" Paxton asked. "You tried to get in here once. It didn't work. Why not go to another MotherCloud?"

"What is this?" Ember asked. "Therapy session? Interrogation? You want to hear my life story?"

"Answer the question."

Ember sighed. "My parents owned a coffee shop a few towns over. Nice little place. I grew up there. When this place went in, all the towns around it withered and died. So did the shop. So did my parents." She looked at her hands in her lap. "I guess you could call it personal, with this one. Maybe too personal." She looked at Paxton. "What are we doing here?"

"What were you planning?"

"It doesn't matter now."

He said it hard and fast: "Tell me. Where's your match?"

"I didn't bring it."

Paxton laughed. "Are you kidding me? You finally got in and you didn't bring it?"

"Are you crazy? Get caught with that on the way in? You know what would've happened to me? I've been trying to find some way to get it smuggled in. Otherwise, I've just been looking for an opportunity to cause some damage." She sighed and looked away. "But no dice. This place is fucking impenetrable."

Paxton reached for his pocket. Confirmed that, yes, it was still there. He removed the thumb drive and turned it over in his hands, running his fingers over the smooth plastic. Ember's eyes went wide. She breathed in, held it.

He didn't know why he'd kept it. He had meant to throw it out the window, back in the car. It hadn't been flagged when he came back into MotherCloud—since he was a blue they'd barely glanced at the screen when he passed through the scanner. Perks. When he got to his room he realized he still had it, and because it was a thumb drive, because it held some kind of value, he put it in the drawer next to the sink rather than the trash.

It was just a little hunk of plastic. And yet he liked having it in the drawer next to the sink, and after he saw Rick, he'd taken to carrying it in his pocket, rubbing his thumb into it when he felt like he needed to calm down and center himself.

He just wanted to keep it close. Carrying something that could hold so much power, it made him feel something. *Good* wasn't the word. He didn't know the word. He just knew the drive was heavier than it looked.

He put it on the desk, closer to him than to her. "What does it do?"

Ember leaned forward, as if to take it, but Paxton put his hand over it.

"It's a virus," she said. "It'll fire thrusters on the Cloud satellites. Push them out of orbit, just a tiny bit. No one will notice, until a few weeks from now, when they break orbit and crash. Cloud grinds to a halt. Shipping data, drone navigation, employment systems, banking. It won't be a fatal blow, but it'll cripple them for a good long time. Maybe long enough something else can take root."

"A lot of people would suffer," Paxton said. "A lot of people would lose their jobs. Their homes."

Ember put on her game face. Eyes narrow, mouth flat, some of the metal returning to her spine. "The system is broken. There's only one way to fix it. Burn it down and start fresh. It's not supposed to feel good."

"What if it doesn't work?"

Ember betrayed a bit of a smile. "Then we tried. Isn't that better than not?"

Paxton's feet ached. His back, too. His stomach felt greasy and bloated from the CloudBurgers. The cherry taste would not go away. He didn't even like cherries.

He pushed the drive toward her and she snatched it, then stuck it into the tablet. Tapped at the screen, which was locked. Paxton leaned across the desk and scanned his watch so it would turn on.

"Go ahead," he said, his voice barely a whisper.

Ember tapped at the face of the tablet as Paxton sat there wishing the door would open, for Dobbs to walk in now, to see it, and he didn't know if it was because he wanted someone to stop what they were doing or because he just wanted to be seen doing it.

Paxton watched. Minutes passed.

Finally, Ember sat back and exhaled hard.

"That's it?" Paxton asked.

She smiled at him, a real smile, the smile of someone who felt a deep and meaningful emotion, and he wanted to bottle that smile up and carry it in his pocket. She said, "You're a hero for doing this."

"No," he said quietly. But then he raised his voice. "No. I am not."

"We can debate later, but now it's time to go," she said.

She stood, moved toward the door. Paxton followed. He didn't know why, but he did. It felt right, in that moment, to follow. She knew he was following but didn't stop him, allowing him to keep pace behind her, to the bank of elevators, where Paxton swiped his watch and they stood there waiting. Ember shifted from foot to foot, like she wanted to break into a run. Paxton kept an eye on the far end of the hallway, hoping nobody would come out and see him.

The doors opened and Dakota and Dobbs stepped off.

They stood there in their tan uniforms like two slabs of sandstone.

They nodded to Paxton, almost in unison, and then turned to Ember, scanning her up and down, like she might be someone they recognized.

Paxton was struck dumb. He didn't know what to say. He felt like he was looking at himself, standing there with Ember, and Dakota and Dobbs, they knew, just knew, what had happened.

The jig was up. Time to go. Follow in Zinnia's footsteps.

Dakota went to say something but Paxton coughed, to force his throat to work again, and said, "New recruit. Got turned around. Escorting her back to the lobby."

Dobbs nodded. "Come on back up when you're done. Got something to talk to you about."

Paxton nodded, holding his breath, and didn't let it go until he and Ember stepped onto the elevator, and the doors closed, and they'd been delivered to the tram.

Standing in rainbow-colored crowds, Paxton felt like he'd been lit by a spotlight, like at any moment every gaze might swing toward him, but nothing happened. He was another shirt moving from one place to the next. Ember stood, staring hard, nearly vibrating, like she was willing herself to not be caught.

They got on the tram and rode it to Incoming and, Paxton being in blue, no one paid them any mind as they made their way toward the rectangle of white light, to the outside world, the heat rising in waves and warping the landscape as they got closer, until they reached the threshold between darkness and sunlight. It was August, easy to forget when you never went outside, so when the sun hit the exposed part of his forearm it baked his skin.

Behind him he felt the cool kiss of air drifting from inside the building, along with anything a person might ever need, available at the touch of a button.

A bed and a roof and a job for life.

Before him was the wide, flat expanse of the world, full of dead towns, no hope or promise of anything but dying of thirst on the long walk to something that might be nothing.

Maybe it was as simple as walking away. Maybe that was the first step. The match to light the fire, and with enough time and oxygen, the whole thing could be burned to the ground.

Could anything so big be so fragile?

Ember stood in the light and turned and fixed him with a stare. It was the kind of stare that made you feel bigger and smaller at the same time. It made you recognize the mistake you'd made but filled you with hope that there was still time to fix it.

Ember asked, "Are you coming?" but Paxton could barely hear it over Zinnia's voice whispering in his ear.

ACKNOWLEDGMENTS

Strap in. There are a lot of people to thank. First and foremost, my agent, Josh Getzler. This is the project that brought us together. He put his faith in me when I had nothing more than the first section and a scattershot pitch. His guidance has been incredible. Thanks are due as well to his brilliant assistant, Jonathan Cobb (who gave me my favorite note on the book), along with everyone at the HSG Agency, with a special shout-out to Soumeya Roberts, for her tireless efforts in selling this book around the world, and Ellen Goff, keeper of the foreign contracts.

Thank you to my editor, Julian Pavia, a master storytelling technician who pushed me past what the book was, and into what it could be. And his assistant, Angeline Rodriguez, who offered her own fantastic insight, on top of diligently handling the burden of all assistants—making sure everything gets done. I'm very lucky to be working with a team as talented and passionate as the one at Crown—huge thanks to Annsley Rosner, Rachel Rokicki, Julie Cepler, Kathleen Quinlan, and Sarah C. Breivogel. And while I am indebted to the agents and editors around the world who put their faith in this book, special thanks are due to Bill Scott-Kerr and the team at Transworld.

Cheers, too, to my film agent, Lucy Stille, for guiding me through a thrilling, head-spinning process. And to Ron Howard, Brian Grazer, and the entire team at Imagine Entertainment, for believing in this book, with special thanks to Katie Donahoe for her guidance and assistance.

Thanks to my parents and my in-laws. I cannot overstate how

much their love and support—including hand-selling me to friends and relatives, and providing frequent child care—has aided me in pursuing my writing career.

Perhaps, most important, my wife deserves thanks at a level I fear I cannot express through earthly means. Amanda has offered her sharp mind and tireless support from day one, and she has made real sacrifices for my writing career. I remain, since the day I met her, in awe of her intelligence, her humor, and her grace.

Thank you to my daughter, who challenges me every single day to be a better person, to want a better world for her to inherit, and to write the kind of book that I hope nudges us in the right direction.

Finally, a brief note on the dedication: Maria Fernandes worked part time at three separate Dunkin' Donuts locations in New Jersey, and in 2014, while sleeping in her car between shifts, accidentally suffocated on gas fumes. She was struggling to pay $550 a month on her basement apartment. That same year, according to the *Boston Globe*, Dunkin' Brands then CEO, Nigel Travis, earned $10.2 million. More than anyone or anything else, Maria's story beats at the heart of this book.

ROB HART is the author of the Ash McKenna crime series and the short-story collection *Take-Out*. He also co-wrote *Scott-Free* with James Patterson. He's worked as a book publisher, a political reporter, and a communications director for a politician, and was a commissioner for the city of New York. He lives on Staten Island with his wife and daughter.

robwhart.com
Twitter: @robwhart
Instagram: @robwhart1